Horace Hayman Wilson

The Vishnu Purana

A System of Hindu Mythology and Tradition Translated from the Original Sanskrit,

and Illustrated by Notes Derived Chiefly from Other Puranas by the Late H.H.

Wilson 1

Horace Hayman Wilson

The Vishnu Purana
 *A System of Hindu Mythology and Tradition Translated from the Original Sanskrit,
and Illustrated by Notes Derived Chiefly from Other Puranas by the Late H.H. Wilson
1*

ISBN/EAN: 9783741177071

Manufactured in Europe, USA, Canada, Australia, Japa

Cover: Foto ©Andreas Hilbeck / pixelio.de

Manufactured and distributed by brebook publishing software
(www.brebook.com)

Horace Hayman Wilson

The Vishnu Purana

THE

VISHNU PURANA:

A SYSTEM

OF

HINDU MYTHOLOGY AND TRADITION.

TRANSLATED

FROM THE ORIGINAL SANSKRIT,

AND

ILLUSTRATED BY NOTES

DERIVED CHIEFLY FROM OTHER PURÁNAS,

BY THE LATE

H. H. WILSON, M.A., F.R.S.,

BODEN PROFESSOR OF SANSKRIT IN THE UNIVERSITY OF OXFORD,
ETC., ETC.

EDITED BY

FITZEDWARD HALL,

M.A., D.C.L. OXON.

VOL. I.

LONDON:

TRÜBNER & CO., 60, PATERNOSTER ROW.

1864.

TO

THE CHANCELLOR, MASTERS, AND SCHOLARS

OF

THE UNIVERSITY OF OXFORD,

THIS WORK

IS RESPECTFULLY INSCRIBED BY

H. H. WILSON,

IN TESTIMONY OF HIS VENERATION FOR

THE UNIVERSITY,

AND IN GRATEFUL ACKNOWLEDGMENT OF THE DISTINCTION

CONFERRED UPON HIM

BY HIS ADMISSION AS A MEMBER,

AND HIS ELECTION

TO THE

BODEN PROFESSORSHIP OF THE SANSKRIT LANGUAGE.

OXFORD,
Feb. 10, 1840.

NOTICE.

—

The Editor defers till the completion of his under-
taking any general remarks that he may have to offer.

———

PREFACE.

THE literature of the Hindus has now been cultivated, for many years, with singular diligence, and, in many of its branches, with eminent success. There are some departments, however, which are yet but partially and imperfectly investigated; and we are far from being in possession of that knowledge which the authentic writings of the Hindus alone can give us of their religion, mythology, and historical traditions.

From the materials to which we have hitherto had access, it seems probable that there have been three principal forms in which the religion of the Hindus has existed, at as many different periods. The duration of those periods, the circumstances of their succession, and the precise state of the national faith at each season, it is not possible to trace with any approach to accuracy. The premises have been too imperfectly determined to authorize other than conclusions of a general and somewhat vague description; and those remain to be hereafter confirmed, or corrected, by more extensive and satisfactory research.

The earliest form under which the Hindu religion appears is that taught in the Vedas. The style of the language, and the purport of the composition, of those works, as far as we are acquainted with them, indicate a date long anterior to that of any other class of Sanskrit writings. It is yet, however, scarcely safe to advance an opinion of the precise belief, or philosophy, which they inculcate. To enable us to judge of their tendency, we have only a general sketch of their arrangement and contents, with a few extracts, by Mr. Colebrooke, in the Asiatic Researches;[1] a few incidental observations by Mr. Ellis, in the same miscellany;[2] and a translation of the first book of the Sanihita, or collection of the prayers of the Rig-veda, by Dr. Rosen;[3] and some of the Upanishads, or speculative treatises, attached to, rather than part of, the Vedas, by Rammohun Roy.[4*] Of the religion taught in the Vedas, Mr. Colebrooke's opinion will probably be received as that which is best entitled to deference; as, certainly, no Sanskrit scholar has been equally conversant with the original works. "The real doctrine of the whole Indian scripture is the unity of the deity, in whom the

---

[1] Vol. VIII., p. 369. †   [2] Vol. XIV., p. 37.

[3] Published by the Oriental Translation Fund Committee.

[4] A translation of the principal Upanishads was published, under the title of Oupnekhat, or Theologia Indica, by Anquetil du Perron; but it was made through the medium of the Persian, and is very incorrect and obscure. A translation of a very different character‡ has been some time in course of preparation by M. Poley.

---

* To insert here a list of the numerous publications bearing on the Vedas, that have appeared since the date of this preface, 1840, would be beside the purpose of my notes.

† Reprinted in Colebrooke's *Miscellaneous Essays*, Vol. I., pp. 9-113.

‡ The kindness of Professor Wilson here mistook a hope for a reality.

universe is comprehended; and the seeming polytheism which it exhibits offers the elements, and the stars and planets, as gods. The three principal manifestations of the divinity, with other personified attributes and energies, and most of the other gods of Hindu mythology, are, indeed, mentioned, or, at least, indicated, in the Vedas. But the worship of deified heroes is no part of that system; nor are the incarnations of deities suggested in any other portion of the text which I have yet seen; though such are sometimes hinted at by the commentators."[1] Some of these statements may, perhaps, require modification; for, without a careful examination of all the prayers of the Vedas, it would be hazardous to assert that they contain no indication whatever of hero-worship; and, certainly, they do appear to allude, occasionally, to the Avatáras, or incarnations, of Vishńu. Still, however, it is true that the prevailing character of the ritual of the Vedas is the worship of the personified elements; of Agni or fire; Indra, the firmament; Váyu, the air; Varuńa, the water; of Áditya, the sun; Soma, the moon; and other elementary and planetary personages. It is also true that the worship of the Vedas is, for the most part, domestic worship, consisting of prayers and oblations offered—in their own houses, not in temples—by individuals, for individual good, and addressed to unreal presences, not to visible types. In a word, the religion of the Vedas was not idolatry.

---

[1] As. Res., Vol. VIII., p. 474.*

* Or *Miscellaneous Essays*, Vol. I., pp. 110 and 111.

It is not possible to conjecture when this more simple and primitive form of adoration was succeeded by the worship of images and types, representing Brahmá, Vishńu, Śiva, and other imaginary beings, constituting a mythological pantheon of most ample extent; or when Ráma and Kríshńa, who appear to have been, originally, real and historical characters, were elevated to the dignity of divinities. Image-worship is alluded to by Manu, in several passages,[1] but with an intimation that those Brahmans who subsist by ministering in temples are an inferior and degraded class. The story of the Rámáyańa and Mahábhárata turns wholly upon the doctrine of incarnations; all the chief dramatis personæ of the poems being impersonations of gods, and demigods, and celestial spirits. The ritual appears to be that of the Vedas; and it may be doubted if any allusion to image-worship occurs. But the doctrine of propitiation by penance and praise prevails throughout; and Vishńu and Śiva are the especial objects of panegyric and invocation. In these two works, then, we trace unequivocal indications of a departure from the elemental worship of the Vedas, and the origin or elaboration of legends which form the great body of the mythological religion of the Hindus. How far they only improved upon the cosmogony and chronology of their predecessors, or in what degree the traditions of families and dynasties may originate with them, are questions that can only be determined when the Vedas and the two works in question shall have been more thoroughly examined.

---

[1] B. III., 152, 164. D. IV., 214.

The different works known by the name of Puránas are evidently derived from the same religious system as the Rámáyana and Mahábhárata, or from the mytho-heroic stage of Hindu belief. They present, however, peculiarities which designate their belonging to a later period, and to an important modification in the progress of opinion. They repeat the theoretical cosmogony of the two great poems; they expand and systematize the chronological computations; and they give a more definite and connected representation of the mythological fictions and the historical traditions. But, besides these and other particulars, which may be derivable from an old, if not from a primitive, era, they offer characteristic peculiarities of a more modern description, in the paramount importance which they assign to individual divinities, in the variety and purport of the rites and observances addressed to them, and in the invention of new legends illustrative of the power and graciousness of those deities, and of the efficacy of implicit devotion to them. Śiva and Vishńu, under one or other form, are almost the sole objects that claim the homage of the Hindus, in the Puráńas; departing from the domestic and elemental ritual of the Vedas, and exhibiting a sectarial fervour and exclusiveness not traceable in the Rámáyana, and only to a qualified extent in the Mahábhárata. They are no longer authorities for Hindu belief, as a whole: they are special guides for separate and, sometimes, conflicting branches of it; compiled for the evident purpose of promoting the preferential, or, in some cases, the sole, worship of Vishńu, or of Śiva.[1]

---

[1] Besides the three periods marked by the Vedas, Heroic

That the Puráńas always bore the character here
given of them may admit of reasonable doubt: that it
correctly applies to them as they now are met with,
the following pages will irrefragably substantiate. It
is possible, however, that there may have been an
earlier class of Puráńas, of which those we now have
are but the partial and adulterated representatives.
The identity of the legends in many of them, and, still
more, the identity of the words—for, in several of them,
long passages are literally the same—is a sufficient
proof that, in all such cases, they must be copied either
from some other similar work, or from a common and
prior original. It is not unusual, also, for a fact to be
stated upon the authority of an 'old stanza', which is
cited accordingly; showing the existence of an earlier
source of information: and, in very many instances,
legends are alluded to, not told; evincing acquaintance
with their prior narration somewhere else. The name
itself, Puráńa, which implies 'old', indicates the object
of the compilation to be the preservation of ancient
traditions; a purpose, in the present condition of the
Puráńas, very imperfectly fulfilled. Whatever weight
may be attached to these considerations, there is no
disputing evidence to the like effect, afforded by other
and unquestionable authority. The description given,
by Mr. Colebrooke,[1] of the contents of a Puráńa is

Poems, and Puráńas, a fourth may be dated from the influence
exercised by the Tantras upon Hindu practice and belief: but we
are yet too little acquainted with those works, or their origin, to
speculate safely upon their consequences.

[1] As. Res., Vol. VII., p. 202.*

---

* Or *Miscellaneous Essays*, Vol. II., pp. 4 and 5, foot-note.

taken from Sanskrit writers. The Lexicon of Amara
Sinha gives, as a synonym of Purána, Pancha-lakshana,
'that which has five characteristic topics'; and there is
no difference of opinion, amongst the scholiasts, as to
what these are. They are, as Mr. Colebrooke mentions:
I. Primary creation, or cosmogony; II. Secondary creation, or the destruction and renovation of worlds,
including chronology; III. Genealogy of gods and
patriarchs; IV. Reigns of the Manus, or periods called
Manwantaras; and, V. History, or such particulars as
have been preserved of the princes of the solar and
lunar races, and of their descendants to modern times.'
Such, at any rate, were the constituent and characteristic portions of a Purána, in the days of Amara Sinha,*
fifty-six years before the Christian era;† and, if the

' The following definition of a Purána is constantly quoted:
it is found in the Vishńu, Matsya, Váyu, and other Puráńas:

सर्गश्च प्रतिसर्गश्च वंशो मन्वन्तराणि च ।
वंशानुचरितं चैव पुराणं पञ्चलक्षणम् ॥

A variation of reading in the beginning of the second line is
noticed by Rámásrama, the scholiast on Amara, भूम्यादिसंहारं,
'Destruction of the earth and the rest, or final dissolution;' in
which case the genealogies of heroes and princes are comprised
in those of the patriarchs.

---

* ?

† That Amarasinha lived at that time, though possible, has not been
proved. Professor Wilson — *Sanskrit Dictionary*, first edition, Preface,
p. v.—asserts that "all tradition concurs in enumerating him amongst
the learned men who, in the metaphorical phraseology of the Hindus,
are denominated the 'nine gems' of the court of Vikramáditya. · · ·
Authorities which assert the contemporary existence of Amara and Vikramáditya might be indefinitely multiplied; and those are equally numerous which class him amongst the 'nine gems'." In the second

Purānas had undergone no change since his time, such
we should expect to find them still. Do they conform

---

edition of his Dictionary, under the word नवरत्न, the Professor explains
the "nine gems" to be: "The nine men of letters at the court of Vikra-
mádítya, or, Dhanwantari, Kshapańaka, Amarasińha, Śanku, Vetálabhatta,
Ghatakarpara, Kálidása, Varáhamihira, and Vararuchi." The tradition
about these ornaments he thinks — *Meghadúta*, second edition, Preface,
p. v. — to be one of those regarding which "there is no reason to dispute
the truth."

The "authorities" spoken of in the first of the preceding extracts are
not specified by Professor Wilson; and they are not known to have
fallen yet in the way of any one else. Those authorities apart, he adduces a stanza about the "nine gems", of which he says, that it "appears
in a great measure traditionary only; as I have not been able to trace
it to any authentic source, although it is in the mouth of every Pandit,
when interrogated on the subject."

The stanza in question occurs in the *Jyotirvidábharana*, near its conclusion, where we find the following verses:

वर्षं श्रुतिस्मृतिविचारविवेचबल्धे
श्रीभारती खधृतिसंमितहेमपीठे ।
अत्तोऽधुना कर्तिारेयं सति मालवेन्द्रे
श्रीविक्रमार्कनृपराजवरे सभासीत् ॥
धातुः शुवान्वरदाविर्मजिर्युदत्तो
विश्रुत्खिलोचनारी घटकर्परात्ख्न: ।
कवेोऽपि सन्ति कवयोऽमरसिंहपूर्वा
यद्वीव विक्रमनृपस्य सभासदोऽमी ॥
मत्तो वराहर्मिाहिर: श्रुतखेनगामा
श्रीवादराथधर्माजित्यकुमारसिंह: ।
श्रीविक्रमार्कनृपसंसदि सन्ति चैते
श्रीवासतत्वकयचस्त्वपरे मदाख्या: ॥
धन्वर्कारि: क्षपणकोऽमरसिंहशङ्कु-
वेतालभट्टघटकर्परकालिदासा: ।
ख्यातो वराहमिहिरो नृपते: सभायां
रत्नानि वै वररुचिर्नव विक्रमस्य ॥

* * * * * * * *
* * * * * * * *
* * * * * * * *
* * * * * * * *

to this description? Not exactly, in any one instance;
to some of them it is utterly inapplicable; to others it
only partially applies. There is not one to which it
belongs so entirely as to the Vishṇu Puráṇa; and it is
one of the circumstances which gives to this work a

याकूतादिपरिच्छदतवरा: कवयभ्वनेके
ज्योतिर्विद: समभवच्च वगाहपूर्वा: ।
श्रीविक्रमार्कनृपसंसदि माध्यमि-
धीरखां नृपसखा विम्र कालिदास: ॥
काव्यपयं सुमानिक्षघुवंशपूर्वं
पूर्वं ततो ननु विषयकृतिखर्मवाद: ।
ज्योतिर्विदाभरखकार्मविधानगाख्यं
श्रीकालिदासकार्वितो हि ततो बभूव ॥
वर्ष: सिन्धुरदर्शनाम्बरगुणैर्याते कली संमिते
मासे माधवसंज्ञके च विहितो ग्रन्थक्रियोपक्रम: ।
नानाबान्विधानगाख्यगदितं ज्ञानं विचीक्षादूरे-
पूर्जे ग्रन्थसमाप्तिरेव विहिता ज्योतिर्विदां प्रीतये ॥

Here we see named, as contemporaries at the court of Vikramáditya, lord of Málava, in the year 3068 of the Kali age, or B. C. 33: Maúí, Aṁśudatta, Jishṇu, Trilochana, and Hari; also Satya, Srutasena, Dádaráyaṇa, Manittha, and Kumárasiṁha, astronomers; and the "nine gems" already particularized.

The writer of the *Jyotirvidábharaṇa* is represented as professing to be one with the author of the *Raghuvaṁśa*. As to Vikramáditya, 160 regions are said to have been subject to his sway. Further, according to some verses of which I have not quoted the original, there were 800 viceroys subordinate to him, of picked warriors he had ten millions, and he possessed 400,000 boats. His victims in battle, among Sákas alone, are multiplied to the whimsical aggregate of 555,555,555. These destroyed, he established his era.

There is every reason for believing the *Jyotirvidábharaṇa* to be not only pseudonymous but of recent composition. And now we are prepared to form an opinion touching the credibility of the tradition, so far as yet traced, which concerns the "nine gems" of Vikramáditya.

In the *Benares Magazine* for 1852, pp. 274-276, I first printed and translated the verses just cited and abstracted. A detailed English version of them has been given by the learned Dr. Bhâu Dâji, in the *Journal of the Bombay Branch of the Royal As. Soc.*, January, 1862, pp. 26 and 27.

more authentic character than most of its fellows can
pretend to. Yet, even in this instance, we have a book
upon the institutes of society and obsequial rites inter-
posed between the Manwantaras and the genealogies
of princes; and a life of Kṛishṇa, separating the latter
from an account of the end of the world; besides the
insertion of various legends of a manifestly popular
and sectarial character. No doubt, many of the Puráṇas, as they now are, correspond with the view
which Colonel Vans Kennedy takes of their purport.
"I cannot discover, in them," he remarks, "any other
object than that of religious instruction." "The description of the earth and of the planetary system, and
the lists of royal races that occur in them," he asserts
to be "evidently extraneous, and not essential circumstances; as they are omitted in some Puráṇas, and very
concisely illustrated, in others; while, on the contrary,
in all the Puráṇas, some or other of the leading principles, rites, and observances of the Hindu religion are
fully dwelt upon, and illustrated, either by suitable
legends, or by prescribing the ceremonies to be practised, and the prayers and invocations to be employed,
in the worship of different deities."[1] Now, however
accurate this description may be of the Puráṇas as they
are, it is clear that it does not apply to what they were
when they were synonymously designated as Pancha-
lakshuṇas or 'treatises on five topics'; not one of which
five is ever specified, by text or comment, to be "religious instruction". In the knowledge of Amara Siṃha,

---

[1] Researches into the Nature and Affinity of Ancient and
Hindu Mythology, p. 153, and note.

the lists of princes were not extraneous and unessential; and their being now so considered by a writer so well acquainted with the contents of the Puráńas as Colonel Vans Kennedy, is a decisive proof that, since the days of the lexicographer, they have undergone some material alteration, and that we have not, at present, the same works, in all respects, that were current, under the denomination of Puráńas, in the century prior to Christianity.

The inference deduced from the discrepancy between the actual form and the older definition of a Puráńa, unfavourable to the antiquity of the extant works generally, is converted into certainty, when we come to examine them in detail. For, although they have no dates attached to them, yet circumstances are sometimes mentioned, or alluded to, or references to authorities are made, or legends are narrated, or places are particularized, of which the comparatively recent date is indisputable, and which enforce a corresponding reduction of the antiquity of the work in which they are discovered. At the same time, they may be acquitted of subservience to any but sectarial imposture. They were pious frauds for temporary purposes: they never emanated from any impossible combination of the Brahmans to fabricate for the antiquity of the entire Hindu system any claims which it cannot fully support. A very great portion of the contents of many, some portion of the contents of all, is genuine and old. The sectarial interpolation, or embellishment, is always sufficiently palpable to be set aside without injury to the more authentic and primitive material; and the Puráńas, although they belong especially to that stage of the Hindu religion in which faith in some one divinity was the prevailing principle, are, also, a valuable record of the form of Hindu belief which came next in order to that of the Vedas; which grafted hero-worship upon the simpler ritual of the latter; and which had been adopted, and was extensively, perhaps universally, established in India, at the time of the Greek invasion. The Hercules of the Greek writers was, indubitably, the Balaráma of the Hindus; and their notices of Mathurá on the Jumna, and of the kingdom of the Suraseni and the Pandæan country, evidence the prior currency of the traditions which constitute the argument of the Mahábhárata, and which are constantly repeated in the Puráńas, relating to the Pándava and Yádava races, to Krishńa and his contemporary heroes, and to the dynasties of the solar and lunar kings.

The theogony and cosmogony of the Puráńas may, probably, be traced to the Vedas. They are not, as far as is yet known, described in detail in those works; but they are frequently alluded to, in a strain more or less mystical and obscure, which indicates acquaintance with their existence, and which seems to have supplied the Puráńas with the groundwork of their systems. The scheme of primary or elementary creation they borrow from the Sánkhya philosophy, which is, probably, one of the oldest forms of speculation on man and nature, amongst the Hindus. Agreeably, however, to that part of the Pauráńik character which there is reason to suspect of later origin, their inculcation of the worship of a favourite deity, they combine the interposition of a creator with the independent evolution of matter, in a somewhat contradictory and unintelligible style. It is evident, too, that their accounts of secondary creation, or the development of the existing forms of things, and the disposition of the universe, are derived from several and different sources; and it appears very likely that they are to be accused of some of the incongruities and absurdities by which the narrative is disfigured, in consequence of having attempted to assign reality and significancy to what was merely metaphor or mysticism. There is, however, amidst the unnecessary complexity of the description, a general agreement, amongst them, as to the origin of things and their final distribution; and, in many of the circumstances, there is a striking concurrence with the ideas which seem to have pervaded the whole of the ancient world, and which we may, therefore, believe to be faithfully represented in the Puráñas.

The pantheism of the Puráñas is one of their invariable characteristics; although the particular divinity who is all things, from whom all things proceed, and to whom all things return, be diversified according to their individual sectarial bias. They seem to have derived the notion from the Vedas; but, in them, the one universal Being is of a higher order than a personification of attributes or elements, and, however imperfectly conceived, or unworthily described, is God. In the Puráñas, the one only Supreme Being is supposed to be manifest in the person of Śiva, or Vishńu, either in the way of illusion, or in sport; and one or other of these divinities is, therefore, also the cause of all that is,—is, himself, all that exists. The identity of God and nature is not a new notion: it was very general

in the speculations of antiquity; but it assumed a new
vigour in the early ages of Christianity, and was carried
to an equal pitch of extravagance by the Platonic
Christians as by the Śaiva or Vaishṅava Hindus. It
seems not impossible that there was some communication between them. We know that there was an
active communication between India and the Red Sea,
in the early ages of the Christian era, and that doctrines, as well as articles of merchandise, were brought
to Alexandria from the former. Epiphanius[1] and Eusebius[2] accuse Scythianus of having imported from
India, in the second century, books on magic, and he-
retical notions leading to Manichæism; and it was at
the same period that Ammonius Saccas instituted the
sect of the new Platonists at Alexandria. The basis of
his heresy was, that true philosophy derived its origin
from the eastern nations. His doctrine of the identity
of God and the universe is that of the Vedas and Puráńas; and the practices he enjoined, as well as their
object, were precisely those described in several of the
Puráńas, under the name of Yoga. His disciples were
taught to exteuuate, by mortification and contemplation, the bodily restraints upon the immortal spirit;
so that, in this life, they might enjoy communion with
the Supreme Being, and ascend, after death, to the
universal Parent.[3] That these are Hindu tenets, the
following pages[4] will testify; and, by the admission of
their Alexandrian teacher, they originated in India.
The importation was, perhaps, not wholly unrequited:

---

[1] Adv. Manichæos.
[2] See Mosheim, I., II., ı.
[3] Hist. Evang.
[4] See Book VI., Chap. VII.

the loan may not have been left unpaid. It is not impossible that the Hindu doctrines received fresh animation from their adoption by the successors of Ammonius, and, especially, by the mystics, who may have prompted, as well as employed, the expressions of the Puráńas. Anquetil du Perron has given,[1] in the introduction to his translation of the 'Oupnekhat', several hymns by Synesius, a bishop of the beginning of the fifth century, which may serve as parallels to many of the hymns and prayers addressed to Vishńu in the Vishńu Puráńa.

But the ascription, to individual and personal deities, of the attributes of the one universal and spiritual Supreme Being, is an indication of a later date than the Vedas, certainly, and, apparently, also, than the Rámáyańa, where Ráma, although an incarnation of Vishńu, commonly appears in his human character alone. There is something of the kind in the Mahábhárata, in respect to Kŕishńa; especially in the philosophical episode known as the Bhagavad Gítá. In other places, the divine nature of Kŕishńa is less decidedly affirmed; in some, it is disputed, or denied; and, in most of the situations in which he is exhibited in action, it is as a prince and warrior, not as a divinity. He exercises no superhuman faculties in the defence of himself or his friends, or in the defeat and destruction of his foes. The Mahábhárata, however, is, evidently, a work of various periods, and requires to be read throughout, carefully and critically, before its weight as an authority can be accurately appreciated. As it is now in

---

[1] Theologia et Philosophia Indica, Dissert., p. xxvi.

type,[1]—thanks to the public spirit of the Asiatic Society of Bengal, and their secretary, Mr. J. Prinsep,—it will not be long before the Sanskrit scholars of the continent will accurately appreciate its value.

The Puráńas are, also, works of evidently different ages, and have been compiled under different circumstances, the precise nature of which we can but imperfectly conjecture from internal evidence and from what we know of the history of religious opinion in India. It is highly probable that, of the present popular forms of the Hindu religion, none assumed their actual state earlier than the time of Śankara Áchárya, the great Śaiva reformer, who flourished, in all likelihood, in the eighth or ninth century. Of the Vaishńava teachers, Rámánuja dates in the twelfth century; Madhwáchárya, in the thirteenth; and Vallabha, in the sixteenth;[2] and the Puráńas seem to have accompanied, or followed, their innovations; being obviously intended to advocate the doctrines they taught. This is to assign to some of them a very modern date, it is true; but I cannot think that a higher can, with justice, be ascribed to them. This, however, applies to some only out of the number, as I shall presently proceed to specify.

Another evidence of a comparatively modern date

---

[1] Three volumes have been printed: the fourth and last is understood to be nearly completed.*

[2] As. Res., Vols. XVI. and XVII. Account of Hindu Sects.†

---

* It was completed in 1839: at least, it bears that date.

† This "Sketch of the Religious Sects of the Hindus", by Professor Wilson, will be found in the first volume of his collected works.

must be admitted in those chapters of the Puráńas which, assuming a prophetic tone, foretell what dynasties of kings will reign in the Kali age. These chapters, it is true, are found but in four of the Puráńas; but they are conclusive in bringing down the date of those four to a period considerably subsequent to Christianity. It is, also, to be remarked that the Váyu, Vishńu, Bhágavata, and Matsya Puráńas, in which these particulars are foretold, have, in all other respects, the character of as great antiquity as any works of their class.[1]

The invariable form of the Puráńas is that of a dialogue, in which some person relates its contents, in reply to the inquiries of another. This dialogue is interwoven with others, which are repeated as having been held, on other occasions, between different individuals, in consequence of similar questions having been asked. The immediate narrator is, commonly, though not constantly, Lomaharshańa or Romaharshańa, the disciple of Vyása, who is supposed to communicate what was imparted to him by his preceptor, as he had heard it from some other sage. Vyása, as will be seen in the body of the work,[2] is a generic title, meaning an 'arranger' or 'compiler'. It is, in this age, applied to Kŕishńa Dwaipáyana, the son of Paráśara,

---

[1] On the history of the composition of the Puráńas, as they now appear, I have hazarded some speculations in my Analysis of the Váyu Puráńa: Journ. Asiatic Society of Bengal, December, 1832.*

[2] Book III., Chapter III.

* See Vol. III. of our author's collected writings.

who is said to have taught the Vedas and Puráńas to
various disciples, but who appears to have been the
head of a college, or school, under whom various
learned men gave to the sacred literature of the Hindus
the form in which it now presents itself. In this task,
the disciples, as they are termed, of Vyása were, rather,
his colleagues and coadjutors; for they were already
conversant with what he is fabled to have taught them;[1]
and, amongst them, Lomaharshańa represents the class
of persons who were especially charged with the record of political and temporal events. He is called
Súta, as if it was a proper name: but it is, more correctly, a title; and Lomaharshańa was 'a Súta', that is,
a bard, or panegyrist, who was created, according to
our text,[2] to celebrate the exploits of princes, and who,
according to the Váyu and Padma Puráńas, has a right,
by birth and profession, to narrate the Puráńas, in preference even to the Brahmans.[3] It is not unlikely,
therefore, that we are to understand, by his being represented as the disciple of Vyása, the institution of
some attempt, made under the direction of the latter,
to collect, from the heralds and annalists of his day,
the scattered traditions which they had imperfectly
preserved: and hence the consequent appropriation of
the Puráńas, in a great measure, to the genealogies of
regal dynasties and descriptions of the universe. However this may be, the machinery has been but loosely

---

[1] See Book III., Chapter III.   [2] Book I., Chapter XIII.
[3] Journ. Royal As. Soc., Vol. V., p. 281.[*]

[*] The article referred to is from the pen of Professor Wilson, and has
been reprinted.

adhered to; and many of the Puránas, like the Vishńu, are referred to a different narrator.

An account is given, in the following work,[1] of a series of Pauráńik compilations of which, in their present form, no vestige appears. Lomaharshańa is said to have had six disciples, three of whom composed as many fundamental Sańhitás, whilst he himself compiled a fourth. By a Sańhitá is generally understood a 'collection' or 'compilation'. The Sańhitás of the Vedas are collections of hymns and prayers belonging to them, arranged according to the judgment of some individual sage, who is, therefore, looked upon as the originator and teacher of each. The Sańhitás of the Puránas, then, should be analogous compilations, attributed, respectively, to Mitrayu, Sáńśapáyana, Akŕitabrańa, and Romaharshańa: no such Pauráńik Sańhitás are now known. The substance of the four is said to be collected in the Vishńu Puráńa, which is, also, in another place,[2] itself called a Sańhitá. But such compilations have not, as far as inquiry has yet proceeded, been discovered. The specification may be accepted as an indication of the Puránas' having existed in some other form, in which they are no longer met with; although it does not appear that the arrangement was incompatible with their existence as separate works; for the Vishńu Puráńa, which is our authority for the four Sańhitás, gives us, also, the usual enumeration of the several Puránas.

There is another classification of the Puránas, alluded to in the Matsya Puráńa, and specified by the Padma

---

PREFACE.

Puráńa, but more fully. It is not undeserving of notice, as it expresses the opinion which native writers entertain of the scope of the Puráńas, and of their recognizing the subservience of these works to the dissemination of sectarian principles. Thus, it is said, in the Uttara Khańda of the Padma,* that the Puráńas, as well as other works, are divided into three classes, according to the qualities which prevail in them. Thus, the Vishńu, Náradíya, Bhágavata, Gáruda, Padma, and Varáha Puráńas are Sáttwika or pure, from the predominance, in them, of the Sattwa quality, or that of goodness and purity. They are, in fact, Vaishńava Puráńas. The Matsya, Kúrma, Linga, Śiva, Skanda, and Agni Puráńas are Támasa, or Puráńas of darkness, from the prevalence of the quality of Tamas, 'ignorance', 'gloom'. They are, indisputably, Śaiva Puráńas. The third series, comprising the Brahmáńda, Brahma Vaivarta, Márkańdeya, Bhavishya, Vámana, and Brahma Puráńas, are designated as Rájasa, 'passionate', from Rajas, the property of passion, which they are supposed to represent. The Matsya does not specify which are the Puráńas that come under these designations, but remarks† that those in which the Máhátmya

----

* Chapter XLII.:

माहात्म्यं चौर्षं तथा लिङ्गं शैवं स्कान्दं तथैव च।
आग्नेयं च षडेतानि तामसानि निबोधत॥
वैष्णवं नारदीयं च तथा भागवतं शुभम्।
गारुडं च तथा पाद्मं वाराहं शुभदर्शने॥
सात्त्विकानि पुराणानि विज्ञेयानि शुभानि वै।
ब्रह्माण्डं ब्रह्मवैवर्तं मार्कण्डेयं तथैव च॥
भविष्यं वामनं ब्राह्मं राजसानि निबोधत।

† Chapter LII.:

of Hari or Vishńu prevails are Sáttwika; those in which
the legends of Agni or Śiva predominate are Támasa:
and those which dwell most on the stories of Brahmá
are Rájasa. I have elsewhere stated[1] that I considered
the Rájasa Puráńas to lean to the Śákta division of the
Hindus, the worshippers of Śakti or the female principle; founding this opinion on the character of the
legends which some of them contain, such as the Durgá
Máhátmya, or celebrated legend on which the worship
of Durgá or Kálí is especially founded, which is a
principal episode of the Márkańdeya. The Brahma
Vaivarta also devotes the greatest portion of its chapters to the celebration of Rádhá, the mistress of Krishńa,
and other female divinities. Colonel Vans Kennedy,
however, objects to the application of the term Śákta
to this last division of the Puráńas; the worship of
Śakti being the especial object of a different class of
works, the Tantras; and no such form of worship being
particularly inculcated in the Brahma Puráńa.[2] This
last argument is of weight in regard to the particular
instance specified; and the designation of Śakti may
not be correctly applicable to the whole class, although
it is to some of the series: for there is no incompatibility in the advocacy of a Tántrika modification of

---

[1] As. Res., Vol. XVI., p. 10. [a]
[2] Asiatic Journal, March, 1837, p. 241.

सात्त्विकेषु पुराणेषु माहात्म्यमधिकं हरेः ।
राजसेषु च माहात्म्यमधिकं ब्रह्मणो विदुः ॥
तद्वदेव च माहात्म्यं तामसेषु शिवस्य च ।
सङ्कीर्णेषु सरस्वत्याः पितॄणां च निगद्यते ॥

[a] Vol. I., p. 13, foot-note, of the author's collective publications.

the Hindu religion by any Puráńa; and it has, unquestionably, been practised in works known as Upapuráńas.
The proper appropriation of the third class of the Puráńas, according to the Padma Puráńa, appears to be
to the worship of Krishńa, not in the character in which
he is represented in the Vishńu and Bhágavata Puráńas,—in which the incidents of his boyhood are only
a portion of his biography, and in which the human
character largely participates, at least in his riper years,
—but as the infant Krishńa, Govinda, Bála Gopála, the
sojourner in Vrindávana, the companion of the cowherds and milkmaids, the lover of Rádhá, or as the
juvenile master of the universe, Jagannátha. The term
Rájasa, implying the animation of passion and enjoyment of sensual delights, is applicable not only to the
character of the youthful divinity, but to those with
whom his adoration in these forms seems to have
originated, the Gosains of Gokul and Bengal, the followers and descendants of Vallabha and Chaitanya, the
priests and proprietors of Jagannáth and Srínáthdwár,
who lead a life of affluence and indulgence, and vindicate, both by precept and practice, the reasonableness of the Rájasa property, and the congruity of temporal enjoyment with the duties of religion.[1]

The Puráńas are uniformly stated to be eighteen in
number. It is said that there are also eighteen Upapuráńas or minor Puráńas: but the names of only a
few of these are specified in the least exceptionable

---

[1] As. Res., Vol. XVI., p. 85. *

---

* Collective Works of Professor Wilson, Vol. I., p. 110.

authorities; and the greater number of the works is not procurable. With regard to the eighteen Puránas, there is a peculiarity in their specification, which is proof of an interference with the integrity of the text, in some of them, at least; for each of them specifies the names of the whole eighteen. Now, the list could not have been complete whilst the work that gives it was unfinished; and in one only, therefore, the last of the series, have we a right to look for it. As, however, there are more last words than one, it is evident that the names must have been inserted in all except one, after the whole were completed. Which of the eighteen is the exception, and truly the last, there is no clue to discover; and the specification is, probably, an interpolation, in most, if not in all.

The names that are specified are commonly the same, and are as follows: 1. Bráhma, 2. Pádma, 3. Vaishńava, 4. Śaiva, 5. Bhágavata, 6. Náradíya, 7. Márkańdeya, 8. Ágneya, 9. Bhavishya, 10. Brahma Vaivarta, 11. Lainga, 12. Váráha, 13. Skánda, 14. Vámana, 15. Kaurma, 16. Mátsya, 17. Gáruda, 18. Brahmáńda.[1] This is from the twelfth book of the Bhágavata, and is the same as occurs in the Vishńu.[2] In other authori-

---

[1] The names are not attributively; the noun substantive, Puráńa, being understood. Thus, Vaishńavam Puráńam means the Puráńa of Vishńu; Śaivam Puráńam, the Puráńa of Śiva; Bráhmam Puráńam, the Puráńa of Brahmá. It is equally correct, and more common, to use the two substantives in apposition, as Vishńu Puráńa, Śiva Puráńa, &c. In the original Sanskrit the nouns are compounded, as Vishńu-puráńa, &c.: but it has not been customary to combine them, in their European shape.

[2] Book III., Chapter VI.

ties there are a few variations. The list of the Kúrma
Puráńa omits the Agni Puráńa, and substitutes the
Váyu.* The Agni leaves out the Śiva, and inserts the
Váyu. The Varáha omits the Garuḍa and Brahmáńḍa,
and inserts the Váyu and Narasiṃha: in this last, it is
singular. The Márkańḍeya agrees with the Vishńu and
Bhágavata, in omitting the Váyu. The Matsya, like
the Agni, leaves out the Śiva.

Some of the Puráńas, as the Agni, Matsya,† Bhágavata,‡ and Padma, also particularize the number of
stanzas which each of the eighteen contains. In one
or two instances they disagree; but, in general, they
concur. The aggregate is stated at 400,000 ślokas, or
1,600,000 lines. These are fabled to be but an abridgment; the whole amount being a krore or ten millions

---

* Professor Wilson's MS. has मार्कण्डेयमथा चैवं; but four MSS. that
I have consulted have मार्कण्डेयमथापरं. And the latter reading is to
be preferred. The *Kúrma* professes, at the end of its list of the Puráńas, to have enumerated eighteen; and, unless it names both the *Váyu*
and the *Agni*, it enumerates but seventeen.

† The particulars from the *Matsya* will be found in the sequel.

‡ The computation of the *Bhágavata*, XII., 13, 4 - 8, is as follows:
Brahma, 10,000 stanzas; *Padma*, 55,000; *Vishńu*, 23,000; *Śiva*, 24,000;
Bhágavata, 18,000; *Nárada*, 25,000; *Márkańḍeya*, 9,000; *Agni*, 15,400;
Bhavishya, 14,500; *Brahma-vaivarta*, 18,000; *Liṅga*, 11,000; *Varáha*,
24,000; *Skanda*, 81,100; *Vámana*, 10,000; *Kúrma*, 17,000; *Matsya*,
14,000; *Garuḍa*, 19,000; *Brahmáńḍa*, 12,000. The total is 400,000.

The *Bhágavata* here calls the *Agni* and the *Garuḍa* by the names of
Váhna and *Sauparńa*.

The *Devi-bhágavata* substitutes, in place of the *Śiva*, the *Váyu*, and
assigns to it 10,600 stanzas. Further, it gives to the *Agni*, 16,000; to
the *Skanda*, 81,000; and to the *Brahmáńḍa*, 12,100.

The *Revá-máhátmya* also has, instead of *Śiva*, *Váyu*, but reckons it
at 24,000 complete; and it likewise allows 16,000 to the *Agni*. To the
Skanda it gives 84,000; and to the *Brahmáńḍa*, 12,200.

For further details, see Burnouf's edition of the *Bhágavata-puráńa*,
Vol. I., Preface, pp. LXXXVI-LXXXIX, foot-note.

of stanzas, or even a thousand millions.* If all the fragmentary portions claiming, in various parts of India, to belong to the Puránas were admitted, their extent would much exceed the lesser, though it would not reach the larger, enumeration. The former is, however, as I have elsewhere stated,[1] a quantity that an individual European scholar could scarcely expect to peruse with due care and attention, unless his whole time were devoted exclusively, for many years, to the task. Yet, without some such labour being achieved, it was clear, from the crudity and inexactness of all that had been hitherto published on the subject, with one exception,[2] that sound views on the subject of Hindu mythology and tradition were not to be expected. Circumstances, which I have already explained in the paper in the Journal of the Royal Asiatic Society, referred to above, enabled me to avail myself of

[1] Journ. Royal As. Soc., Vol. V., p. 61.†

[2] I allude to the valuable work of Colonel Vans Kennedy, Researches into the Nature and Affinity of Ancient and Hindu Mythology. However much I may differ from that learned and industrious writer's conclusions, I must do him the justice to admit that he is the only author who has discussed the subject of the mythology of the Hindus on right principles, by drawing his materials from authentic sources.

* So says the *Matsya-puráńa*, LII., *ad init.*:

पुराणं सर्वशास्त्राणां प्रथमं ब्रह्मणा स्मृतम् ।
अनन्तरं च वक्त्रेभ्यो वेदास्तस्य विनिर्गताः ॥
पुराणमेकमेवासीत्तदा कल्पान्तरे ऽनघ ।
त्रिवर्गसाधनं पुण्यं शतकोटिप्रविस्तरम् ॥

† See Professor Wilson's collective works, Vol. III.

competent assistance, by which I made a minute abstract of most of the Puráńas. In course of time I hope to place a tolerably copious and connected analysis of the whole eighteen before Oriental scholars, and, in the meanwhile, offer a brief notice of their several contents.

In general, the enumeration of the Puráńas is a simple nomenclature, with the addition, in some cases, of the number of verses; but to these the Matsya Puráńa* joins the mention of one or two circumstances peculiar to each, which, although scanty, are of value, as offering means of identifying the copies of the Puráńas now found with those to which the Matsya refers, or of discovering a difference between the present and the past. I shall, therefore, prefix the passage descriptive of each Puráńa, from the Matsya. It is necessary to remark, however, that, in the comparison instituted between that description and the Puráńa as it exists, I necessarily refer to the copy or copies which I employed for the purpose of examination and analysis, and which were procured, with some trouble and cost, in Benares and Calcutta. In some instances my manuscripts have been collated with others from different parts of India; and the result has shown that, with regard at least to the Brahma, Vishńu, Váyu, Matsya, Padma, Bhágavata, and Kúrma Puráńas, the same works, in all essential respects, are generally current under the same appellations. Whether this is invariably the case, may be doubted; and further inquiry may possibly show that I have been obliged to con-

---

* Chapter LII.

tent myself with mutilated or unauthentic works.[1] It is with this reservation, therefore, that I must be understood to speak of the concurrence or disagreement of any Puráńa with the notice of it which the Matsya Puráńa has preserved.

1. Brahma Puráńa. "That, the whole of which was formerly repeated by Brahmá to Maríchi, is called the Bráhma Puráńa, and contains ten thousand stanzas."[2] In all the lists of the Puráńas, the Brahma is placed at the head of the series, and is, thence, sometimes also entitled the Ádi or 'first' Puráńa. It is also designated as the Saura; as it is, in great part, appropriated to the worship of Súrya, 'the sun'. There are, however, works bearing these names which belong to the class of Upapuráńas, and which are not to be confounded with the Brahma. It is usually said, as above, to contain ten thousand ślokas; but the number actually occurring is between seven and eight thousand. There is a supplementary or concluding section, called the Brahmottara Puráńa, and which is different from a portion of the Skanda called the Brahmottara Khańḍa, which contains about three thousand stanzas more. But

---

[1] Upon examining the translations of different passages from the Puráńas, given by Colonel Vans Kennedy in the work mentioned in a former note, and comparing them with the text of the manuscripts I have consulted, I find such an agreement as to warrant the belief, that there is no essential difference between the copies in his possession and in mine. The varieties which occur in the MSS. of the East India Company's Library will be noticed in the text.

[2] ब्रह्मणाभिहितं पूर्वं यावदास्यं मरीचये।
मार्त्तं तु यदाख्यातं पुराणं परिकीर्तितम्॥

there is every reason to conclude that this is a distinct and unconnected work.

The immediate narrator of the Brahma Puráńa is Lomaharshańa, who communicates it to the Rishis or sages assembled at Naimishárańya, as it was originally revealed by Brahmá, not to Maríchi, as the Matsya affirms, but to Daksha, another of the patriarchs. Hence its denomination of the Brahma Puráńa.

The early chapters of this work give a description of the creation, an account of the Manwantaras, and the history of the solar and lunar dynasties to the time of Kríshńa, in a summary manner, and in words which are common to it and several other Puráńas. A brief description of the universe succeeds; and then come a number of chapters relating to the holiness of Orissa, with its temples and sacred groves dedicated to the sun, to Śiva, and Jagannátha, the latter especially. These chapters are characteristic of this Puráńa, and show its main object to be the promotion of the worship of Kríshńa as Jagannátha.[1] To these particulars

---

[1] Colonel Vans Kennedy objects to this character of the Brahma Puráńa, and observes that it contains only two short descriptions of pagodas, the one of Końáditya, the other of Jagannátha. In that case, his copy must differ considerably from those I have met with; for, in them, the description of Purushottama Kshetra, the holy land of Orissa, runs through forty chapters, or one third of the work. The description, it is true, is interspersed, in the usual rambling strain of the Puráńas, with a variety of legends, some ancient, some modern; but they are intended to illustrate some local circumstance, and are, therefore, not incompatible with the main design, the celebration of the glories of Purushottama Kshetra. The specification of the temple of Jagannátha, how-

succeeds a life of Kŕishńa, which is, word for word, the same as that of the Vishńu Puráńa; and the compilation terminates with a particular detail of the mode in which Yoga or contemplative devotion, the object of which is still Vishńu, is to be performed. There is little, in this, which corresponds with the definition of a Pancha-lakshańa Puráńa; and the mention of the temples of Orissa, the date of the original construction of which is recorded,[1] shows that it could not have been compiled earlier than the thirteenth or fourteenth century.

The Uttara Khańda of the Brahma Puráńa bears still more entirely the character of a Máhátmya or local legend; being intended to celebrate the sanctity of the Balajá river, conjectured to be the same as the Banás in Marwar. There is no clue to its date: but it is clearly modern; grafting personages and fictions of its own invention on a few hints from older authorities.[2]

2. Padma Puráńa. "That which contains an account of the period when the world was a golden lotos (padma), and of all the occurrences of that time, is, therefore, called the Pádma by the wise. It contains fifty-five thousand stanzas."[3] The second Puráńa, in

ever, is, of itself, sufficient, in my opinion, to determine the character and era of the compilation.

[1] See Account of Orissa Proper, or Cuttack, by A. Stirling, Esq.: Asiatic Res., Vol. XV., p. 305.

[2] See Analysis of the Brahma Puráńa: Journ. Royal As. Soc., Vol. V., p. 65.

[3] एतदेव यदा पद्मभूरित्यभवत् जगत् ।
तदुत्पत्त्यादिवर्णं महत्याद्यनिबद्धने भूमिः ॥
पाद्म तत्सर्वपपाद्यस्तु सर्वसाधीर क्रमे ।

the usual lists, is always the Pádma, a very voluminous work, containing, according to its own statement, as well as that of other authorities, fifty-five thousand slokas; an amount not far from the truth. These are divided amongst five books, or Khańdas: 1. The Srishḍi Khańda or section on creation; 2. The Bhúmí Khańda, description of the earth; 3. The Swarga Khańda, chapter on heaven; 4. Pátála Khańda, chapter on the regions below the earth; and 5. the Uttara Khańda, last or supplementary chapter. There is also current a sixth division, the Kriyá Yoga Sára, a treatise on the practice of devotion.

The denominations of these divisions of the Padma Puráńa convey but an imperfect and partial notion of their contents. In the first, or section which treats of creation, the narrator is Ugrasrvas, the Súta, the son of Lomaharshańa, who is sent, by his father, to the Rishis at Naimishárańya, to communicate to them the Puráńa, which, from its containing an account of the lotos (padma) in which Brahmá appeared at creation, is termed the Pádma, or Padma Puráńa. The Súta repeats what was originally communicated by Brahmá to Pulastya, and by him to Bhíshma. The early chapters narrate the cosmogony, and the genealogy of the patriarchal families, much in the same style, and often in the same words, as the Vishńu; and short accounts of the Manwantaras and regal dynasties: but these, which are legitimate Pauráńik matters, soon make way for new and unauthentic inventions, illustrative of the virtues of the lake of Pushkara or Pokher, in Ajmir, as a place of pilgrimage.

The Bhúmí Khańda, or section of the earth, defers

any description of the earth until near its close; filling up one hundred and twenty-seven chapters with legends of a very mixed description, some ancient, and common to other Puráńas, but the greater part peculiar to itself, illustrative of Tirthas, either figuratively so termed,—as a wife, a parent, or a Guru, considered as a sacred object,—or places to which actual pilgrimage should be performed.

The Swarga Khańda describes, in the first chapters, the relative positions of the Lokas or spheres above the earth; placing above all, Vaikuńtha, the sphere of Vishńu: an addition which is not warranted by what appears to be the oldest cosmology.[1] Miscellaneous notices of some of the most celebrated princes then succeed, conformably to the usual narratives; and these are followed by rules of conduct for the several castes, and at different stages of life. The rest of the book is occupied by legends of a diversified description, introduced without much method or contrivance; a few of which, as Daksha's sacrifice, are of ancient date. but of which the most are original and modern.

The Pátála Khańda devotes a brief introduction to the description of Pátála, the regions of the snake-gods. But, the name of Ráma having been mentioned, Sesha, who has succeeded Pulastya as spokesman, proceeds to narrate the history of Ráma, his descent, and his posterity; in which the compiler seems to have taken the poem of Kálidása, the Raghu Vanśa, for his chief authority. An originality of addition may be suspected, however, in the adventures of the horse des-

---

[1] See Book II., Chapter VII.

tined by Ráma for an Aswamedha, which form the
subject of a great many chapters. When about to be
sacrificed, the horse turns out to be a Brahman, condemned, by an imprecation of Durvásas, a sage, to assume the equine nature, and who, by having been
sanctified by connexion with Ráma, is released from
his metamorphosis, and despatched, as a spirit of light,
to heaven. This piece of Vaishńava fiction is followed
by praises of the Srí Bhágavata, an account of Krishńa's
juvenilities, and the merits of worshipping Vishńu.
These accounts are communicated through a machinery
borrowed from the Tantras: they are told by Sadásiva
to Párvatí, the ordinary interlocutors of Tántrika compositions.

The Uttara Khańda is a most voluminous aggregation of very heterogeneous matters; but it is consistent
in adopting a decidedly Vaishńava tone, and admitting
no compromise with any other form of faith. The chief
subjects are first discussed in a dialogue between king
Dilípa and the Muni Vasishtha; such as the merits of
bathing in the month of Mágha, and the potency of
the Mantra or prayer addressed to Lakshmí Náráyańa.
But the nature of Bhakti, faith in Vishńu—the use of
Vaishńava marks on the body—the legends of Vishńu's
Avatáras, and especially of Ráma—and the construction of images of Vishńu—are too important to be
left to mortal discretion. They are explained by Siva
to Párvatí, and wound up by the adoration of Vishńu
by those divinities. The dialogue then reverts to the
king and the sage; and the latter states why Vishńu is
the only one of the triad entitled to respect; Siva being
licentious, Brahmá arrogant, and Vishńu alone pure.

Vasishtha then repeats, after Śiva, the Máhátmya of
the Bhagvad Gítá; the merit of each book of which
is illustrated by legends of the good consequences, to
individuals, from perusing or hearing it. Other Vaishńava Máhátmyas occupy considerable portions of
this Khańda, especially the Kárttika Máhátmya, or
holiness of the month Kárttika; illustrated, as usual,
by stories, a few of which are of an early origin, but
the greater part modern, and peculiar to this Puráńa.[1]

The Kriyá Yoga Sára is repeated, by Súta, to the
Rishis, after Vyása's communication of it to Jaimini,
in answer to an inquiry how religious merit might be
secured in the Kali age, in which men have become
incapable of the penances and abstraction by which
final liberation was formerly to be attained. The answer
is, of course, that which is intimated in the last book
of the Vishńu Puráńa—personal devotion to Vishńu.
Thinking of him, repeating his names, wearing his
marks, worshipping in his temples, are a full substitute
for all other acts of moral, or devotional, or contemplative, merit.

The different portions of the Padma Puráńa are, in
all probability, as many different works, neither of
which approaches to the original definition of a Puráńa.
There may be some connexion between the three first
portions, at least as to time: but there is no reason to
consider them as of high antiquity. They specify
the Jainas, both by name and practices; they talk of
Mlechchhas, "barbarians", flourishing in India: they

---

[1] One of them, the story of Jalandhara, is translated by
Colonel Vans Kennedy: Researches into the Nature and Affinity
of Ancient and Hindu Mythology, Appendix D.

XXXIV   PREFACE.

commend the use of the frontal and other Vaishńava
marks; and they notice other subjects which, like these,
are of no remote origin. The Pátála Khańda dwells
copiously upon the Bhágavata, and is, consequently,
posterior to it. The Uttara Khańda is intolerantly
Vaishńava, and is, therefore, unquestionably modern.
It enjoins the veneration of the Sálagráma stone and
Tulasí plant, the use of the Tapta-mudra, or stamping
with a hot iron the name of Vishńu on the skin, and a
variety of practices and observances undoubtedly no
part of the original system. It speaks of the shrines
of Śríranga and Venkatádri in the Dekhin, temples that
have no pretension to remote antiquity; and it names
Haripura on the Tungabhadrá, which is, in all likelihood,
the city of Vijayanagara, founded in the middle of the
fourteenth century. The Kriyá Yoga Sára is equally
a modern, and, apparently, a Bengali composition. No
portion of the Padma Puráńa is, probably, older than
the twelfth century; and the last parts may be as recent
as the fifteenth or sixteenth.[1]

3. Vishńu Puráńa. "That in which Parásara, beginning with the events of the Varáha Kalpa, expounds
all duties, is called the Vaishńava: and the learned know
its extent to be twenty-three thousand stanzas."[2] The

---

[1] The grounds of these conclusions are more particularly
detailed in my Analysis of the Padma Puráńa: J. R. As. Soc.,
Vol. V., p. 280.

[2] वराहकल्पानुचरितमखिलं यत्र पठ्यते ।
यस्माद् धर्माखिलांसंयुतं वैष्णवं विदुः ॥
* * * * * * * *
* * * * * * * *
त्रयोविंशतिसाहस्रं लक्षणायं विदुर्बुधाः ।

third Puráńa of the lists is that which has been selected
for translation, the Vishńu. It it unnecessary, therefore, to offer any general summary of its contents; and
it will be convenient to reserve any remarks upon its
character and probable antiquity, for a subsequent page.
It may here be observed, however, that the actual
number of verses contained in it falls far short of the
enumeration of the Matsya, with which the Bhágavata
concurs. Its actual contents are not seven thousand
stanzas. All the copies—and, in this instance, they are
not fewer than seven in number,—procured both in
the east and in the west of India, agree; and there is
no appearance of any part being wanting. There is a
beginning, a middle, and an end, in both text and comment; and the work, as it stands, is, incontestably,
entire. How is the discrepancy to be explained?

4. Váyu Puráńa. "The Puráńa in which Váyu has
declared the laws of duty, in connexion with the Sweta
Kalpa, and which comprises the Máhátmya of Rudra,
is the Váyaviya Puráńa: it contains twenty-four thousand verses."[1] The Siva or Saiva Puráńa is, as above
remarked, omitted in some of the lists; and, in general,
when that is the case, it is replaced by the Váyu or
Váyaviya. When the Siva is specified, as in the Bhágavata, then the Váyu is omitted;[*] intimating the possible identity of these two works.[†] This, indeed, is

---

[1] श्वेतकल्पमधीकृत्य धर्मान्वायुरिहाब्रवीत् ।
वायवीयं काबुद्धमाहात्म्यसंयुतम् ॥
चतुर्विंशत्सहस्राणि पुराणं तदिहोच्यते ।

---

* See p. XXIV. *supra*.
† This identity is distinctly asserted in the *Revá-máhátmya*, as follows:

confirmed by the Matsya, which describes the Váya-víya Puráńa as characterized by its account of the greatness of Rudra or Śiva: and Bálam Bhaṭṭa[1] mentions, that the Váyavíya is also called the Śaiva, though, according to some, the latter is the name of an Upapuráńa.[2] Colonel Vans Kennedy observes, that, in the west of India, the Śaiva is considered to be an Upa or 'minor' Puráńa.[3]

Another proof that the same work is intended by the authorities here followed, the Bhágavata and Matsya, under different appellations, is their concurrence in the extent of the work; each specifying its verses to be twenty-four thousand. A copy of the Śiva Puráńa, of which an index and analysis have been prepared, does not contain more than about seven thousand. It cannot, therefore, be the Śiva Puráńa of the Bhágavata: and we may safely consider that to be the same as the Váyavíya of the Matsya.[4]

---

[1] Commentary on the Mitákshará, Vyavahára Kánda.

[2] As. Journ., March, 1837, p. 242, note.

[3] Analysis of the Váyu Puráńa: Journ. As. Soc. of Bengal, December, 1832.

चतुर्थं वायुना प्रोक्तं वायवीयमिति श्रुतम् ।
शिवभक्तिसमायोगाच्छैवं तत्परिरक्षता ॥

[4] For accounts of works entitled *Śiva-puráńa* and *Laghu-śiva-puráńa,* see *Catalog. Cod. Manuscript. Sanscrit. Postvedic. Bodleian.,* &c., §§ 113, 127, and 129.

Regarding the first, described in § 113, Dr. Aufrecht observes: "De libro ipso, quem ad celebrandum cultum Laingicum scriptum esse vides, in praesentia nihil temere asseveraverim; expectandum enim est, dum de Skandapuráńae parte, quae Śivamáhátmya appellatur, accuratiora audiamus. Ex quo libellum nostrum desumtum esse, iis quae infra dicta sunt, suspicari possis."

The Váyu Puráńa is narrated, by Súta, to the Rishis at Naimishárańya, as it was formerly told, at the same place, to similar persons, by Váyu; a repetition of circumstances not uncharacteristic of the inartificial style of this Puráńa. It is divided into four Pádas, termed, severally, Prakriyá, Upodgháta, Anushanga, and Upasamhára; a classification peculiar to this work. These are preceded by an index, or heads of chapters, in the manner of the Mahábhárata and Rámáyańa—another peculiarity.

The Prakriyá portion contains but a few chapters, and treats, chiefly, of elemental creation, and the first evolutions of beings, to the same purport as the Vishńu, but in a more obscure and unmethodical style. The Upodgháta then continues the subject of creation, and describes the various Kalpas or periods during which the world has existed; a greater number of which is specified by the Saiva, than by the Vaishńava, Puráńas. Thirty-three are here described, the last of which is the Sweta or 'white' Kalpa, from Siva's being born, in it, of a white complexion. The genealogies of the patriarchs, the description of the universe, and the incidents of the first six Manwantaras are all treated of in this part of the work; but they are intermixed with legends and praises of Siva, as the sacrifice of Daksha, the Maheswara Máhátmya, the Nílakańtha Stotra, and others. The genealogies, although, in the main, the same as those in the Vaishńava Puráńas, present some variations. A long account of the Pitris or progenitors is also peculiar to this Puráńa; as are stories of some of the most celebrated Rishis who were engaged in the distribution of the Vedas.

The third division commences with an account of
the seven Rishis and their descendants, and describes
the origin of the different classes of creatures from the
daughters of Daksha, with a profuse copiousness of
nomenclature, not found in any other Puráńa. With
exception of the greater minuteness of detail, the particulars agree with those of the Vishńu Puráńa. A
chapter then occurs on the worship of the Pitris; another,
on Tírthas or places sacred to them; and several, on
the performance of Śráddhas, constituting the Śráddha
Kalpa. After this comes a full account of the solar and
lunar dynasties, forming a parallel to that in the following pages, with this difference, that it is, throughout,
in verse, whilst that of our text, as noticed in its place,
is, chiefly, in prose. It is extended, also, by the insertion
of detailed accounts of various incidents, briefly noticed
in the Vishńu, though derived, apparently, from a common original. The section terminates with similar
accounts of future kings, and the same chronological
calculations, that are found in the Vishńu.

The last portion, the Upasaṁhára, describes briefly
the future Manwantaras, the measures of space and
time, the end of the world, the efficacy of Yoga, and the
glories of Śivapura, or the dwelling of Śiva, with whom
the Yogin is to be united. The manuscript concludes
with a different history of the successive teachers of
the Váyu Puráńa, tracing them from Brahmá to Váyu,
from Váyu to Brihaspati, and from him, through various
deities and sages, to Dwaipáyana and Súta.

The account given of this Puráńa in the Journal of
the Asiatic Society of Bengal was limited to something
less than half the work; as I had not then been able to

procure a larger portion. I have now a more complete
one of my own; and there are several copies in the
East India Company's library, of the like extent. One,
presented by His Highness the Guicowar, is dated
Samvat 1540, or A. D. 1483, and is, evidently, as old
as it professes to be. The examination I have made
of the work confirms the view I formerly took of it;
and, from the internal evidence it affords, it may, perhaps, be regarded as one of the oldest and most authentic specimens extant of a primitive Puráña.

It appears, however, that we have not yet a copy of
the entire Váyu Puráña. The extent of it, as mentioned
above, should be twenty-four thousand verses. The
Guicowar MS. has but twelve thousand, and is denominated the Púrvárdha or first portion. My copy is
of the like extent. The index also shows, that several
subjects remain untold; as, subsequently to the description of the sphere of Śiva, and the periodical dissolution
of the world, the work is said to contain an account
of a succeeding creation, and of various events that
occurred in it, as the birth of several celebrated Ŕishis,
including that of Vyása, and a description of his distribution of the Vedas; an account of the enmity between
Vasishṭha and Viśwámitra; and a Naimishárañya Máhátmya. These topics are, however, of minor importance, and can scarcely carry the Puráña to the whole
extent of the verses which it is said to contain. If the
number is accurate, the index must still omit a considerable portion of the subsequent contents.

5. Śrí Bhágavata Puráña. "That in which ample
details of duty are described, and which opens with
(an extract from) the Gáyatrí; that in which the death

of the Asura Vṛitra is told, and in which the mortals
and immortals of the Sáraswata Kalpa, with the events
that then happened to them in the world, are related;
that is celebrated as the Bhágavata, and consists of
eighteen thousand verses." ¹ The Bhágavata is a work
of great celebrity in India, and exercises a more direct
and powerful influence upon the opinions and feelings
of the people than, perhaps, any other of the Puráńas.
It is placed the fifth in all the lists; but the Padma
Puráńa ranks it as the eighteenth, as the extracted
substance of all the rest. According to the usual specification, it consists of eighteen thousand ślokas, distributed amongst three hundred and thirty-two chapters,
divided into twelve Skandhas or books. It is named
Bhágavata from its being dedicated to the glorification
of Bhagavat or Vishńu.

The Bhágavata is communicated to the Rishis at Naimishárańya, by Súta, as usual: but he only repeats what
was narrated by Śuka, the son of Vyása, to Parikshit,
the king of Hastinápura, the grandson of Arjuna. Having
incurred the imprecation of a hermit, by which he was
sentenced to die of the bite of a venomous snake at
the expiration of seven days, the king, in preparation
for this event, repairs to the banks of the Ganges,
whither also come the gods and sages, to witness his

---

¹ यत्राधिकृत्य गायत्रीं वर्ण्यते धर्मविस्तरः ।
वृत्रासुरवधोपेतं तद्भागवतमुच्यते ॥
सारस्वतस्य कल्पस्य मध्ये ये स्युर्नरामराः ।
तद्वृत्तान्तोद्भवं लोके तद्भागवतमुच्यते ॥
* * * * * * * *
* * * * * * * *
अष्टादश सहस्राणि पुराणं तत्प्रकीर्तितम् ।

death. Amongst the latter is Śuka; and it is in reply to Parikshit's question, what a man should do who is about to die, that he narrates the Bhágavata, as he had heard it from Vyása: for nothing secures final happiness so certainly, as to die whilst the thoughts are wholly engrossed by Vishńu.

The course of the narration opens with a cosmogony, which, although, in most respects, similar to that of other Puráńas, is more largely intermixed with allegory and mysticism, and derives its tone more from the Vedánta than the Sánkhya philosophy. The doctrine of active creation by the Supreme, as one with Vásudeva, is more distinctly asserted, with a more decided enunciation of the effects being resolvable into Máyá or illusion. There are, also, doctrinal peculiarities highly characteristic of this Puráńa; amongst which is the assertion, that it was originally communicated by Brahmá to Nárada, that all men whatsoever, Hindus of every caste, and even Mlechchhas, outcasts or barbarians, might learn to have faith in Vásudeva.

In the third book, the interlocutors are changed to Maitreya and Vidura, the former of whom is the disciple, in the Vishńu Puráńa; the latter was the half-brother of the Kuru princes. Maitreya, again, gives an account of the Śrishti-lílá or sport of creation, in a strain partly common to the Puráńas, partly peculiar; although he declares he learned it from his teacher Paráśara, at the desire of Pulastya:[1] referring, thus, to the fabulous origin of the Vishńu Puráńa, and furnishing evidence of its priority. Again, however, the

---

[1] See Book I., Chapter I., *ad finem.*

authority is changed: and the narrative is said to have been that which was communicated by Śesha to the Nágas. The creation of Brahmá is then described, and the divisions of time are explained. A very long and peculiar account is given of the Varáha incarnation of Vishńu, which is followed by the creation of the Prajápatis and Swáyambhuva, whose daughter Devahúti is married to Kardama Rishi; an incident peculiar to this work, as is that which follows, of the Avatára of Vishńu as Kapila the son of Kardama and Devahúti, the author of the Sánkhya philosophy, which he expounds, after a Vaishńava fashion, to his mother, in the last nine chapters of this section.

The Manwantara of Swáyambhuva, and the multiplication of the patriarchal families, are next described with some peculiarities of nomenclature, which are pointed out in the notes to the parallel passages of the Vishńu Puráńa. The traditions of Dhruva, Veńa, Príthu, and other princes of this period, are the other subjects of the fourth Skandha, and are continued, in the fifth, to that of the Bharata who obtained emancipation. The details generally conform to those of the Vishńu Puráńa; and the same words are often employed; so that it would be difficult to determine which work had the best right to them, had not the Bhágavata itself indicated its obligations to the Vishńu. The remainder of the fifth book is occupied with the description of the universe; and the same conformity with the Vishńu continues.

This is only partially the case with the sixth book, which contains a variety of legends of a miscellaneous description, intended to illustrate the merit of worship-

ping Vishńu. Some of them belong to the early stock;
but some are, apparently, novel. The seventh book is,
mostly, occupied with the legend of Prahláda. In the
eighth, we have an account of the remaining Manwantaras; in which, as happening in the course of them, a
variety of ancient legends are repeated, as the battle
between the king of the elephants and an alligator, the
churning of the ocean, and the dwarf and fish Avatáras.
The ninth book narrates the dynasties of the Vaivaswata Manwantara, or the princes of the solar and lunar
races to the time of Kŕishńa.[1] The particulars conform,
generally, with those recorded in the Vishńu.

The tenth book is the characteristic part of this
Puráńa, and the portion upon which its popularity is
founded. It is appropriated entirely to the history of
Kŕishńa, which it narrates much in the same manner
as the Vishńu, but in more detail; holding a middle
place, however, between it and the extravagant prolixity
with which the Hari Vaṃśa repeats the story. It is not
necessary to particularize it further. It has been translated into, perhaps, all the languages of India, and is
a favourite work with all descriptions of people.

The eleventh book describes the destruction of the
Yádavas and death of Kŕishńa. Previous to the latter
event, Kŕishńa instructs Uddhava in the performance
of the Yoga; a subject consigned, by the Vishńu, to
the concluding passages. The narrative is much

---

[1] A translation of the ninth, by Captain Fell, was published
in Calcutta, in different numbers of the Monthly and Quarterly
Magazine, in 1823 and 1824. The second volume of Maurice's
Ancient History of Hindostan contains a translation, by Mr. Halhed,
of the tenth book, made through the medium of a Persian version.

the same, but something more summary than that of
the Vishńu. The twelfth book continues the lines of
the kings of the Kali age, prophetically, to a similar
period as the Vishńu, and gives a like account of the
deterioration of all things and their final dissolution.
Consistently with the subject of the Puráńa, the serpent
Takshaka bites Parikshit, and he expires: and the work
should terminate; or the close might be extended to the
subsequent sacrifice of Janamejaya, for the destruction
of the whole serpent race. There is a rather awkwardly
introduced description, however, of the arrangement
of the Vedas and Puráńas by Vyása, and the legend of
Márkańdeya's interview with the infant Kŕishńa, during
a period of worldly dissolution. We then come to the
end of the Bhágavata, in a series of encomiastic com-
mendations of its own sanctity and efficacy to salvation.

Mr. Colebrooke observes, of the Bhágavata Puráńa:
"I am, myself, inclined to adopt an opinion supported
by many learned Hindus, who consider the celebrated
Srí Bhágavata as the work of a grammarian [Bopadeva],
supposed to have lived about six hundred years ago."[1]
Colonel Vans Kennedy considers this an incautious
admission; because "it is unquestionable that the number
of the Puráńas have been always held to be eighteen;
but, in most of the Puráńas, the names of the eighteen
are enumerated, amongst which the Bhágavata is invariably included; and, consequently, if it were composed only six hundred years ago, the others must be

---

[1] As. Res., Vol. VIII., p. 467. *

* *Miscellaneous Essays*, Vol. I., p. 104.

of an equally modern date."[1] Some of them are, no doubt, more recent; but, as already remarked, no weight can be attached to the specification of the eighteen names; for they are always complete: each Puráńa enumerates all.* Which is the last? Which had the opportunity of naming its seventeen predecessors, and adding itself? The argument proves too much. There can be little doubt that the list has been inserted, upon the authority of tradition, either by some improving transcriber, or by the compiler of a work more recent than the eighteen genuine Puráńas. The objection is also rebutted by the assertion, that there was another Puráńa to which the name applies, and which is still to be met with, the Deví Bhágavata.

For the authenticity of the Bhágavata is one of the few questions, affecting their sacred literature, which Hindu writers have ventured to discuss. The occasion is furnished by the text itself. In the fourth chapter of the first book, it is said that Vyása arranged the Vedas, and divided them into four, and that he then compiled the Itihása and Puráńas, as a fifth Veda. The Vedas he gave to Paila and the rest; the Itihása and Puráńas, to Lomaharshańa, the father of Súta.[2] Then,

---

[1] Researches into the Nature and Affinity of Ancient and Hindu Mythology, p. 155, note.

[2] Book I., Chapter IV., 19-22.†

---

* But see the editor's second note in p. LIV. *infra*.

† चातुर्होत्रं कर्म शुद्धं प्रजानां वीक्ष्य वैदिकम् ।
व्यदधाद्यज्ञसंतत्यै वेदमेकं चतुर्विधम् ॥
ऋग्यजुःसामाथर्वाख्या वेदाश्चत्वार उद्धृताः ।
इतिहासपुराणं च पञ्चमो वेद उच्यते ॥

reflecting that these works may not be accessible to
women, Súdras, and mixed castes, he composed the
Bhárata, for the purpose of placing religious knowledge
within their reach. Still, he felt dissatisfied, and wan-
dered, in much perplexity, along the banks of the
Saraswatí, where his hermitage was situated, when
Nárada paid him a visit. Having confided to him his
secret and seemingly causeless dissatisfaction, Nárada
suggested that it arose from his not having sufficiently
dwelt, in the works he had finished, upon the merit of
worshipping Vásudeva. Vyása at once admitted its
truth, and found a remedy for his uneasiness in the
composition of the Bhágavata, which he taught to Śuka,
his son.[1] Here, therefore, is the most positive assertion
that the Bhágavata was composed subsequently to the
Puráńas, and given to a different pupil, and was not,
therefore, one of the eighteen of which Romaharshańa,
the Súta, was, according to all concurrent testimonies,
the depositary. Still, the Bhágavata is named amongst
the eighteen Puráńas, by the inspired authorities: and
how can these incongruities be reconciled?

The principal point in dispute seems to have been
started by an expression of Śrídhara Swámin, a commentator on the Bhágavata, who, somewhat incautiously,
made the remark, that there was no reason to suspect

---

[1] Book I., 7, 8.

नवर्वेदधरः पैलः सामगो जैमिनिः कविः ।
वैशम्पायन एवैको निष्णातो वह्वृचोऽजुन ॥
वर्याणि ... आसीत्सुमन्तुर्दारुणो मुनिः ।
इतिहासपुराणानां पिता मे रोमहर्षणः ॥

that, by the term Bhágavata, any other work than the subject of his labours was intended. This was, therefore, an admission that some suspicions had been entertained of the correctness of the nomenclature, and that an opinion had been expressed, that the term belonged, not to the Śrí Bhágavata, but to the Deví Bhágavata; to a Śaiva, not a Vaishńava, composition. With whom doubts prevailed prior to Śrídhara Swámin, or by whom they were urged, does not appear; for, as far as we are aware, no works, anterior to his date, in which they are advanced have been met with. Subsequently, various tracts have been written on the subject. There are three in the library of the East India Company: the Durjana Mukha Chapeṭiká, 'A slap of the face for the vile', by Rámáśrama; the Durjana Mukha Mahá Chapeṭiká,* 'A great slap of the face for the wicked', by Káśinátha Bhaṭṭa; and the Durjana Mukha Padma Páduká, 'A slipper' for the same part of the same persons, by a nameless disputant. The first maintains the authenticity of the Bhágavata; the second asserts, that

* The postscript of this tract has *Durjana-mukha-chapeṭiká.* In the MS., Professor Wilson has noted, that it is referred to, in the *Durjana-mukha-padma-páduká,* under a longer title, that given in the text. Burnouf—who, in the preface to the first volume of his *Bhágavata-puráńa,* has translated and annotated the three treatises named above—remarks as follows on that reference: "Le traité auquel notre auteur fait allusion paraît être le même que celui que j'ai placé le troisième, et qui est consacré tout entier à prouver cette thèse, que quand les Puráńas parlent du Bhágavata, c'est le Dévibhágavata qu'ils entendent désigner, et non pas notre Çri Bhágavata, qui fait autorité pour les Vâichńavas. Cependant le passage sur lequel porte la présente note comme ce traité: *Un grand soufflet, etc.;* ce qui ferait supposer qu'il existe deux traités de ce genre, dont l'un serait plus étendu que l'autre, et dont nous ne posséderions que le plus court, c'est-à-dire celui qui est traduit plus bas." P. LXXVII.

the Deví Bhágavata is the genuine Puráńa; and the
third replies to the arguments of the first. There is,
also, a work by Purushottama, entitled 'Thirteen arguments for dispelling all doubts of the character of the
Bhágavata' (Bhágavata swarúpa vishaya śanká nirása
trayodaśa); whilst Bálam-Bhatta, a commentator on the
Mitákshará, indulging in a dissertation on the meaning
of the word Puráńa, adduces reasons for questioning
the inspired origin of this Puráńa.

The chief arguments in favour of the authenticity
of this Puráńa are, the absence of any reason why
Bopadeva, to whom it is attributed, should not have
put his own name to it; its being included in all lists
of the Puráńas, sometimes with circumstances that
belong to no other Puráńa; and its being admitted to
be a Puráńa, and cited as authority, or made the subject of comment, by writers of established reputation,
of whom Śankara Achárya is one: and he lived long
before Bopadeva. The reply to the first argument is
rather feeble; the controversialists being unwilling,
perhaps, to admit the real object, the promotion of new
doctrines. It is, therefore, said, that Vyása was an incarnation of Náráyańa; and the purpose was to propitiate his favour. The insertion of a Bhágavata amongst
the eighteen Puráńas is acknowledged; but this, it is
said, can be the Deví Bhágavata alone: for the circumstances apply more correctly to it than to the Vaishńava
Bhágavata. Thus, a text is quoted, by Kásínátha, from
a Puráńa—he does not state which—that says, of the
Bhágavata, that it contains eighteen thousand verses,
twelve books, and three hundred and thirty-two chap-

ters.* Kásínátha asserts that the chapters of the Srí
Bhágavata are three hundred and thirty-five, and that
the numbers apply, throughout, only to the Devi Bhágavata. It is also said that the Bhágavata contains an
account of the acquirement of holy knowledge by
Hayagríva; the particulars of the Sáraswata Kalpa; a
dialogue between Ambarísha and Suka: and that it
commences with the Gáyatrí, or, at least, a citation of
it. These all apply to the Deví Bhágavata alone, except
the last: but it also is more true of the Saiva than of
the Vaishñava work; for the latter has only one word
of the Gáyatrí, dhímahi, 'we meditate'; whilst the
former to dhímahi adds, Yo nah prachodayát, 'who
may enlighten us.' To the third argument it is, in the
first place, objected, that the citation of the Bhágavata
by modern writers is no test of its authenticity; and,
with regard to the more ancient commentary of Sankara Áchárya, it is asked, "Where is it?" Those who
advocate the sanctity of the Bhágavata reply: "It was
written in a difficult style, and became obsolete, and
is lost." "A very unsatisfactory plea", retort their
opponents; "for we still have the works of Sankara,
several of which are quite as difficult as any in the
Sanskrit language." The existence of this comment,
too, rests upon the authority of Mádhwa or Mádha-

* यस्मो ऽध्याहृत्य सारस्यं सारादपि समुद्धृतम् ।
एकवीजमभूद्विद्या अथ भूतविधारणा ।
आत्मा च समारब्धार्थं भागवतं विदुः ।
सन्ख्या तादृश एतावत् ऋद्वेन विरिता: शुभा: ॥
पार्षद्यविभूतं पूर्वकभाषा: परिकीर्तिता: ।

The first three of these five verses are quoted, professedly from the *Pu-
rāṇārṇava*, near the beginning of Chitsukha's *Bhágavata-tattwa-sangraha*.

va," who, in a commentary of his own, asserts that he has consulted eight others. Now, amongst these is one by the monkey Hanumat; and, although a Hindu disputant may believe in the reality of such a composition, yet we may receive its citation as a proof that Mádhwa was not very scrupulous in the verification of his authorities.

There are other topics urged, in this controversy, on both sides, some of which are simple enough, some are ingenious: but the statement of the text is, of itself, sufficient to show, that, according to the received opinion, of all the authorities, of the priority of the eighteen Puráńas to the Bhárata, it is impossible that the Srí Bhágavata, which is subsequent to the Bhárata, should be of the number; and the evidence of style, the superiority of which to that of the Puráńas in general is admitted by the disputants, is also proof that it is the work of a different hand. Whether the Deví Bhágavata have a better title to be considered as an original composition of Vyása, is equally questionable; but it cannot be doubted that the Srí Bhágavata is the product of uninspired erudition. There does not seem to be any other ground than tradition for ascribing it to Bopadeva the grammarian: but there is no reason to call the tradition in question. Bopadeva flourished at the court of Hemádri, Raja of Devagiri, Deogur or Dowlutabad, and must, consequently, have lived prior to the conquest of that principality by the Mohammedans in the fourteenth century. The date of the

---

* See Burnouf's edition of the *Bhágavata-puráńa*, Vol. I., Preface p. LXII., note.

twelfth century,[*] commonly assigned to him, is, probably, correct, and is that of the Bhágavata Puráńa.

6. Nárada or Náradíya Puráńa. "Where Nárada has described the duties which were observed in the Brihat Kalpa, that is called the Náradíya, having twenty-five thousand stanzas."[1] If the number of verses be here correctly stated, the Puráńa has not fallen into my hands. The copy I have analysed contains not many more than three thousand slokas. There is another work, which might be expected to be of greater extent, the Brihan Náradíya or great Nárada Puráńa; but this, according to the concurrence of three copies in my possession, and of five others in the Company's library, contains but about three thousand five hundred verses. It may be doubted, therefore, if the Nárada Puráńa of the Matsya exists.[2]

According to the Matsya, the Nárada Puráńa is related

यत्र नारदो धर्मानुपृक्तिस्वानवानि ।
पर्वनिघ्नसत्कानि नारदीयं तदुच्यते ॥

[1] The description of Vishńu, translated by Colonel Vans Kennedy (Researches into the Nature and Affinity of Ancient and Hindu Mythology, p. 200) from the Náradíya Puráńa, occurs in my copy of the Brihan Náradíya. There is no Nárada Puráńa in the East India Company's library, though, as noticed in the text, several of the Brihan Náradíya. There is a copy of the Rukmángada Charitra, said to be a part of the Śrí Nárada Puráńa.

[*] Burnouf—*Bhágavata-puráńa*, Vol. I., Preface, p. LXIII., first note, and pp. XCVII. *et seq.*—would place Bopadeva in the second half of the thirteenth century.

I follow the western and southern pandits in preferring Bopadeva to Vopadeva, as the name is ordinarily exhibited.

Touching Bopadeva and Hemádri, see Dr. Aufrecht's *Catalog. Cod. Manuscript.*, &c., pp. 37 and 38.

d*

by Nárada, and gives an account of the Bríhat Kalpa.
The Náradíya Puráńa is communicated, by Nárada, to
the Rishis at Naimishárańya, on the Gomatí river. The
Bríhan Náradíya is related to the same persons, at the
same place, by Súta, as it was told by Nárada to Sanatkumára. Possibly, the term Bríhat may have been suggested by the specification which is given in the Matsya:
but there is no description, in it, of any particular Kalpa
or day of Brahmá.

From a cursory examination of these Puráńas it is
very evident that they have no conformity to the definition of a Puráńa, and that both are sectarial and modern
compilations, intended to support the doctrine of Bhakti
or faith in Vishńu. With this view, they have collected
a variety of prayers addressed to one or other form of
that divinity; a number of observances and holydays
connected with his adoration; and different legends,
some, perhaps, of an early, others of a more recent,
date, illustrative of the efficacy of devotion to Hari.
Thus, in the Nárada, we have the stories of Dhruva
and Prahláda: the latter told in the words of the Vishńu:
whilst the second portion of it is occupied with a legend
of Mohiní, the will-born daughter of a king called Rukmángada; beguiled by whom, the king offers to perform
for her whatever she may desire. She calls upon him
either to violate the rule of fasting on the eleventh day
of the fortnight, a day sacred to Vishńu, or to put his
son to death; and he kills his son, as the lesser sin of
the two. This shows the spirit of the work. Its date
may also be inferred from its tenor; as such monstrous
extravagancies in praise of Bhakti are, certainly, of modern origin. One limit it furnishes, itself; for it refers

to Śuka and Parikshit, the interlocutors of the Bhágavata; and it is, consequently, subsequent to the date
of that Puráńa. It is, probably, considerably later: for
it affords evidence that it was written after India was
in the hands of the Mohammedans. In the concluding
passage it is said: "Let not this Puráńa be repeated in
the presence of the 'killers of cows' and contemners
of the gods." It is, possibly, a compilation of the sixteenth or seventeenth century.

The Bṛihan Náradíya is a work of the same tenor
and time. It contains little else than panegyrical prayers
addressed to Vishńu, and injunctions to observe various
rites, and keep holy certain seasons, in honour of him.
The earlier legends introduced are the birth of Márkańdeya, the destruction of Sagara's sons, and the dwarf
Avatára; but they are subservient to the design of the
whole, and are rendered occasions for praising Náráyańa. Others, illustrating the efficacy of certain
Vaishńava observances, are puerile inventions, wholly
foreign to the more ancient system of Pauráńik fiction.
There is no attempt at cosmogony, or patriarchal or
regal genealogy. It is possible that these topics may
be treated of in the missing stanzas: but it seems more
likely that the Nárada Puráńa of the lists has little in
common with the works to which its name is applied
in Bengal and Hindusthán.

7. Márkańda or Márkańdeya Puráńa. "That Puráńa
in which, commencing with the story of the birds that
were acquainted with right and wrong, everything is
narrated fully by Márkańdeya, as it was explained by
holy sages, in reply to the question of the Muni, is
called the Márkańdeya, containing nine thousand ver

ses."[1] This is so called from its being, in the first instance, narrated by Márkańdeya Muni, and. in the second place, by certain fabulous birds; thus far agreeing with the account given of it in the Matsya. That, as well as other authorities, specify its containing nine thousand stanzas; but my copy closes with a verse affirming that the number of verses recited by the Muni was six thousand nine hundred; and a copy in the East India Company's library has a similar specification. The termination is, however, somewhat abrupt; and there is no reason why the subject with which it ends should not have been carried on further. One copy in the Company's library, indeed, belonging to the Guicowar's collection, states, at the close, that it is the end of the first Khańda or section. If the Puráńa was ever completed, the remaining portion of it appears to be lost.[*]

Jaimini, the pupil of Vyása, applies to Márkańdeya to be made acquainted with the nature of Vásudeva, and for an explanation of some of the incidents described in the Mahábhárata; with the ambrosia of which divine poem, Vyása, he declares, has watered the whole world: a reference which establishes the priority of the Bhárata to the Márkańdeya Puráńa, however incom-

---

यदाधिकृत्व बहुणीमलीधर्मविचारख्णाम् ।
व्याख्यातं यदुणिमये चविविभिर्धर्मचारिदभि: ॥
मार्कण्डेयेन कथितं तत्त्वं विस्तरेन तु ।
पुरानं नवसाहस्रं मार्कण्डेयमिनुच्यते ॥ [†]

* See the Rev. Krishnamohan Banerjea's edition of the *Márkańdeya-puráńa*, Introduction, pp. 26, 31, and 32.

† Two MSS. of the *Matsya-puráńa*, out of four within my reach, omit the second and third lines. The other two give the second as follows:

व्याख्यातं यैमिनिमये यचविभिर्धर्मचारिदभि: ।

patible this may be with the tradition, that, having finished the Puránas, Vyása wrote the poem.[*]

Márkańdeya excuses himself, saying he has a religious rite to perform; and he refers Jaimini to some very sapient birds who reside in the Vindhya mountains; birds of a celestial origin, found, when just born, by the Muni Samíka, on the field of Kurukshetra, and brought up, by him, along with his scholars: in consequence of which, and by virtue of their heavenly descent, they became profoundly versed in the Vedas and a knowledge of spiritual truth. This machinery is borrowed from the Mahábhárata, with some embellishment. Jaimini, accordingly, has recourse to the birds, Pingáksha and his brethren, and puts to them the questions he had asked of the Muni: "Why was Vásudeva born as a mortal? How was it that Draupadí was the wife of the five Páńdus? Why did Baladeva do penance for Brahmanicide? And why were the children of Draupadí destroyed, when they had Kŕishńa and Arjuna to defend them?" The answers to these inquiries occupy a number of chapters, and form a sort of supple-

---

[*] In his account of the *Márkańdeya-puráńa*, Professor Banerjea says: "We cannot help noticing, in this place, the dignity imputed to the work under review. It is classed in the same category with the Vedas, and described as an immediate product from Brahmá's mouth. Although a Puráńa, it is not attributed to Vyása, whom other Sástras consider as the author of all works bearing that title. The Márkańdeya, however, does not acknowledge him as its composer, editor, or compiler. It claims equal honour, in this respect, with the Vedas themselves."

Again, with reference to the list spoken of in pp. XXIII. and XLV., *supra*: "As far as we have seen Bengal Manuscripts, the Márkańdeya presents a singular exception to this hackneyed enumeration of the eighteen Puráńas, and the celebration of Vyása's name as the author of them all. The Maithila manuscripts, as they are commonly called, are not so chaste." *Ibid.*, Preface, pp. 15 and 16.

ment to the Mahábhárata; supplying, partly by invention, perhaps, and partly by reference to equally ancient authorities, the blanks left in some of its narrations.

Legends of Vítrásura's death, Baladeva's penance, Harischandra's elevation to heaven, and the quarrel between Vasishtha and Viśwámitra, are followed by a discussion respecting birth, death, and sin; which leads to a more extended description of the different hells than is found in other Puráñas. The account of creation which is contained in this work is repeated, by the birds, after Márkañdeya's account of it to Kraushtínki, and is confined to the origin of the Vedas and patriarchal families, amongst whom are new characters, as Duhsaha and his wife Márshtí, and their descendants; allegorical personages, representing intolerable iniquity and its consequences. There is then a description of the world, with, as usual to this Puráña, several singularities, some of which are noticed in the following pages. This being the state of the world in the Swáyaṁbhuva Manwantara, an account of the other Manwantaras succeeds, in which the births of the Manus, and a number of other particulars, are peculiar to this work. The present or Vaivaswata Manwantara is very briefly passed over; but the next, the first of the future Manwantaras, contains the long episodical narrative of the actions of the goddess Durgá, which is the especial boast of this Puráña, and is the text-book of the worshippers of Kálí, Chañdí, or Durgá, in Bengal. It is the Chañdí Pátha, or Durgá Máhátmya, in which the victories of the goddess over different evil beings or Asuras are detailed with considerable power and spirit. It is read daily in the temples of Durgá, and furnishes the pomp and circumstance of the great festival of Bengal, the Durgá pújá, or public worship of that goddess.[1]

After the account of the Manwantaras is completed, there follows a series of legends, some new, some old, relating to the Sun and his posterity; continued to Vaivaswata Manu and his sons, and their immediate descendants; terminating with Dama, the son of Narishyanta.[2] Of most of the persons noticed the work narrates particulars not found elsewhere.

This Puráňa has a character different from that of all the others. It has nothing of a sectarial spirit, little of a religious tone; rarely inserting prayers and invocations to any deity; and such as are inserted are brief and moderate. It deals little in precepts, ceremonial or moral. Its leading feature is narrative; and it presents an uninterrupted succession of legends, most of which, when ancient, are embellished with new circumstances, and, when new, partake so far of the spirit of the old, that they are disinterested creations of the imagination, having no particular motive, being designed to recommend no special doctrine or observance. Whether they are derived from any other source, or whether they are original inventions, it is not possible to ascertain. They are, most probably, for the greater part, at least, original; and the whole has been narrated in the compiler's own manner; a manner superior to that of the Puráñas in general, with exception of the Bhágavata.

---

[1] A translation into English, by a Madras Pandit, Kávali Venkáta Rámaswámin, was published at Calcutta, in 1823.

[2] See Vishňu Puráňa, Book IV., Chapter I.

It is not easy to conjecture a date for this Puráńa. It is subsequent to the Mahábhárata: but how long subsequent, is doubtful. It is, unquestionably, more ancient than such works as the Brahma, Padma, and Náradíya Puráńas: and its freedom from sectarial bias is a reason for supposing it anterior to the Bhágavata. At the same time, its partial conformity to the definition of a Puráńa, and the tenor of the additions which it has made to received legends and traditions, indicate a not very remote age; and, in the absence of any guide to a more positive conclusion, it may, conjecturally, be placed in the ninth or tenth century.

8. Agni Puráńa. "That Puráńa which describes the occurrences of the Ísána Kalpa, and was related by Agni to Vasishtha, is called the Ágneya. It consists of sixteen thousand stanzas."[1] The Agni or Ágneya Puráńa derives its name from its having being communicated, originally, by Agni, the deity of fire, to the Muni Vasishtha, for the purpose of instructing him in the twofold knowledge of Brahma.[2] By him it was taught to Vyása, who imparted it to Súta; and the latter is represented as repeating it to the Rishis at Naimishá-rańya. Its contents are variously specified as sixteen thousand, fifteen thousand, or fourteen thousand, stanzas. The two copies which were employed by me contain about fifteen thousand slokas. There are two, in the

---

[1] यदाग्नेयार्थं कल्पपुराणमधिकृतं च ।
वसिष्ठायादिका श्रीतमाग्नेयं नमपर्चे ॥
* * * * * * * *
* * * * * * * *
तत्र पौरस्वार्थं सर्वकल्पुस्खमद्रु ।

[2] See Book VI., Chapter V.

Company's library, which do not extend beyond twelve thousand verses; but they are, in many other respects, different from mine. One of them was written at Agra, in the reign of Akbar, in A. D. 1589.

The Agni Puráńa, in the form in which it has been obtained in Bengal and at Benares, presents a striking contrast to the Márkańdeya. It may be doubted if a single line of it is original. A very great proportion of it may be traced to other sources; and a more careful collation—if the task was worth the time it would require—would probably discover the remainder.

The early chapters of this Puráńa[1] describe the Avatáras, and, in those of Ráma and Kríshńa, avowedly follow the Rámáyańa and Mahábhárata. A considerable portion is then appropriated to instructions for the performance of religious ceremonies; many of which belong to the Tántrika ritual, and are, apparently, transcribed from the principal authorities of that system. Some belong to mystical forms of Śaiva worship, little known in Hindusthán, though, perhaps, still practised in the south. One of these is the Dikshá or initiation of a novice: by which, with numerous ceremonies and invocations, in which the mysterious monosyllables of the Tantras are constantly repeated, the disciple is transformed into a living personation of Śiva, and receives, in that capacity, the homage of his Guru. Inter-

---

[1] Analysis of the Agni Puráńa: Journal of the Asiatic Society of Bengal, March, 1832.[*] I have there stated, incorrectly, that the Agni is a Vaishńava Puráńa. It is one of the Támasa or Śaiva class, as mentioned above.

[*] See Professor Wilson's collected works, Vol. III.

spersed with these are chapters descriptive of the earth
and of the universe, which are the same as those of
the Vishńu Puráńa: and Máhátmyas or legends of holy
places, particularly of Gayá. Chapters on the duties
of kings and on the art of war then occur, which have
the appearance of being extracted from some older
work, as is, undoubtedly, the chapter on judicature,[*]
which follows them, and which is the same as the text
of the Mitákshará. Subsequent to these we have an
account of the distribution and arrangement of the
Vedas and Puráńas, which is little else than an abridgment of the Vishńu; and, in a chapter on gifts, we have
a description of the Puráńas, which is precisely the
same, and in the same situation, as the similar subject
in the Matsya Puráńa. The genealogical chapters are
meagre lists, differing, in a few respects, from those
commonly received, as hereafter noticed, but unaccom-
panied by any particulars such as those recorded or
invented in the Márkańdeya. The next subject is medicine, compiled, avowedly, but injudiciously, from the
Sauśruta. A series of chapters on the mystic worship
of Śiva and Deví follows; and the work winds up with
treatises on rhetoric, prosody, and grammar, according
to the Sútras of Pingala and Páńini.

The cyclopædical character of the Agni Puráńa, as
it is now described, excludes it from any legitimate
claims to be regarded as a Puráńa, and proves that its

---

[*] According to Dr. Aufrecht: "Haec pars, paucis mutatis et additis,
ex Yájnavalkyae legum codice desumta est." Then follows "Rigvidhánam,
i. e., Rigvedi hymni sive disticha ad varias superstitiones adhibenda.
Haec pars e Rigvidhána libello, qui et ipse serae originis indicia prae se
fert excerpta est, multique versus ad literam cum illo consentiunt."
Catalog. Cod. Manuscript., &c., p. 7.

origin cannot be very remote. It is subsequent to the
Itihásas, to the chief works on grammar, rhetoric, and
medicine, and to the introduction of the Tántrika
worship of Deví. When this latter took place, is yet
far from determined; but there is every probability
that it dates long after the beginning of our era. The
materials of the Agni Puráńa are, however, no doubt,
of some antiquity. The medicine of Suśruta is considerably older than the ninth century; and the grammar of Páńini probably precedes Christianity. The
chapters on archery and arms, and on regal administ-
ration, are also distinguished by an entirely Hindu
character, and must have been written long anterior
to the Mohammedan invasion. So far the Agni Puráńa
is valuable, as embodying and preserving relics of
antiquity, although compiled at a more recent date.

Colonel Wilford[1] has made great use of a list of
kings derived from an appendix to the Agni Puráńa,
which professes to be the sixty-third or last section.
As he observes, it is seldom found annexed to the
Puráńa. I have never met with it, and doubt its ever
having formed any part of the original compilation.
It would appear, from Colonel Wilford's remarks, that
this list notices Mohammed as the institutor of an era:
but his account of this is not very distinct. He mentions, explicitly, however, that the list speaks of Sáliváhana and Vikramáditya: and this is quite sufficient
to establish its character. The compilers of the Puráńas
were not such bunglers as to bring within their chro-

---

[1] Essay on Vikramáditya and Sáliváhana: As. Res., Vol. IX ,
p. 131.

nology so well known a personage as Vikramáditya.
There are, in all parts of India, various compilations
ascribed to the Puránas, which never formed any portion of their contents, and which, although offering,
sometimes, useful local information, and valuable as
preserving popular traditions, are not, in justice, to be
confounded with the Puránas, so as to cause them to
be charged with even more serious errors and ana-
chronisms than those of which they are guilty.

The two copies of this work in the library of the
East India Company appropriate the first half to a
description of the ordinary and occasional observances
of the Hindus, interspersed with a few legends. The
latter half treats exclusively of the history of Ráma.

9. Bhavishya Purána. "The Purána in which Brahmá,
having described the greatness of the sun, explained to
Manu the existence of the world, and the characters
of all created things, in the course of the Aghora Kalpa,
that is called the Bhavishya; the stories being, for the
most part, the events of a future period. It contains
fourteen thousand five hundred stanzas."[1] This Purána,
as the name implies, should be a book of prophecies,
foretelling what will be (bhavishyati), as the Matsya
Purána intimates. Whether such a work exists, is
doubtful. The copies, which appear to be entire, and
of which there are three in the library of the East
India Company, agreeing, in their contents, with two

---

[1] यत्राधिकृत्य माहात्म्यमादित्यस्य चतुर्मुख: ।
अघोरकल्पनामानयप्रद्येन धर्मास्थितम् ॥
अभवे भवयामास भूतग्रामस्य लक्षणम् ।
चतुर्दश सहस्राणि तथा पञ्च शतानि च ॥
भविष्यचरितप्रायं भविष्यं तद्विदो विदुः ।

in my possession, contain about seven thousand stanzas. There is another work, entitled the Bhavishyottara, as if it was a continuation or supplement of the former, containing, also, about seven thousand verses: but the subjects of both these works are but to a very imperfect degree analogous to those to which the Matsya alludes.[1]

The Bhavishya Puráńa, as I have it, is a work in a hundred and twenty-six short chapters, repeated by Sumantu to Śatáníka, a king of the Páńdu family. He notices, however, its having originated with Swayambhu or Brahmá, and describes it as consisting of five parts; four dedicated, it should seem, to as many deities, as they are termed, Bráhma, Vaishńava, Śaiva, and Twáshťra; whilst the fifth is the Pratisarga or repeated creation. Possibly, the first part only may have come into my hands: although it does not so appear by the manuscript.

Whatever it may be, the work in question is not a Puráńa. The first portion, indeed, treats of creation; but it is little else than a transcript of the words of the first chapter of Manu. The rest is entirely a manual of religious rites and ceremonies. It explains the ten Saṁskáras or initiatory rites; the performance of the Sandhyá; the reverence to be shown to a Guru; the duties of the different Áśramas and castes; and enjoins a number of Vratas or observances of fasting and the

---

[1] Colonel Vans Kennedy states that he had "not been able to procure the Bhavishya Puráńa, nor even to obtain any account of its contents." Researches into the Nature and Affinity of Ancient and Hindu Mythology, p. 153, note.

like, appropriate to different lunar days. A few legends
enliven the series of precepts. That of the sage Chya-
vana is told at considerable length, taken, chiefly, from
the Mahábhárata. The Nága Panchamí, or fifth lunation
sacred to the serpent-gods, gives rise to a description
of different sorts of snakes. After these, which occupy
about one third of the chapters, the remainder of them
conform, in subject, to one of the topics referred to by
the Matsya. They chiefly represent conversations between Kríshńa, his son Sámba,—who had become a leper
by the curse of Durvásas,—Vasishtha, Nárada, and
Vyása, upon the power and glory of the Sun, and the
manner in which he is to be worshipped. There is
some curious matter in the last chapters, relating to
the Magas, silent worshippers of the sun, from Sáka-
dwípa; as if the compiler had adopted the Persian term
Magh, and connected the fire-worshippers of Iran with
those of India. This is a subject, however, that requires
further investigation.

The Bhavishyottara is, equally with the preceding,
a sort of manual of religious offices; the greater portion
being appropriated to Vratas, and the remainder, to
the forms and circumstances with which gifts are to
be presented. Many of the ceremonies are obsolete,
or are observed in a different manner, as the Rathayátrá or car-festival, and the Madanotsava or festival
of spring. The descriptions of these throw some light
upon the public condition of the Hindu religion at a
period probably prior to the Mohammedan conquest.
The different ceremonies are illustrated by legends,
which are, sometimes, ancient; as, for instance, the destruction of the god of love by Śiva, and his thence

becoming Ananga, the disembodied lord of hearts. The work is supposed to be communicated by Krishńa to Yudhishthira, at a great assemblage of holy persons at the coronation of the latter, after the conclusion of the Great War.

10. Brahma Vaivarta Puráńa. "That Puráńa which is related by Sávarńi to Náradu, and contains the account of the greatness of Krishńa, with the occurrences of the Rathantara Kalpa, where, also, the story of Brahma-varáha is repeatedly told, is called the Brahma Vaivarta, and contains eighteen thousand stanzas."[1] The account here given of the Brahma Vaivarta Puráńa agrees with its present state, as to its extent. The copies rather exceed than fall short of eighteen thousand stanzas. It also correctly represents its comprising a Máhátmya or legend of Krishńa; but it is very doubtful, nevertheless, if the same work is intended.

The Brahma Vaivarta, as it now exists, is narrated, not by Sávarńi, but the Rishi Náráyańa, to Nárada, by whom it is communicated to Vyása: he teaches it to Súta; and the latter repeats it to the Rishis at Naimishárańya. It is divided into four Khańdas or books, the Bráhma, Prakriti, Gańeśa, and Krishńa Janma Khańdas; dedicated, severally, to describe the acts of Brahmá, Deví, Gańeśa, and Krishńa; the latter, however, throughout absorbing the interest and importance of the work. In none of these is there any account of

---

[1] रथान्तरं कल्पवृत्तं पुराणमभिधीयते यत् ।
सावर्णिना नारदाय ब्रह्माणमनुवर्णितम् ॥
यत्र ब्रह्महरारूपं वर्णितं स्वल्पमेव तु ।
तद्‌ब्राह्मवैवर्तमिति तद्विद्धि द्विजसत्तम ॥

the Varáha Avatára of Vishńu,—which seems to be intended by the Matsya,—nor any reference to a Rathantara Kalpa. It may also be observed, that, in describing the merit of presenting a copy of this Puráńa, the Matsya adds: "Whoever makes such gift is honoured in the Brahma-loka";* a sphere which is of very inferior dignity to that to which a worshipper of Krishńa is taught to aspire by this Puráńa. The character of the work is, in truth, so decidedly sectarial, and the sect to which it belongs so distinctly marked,— that of the worshippers of the juvenile Krishńa and Rádhá, a form of belief of known modern origin,—that it can scarcely have found a notice in a work to which, like the Matsya, a much more remote date seems to belong. Although, therefore, the Matsya may be received in proof of there having been a Brahma Vaivarta Puráńa at the date of its compilation, dedicated especially to the honour of Krishńa, yet we cannot credit the possibility of its being the same we now possess.

Although some of the legends believed to be ancient are scattered through the different portions of this Puráńa, yet the great mass of it is taken up with tiresome descriptions of Vrindávana and Goloka, the dwellings of Krishńa on earth and in heaven; with endless repetitions of prayers and invocations addressed to him; and with insipid descriptions of his person and sports, and the love of the Gopís and of Rádhá towards him. There are some particulars of the origin of the

* पुराणं ब्रह्मवैवर्त्तं यो दद्यात्काञ्चनान्वितं च ।
पौर्णमास्यां च भवेत् (?) ब्रह्मलोके महीयते ॥

artificer castes,—which is of value, because it is cited as authority in matters affecting them,—contained in the Bráhma Khańda; and, in the Prakṛiti and Gańeśa Khańdas, are legends of those divinities, not wholly, perhaps, modern inventions, but of which the source has not been traced. In the life of Kṛishńa, the incidents recorded are the same as those narrated in the Vishńu and the Bhágavata; but the stories, absurd as they are, are much compressed, to make room for original matter still more puerile and tiresome. The Brahma Vaivarta has not the slightest title to be regarded as a Puráńa.[1]

11. Linga Puráńa. "Where Maheśwara, present in the Agni Linga, explained (the objects of life) virtue, wealth, pleasure, and final liberation at the end of the Agni Kalpa,[2] that Puráńa, consisting of eleven thousand stanzas, was called the Lainga by Brahmá himself."[?]

The Linga Puráńa conforms, accurately enough, to this description. The Kalpa is said to be the Íśána: but this is the only difference. It consists of eleven thousand stanzas. It is said to have been originally composed by Brahmá; and the primitive Linga is a

---

[1] Analysis of the Brahma Vaivarta Puráńa: Journal of the Asiatic Society of Bengal, June, 1832.†

> यत्राग्निलिङ्गमध्यस्थः साच देवो महेश्वरः ।
> धर्मार्थकामसोपार्गमाचेयमधिकृत च ।
> कल्यान्ते निर्जगाद मुरारं ब्रह्मा स्वयम् ।
> लैङ्गाद्यमाख्यं * * * * * * * * ॥

[?] Instead of Professor Wilson's कल्यान्ते &c., one of the MSS. I have seen has कल्यान्तनीर्*; another, कल्यानालिङ्ग*; and another, कल्य महिङ्ग*; while the fourth is here corrupt past mending by conjecture.
† See Professor Wilson's collected works, Vol. III.

o*

pillar of radiance, in which Maheśwara is present. The work is, therefore, the same as that referred to by the Matsya.

A short account is given, in the beginning, of elemental and secondary creation, and of the patriarchal families; in which, however, Śiva takes the place of Vishńu, as the indescribable cause of all things. Brief accounts of Śiva's incarnations and proceedings in different Kalpas next occur, offering no interest, except as characteristic of sectarial notions. The appearance of the great fiery Linga takes place, in the interval of a creation, to separate Vishńu and Brahmá, who not only dispute the palm of supremacy, but fight for it; when the Linga suddenly springs up, and puts them both to shame; as, after travelling upwards and downwards for a thousand years in each direction, neither can approach to its termination. Upon the Linga the sacred monosyllable Om is visible; and the Vedas proceed from it, by which Brahmá and Vishńu become enlightened, and acknowledge and eulogize the superior might and glory of Śiva.

A notice of the creation in the Padma Kalpa then follows; and this leads to praises of Śiva by Vishńu and Brahmá. Śiva repeats the story of his incarnations, twenty-eight in number; intended as a counterpart, no doubt, to the twenty-four Avatáras of Vishńu, as described in the Bhágavata; and both being amplifications of the original ten Avatáras, and of much less merit as fictions. Another instance of rivalry occurs in the legend of Dadhíchi, a Muni, and worshipper of Śiva. In the Bhágavata, there is a story of Ambarísha being defended against Durvásas by the discus of Vishńu, against which that Śaiva sage is helpless. Here, Vishńu hurls his discus at Dadhíchi: but it falls, blunted, to the ground; and a conflict ensues, in which Vishńu and his partisans are all overthrown by the Muni.

A description of the universe, and of the regal dynasties of the Vaivaswata Manwantara to the time of Kŕishńa, runs through a number of chapters, in substance, and, very commonly, in words, the same as in other Puráńas; after which the work resumes its proper character, narrating legends, and enjoining rites, and reciting prayers, intending to do honour to Śiva under various forms. Although, however, the Linga holds a prominent place amongst them, the spirit of the worship is as little influenced by the character of the type as can well be imagined. There is nothing like the phallic orgies of antiquity: it is all mystical and spiritual. The Linga is twofold, external and internal. The ignorant, who need a visible sign, worship Śiva through a 'mark' or 'type'—which is the proper meaning of the word 'Linga'—of wood, or stone: but the wise look upon this outward emblem as nothing, and contemplate, in their minds, the invisible, inscrutable type, which is Śiva himself. Whatever may have been the origin of this form of worship in India, the notions upon which it was founded, according to the impure fancies of European writers, are not to be traced in even the Śaiva Puráńas.

Data for conjecturing the era of this work are defective. But it is more a ritual than a Puráńa; and the Pauráńik chapters which it has inserted, in order to keep up something of its character, have been, evidently, borrowed for the purpose. The incarnations of Śiva,

and their 'pupils', as specified in one place, and the
importance attached to the practice of the Yoga, render
it possible that, under the former, are intended those
teachers of the Śaiva religion who belong to the Yoga
school,[1] which seems to have flourished about the
eighth or ninth centuries. It is not likely that the work
is earlier: it may be considerably later. It has preserved, apparently, some Śaiva legends of an early
date; but the greater part is ritual and mysticism of
comparatively recent introduction.

12. Varáha Puráńa. "That in which the glory of
the great Varáha is predominant, as it was revealed to
Earth by Vishńu, in connexion, wise Munis, with the
Mánava Kalpa, and which contains twenty-four thousand verses, is called the Váráha Puráńa."[2]

It may be doubted if the Varáha Puráńa of the present day is here intended. It is narrated by Vishńu
as Varáha, or in the boar incarnation, to the personified
Earth. Its extent, however, is not half that specified:
little exceeding ten thousand stanzas. It furnishes, also,
itself, evidence of the prior currency of some other
work, similarly denominated; as, in the description of
Mathurá contained in it, Sumantu, a Muni, is made to
observe: "The divine Varáha in former times expounded
a Puráńa, for the purpose of solving the perplexity of
Earth."

---

[1] See Asiatic Researches, Vol. XVII., p. 187.[*]

[2] महावराहस्य पुनर्माहात्म्यमधिकृत्य च ।
विष्णुनाभिहितं भूम्यै महावाराहमुच्यते ॥
मानवस्य च कल्पस्य प्रसङ्गेन मुनीश्वराः ।
चतुर्विंशतिसाहस्रं तद्वाराहमिहोच्यते ॥

[*] See Professor Wilson's collective works, Vol. I., p. 305.

Nor can the Varáha Puráńa be regarded as a Puráńa agreeably to the common definition; as it contains but a few scattered and brief allusions to the creation of the world and the reign of kings: it has no detailed genealogies, either of the patriarchal or regal families, and no account of the reigns of the Manus. Like the Linga Puráńa, it is a religious manual, almost wholly occupied with forms of prayer and rules for devotional observances, addressed to Vishńu; interspersed with legendary illustrations, most of which are peculiar to itself, though some are taken from the common and ancient stock. Many of them, rather incompatibly with the general scope of the compilation, relate to the history of Śiva and Durgá.[1] A considerable portion of the work is devoted to descriptions of various Tírthas, places of Vaishńava pilgrimage; and one of Mathurá enters into a variety of particulars relating to the shrines of that city, constituting the Mathurá Máhátmya.

In the sectarianism of the Varáha Puráńa there is no leaning to the particular adoration of Kŕishńa; nor are the Rathayátrá and Janmáshtamí included amongst the observances enjoined. There are other indications of its belonging to an earlier stage of Vaishńava worship; and it may, perhaps, be referred to the age of Rámánuja, the early part of the twelfth century.

---

[1] One of these is translated by Colonel Vans Kennedy, the origin of the three Śaktis or goddesses, Saraswatí, Lakshmí, and Párvatí. Researches into the Nature and Affinity of Ancient and Hindu Mythology, p. 209. The Tri Śakti Máhátmya occurs, as he gives it, in my copy, and is, so far, an indication of the identity of the Varáha Puráńa in the different MSS.

13. Skanda Purána. "The Skánda Puráńa is that in which the six-faced deity (Skanda) has related the events of the Tatpurusha Kalpa, enlarged with many tales, and subservient to the duties taught by Maheśwara. It is said to contain eighty-one thousand one hundred stanzas: so it is asserted amongst mankind."[1]

It is uniformly agreed that the Skanda Puráńa, in a collective form, has no existence; and the fragments, in the shape of Saṁhitás, Khańdas, and Máhátmyas, which are affirmed, in various parts of India, to be portions of the Puráńa, present a much more formidable mass of stanzas than even the immense number of which it is said to consist. The most celebrated of these portions, in Hindusthán, is the Kásí Khańda, a very minute description of the temples of Śiva in or adjacent to Benares, mixed with directions for worshipping Maheśwara, and a great variety of legends explanatory of its merits and of the holiness of Kásí. Many of them are puerile and uninteresting; but some are of a higher character. The story of Agastya records, probably, in a legendary style, the propagation of Hinduism in the south of India; and, in the history of Divodása, king of Kásí, we have an embellished tradition of the temporary depression of the worship of Śiva, even in its metropolis, before the ascendancy of the followers of Buddha.[2] There is every reason to believe the greater

---

[1] यत्र माहेश्वरात्प्रसंगोपधिकृत्य च षड्मुखः ।
वक्ष्ये तत्पुरुषे कल्पं चरितैरुपबृंहितम् ॥
स्कान्दं नाम पुराणं तन्महाकार्तिनिर्मितम् ।
बहुलाभि वर्णं षष्टिमिति मर्त्येषु वदति ॥

[2] The legend is translated by Colonel Vans Kennedy: Re-

pa[illegible] of the contents of the Kásí Khańda anterior to th[illegible]rst attack upon Benares by Mahmud of Ghizni. T[illegible] Kásí Khańda alone contains fifteen thousand stanzas. [illegible]other considerable work ascribed, in Upper India, [illegible] Skanda Puráńa, is the Utkala Khańda, giving [illegible]count of the holiness of Orissa, and the Kshetra-[illegible]urushottama or Jagannátha. The same vicinage [illegible] site of temples, once of great magnificence and [illegible]t, dedicated to Śiva, as Bhuvaneśwara, which [illegible] an excuse for attaching an account of a Vaish-[illegible] Tirtha to an eminently Śaiva Puráńa. There can [illegible]tle doubt, however, that the Utkala Khańda is [illegible]rrantably included amongst the progeny of the [illegible]t work. Besides these, there is a Brahmottara [illegible]ńda, a Revá Khańda, a Śiva Rahasya Khańda, a [illegible]vat Khańda, and others. Of the Samhitás the [illegible]f are the Súta Samhitá, Sanatkumára Samhitá, [illegible]a Samhitá, and Kapila Samhitá: there are several [illegible]r works denominated Samhitás. The Máhátmyas [illegible]more numerous still.[1] According to the Súta Sam-[illegible], as quoted by Colonel Vans Kennedy,[2] the Skanda

[illegible] into the Nature and Affinity of Ancient and Hindu My-[illegible], Appendix D.

[illegible] a list of reputed portions of the Skanda Puráńa in the [illegible]sion of my friend, Mr. C. P. Brown, of the Civil Service of [illegible]ras, the Samhitás are seven, the Khańdas, twelve, besides parts denominated Gítá, Kalpa, Stotra, &c. In the collection of Colonel Mackenzie, amongst the Máhátmyas, thirty-six are said to belong to the Skanda Puráńa. Vol. I., p. 61. In the library at the India House are two Samhitás, the Súta and Sanatkumára, fourteen Khańdas, and twelve Máhátmyas.

[2] Researches into the Nature and Affinity of Ancient and Hindu Mythology, p. 154, note.

Puráńa contains six Samhitás, five hundred Khańdas, and five hundred thousand stanzas; more than is even attributed to all the Puráńas. He thinks, judging from internal evidence, that all the Khańdas and Samhitás may be admitted to be genuine, though the Máhátmyas have rather a questionable appearance. Now, one kind of internal evidence is the quantity; and, as no more than eighty-one thousand one hundred stanzas have ever been claimed for it,[*] all in excess above that amount must be questionable. But many of the Khańdas, the Kásí Khańda, for instance, are quite as local as the Máhátmyas; being legendary stories relating to the erection and sanctity of certain temples, or groups of temples, and to certain Lingas; the interested origin of which renders them, very reasonably, objects of suspicion. In the present state of our acquaintance with the reputed portions of the Skanda Puráńa, my own views of their authenticity are so opposed to those entertained by Colonel Vans Kennedy, that, instead of admitting all the Samhitás and Khańdas to be genuine, I doubt if any one of them was ever a part of the Skanda Puráńa.

14. Vámana Puráńa. "That in which the four-faced Brahmá taught the three objects of existence, as subservient to the account of the greatness of Trivikrama, which treats, also, of the Síva Kalpa, and which consists of ten thousand stanzas, is called the Vámana Puráńa."[1]

---

[1] त्रिविक्रमस्य माहात्म्यमधिकृत्य चतुर्मुख: ।
विवर्णमभ्यधात्राच्च वामनं परिकीर्तितम् ।
पुरतो दशसाहस्रं ख्यातं† अध्यात्मनं शिवम् ।

---

[*] But see the end of my third note in p. XXIV., *supra*.

† Professor Wilson here omitted a word of two syllables —,probably,

The Vámana Puráña contains an account of the dwarf incarnation of Vishñu: but it is related by Pulastya to Nárada, and extends to but about seven thousand stanzas. Its contents scarcely establish its claim to the character of a Puráña.[1]

There is little or no order in the subjects which this work recapitulates, and which arise out of replies made by Pulastya to questions put, abruptly and unconnectedly, by Nárada. The greater part of them relate to the worship of the Linga; a rather strange topic for a Vaishñava Puráña, but engrossing the principal part of the compilation. They are, however, subservient to the object of illustrating the sanctity of certain holy places; so that the Vámana Puráña is little else than a succession of Máhátmyas. Thus, in the opening, almost, of the work occurs the story of Daksha's sacrifice, the object of which is to send Śiva to Pápamochana Tírtha, at Benares, where he is released from the sin of Brahmanicide. Next comes the story of the burning of Kámadeva, for the purpose of illustrating the holiness of a Śiva-linga at Kedáreśwara in the Himalaya, and of Badarikáśrama. The larger part of the work consists of the Saro-máhátmya, or legendary exemplifications of the holiness of Sthánu Tírtha; that

---

[1] From the extracts from the Vámana Puráña translated by Colonel Vans Kennedy, pp. 293, et seq., it appears that his copy so far corresponds with mine; and the work is, therefore, probably, the same. Two copies in the Company's library also agree with mine.

वामन. Instead of this, one of the four MSS. of the *Matsya-puráña* in the India Office Library has कौर्मं, and two have मूलं.

is, of the sanctity of various Lingas and certain pools
at Thanesar and Kurukhet, the country north-west
from Delhi. There are some stories, also, relating to
the holiness of the Godávarí river: but the general
site of the legends is in Hindusthán. In the course of
these accounts, we have a long narrative of the marriage of Śiva with Umá, and the birth of Kárttikeya.
There are a few brief allusions to creation and the
Manwantaras; but they are merely incidental: and all
the five characteristics of a Puráńa are deficient.   In
noticing the Swárochisha Manwantara, towards the
end of the book, the elevation of Bali as monarch of
the Daityas, and his subjugation of the universe, the
gods included, are described; and this leads to the
narration that gives its title to the Puráńa, the birth
of Krishńa as a dwarf, for the purpose of humiliating
Bali by fraud, as he was invincible by force. The story
is told as usual; but the scene is laid at Kurukshetra.

A more minute examination of this work than that
which has been given to it, might, perhaps, discover
some hint from which to conjecture its date. It is of
a more tolerant character than the Puráńas, and divides
its homage between Śiva and Vishńu with tolerable
impartiality. It is not connected, therefore, with any
sectarial principles, and may have preceded their introduction. It has not, however, the air of any antiquity; and its compilation may have amused the leisure
of some Brahman of Benares three or four centuries ago.

15. Kúrma Puráńa. "That in which Janárdana, in
the form of a tortoise, in the regions under the earth,
explained the objects of life — duty, wealth, pleasure,
and liberation — in communication with Indradyumna

and the Rishis in the proximity of Śakra, which refers to the Lakshmí Kalpa, and contains seventeen thousand stanzas, is the Kúrma Puráńa."[1]

In the first chapter of the Kúrma Puráńa, it gives an account of itself, which does not exactly agree with this description. Súta, who is repeating the narration, is made to say to the Rishis: "This most excellent Kaurma Puráńa is the fifteenth. Saṁhitás are fourfold, from the variety of the collections. The Bráhmí, Bhágavatí, Saurí, and Vaishńaví are well known as the four Saṁhitás which confer virtue, wealth, pleasure, and liberation. This is the Bráhmí Saṁhitá, conformable to the four Vedas; in which there are six thousand ślokas; and, by it, the importance of the four objects of life, O great sages, holy knowledge and Parameśwara is known."[2] There is an irreconcilable difference in this specification of the number of stanzas and that

---

[1] यत्र धर्मार्थकामानां मोक्षस्य च रक्षानते ।
माहात्म्यं कथयामास कूर्मरूपी जनार्दनः ॥
एकभुजप्रसङ्गेन ऋषिभिः† ब्रह्मविधौ ।
तस्मद्य सहस्राणि लक्ष्मीकल्पानुवर्तिनम् ॥

[2] एतद् तु पञ्चदशमं पुराणं कौर्मसुफलम् ।
चतुर्धा संस्थितं पुण्यं संहितानां प्रभेदनः ॥
ब्राह्मी भागवती सौरी वैष्णवी च प्रकीर्तिताः ।
चतस्रः संहिताः पुण्या धर्मकामार्थमोक्षदाः ॥
एषा तु संहिता ब्राह्मी चतुर्वेदैश्च संमिता ।
भवन्ति चतुस्राणि लोकानामय संख्यया ॥
यत्र धर्मार्थकामानां मोक्षस्य च मुनीश्वराः ।
माहात्म्यमखिलं सम्यक् भावति परमेश्वरः ॥

So read the best MSS. of the *Kúrma-puráńa* that are at present accessible to me.

† One of the four I. O. L. MSS. of the *Matsya-puráńa* has ऋषिभिः ।

given above. It is not very clear what is meant by a
Saṁhitá, as here used. A Saṁhitá, as observed above
(p. XIX.), is something different from a Puráńa. It may
be an assemblage of prayers and legends, extracted,
professedly, from a Puráńa, but is not, usually, applicable to the original. The four Saṁhitás here specified
refer rather to their religious character than to their
connexion with any specific work; and, in fact, the
same terms are applied to what are called Saṁhitás
of the Skanda. In this sense, a Puráńa might be also
a Saṁhitá; that is, it might be an assemblage of formulæ
and legends belonging to a division of the Hindu system; and the work in question, like the Vishńu Puráńa,
does adopt both titles. It says: "This is the excellent
Kaurma Puráńa, the fifteenth (of the series)." And
again: "This is the Bráhmí Saṁhitá." At any rate, no
other work has been met with pretending to be the
Kúrma Puráńa.

With regard to the other particulars specified by
the Matsya, traces of them are to be found. Although,
in two accounts of the traditional communication of
the Puráńa, no mention is made of Vishńu as one of
the teachers, yet Súta repeats, at the outset, a dialogue
between Vishńu, as the Kúrma, and Indradyumna, at
the time of the churning of the ocean; and much of
the subsequent narrative is put into the mouth of the
former.

The name, being that of an Avatára of Vishńu, might
lead us to expect a Vaishńava work: but it is always,
and correctly, classed with the Saiva Puráńas; the
greater portion of it inculcating the worship of Siva
and Durgá. It is divided into two parts, of nearly

equal length. In the first part, accounts of the creation, of the Avatáras of Vishńu, of the solar and lunar dynasties of the kings to the time of Kŕishńa, of the universe, and of the Manwantaras, are given, in general in a summary manner, but, not unfrequently, in the words employed in the Vishńu Puráńa. With these are blended hymns addressed to Maheśwara by Brahmá and others; the defeat of Andhakásura by Bhairava; the origin of four Śaktis, Maheśwarí, Sivá, Sati, and Haimavatí, from Śiva; and other Śaiva legends. One chapter gives a more distinct and connected account of the incarnations of Śiva, in the present age, than the Linga; and it wears, still more, the appearance of an attempt to identify the teachers of the Yoga school with personations of their preferential deity. Several chapters form a Káśí Máhátmya, a legend of Benares. In the second part there are no legends. It is divided into two parts, the Íswara Gítá[1] and Vyása Gítá. In the former, the knowledge of god, that is, of Śiva, through contemplative devotion, is taught. In the latter, the same object is enjoined through works, or observance of the ceremonies and precepts of the Vedas.

The date of the Kúrma Puráńa cannot be very remote; for it is, avowedly, posterior to the establishment of the Tántrika, the Śákta, and the Jaina sects. In the twelfth chapter it is said: "The Bhairava, Váma, Árhata,

---

[1] This is also translated by Colonel Vans Kennedy (Researches into the Nature and Affinity of Ancient and Hindu Mythology, Appendix D., p. 444); and, in this instance, as in other passages quoted by him from the Kúrma, his MS. and mine agree.

and Yámala Sástras are intended for delusion." There
is no reason to believe that the Bhairava and Yámala
Tantras are very ancient works, or that the practices
of the left-hand Sáktas, or the doctrines of Arhat or
Jina, were known in the early centuries of our era.

16. Matsya Puráña. "That in which, for the sake
of promulgating the Vedas, Vishńu, in the beginning
of a Kalpa, related to Manu the story of Narasinha
and the events of seven Kalpas; that, O sages, know
to be the Mátsya Puráña, containing twenty thousand
stanzas."[1]

We might, it is to be supposed, admit the description
which the Matsya gives of itself to be correct; and yet,
as regards the number of verses, there seems to be a
misstatement. Three very good copies—one in my
possession, one in the Company's library, and one in
the Radcliffe library—concur in all respects, and in
containing no more than between fourteen and fifteen
thousand stanzas. In this case the Bhágavata is nearer
the truth, when it assigns to it fourteen thousand. We
may conclude, therefore, that the reading of the passage
is, in this respect, erroneous.* It is correctly said, that

---

[1] सुनीला यत्र व्याख्यातो मत्स्यार्थ जनार्दन: ।
मात्स्यरूपेण मनवे नरसिंघस्य वर्षणम् ॥
सप्तकल्पानुवृत्तान्तसमायुक्तं सुनिश्चिता: ।
तन्मात्स्यमिति वाणीभिः सहस्राणि विंशति ॥

---

* Two out of the four I. O. L. MSS. of the *Matsya-puráña*—see the
last line of the Sanskrit quoted in this page—give चतुर्दश सहस्राणि,
"fourteen thousand"; and the others exhibit evident corruptions of the
same reading. That this reading is to be preferred, we have, besides
the evidence, adduced by Professor Wilson, of the *Bhágavata-puráña*,
that of the *Deví-bhágavata* and *Revá-mdhátmya*.

the subjects of the Puráña were communicated by Vishńu, in the form of a fish, to Manu.

The Puráña, after the usual prologue of Súta and the Ŕishis, opens with the account of the Matsya or 'fish' Avatára of Vishńu, in which he preserves a king, named Manu, with the seeds of all things, in an ark, from the waters of that inundation which, in the season of a Pralaya, overspreads the world. This story is told in the Mahábhárata, with reference to the Matsya as its authority; from which it might be inferred, that the Puráña was prior to the poem. This, of course, is consistent with the tradition that the Puráñas were first composed by Vyása. But there can be no doubt that the greater part of the Mahábhárata is much older than any extant Puráña. The present instance is, itself, a proof; for the primitive simplicity with which the story of the fish Avatára is told in the Mahábhárata, is of a much more antique complexion than the mysticism and extravagance of the actual Matsya Puráña. In the former, Manu collects the seeds of existing things in the ark; it is not said how: in the latter, he brings them all together by the power of Yoga. In the latter, the great serpents come to the king, to serve as cords wherewith to fasten the ark to the horn of the fish: in the former, a cable made of ropes is more intelligibly employed for the purpose.

Whilst the ark floats, fastened to the fish, Manu enters into conversation with him; and his questions and the replies of Vishńu form the main substance of the compilation. The first subject is the creation, which is that of Brahmá and the patriarchs. Some of the details are the usual ones; others are peculiar, especially those relating to the Pitŕis or progenitors. The regal dynasties are next described; and then follow chapters on the duties of different orders. It is in relating those of the householder, in which the duty of making gifts to Brahmans is comprehended, that we have the specification of the extent and subjects of the Puráńas. It is meritorious to have copies made of them, and to give these away on particular occasions. Thus, it is said, of the Matsya: "Whoever gives it away at either equinox, along with a golden fish and a milch cow, gives away the whole earth;"* that is, he reaps a like reward, in his next migration. Special duties of the householder—Vratas or occasional acts of piety—are then described at considerable length, with legendary illustrations. The account of the universe is given in the usual strain. Śaiva legends ensue: as the destruction of Tripurásura; the war of the gods with Táraka and the Daityas, and the consequent birth of Kárttikeya, with the various circumstances of Umá's birth and marriage, the burning of Kámadeva, and other events involved in that narrative; the destruction of the Asuras Maya and Andhaka; the origin of the Mátŕis, and the like; interspersed with the Vaishńava legends of the Avatáras. Some Máhátmyas are also introduced; one of which, the Narmadá Máhátmya, contains some interesting particulars. There are various chapters on law and morals, and one which furnishes directions for building houses and making images. We then have an account of the kings of future periods; and the Puráńa concludes with a chapter on gifts.

---

* विष्णुवे हेमनात्स्येन धेन्वा चैव समन्वितम् ।
यो दद्यात्पृथिवी तेन दत्ता भवति पार्थिव ॥

The Matsya Puráńa, it will be seen, even from this brief sketch of its contents, is a miscellaneous compilation, but including, in its contents, the elements of a genuine Puráńa. At the same time, it is of too mixed a character to be considered as a genuine work of the Puárańik class; and, upon examining it carefully, it may be suspected that it is indebted to various works, not only for its matter, but for its words. The genealogical and historical chapters are much the same as those of the Vishńu; and many chapters, as those on the Pitŕis and Śráddhas, are precisely the same as those of the Śrishti Khańda of the Padma Puráńa. It has drawn largely also from the Mahábhárata. Amongst other instances, it is sufficient to quote the story of Sávitrí, the devoted wife of Satyavat, which is given in the Matsya in the same manner, but considerably abridged.

Although a Śaiva work, it is not exclusively so; and it has not such sectarial absurdities as the Kúrma and Linga. It is a composition of considerable interest; but, if it has extracted its materials from the Padma,—which it also quotes on one occasion, the specification of the Upapuráńas,—it is subsequent to that work, and, therefore, not very ancient. ·

17. Garuda Puráńa. "That which Vishńu recited in the Gáruda Kalpa, relating, chiefly, to the birth of Garuda from Vinatá, is here called the Gáruda Puráńa; and in it there are read nineteen thousand verses."[1]

---

[1] यदा च नारदे अस्मै विनतानन्दनोद्भवम् । वर्णिकावारवीर्दिव्यधुर्मारद्वं नदिदोष्यमे ॥ तद्हादय वैर्व च मशुकाखीव पद्यते ।

---

[2] विनतानन्दनोद्भवं seems to be the more ordinary reading.

The Garuḍa Puráṇa which has been the subject of my examination corresponds in no respect with this description, and is, probably, a different work, though entitled the Garuḍa Puráṇa. It is identical, however, with two copies in the Company's library. It consists of no more than about seven thousand stanzas; it is repeated by Brahmá to Indra; and it contains no account of the birth of Garuḍa. There is a brief notice of the creation; but the greater part is occupied with the description of Vratas or religious observances, of holydays, of sacred places dedicated to the sun, and with prayers from the Tántrika ritual, addressed to the sun, to Śiva, and to Vishṇu. It contains, also, treatises on astrology, palmistry, and precious stones, and one, still more extensive, on medicine. The latter portion, called the Preta Kalpa, is taken up with directions for the performance of obsequial rites. There is nothing, in all this, to justify the application of the name. Whether a genuine Garuḍa Puráṇa exists is doubtful. The description given in the Matsya is less particular than even the brief notices of the other Puráṇas, and might have easily been written without any knowledge of the book itself; being, with exception of the number of stanzas, confined to circumstances that the title alone indicates.

18. Brahmáṇḍa Puráṇa.* "That which has declared, in twelve thousand two hundred verses, the magnificence of the egg of Brahmá, and in which an account

---

* A very popular work which is considered to be a part of the *Brahmáṇḍa-puráṇa*, is the *Adhyátma-rámáyaṇa*. It has been lithographed, with the commentary of Nágeśa Bhaṭṭa, at Bombay. For some account of it, see Prof. Aufrecht's *Catalog. Cod. Manuscript.* &c., pp. 18 and 19.

of the future Kalpas is contained, is called the Brahmánda Puráńa, and was revealed by Brahmá."[1*]

The Brahmánda Puráńa is usually considered to be
in much the same predicament as the Skanda, no longer
procurable in a collective body, but represented by a
variety of Khańdas and Máhátmyas, professing to be
derived from it. The facility with which any tract
may be thus attached to the non-existent original, and
the advantage that has been taken of its absence to
compile a variety of unauthentic fragments, have given
to the Brahmáńda, Skanda, and Padma, according to
Colonel Wilford, the character of being "the Puráńas
of thieves or impostors."[2] This is not applicable to
the Padma, which, as above shown, occurs entire and
the same in various parts of India. The imposition of
which the other two are made the vehicles can deceive
no one; as the purpose of the particular legend is
always too obvious to leave any doubt of its origin.

Copies of what profess to be the entire Brahmáńda
Puráńa are sometimes, though rarely, procurable. I
met with one in two portions, the former containing
one hundred and twenty-four chapters, the latter,
seventy-eight; and the whole containing about the
number of stanzas assigned to the Puráńa. The first

---

[1] यच† ब्रह्माण्डमाहात्म्यमधिकृत्यात्रयीतनुः ।
तच दादशसाहस्रं पुराणं विधृताधिकम् ॥
अविकाराां च कल्याणां ब्रूयते यच विस्तरे: ।
तद्ब्रह्माण्डपुराणं च ब्रह्मणा समुदाहृतम् ॥

[2] As. Res., Vol. VIII., p. 252.

---

* ?

† The four I. O. L. MSS. of the *Matsya* have भाण्ड°, not यच.

and largest portion, however, proved to be the same as the Váyu Puráńa, with a passage occasionally slightly varied, and at the end of each chapter the common phrase 'Iti Brahmáńḍa Puráńe' substituted for 'Iti Váyu Puráńe'. I do not think there was any intended fraud in the substitution. The last section of the first part of the Váyu Puráńa is termed the Brahmáńḍa section, giving an account of the dissolution of the universe: and a careless or ignorant transcriber might have taken this for the title of the whole. The checks to the identity of the work have been honestly preserved, both in the index and the frequent specification of Váyu as the teacher or narrator of it.

The second portion of this Brahmáńḍa is not any part of the Váyu: it is, probably, current in the Dakhin as a Saṁhitá or Khańḍa. Agastya is represented as going to the city Kánchí (Conjeveram), where Vishńu, as Hayagríva, appears to him, and, in answer to his inquiries, imparts to him the means of salvation, the worship of Paraśakti. In illustration of the efficacy of this form of adoration, the main subject of the work is an account of the exploits of Lalitá Deví, a form of Durgá, and her destruction of the demon Bháńḍásura. Rules for her worship are also given, which are decidedly of a Śákta or Tántrika description; and this work cannot be admitted, therefore, to be part of a genuine Puráńa.

The Upapuráńas, in the few instances which are known, differ little, in extent or subject, from some of those to which the title of Puráńa is ascribed. The Matsya enumerates but four; but the Deví Bhágavata has a more complete list, and specifies eighteen. They

are: 1. The Sanatkumára, 2. Nárasinha,[*] 3. Náradíya,
4. Śiva, 5. Durvásasa, 6. Kápila, 7. Mánava, 8. Auśanasa, 9. Váruńa, 10. Kúliká, 11. Śámba, 12. Nandi,
13. Saura, 14. Párásara, 15. Áditya, 16. Máheśwara,
17. Bhágavata, 18. Vásishtha. The Matsya observes,
of the second, that it is named in the Padma Puráńa,[†]
and contains eighteen thousand verses. The Nandi it
calls Nandá, and says, that Kárttikeya tells, in it, the
story of Nandá.[‡] A rather different list is given in the
Revá Khańda; or: 1. Sanatkumára, 2. Nárasinha,
3. Nandá, 4. Śivadharma, 5. Daurvásasa, 6. Bhavishya,
related by Nárada or Náradíya, 7. Kápila, 8. Mánava,
9. Auśanasa, 10. Bruhmáńda, 11. Váruńa, 12. Káliká,
13. Máheśwara, 14. Śámba, 15. Saura, 16. Párásara,
17. Bhágavata, 18. Kaurma. These authorities, however, are of questionable weight; having in view, no
doubt, the pretensions of the Deví Bhágavata to be
considered as the authentic Bhágavata.

Of these Upapuráńas few are to be procured. Those
in my possession are the Śiva, considered as distinct
from the Váyu, the Kúliká, and, perhaps, one of the
Náradíyas, as noticed above. I have, also, three of the

---

* For an account of the *Narasinha-puráńa*, see Prof. Aufrecht's *Catalog.
Cod. Manuscript.*, &c., pp. 62 and 63.

† In the *Revá-máhátmya*, it is thus spoken of:

दितीयं नारसिंहं च पुराणं पद्मसंज्ञितं ।
: पाद्मे पुराणे यत्प्रोक्तं नरसिंहोपवर्णनम् ।
तथाप्रादुर्भवार्थं नारसिंहमिहोच्यते ॥
नन्दा च एव माहात्म्यं कार्त्तिकेयेन यत्कृतं ।
नन्दापुराणं माहेश्वरास्थानमिति कीर्त्यते ॥

Three of the I. O. L. copies of the *Matsya-puráńa* mention, besides
the *Narasinha* and the *Nandá*, the *Śámba* and the *Áditya*; while one
copy omits the *Śámba*. It seems that the Oxford MS. omits the *Áditya*.
See Prof. Aufrecht's *Catalog. Cod. Manuscript.*, &c., p. 40.

Skandhas of the Deví Bhágavata, which, most undoubtedly, is not the real Bhágavata, supposing that any Puráña so named preceded the work of Bopadeva. There can be no doubt that in any authentic list the name of Bhágavata does not occur amongst the Upapuráñas: it has been put there to prove that there are two works so entitled, of which the Puráña is the Deví Bhágavata, the Upapuráña, the Srí Bhágavata. The true reading should be Bhárgava,* the Puráña of Bhrígu: and the Deví Bhágavata is not even an Upapuráña. It is very questionable if the entire work, which, as far as it extends, is eminently a Sákta composition, ever had existence.†

The Śiva Upapuráña contains about six thousand stanzas, distributed into two parts. It is related by Sanatkumára to Vyúsa and the Rishis at Naimishárañya; and its character may be judged of from the questions to which it is a reply. "Teach us", said the Rishis, "the rules of worshipping the Linga, and of the god of gods adored under that type: describe to us his various forms, the places sanctified by him, and the prayers with which he is to be addressed." In answer, Sanatkumára repeats the Śiva Puráña, containing the birth of Vishńu and Brahmá; the creation and divisions of the universe; the origin of all things from the Linga; the rules of worshipping it and Śiva; the sanctity of

---

* This suggestion is offered by the anonymous author of the *Durjana-mukha-padma-páduká*. See Burnouf's *Bhágavata-purána*, Vol. 1., Preface, p. LXXVII.

† The editor saw, at Benares, about twelve years ago, a manuscript of the *Deví-bhágavata*, containing some 18,000 *ślokas*. Its owner, a learned Brahman, maintained that his copy was complete. To collect its various parts, he had travelled during many years, and over a large part of India.

times, places, and things, dedicated to him; the delusion of Brahmá and Vishńu by the Linga; the rewards of offering flowers and the like to a Linga; rules for various observances in honour of Mahádeva; the mode of practising the Yoga; the glory of Benares and other Saiva Tírthas; and the perfection of the objects of life by union with Maheśwara. These subjects are illustrated, in the first part, with very few legends; but the second is made up, almost wholly, of Saiva stories, as the defeat of Tripurásura; the sacrifice of Daksha; the births of Kárttikeya and Gańeśa, (the sons of Siva), and Nandi and Bhŕingaríti (his attendants), and others; together with descriptions of Benares and other places of pilgrimage, and rules for observing such festivals as the Sivarátri. This work is a Saiva manual, not a Puráńa.

The Káliká Puráńa contains about nine thousand stanzas, in ninety-eight chapters, and is the only work of the series dedicated to recommend the worship of the bride of Siva. in one or other of her manifold forms, as Girijá, Deví, Bhadrakálí, Kálí, Mahámáyá. It belongs, therefore, to the Sákta modification of Hindu belief, or the worship of the female powers of the deities. The influence of this worship shows itself in the very first pages of the work, which relate the incestuous passion of Brahmá for his daughter Sandhyá, in a strain that has nothing analogous to it in the Váyu, Linga, or Siva Puráńas.

The marriage of Siva and Párvatí is a subject early described, with the sacrifice of Daksha, and the death of Satí. And this work is authority for Siva's carrying the dead body about the world, and the origin of the

Píthasthánas or places where the different members
of it were scattered, and where Lingas were, consequently, erected. A legend follows of the births of
Bhairava and Vetála, whose devotion to different forms
of Deví furnishes occasion to describe, in great detail,
the rites and formulæ of which her worship consists,
including the chapters on sanguinary sacrifices, translated in the Asiatic Researches.* Another peculiarity
in this work is afforded by very prolix descriptions of
a number of rivers and mountains at Kámarúpa Tírtha,
in Assam, and rendered holy ground by the celebrated
temple of Durgá in that country, as Kámákshí or Ká-
mákshyá. It is a singular, and yet uninvestigated, circumstance, that Assam, or, at least, the north-east of
Bengal, seems to have been, in a great degree, the
source from which the Tántrika and Śákta corruptions
of the religion of the Vedas and Puráńas proceeded.

The specification of the Upapuráńas, whilst it names
several of which the existence is problematical, omits
other works bearing the same designation, which are
sometimes met with. Thus, in the collection of Colonel
Mackenzie,[1] we have a portion of the Bhárgava, and a
Mudgala Puráńa, which is, probably, the same with
the Gańeśa Upapuráńa, cited by Colonel Vans Kennedy.[2]
I have, also, a copy of the Gańeśa Puráńa,† which

---

[1] Mackenzie Collection, Vol. I., pp. 50, 51.

[2] Researches into the Nature and Affinity of Ancient and Hindu
Mythology, p. 251.

---

* Vol. V., pp. 371, et seq.

† For Dr. J. Stevenson's "Analysis of the Gańeśa Puráńa, with special
reference to the History of Buddhism", see *Journal of the Royal Asiatic
Society*, Vol. VIII., pp. 319-329.

seems to agree with that of which he speaks; the second
portion being entitled the Krídá Khańda, in which the
pastimes of Gańeśa, including a variety of legendary
matters, are described. The main subject of the work
is the greatness of Gańeśa; and prayers and formulæ
appropriate to him are abundantly detailed. It appears
to be a work originating with the Gáńapatya sect, or
worshippers of Gańeśa. There is, also, a minor Puráńa
called Ádi or 'first', not included in the list. This is a
work, however, of no great extent or importance, and
is confined to a detail of the sports of the juvenile
Krishńa.

From the sketch thus offered of the subjects of the
Puráńas, and which, although admitting of correction,
is believed to be, in the main, a candid and accurate
summary, it will be evident, that, in their present condition, they must be received with caution, as authorities
for the mythological religion of the Hindus at any
remote period. They preserve, no doubt, many ancient
notions and traditions; but these have been so much
mixed up with foreign matter, intended to favour the
popularity of particular forms of worship, or articles
of faith, that they cannot be unreservedly recognized
as genuine representations of what we have reason to
believe the Puráńas originally were.

The safest sources, for the ancient legends of the
Hindus, after the Vedas, are, no doubt, the two great
poems, the Rámáyańa and Mahábhárata. The first
offers only a few; but they are of a primitive character.
The Mahábhárata is more fertile in fiction; but it is
more miscellaneous; and much that it contains is of
equivocal authenticity and uncertain date. Still, it

affords many materials that are genuine; and it is,
evidently, the great fountain from which most, if not
all, of the Puránas have drawn; as it intimates, itself,
when it declares, that there is no legend current in the
world which has not its origin in the Mahábhárata.[1]

A work of some extent, professing to be part of the
Mahábhárata, may, more accurately, be ranked with the
Pauránik compilations of least authenticity and latest
origin. The Hari Vamśa is chiefly occupied with the
adventures of Krishńa; but, as introductory to his era,
it records particulars of the creation of the world, and
of the patriarchal and regal dynasties. This is done
with much carelessness and inaccuracy of compilation;
as I have had occasion, frequently, to notice, in the
following pages. The work has been very industriously
translated by M. Langlois.

A comparison of the subjects of the following pages
with those of the other Puránas will sufficiently show,
that, of the whole series, the Vishńu most closely conforms to the definition of a Pancha-lakshańa Puráńa,
or one which treats of five specified topics. It comprehends them all; and, although it has infused a portion of extraneous and sectarial matter, it has done so
with sobriety and with judgment, and has not suffered
the fervour of its religious zeal to transport it into
very wide deviations from the prescribed path. The
legendary tales which it has inserted are few, and are
conveniently arranged, so that they do not distract the

जनाश्रितिविदूमाखानं कथा भूवि न विद्यते ।

'Unconnected with this narrative, no story is known upon
earth.' *Adi-parvan*, 307.

attention of the compiler from objects of more permanent interest and importance.

The first book of the six, into which the work is divided, is occupied chiefly with the details of creation, primary (Sarga) and secondary (Pratisarga); the first explaining how the universe proceeds from Prakŕiti or eternal crude matter; the second, in what manner the forms of things are developed from the elementary substances previously evolved, or how they reappear after their temporary destruction. Both these creations are periodical; but the termination of the first occurs only at the end of the life of Brahmá, when not only all the gods and all other forms are annihilated, but the elements are again merged into primary substance, besides which, one only spiritual being exists. The latter takes place at the end of every Kalpa or day of Brahmá, and affects only the forms of inferior creatures, and lower worlds; leaving the substance of the universe entire, and sages and gods unharmed. The explanation of these events involves a description of the periods of time upon which they depend, and which are, accordingly, detailed. Their character has been a source of very unnecessary perplexity to European writers; as they belong to a scheme of chronology wholly mythological, having no reference to any real or supposed history of the Hindus, but applicable, according to their system, to the infinite and eternal revolutions of the universe. In these notions, and in that of the coeternity of spirit and matter, the theogony and cosmogony of the Puráńas, as they appear in the Vishńu Puráńa, belong to and illustrate systems of high antiquity, of which we have only fragmentary traces in the records of other nations.

The course of the elemental creation is, in the Vishńu, as in other Puráńas, taken from the Sánkhya philosophy; but the agency that operates upon passive matter is confusedly exhibited, in consequence of a partial adoption of the illusory theory of the Vedánta philosophy, and the prevalence of the Pauráńik doctrine of pantheism. However incompatible with the independent existence of Pradhána or crude matter, and however incongruous with the separate condition of pure spirit or Purusha, it is declared, repeatedly, that Vishńu, as one with the supreme being, is not only spirit, but crude matter, and not only the latter, but all visible substance, and Time. He is Purusha, 'spirit'; Pradhána, 'crude matter'; Vyakta, 'visible form'; and Kála, 'time'. This cannot but be regarded as a departure from the primitive dogmas of the Hindus, in which the distinctness of the Deity and his works was enunciated; in which, upon his willing the world to be, it was; and in which his interposition in creation, held to be inconsistent with the quiescence of perfection, was explained away by the personification of attributes in action, which afterwards came to be considered as real divinities, Brahmá, Vishńu, and Śiva, charged, severally, for a given season, with the creation, preservation, and temporary annihilation of material forms. These divinities are, in the following pages, consistently with the tendency of a Vaishńava work, declared to be no other than Vishńu. In Śaiva Puráńas, they are, in like manner, identified with Śiva; the Puráńas thus displaying and explaining the seeming incompatibility, of which there are traces in other ancient mythologies, between three distinct hypostases of one superior deity, and the identification of one or other of those hypostases with their common and separate original.

After the world has been fitted for the reception of living creatures, it is peopled by the will-engendered sons of Brahmá, the Prajápatis or patriarchs, and their posterity. It would seem as if a primitive tradition of the descent of mankind from seven holy personages had at first prevailed, but that, in the course of time, it had been expanded into complicated, and not always consistent, amplification. How could these Rishis or patriarchs have posterity? It was necessary to provide them with wives. In order to account for their existence, the Manu Swáyambhuva and his wife Satarupá were added to the scheme; or Brahmá becomes twofold, male and female; and daughters are then begotten, who are married to the Prajápatis. Upon this basis various legends of Brahmá's double nature, some, no doubt, as old as the Vedas, have been constructed. But, although they may have been derived, in some degree, from the authentic tradition of the origin of mankind from a single pair, yet the circumstances intended to give more interest and precision to the story are, evidently, of an allegorical or mystical description, and conduced, in apparently later times, to a coarseness of realization which was neither the letter nor spirit of the original legend. Swáyambhuva, the son of the self-born or uncreated, and his wife Satarupá, the hundred-formed or multiform, are, themselves, allegories; and their female descendants, who become the wives of the Rishis, are Faith, Devotion, Content, Intelligence, Tradition, and the like; whilst, amongst their posterity, we have the different phases of the moon and the sacrificial fires. In another creation, the chief source of creatures is the patriarch Daksha (ability), whose daughters—Virtues, or Passions, or Astronomical Phenomena—are the mothers of all existing things. These legends, perplexed as they appear to be, seem to admit of allowable solution, in the conjecture that the Prajápatis and Rishis were real personages, the authors of the Hindu system of social, moral, and religious obligations, and the first observers of the heavens, and teachers of astronomical science.

The regal personages of the Swáyambhuva Manwantara are but few; but they are described, in the outset, as governing the earth in the dawn of society, and as introducing agriculture and civilization. How much of their story rests upon a traditional remembrance of their actions, it would be useless to conjecture; although there is no extravagance in supposing that the legends relate to a period prior to the full establishment, in India, of the Brahmanical institutions. The legends of Dhruva and Prahláda, which are intermingled with these particulars, are, in all probability, ancient; but they are amplified, in a strain conformable to the Vaishńava purport of this Puráńa, by doctrines and prayers asserting the identity of Vishńu with the Supreme. It is clear that the stories do not originate with this Puráńa. In that of Prahláda, particularly, as hereafter pointed out, circumstances essential to the completeness of the story are only alluded to, not recounted; showing, indisputably, the writer's having availed himself of some prior authority for his narration.

The second book opens with a continuation of the kings of the first Manwantara; amongst whom, Bharata is said to have given a name to India, called, after him, Bhárata-varsha. This leads to a detail of the geographical system of the Puráńas, with mount Meru, the seven circular continents, and their surrounding oceans, to the limits of the world; all of which are mythological fictions, in which there is little reason to imagine that any topographical truths are concealed. With regard to Bhárata or India, the case is different. The mountains and rivers which are named are readily verifiable; and the cities and nations that are particularized may, also, in many instances, be proved to have had a real existence. The list is not a very long one, in the Vishńu Puráńa, and is, probably, abridged from some more ample detail, like that which the Mahábhárata affords, and which, in the hope of supplying information with respect to a subject yet imperfectly investigated, the ancient political condition of India, I have inserted and elucidated.

The description which this book also contains of the planetary and other spheres, is equally mythological, although occasionally presenting practical details and notions in which there is an approach to accuracy. The concluding legend of Bharata—in his former life, the king so named, but now a Brahman, who acquires true wisdom, and thereby attains liberation—is, palpably, an invention of the compiler, and is peculiar to this Puráńa.

The arrangement of the Vedas and other writings considered sacred by the Hindus,—being, in fact, the authorities of their religious rites and belief,—which is described in the beginning of the third book, is of much importance to the history of Hindu literature and of the Hindu religion. The sage Vyása is here represented, not as the author, but the arranger or compiler, of the Vedas, the Itihásas, and Puránas. His name denotes his character, meaning the 'arranger' or 'distributor';[*] and the recurrence of many Vyásas, many individuals who new-modelled the Hindu scriptures, has nothing, in it, that is improbable, except the fabulous intervals by which their labours are separated. The rearranging, the refashioning, of old materials is nothing more than the progress of time would be likely to render necessary. The last recognized compilation is that of Kríshńa Dwaipáyana, assisted by Brahmans who were already conversant with the subjects respectively assigned to them. They were the members of a college, or school, supposed, by the Hindus, to have flourished in a period more remote, no doubt, than the truth, but not at all unlikely to have been instituted at some time prior to the accounts of India which we owe to Greek writers, and in which we see enough of the system to justify our inferring that it was then entire. That there have been other Vyásas and other schools since that date, that Brahmans unknown to

---

[*] *Mahábhárata*, *Ádi-parvan*, 2417 :

विभाग वेदान्यासात् महाभारत इति स्मृत: ।

"Inasmuch as he arranged the mass of the Vedas, he is styled Vyása." Again, *ibid.*, *Ádi-parvan*, 4236 :

यो बभ्र वेदांगुरूखपसा मनुषागृषि: ।
तीयो बालसनाषिदे वार्त्तांगाक्षसमेत च ॥

These two passages are referred to in Lassen's *Indische Alterthumskunde*, Vol. I., p. 679, note 2.

See, further, *Original Sanskrit Texts*, Part II., p. 177, and Part. III., pp. 20, *et seq.*, and p. 190.

fame have remodelled some of the Hindu scriptures,
and, especially, the Puránas, cannot reasonably be con-
tested, after dispassionately weighing the strong internal evidence, which all of them afford, of the intermix-
ture of unauthorized and comparatively modern ingredients. But the same internal testimony furnishes
proof, equally decisive, of the anterior existence of
ancient materials; and it is, therefore, as idle as it is
irrational, to dispute the antiquity or authenticity of
the greater portion of the contents of the Puránas,
in the face of abundant positive and circumstantial
evidence of the prevalence of the doctrines which they
teach, the currency of the legends which they narrate,
and the integrity of the institutions which they describe,
at least three centuries before the Christian era. But
the origin and development of their doctrines, traditions, and institutions were not the work of a day;
and the testimony that establishes their existence three
centuries before Christianity, carries it back to a much
more remote antiquity, to an antiquity that is, probably,
not surpassed by any of the prevailing fictions, institutions, or belief, of the ancient world.

The remainder of the third book describes the leading institutions of the Hindus, the duties of castes, the
obligations of different stages of life, and the celebration of obsequial rites, in a short but primitive strain,
and in harmony with the laws of Manu. It is a distinguishing feature of the Vishńu Puráńa, and it is
characteristic of its being the work of an earlier period
than most of the Puráńas, that it enjoins no sectarial
or other acts of supererogation; no Vratas, occasional
self-imposed observances; no holydays, no birthdays

of Kríshńa, no nights dedicated to Lakshmí; no sacrifices or modes of worship other than those conformable to the ritual of the Vedas. It contains no Máhátmyas or golden legends, even of the temples in which Vishńu is adored.

The fourth book contains all that the Hindus have of their ancient history. It is a tolerably comprehensive list of dynasties and individuals: it is a barren record of events. It can scarcely be doubted, however, that much of it is a genuine chronicle of persons, if not of occurrences. That it is discredited by palpable absurdities in regard to the longevity of the princes of the earlier dynasties, must be granted; and the particulars preserved of some of them are trivial and fabulous. Still, there is an inartificial simplicity and consistency in the succession of persons, and a possibility and probability in some of the transactions, which give to these traditions the semblance of authenticity, and render it likely, that they are not altogether without foundation. At any rate, in the absence of all other sources of information, the record, such as it is, deserves not to be altogether set aside. It is not essential to its credibility, or its usefulness, that any exact chronological adjustment of the different reigns should be attempted. Their distribution amongst the several Yugas, undertaken by Sir William Jones, or his Pandits, finds no countenance from the original texts, further than an incidental notice of the age in which a particular monarch ruled, or the general fact that the dynasties prior to Kríshńa precede the time of the Great War and the beginning of the Kali age; both which events we are not obliged, with the Hindus, to

place five thousand years ago. To that age the solar
dynasty of princes offers ninety-three descents, the
lunar, but forty-five; though they both commence at
the same time. Some names may have been added
to the former list, some omitted in the latter; and it
seems most likely, that, notwithstanding their syn-
chronous beginning, the princes of the lunar race
were subsequent to those of the solar dynasty. They
avowedly branched off from the solar line; and the
legend of Sudyumna,[1] that explains the connexion, has
every appearance of having been contrived for the
purpose of referring it to a period more remote than
the truth. Deducting, however, from the larger number
of princes a considerable proportion, there is nothing
to shock probability in supposing, that the Hindu dynasties and their ramifications were spread through
an interval of about twelve centuries anterior to the
war of the Mahábhárata, and, conjecturing that event
to have happened about fourteen centuries before
Christianity, thus carrying the commencement of the
regal dynasties of India to about two thousand six
hundred years before that date. This may, or may
not, be too remote;[2] but it is sufficient, in a subject

---

[1] Book IV., Chapter I.

[2] However incompatible with the ordinary computation of the
period that is supposed to have elapsed between the flood and
the birth of Christ, this falls sufficiently within the larger limits
which are now assigned, upon the best authorities, to that period.
As observed by Mr. Milman, in his note on the annotation of
Gibbon (II., 301), which refers to this subject: "Most of the more
learned modern English protestants, as Dr. Hales, Mr. Faber,
Dr. Russell, as well as the continental writers, adopt the larger

where precision is impossible, to be satisfied with the
general impression, that, in the dynasties of kings detailed in the Puráńas, we have a record which, although
it cannot fail to have suffered detriment from age, and
may have been injured by careless or injudicious compilation, preserves an account, not wholly undeserving
of confidence, of the establishment and succession of
regular monarchies, amongst the Hindus, from as early
an era, and for as continuous a duration, as any in the
credible annals of mankind.

The circumstances that are told of the first princes
have evident relation to the colonization of India, and
the gradual extension of the authority of new races
over an uninhabited or uncivilized region. It is commonly admitted, that the Brahmanical religion and civilization were brought into India from without.[1] Certainly, there are tribes on the borders, and in the heart
of the country, who are still not Hindus; and passages
in the Rámáyańa, and Mahábhárata, and Manu, and
the uniform traditions of the people themselves, point
to a period when Bengal, Orissa, and the whole of the
Dakhin were inhabited by degraded or outcaste, that
is, by barbarous, tribes. The traditions of the Puráńas

chronology." To these may be added the opinion of Dr. Mill,
who, for reasons which he has fully detailed, identifies the commencement of the Kali age of the Hindus, B. C. 3102, with the
era of the deluge. Christa Sangita, Introd., supplementary note.

[1] Sir William Jones on the Hindus (As. Res., Vol. III.);
Klaproth, Asia Polyglotta; Colonel Vans Kennedy, Researches
into the Origin and Affinity of the Principal Languages of Asia
and Europe; A. von Schlegel, Origines des Hindous (Transactions
of the Royal Society of Literature).

confirm these views: but they lend no assistance to
the determination of the question whence the Hindus
came; whether from a central Asiatic nation, as Sir
William Jones supposed, or from the Caucasian mountains, the plains of Babylonia, or the borders of the
Caspian, as conjectured by Klaproth, Vans Kennedy,
and Schlegel. The affinities of the Sanskrit language
prove a common origin of the now widely scattered
nations amongst whose dialects they are traceable, and
render it unquestionable that they must all have spread
abroad from some centrical spot in that part of the
globe first inhabited by mankind, according to the
inspired record. Whether any indication of such an
event be discoverable in the Vedas, remains to be determined; but it would have been obviously incompatible with the Pauránik system to have referred the
origin of Indian princes and principalities to other than
native sources. We need not, therefore, expect, from
them, any information as to the foreign derivation of
the Hindus.

We have, then, wholly insufficient means for arriving
at any information concerning the ante-Indian period
of Hindu history, beyond the general conclusion derivable from the actual presence of barbarous and, apparently, aboriginal tribes—from the admitted progressive
extension of Hinduism into parts of India where it did
not prevail when the code of Manu was compiled—from
the general use of dialects in India, more or less copious,
which are different from Sanskrit—and from the affinities of that language with forms of speech current
in the western world—that a people who spoke Sanskrit, and followed the religion of the Vedas, came into

India, in some very distant age, from lands west of the
Indus. Whether the date and circumstances of their
immigration will ever be ascertained, is extremely
doubtful: but it is not difficult to form a plausible out-
line of their early site and progressive colonization.

The earliest seat of the Hindus, within the confines
of Hindusthán, was, undoubtedly, the eastern confines
of the Punjab. The holy land of Manu and the Puránas
lies between the Drishadwatí and Saraswatí rivers,—the
Caggar and Sursooty of our barbarous maps. Various
adventures of the first princes and most famous sages
occur in this vicinity; and the Ásramas or religious
domiciles of several of the latter are placed on the
banks of the Saraswatí. According to some authorities,
it was the abode of Vyása, the compiler* of the Vedas
and Puránas; and, agreeably to another, when, on one
occasion, the Vedas had fallen into disuse and been
forgotten, the Brahmans were again instructed in them
by Sáraswata, the son of Saraswatí.[1] One of the most
distinguished of the tribes of the Brahmans is known
as the Sáraswata;[2] and the same word is employed, by
Mr. Colebrooke, to denote that modification of Sanskrit
which is termed generally Prakrit, and which, in this
case, he supposes to have been the language of the
Sáraswata nation, "which occupied the banks of the
river Saraswatí."[3] The river itself receives its appella-

---

[1] See Book III., Chapter VI., note *ad finem.*

[2] As. Res., Vol. V., p. 55.†

[3] *Ibid.*, Vol., VII., p. 219.‡

---

* See my note in p. XCVIII., *supra.*

† *Miscellaneous Essays*, Vol. II., p. 179.

‡ *Ibid.*, Vol. II., p. 21.

tion from Saraswati, the goddess of learning, under whose auspices the sacred literature of the Hindus assumed shape and authority. These indications render it certain, that, whatever seeds were imported from without, it was in the country adjacent to the Saraswatí river that they were first planted, and cultivated, and reared, in Hindusthán.

The tract of land thus assigned for the first establishment of Hinduism in India, is of very circumscribed extent, and could not have been the site of any numerous tribe or nation. The traditions that evidence the early settlement of the Hindus in this quarter, ascribe to the settlers more of a philosophical and religious, than of a secular, character, and combine, with the very narrow bounds of the holy land, to render it possible, that the earliest emigrants were the members, not of a political, so much as of a religious, community; that they were a colony of priests, not in the restricted sense in which we use the term, but in that in which it still applies in India, to an Agrahára, a village or hamlet of Brahmans, who, although married, and having families, and engaging in tillage, in domestic duties, and in the conduct of secular interests affecting the community, are, still, supposed to devote their principal attention to sacred study and religious offices. A society of this description, with its artificers and servants, and, perhaps, with a body of martial followers, might have found a home in the Brahmávarta of Manu, the land which, thence, was entitled 'the holy', or, more literally, 'the Brahman, region', and may have communicated to the rude, uncivilized, unlettered, aborigines the rudiments of social organization, literature, and religion; partly, in all probability, brought along with them, and partly devised and fashioned, by degrees, for the growing necessities of new conditions of society. Those with whom this civilization commenced would have had ample inducements to prosecute their successful work; and, in the course of time, the improvement which germinated on the banks of the Saraswatí was extended beyond the borders of the Jumna and the Ganges.

We have no satisfactory intimation of the stages by which the political organization of the people of Upper India traversed the space between the Saraswatí and the more easterly region, where it seems to have taken a concentrated form, and whence it diverged, in various directions, throughout Hindusthán. The Manu of the present period, Vaivaswata, the son of the Sun, is regarded as the founder of Ayodhyá; and that city continued to be the capital of the most celebrated branch of his descendants, the posterity of Ikshwáku. The Vishńu Puráńa evidently intends to describe the radiation of conquest or colonization from this spot, in the accounts it gives of the dispersion of Vaivaswata's posterity; and, although it is difficult to understand what could have led early settlers in India to such a site, it is not inconveniently situated as a commanding position whence emigrations might proceed to the east, the west, and the south. This seems to have happened. A branch from the house of Ikshwáku spread into Tirhoot, constituting the Maithila kings; and the posterity of another of Vaivaswata's sons reigned at Vaisálí, in Southern Tirhoot, or Sarun.

The most adventurous emigrations, however, took place through the lunar dynasty, which, as observed above, originates from the solar; making, in fact, but one race and source for the whole. Leaving out of consideration the legend of Sudyumna's double transformation, the first prince of Pratishthána, a city south from Ayodhyá, was one of Vaivaswata's children, equally with Ikshwáku. The sons of Purúravas, the second of this branch, extended, by themselves, or their posterity, in every direction: to the east, to Kásí, Magadhá, Benares, and Behar; southwards, to the Vindhya hills, and, across them, to Vidarbha or Berar; westwards, along the Narmadá, to Kusásthalí or Dwáraká in Gujerat; and, in a north-westerly direction, to Mathurá and Hastinápura. These movements are very distinctly discoverable amidst the circumstances narrated in the fourth book of the Vishńu Puráńa, and are precisely such as might be expected from a radiation of colonies from Ayodhyá. Intimations also occur of settlements in Banga, Kalinga, and the Dakhin: but they are brief and indistinct, and have the appearance of additions subsequent to the comprehension of those countries within the pale of Hinduism.

Besides these traces of migration and settlement, several curious circumstances, not likely to be unauthorized inventions, are hinted in these historical traditions. The distinction of castes was not fully developed prior to the colonization. Of the sons of Vaivaswata, some, as kings, were Kshatriyas; but one founded a tribe of Brahmans, another became a Vaisya, and a fourth, a Súdra. It is also said, of other princes, that they established the four castes amongst their subjects.[1] There are, also, various notices of Brahmanical Gotras or families, proceeding from Kshatriya races;[2] and there are several indications of severe struggles between the two ruling castes, not for temporal, but for spiritual, dominion, the right to teach the Vedas. This seems to be the especial purport of the inveterate hostility that prevailed between the Brahman Vasishṭha and the Kshatriya Viśwámitra, who, as the Rámáyaṇa relates, compelled the gods to make him a Brahman also, and whose posterity became very celebrated as the Kauśika Brahmans. Other legends, again, such as Daksha's sacrifice, denote sectarial strife; and the legend of Paraśuráma reveals a conflict even for temporal authority, between the two ruling castes. More or less weight will be attached to these conjectures, according to the temperament of different inquirers. But, even whilst fully aware of the facility with which plausible deductions may cheat the fancy, and little disposed to relax all curb upon the imagination, I find it difficult to regard these legends as wholly unsubstantial fictions, or devoid of all resemblance to the realities of the past.

After the date of the great war, the Vishṇu Puráṇa, in common with those Puráṇas which contain similar lists, specifies kings and dynasties with greater precision, and offers political and chronological particulars to which, on the score of probability, there is nothing to object. In truth, their general accuracy has been incontrovertibly established. Inscriptions on columns

---

[1] See Book IV., Chapters VIII. and XVIII., &c.

[2] See Book IV., Chapter XIX.

of stone or rocks, on coins, deciphered only of late years, through the extraordinary ingenuity and perseverance of Mr. James Prinsep, have verified the names of races and titles of princes—the Gupta and Andhra Rajas, mentioned in the Puránas—and have placed beyond dispute the identity of Chandragupta and Sandrocoptus; thus giving us a fixed point from which to compute the date of other persons and events. Thus, the Vishńu Puráńa specifies the interval between Chandragupta and the Great War to be eleven hundred years; and the occurence of the latter little more than fourteen centuries B. C., as shown in my observations on the passage,[1] remarkably concurs with inferences of the like date from different premises. The historical notices that then follow are considerably confused; but they probably afford an accurate picture of the political distractions of India at the time when they were written: and much of the perplexity arises from the corrupt state of the manuscripts, the obscure brevity of the record, and our total want of the means of collateral illustration.

The fifth book of the Vishńu Puráńa is exclusively occupied with the life of Kŕishńa. This is one of the distinguishing characteristics of the Puráńa, and is one argument against its antiquity. It is possible, though not yet proved, that Kŕishńa, as an Avatára of Vishńu, is mentioned in an indisputably genuine text of the Vedas. He is conspicuously prominent in the Mahábhárata, but very contradictorily described there. The part that he usually performs is that of a mere mortal;

---

[1] See Book IV., Chapter XXIV.

although the passages are numerous that attach divinity
to his person. There are, however, no descriptions, in
the Mahábhárata, of his juvenile frolics, of his sports
in Vrindávana, his pastimes with the cow-boys, or even
his destruction of the Asuras sent to kill him. These
stories have, all, a modern complexion; they do not
harmonize with the tone of the ancient legends, which
is, generally, grave, and, sometimes, majestic. They are
the creations of a puerile taste and grovelling imagination. These chapters of the Vishńu Puráńa offer some
difficulties as to their originality. They are the same
as those on the same subject in the Brahma Puráńa:
they are not very dissimilar to those of the Bhágavata.
The latter has some incidents which the Vishńu has
not, and may, therefore, be thought to have improved
upon the prior narrative of the latter. On the other
hand, abridgment is equally a proof of posteriority as
amplification. The simpler style of the Vishńu Puráńa
is, however, in favour of its priority; and the miscellaneous composition of the Brahma Puráńa renders it
likely to have borrowed these chapters from the Vishńu.
The life of Kŕishńa in the Hari Vańśa and the Brahma
Vaivarta are, indisputably, of later date.

The last book contains an account of the dissolution
of the world, in both its major and minor cataclysms;
and, in the particulars of the end of all things by fire
and water, as well as in the principle of their perpetual
renovation, presents a faithful exhibition of opinions
that were general in the ancient world.[1] The meta-

---

[1] Dr. Thomas Burnet has collected the opinions of the ancient
world on this subject, tracing them, as he says, "to the earliest

physical annihilation of the universe, by the release of
the spirit from bodily existence, offers, as already remarked, other analogies to doctrines and practices
taught by Pythagoras and Plato, and by the Platonic
Christians of later days.

The Vishńu Puráńa has kept very clear of particulars from which an approximation to its date may be
conjectured. No place is described of which the sacred-
ness has any known limit, nor any work cited of probable recent composition. The Vedas, the Puráńas,
other works forming the body of Sanskrit literature,
are named; and so is the Mahábhárata, to which, therefore, it is subsequent. Both Bauddhas and Jainas are
adverted to. It was, therefore, written before the
former had disappeared. But they existed, in some
parts of India, as late as the twelfth century, at least;
and it is probable that the Puráńa was compiled before
that period. The Gupta kings reigned in the seventh
century.* The historical record of the Puráńa which
mentions them was, therefore, later: and there seems
little doubt that the same alludes to the first incursions
of the Mohammedans, which took place in the eighth
century; which brings it still lower. In describing the
latter dynasties, some, if not all, of which were, no
doubt, contemporary, they are described as reigning,

people, and the first appearances of wisdom after the Flood."
Sacred Theory of the Earth, Book III., Chapter III. The Hindu
account explains what is imperfect or contradictory in ancient
tradition, as banded down from other and less carefully per-
petuated sources.

* More recent researches have rendered this conclusion doubtful.

altogether, one thousand seven hundred and ninety-six years. Why this duration should have been chosen does not appear; unless, in conjunction with the number of years which are said to have elapsed between the Great War and the last of the Andhra dynasty, which preceded these different races, and which amounted to two thousand three hundred and fifty, the compiler was influenced by the actual date at which he wrote. The aggregate of the two periods would be the Kali year 4146, equivalent to A. D. 1045. There are some variety and indistinctness in the enumeration of the periods which compose this total: but the date which results from it is not unlikely to be an approximation to that of the Vishṇu Purāṇa.

It is the boast of inductive philosophy, that it draws its conclusions from the careful observation and accumulation of facts; and it is, equally, the business of all philosophical research to determine its facts before it ventures upon speculation. This procedure has not been observed in the investigation of the mythology and traditions of the Hindus. Impatience to generalize has availed itself greedily of whatever promised to afford materials for generalization; and the most erroneous views have been confidently advocated, because the guides to which their authors trusted were ignorant or insufficient. The information gleaned by Sir William Jones was gathered in an early season of Sanskrit study, before the field was cultivated. The same may be said of the writings of Paolino da S. Bartolomeo,[1] with the further disadvantage of his having

---

[1] Systema Brahmanicum, &c.

been imperfectly acquainted with the Sanskrit language
and literature, and his veiling his deficiencies under
loftiness of pretension and a prodigal display of mis-
applied erudition. The documents to which Wilford[1]
trusted proved to be, in great part, fabrications, and,
where genuine, were mixed up with so much loose and
unauthenticated matter, and so overwhelmed with
extravagance of speculation, that his citations need to
be carefully and skilfully sifted, before they can be
serviceably employed. The descriptions of Ward[2] are
too deeply tinctured by his prejudices to be implicitly
confided in; and they are also derived, in a great
measure, from the oral or written communications of
Bengali pandits, who are not, in general, very deeply
read in the authorities of their mythology. The accounts of Polier[3] were, in like manner, collected from
questionable sources: and his Mythologie des Indous
presents an heterogeneous mixture of popular and Pauránik tales, of ancient traditions, and legends apparently invented for the occasion, which renders the
publication worse than useless, except in the hands of
those who can distinguish the pure metal from the alloy.
Such are the authorities to which Maurice, Faber, and
Creuzer have exclusively trusted, in their description
of the Hindu mythology; and it is no marvel that there
should have been an utter confounding of good and
bad in their selection of materials, and an inextricable

---

[1] Asiatic Researches.

[2] View of the History, Literature, and Religion of the Hindoos,
with a Description of their Manners and Customs.

[3] Mythologie des Indous, edited by la Chanoinesse de Polier.

mixture of truth and error in their conclusions. Their labours, accordingly, are far from entitled to that confidence which their learning and industry would, else, have secured; and a sound and comprehensive survey of the Hindu system is still wanting to the comparative analysis of the religious opinions of the ancient world, and to a satisfactory elucidation of an important chapter in the history of the human race. It is with the hope of supplying some of the necessary means for the accomplishment of these objects, that the following pages have been translated.

The translation of the Vishńu Puráńa has been made from a collation of various manuscripts in my possession. I had three, when I commenced the work; two in the Devanagari, and one in the Bengali, character. A fourth, from the west of India, was given to me by Major Jervis, when some progress had been made; and, in conducting the latter half of the translation through the press, I have compared it with three other copies in the library of the East India Company. All these copies closely agree; presenting no other differences than occasional varieties of reading, owing, chiefly, to the inattention or inaccuracy of the transcriber. Four of the copies were accompanied by a commentary, essentially the same, although occasionally varying, and ascribed, in part, at least, to two different scholiasts. The annotations on the first two books and the fifth are, in two MSS., said to be the work of Śrídhara Yati, the disciple of Parónanda Nrihari, and who is, therefore, the same as Śrídhara Swámin, the commentator on the Bhágavata. In the other three books, these two MSS. concur with other two in naming the commentator Ratnagarbha Bhattáchárya, who, in those two, is the author of the notes on the entire work. The introductory verses[*] of his comment specify him to be the disciple of Vidyáváchaspati, the son of Hiranyagarbha, and grandson of Mádhava, who composed his commentary by desire of Súryákara, son of Ratinátha Misra, son of Chandrákara, hereditary ministers of some sovereign who is not particularized. In the illustrations which are attributed to these different writers, there is so much conformity, that one or other is largely indebted to his predecessor. They both refer to earlier commentaries. Srídhara cites the works of Chitsukha Yogin and others, both more extensive and more concise; between which, his own, which he terms Átma- or Swa-prakása, 'self-illuminator',

---

[*] The verses referred to are as follows:

हिरण्यगर्भतनयो माधवख्यातिमाश्रयः ।
श्रीगर्भगर्भसंभूते विद्यावाचस्पतिर्द्विजः ॥
पुराणसंहितासारं पीठस्वादिष्टवं वरात् ।
परापरमुनिज्ञबे पुराणं पञ्चलक्षणम् ॥
बहुहृद्य पदं तद्दीक्षया कृतया स्वयम् ।
श्रीसूर्याकरमिश्रातियत्नः संकुलीकृतम् ॥

At the end of Ratnagarbha's commentary we read:

यदूख यच्चख कुटपदपदार्थातिनिपुणा
न केषामप्यर्थः स्फुरति वनि चण्डेहिनिगिरे ।
ततो विद्यावाधर्षातियधनदीपावलिमता
मया व्याख्यार्थांभुदि कुरुत सज्जाः साहदशाः ॥
चन्द्राकरश्च तनयो रतिनाथार्मिश्रः
गोणीभूमव्वच्छदभूदच तत्सुतोन ।
सूर्याकरेण नृपमन्त्रिवरेण यत्ना-
त्संग्रार्थिनो विहितमाचरणब्व टीकाम् ॥

holds an intermediate character.* Ratnagarbha entitles his, Vaishńavákúta-chandriká, 'the moonlight of devotion to Vishńu.' The dates of these commentators are not ascertainable, as far as I am aware, from any of the particulars which they have specified.

In the notes which I have added to the translation, I have been desirous, chiefly, of comparing the statements of the text with those of other Puráńas, and pointing out the circumstances in which they differ or agree; so as to render the present publication a sort of concordance to the whole; as it is not very probable that many of them will be published or translated. The Index that follows† has been made sufficiently copious to answer the purposes of a mythological and historical dictionary, as far as the Puráńas, or the greater number of them, furnish materials.

In rendering the text into English, I have adhered to it as literally as was compatible with some regard to the usages of English composition. In general, the original presents few difficulties. The style of the Puráńas is, very commonly, humble and easy; and the narrative is plainly and unpretendingly told. In the addresses to the deities, in the expatiations upon the divine nature, in the descriptions of the universe, and

* Srídhara, at the opening of his commentary, writes thus:

श्रीमच्चित्सुखयोगिमुख्यरचितव्याख्यां निरीक्ष्य स्फुटं
सन्मार्गेण सुबोधसंयुतमिमामात्मप्रकाशाभिधाम् ।
श्रीमद्विष्णुपुराणसारविवृतिं कर्तुं यतिः श्रीधर-
स्वामी सद्गुरुपादपद्ममधुपः साधुः सुधीयुक्तये ॥
श्रीमद्विष्णुपुराणस्य व्याख्यां सम्यगतिविस्तराम् ।
मायानालोक्य तद्व्याख्या मध्यमेयं विधीयते ॥

† A new and amplified Index will be given at the end of the last volume.

in argumentative and metaphysical discussion, there occur passages in which the difficulty arising from the subject itself is enhanced by the brief and obscure manner in which it is treated. On such occasions, I derived much aid from the commentary. But it is possible that I may have, sometimes, misapprehended and misrepresented the original; and it is, also, possible that I may have sometimes failed to express its purport with sufficient precision to have made it intelligible. I trust, however, that this will not often be the case, and that the translation of the Vishńu Puráńa will be of service and of interest to the few who, in these times of utilitarian selfishness, conflicting opinion, party virulence, and political agitation, can find a resting-place for their thoughts in the tranquil contemplation of those yet living pictures of the ancient world which are exhibited by the literature and mythology of the Hindus.

CONTENTS.

BOOK I.

CHAPTER I.

CHAPTER II.

CHAPTER III.

CHAPTER IV.

CHAPTER V.

CHAPTER VI.

CHAPTER VII.

CHAPTER VIII.

CHAPTER IX.

CHAPTER X.

CHAPTER XI.

CHAPTER XII.

CHAPTER XIII.

CHAPTER XIV.

CHAPTER XV.

CHAPTER XVI.

CHAPTER XVII.

CHAPTER XVIII.

CHAPTER XIX.

CHAPTER XX.

CHAPTER XXI.

CHAPTER XXII.

BOOK II.

CHAPTER I.

CHAPTER II.

CHAPTER III.

CHAPTER IV.

CHAPTER X.

CHAPTER XI.

CHAPTER XII.

CHAPTER XIII.

CHAPTER XIV.

CHAPTER XV.

CHAPTER XVI.

BOOK III.

CHAPTER I.

CHAPTER II.

CHAPTER III.

CHAPTER IV.

CHAPTER V.

CHAPTER VI.

CHAPTER VII.

CHAPTER VIII.

CHAPTER IX.

CHAPTER X.

CHAPTER XI.

CHAPTER XII.

CHAPTER XIII.

CHAPTER II.

CHAPTER III.

CHAPTER IV.

CHAPTER V.

CHAPTER VI.

CHAPTER VII.

CHAPTER VIII.

CHAPTER IX.

CHAPTER X.

CHAPTER XI.

CHAPTER XII.

CHAPTER XIII.

Satrájit gives it to Prasena, who is killed by a lion: the lion killed by the bear Jámbavat. Krishńa, suspected of killing Prasena, goes to look for him in the forests: traces the bear to his cave: fights with him for the jewel: the contest prolonged: supposed, by his companions, to be slain: he overthrows Jámbavat and marries his daughter Jámbavatí: returns, with her and the jewel, to Dwáraká: restores the jewel to Satrájit and marries his daughter Satyabhámá. Satrájit murdered by Satadhanwan: avenged by Krishńa. Quarrel between Krishńa and Balaráma. Akrúra possessed of the jewel: leaves Dwáraká. Public calamities. Meeting of the Yáduvas. Story of Akrúra's birth: he is invited to return: accused, by Krishńa, of having the Syamantaka jewel: produces it in full assembly: it remains in his charge: Krishńa acquitted of having purloined it.

CHAPTER XIV.

Descendants of Sini, of Anamitra, of Swaphalka and Chitraka, of Andhaka. The children of Devaka and Ugrasena. The descendants of Bhajamána. Children of Súra: his son Vasudeva: his daughter Prithá married to Páńdu: her children, Yudhishthira and his brothers; also Karńa, by Áditya. The sons of Páńdu by Mádri. Husbands and children of Súra's other daughters. Previous births of Sisupála.

CHAPTER XV.

Explanation of the reason why Sisupála, in his previous births as Hirańyakasipu and Rávaňa, was not identified with Vishńu, on being slain by him, and was so identified, when killed as Sisupála. The wives of Vasudeva: his children: Balaráma and Krishńa his sons by Devaki: born, apparently, of Rohiní and Yasodá. The wives and children of Krishńa. Multitude of the descendants of Yadu.

CHAPTER XVI.

Descendants of Turvasu.

CHAPTER XVII.

Descendants of Druhyu.

CHAPTER XVIII.

CHAPTER XIX.

CHAPTER XX.

CHAPTER XXI.

CHAPTER XXII.

CHAPTER XXIII.

CHAPTER XXIV.

CHAPTER XVII.

CHAPTER XVIII.

CHAPTER XIX.

CHAPTER XX.

CHAPTER XXI.

CHAPTER XXII.

CHAPTER XXIII.

CHAPTER XXIV.

CHAPTER XXV.

CHAPTER XXVI.

CHAPTER XXVII.

CHAPTER XXVIII.

CHAPTER XXIX.

BOOK VI.

CHAPTER I.

CHAPTER II.

CHAPTER III.

CHAPTER IV.

CHAPTER V.

CHAPTER VI.

CHAPTER VII.

CHAPTER VIII.

VISHŃU PURÁŃA.

BOOK I.

CHAPTER I.

Invocation. Maitreya inquires of his teacher, Paráśara, the
origin and nature of the universe. Paráśara performs a rite
to destroy the demons: reproved by Vasishťha, he desists:
Pulastya appears, and bestows upon him divine knowledge:
he repeats the Vishńu Puráńa. Vishńu the origin, existence,
and end of all things.

Oṁ! GLORY TO VÁSUDEVA.[1]—Victory be to thee,
Puńdaríkáksha; adoration be to thee, Viśwabhávana;

---

[1] ओम् । नमो वासुदेवाय । An address of this kind, to one
or other Hindu divinity, usually introduces Sanskrit compositions,
especially those considered sacred. The first term of this Mantra
or brief prayer, Om or Onkára, is well known as a combination
of letters invested by Hindu mysticism with peculiar sanctity.
In the Vedas, it is said to comprehend all the gods; and, in the
Puráńas, it is directed to be prefixed to all such formulæ as
that of the text. Thus, in the Uttara Khańda* of the Padma
Puráńa: 'The syllable Om, the mysterious name, or Brahma, is
the leader of all prayers: let it, therefore, O lovely-faced,
(Śiva addresses Durgá,) be employed in the beginning of all
prayers':

ओंकार: प्रवदी ब्रह्म सर्वमन्त्रेषु नायक: ।
तादी सर्वं पूजीत मन्त्राद्यं च शुभाननं ॥

* Chapter XXXII.

L   1

glory be to thee, Hrishíkeśa, Mahápurusha and Púrvaja.[1]

According to the same authority, one of the mystical imports of
the term is the collective enunciation of Vishńu, expressed by A;
of Śrí, his bride, intimated by U; and of their joint worshipper,
designated by M. A whole chapter of the Váyu Puráńa is devoted to this term. A text of the Vedas is there cited: ओमि-
त्येकाक्षरं ब्रह्म । 'Om, the monosyllable Brahma'; the latter
meaning either the supreme being, or the Vedas collectively, of
which this monosyllable is the type. It is also said to typify
the three spheres of the world, the three holy fires, the three
steps of Vishńu, &c.:

ओमित्येतत्त्रयो वेदास्त्रयो लोकास्त्रयो ऽग्नयः ।[*]
विष्णुस्त्रिमात्रस्त्रयस्ते चक्षणानि चत्वारि च ॥

Frequent meditation upon it and repetition of it ensure release
from worldly existence:

एतदक्षरं ब्रह्म परमोंकारसंज्ञितम् ।
यच्च वेद्यते सम्यग् ध्यायति वा पुनः ॥
संसारचक्रमुत्सृज्य मुक्तपद्मवदच्युतः ।
यच्च निर्मुक्तं ज्ञानं शिवं मार्गोपलम्भयः ॥

See, also, Manu, II., 76. Vásudeva, a name of Vishńu or Krishńa,
is, according to its grammatical etymology, a patronymic derivative implying son of Vasudeva. The Vaishńava Puráńas,
however, devise other explanations. See the next chapter, and,
again, b. VI., c. 5.

[1] In this stanza occurs a series of the appellations of Vishńu:
1. Puńdaríkáksha (पुण्डरीकाक्ष), having eyes like a lotos, or
heart-pervading: or Puńdaríka is explained supreme glory, and
Aksha, imperishable. The first is the most usual etymon. 2. Viśwabhávana (विश्वभावन), the creator of the universe, or the
cause of the existence of all things. 3. Hrishíkeśa (हृषीकेश),

---

[*] This verse is also found in the *Márkańdeya-puráńa*, XLII., 8; p. 241 of
the edition in the *Bibliotheca Indica*.

May that Vishńu, who is the existent, imperishable
Brahma; who is Íswara;[1] who is spirit;[2] who, with the
three qualities,[3] is the cause of creation, preservation,
and destruction; who is the parent of nature, intellect,

---

lord of the senses.[*] 4. Mahápurusha (महापुरुष), great or supreme spirit; Purusha meaning that which abides or is quiescent
in body (puri śete). 5. Púrvaja (पूर्वज), produced or appearing
before creation; the Orphic πρωτόγονος. In the fifth book,
c. 18, Vishńu is described by five appellations which are considered analogous to these; or: 1. Bhútátman (भूतात्मन्), one with
created things, or Puńdaríkáksha; 2. Pradhánátman (प्रधानात्मन्),
one with crude nature, or Viswabhávana; 3. Indriyátman (इन्द्रि-
यात्मन्), one with the senses, or Hríshikeśa; 4. Parmátman (पर-
मात्मन्), supreme spirit, or Mahápurusha; and Átman (आत्मन्),
soul, living soul, animating nature and existing before it, or
Púrvaja.

[1] Brahma (ब्रह्म), in the neuter form, is abstract supreme
spirit; and Íswara (ईश्वर) is the deity in his active nature,
he who is able to do or leave undone, or to do anything in any
other manner than that in which it is done: कर्तुमकर्तुमन्यथा वा
समर्थः ।

[2] Puns (पुंस्), which is the same with Purusha, incor-
porated spirit. By this, and the two preceding terms, also, the
commentator understands the text to signify, that Vishńu is any
form of spiritual being that is acknowledged by different philosophical systems; or that he is the Brahma of the Vedánta,
the Íswara of the Pátanjala, and the Purusha of the Sánkhya,
school.

[3] The three qualities, to which we shall have further occasion
to advert, are: Sattwa (सत्त्व), goodness or purity, knowledge,

---

[*] In the *Mahábhárata*, *Udyoga-parvas*, 2564 and 2567, Puńdaríkáksha
and Hríshikeśa are explained to a very different purport. The stanzas
are quoted and translated in Muir's *Original Sanskrit Texts*, Part IV.,
pp. 162 and 163.

and the other ingredients of the universe;[1] be to us the bestower of understanding, wealth, and final emancipation.

Having adored Vishńu,[2] the lord of all, and paid

---

quiescence; Rajas (रजस्), foulness, passion, activity; and Tamas (तमस्), darkness, ignorance, inertia. *

[1] Pradhánabuddhyádijagatprapanchasúh (प्रधानबुद्ध्यादिजगत्प्रपञ्चसूः). This predicate of the deity distinguishes most of the Puráńas from several of the philosophical systems, which maintain, as did the earliest Grecian systems of cosmogony, the eternal and independent existence of the first principle of things, as nature, matter, or chaos. Accordingly, the commentator notices the objection. Pradhána being without beginning, it is said, How can Vishńu be its parent? To which he replies, that this is not so; for, in a period of worldly destruction (Pralaya), when the creator desists from creating, nothing is generated by virtue of any other energy or parent. Or, if this be not satisfactory, then the text may be understood to imply that Intellect (Buddhi), &c., are formed through the materiality of crude nature or Pradhána.

[2] Vishńu is commonly derived, in the Puráńas, from the root Vis (विश्), to enter; entering into or pervading the universe: agreeably to the text of the Vedas: तत्सृष्ट्वा तदेवानुप्राविशत् । 'Having created that (world), he then afterwards enters into it;' being, as our comment observes, undistinguished by place, time, or property: देशकालरूपी चायदेहाभावात् । According to the Matsya P., the name alludes to his entering into the mundane egg: according to the Padma P., to his entering into, or combining with, Prakriti, as Purusha or spirit:

स एव भगवान्विष्णुः प्रधानात्माधिवेश इ ।

In the Moksha Dharma of the Mahábhárata, s. 165, the word is derived from the root vi (वी), signifying motion, pervasion,

---

* See the editor's second note in p. 26, and note in p. 33, *infra.*

reverence to Brahmá and the rest;[1] having also saluted the spiritual preceptor;[2] I will narrate a Puráńa equal in sanctity to the Vedas.

---

production, radiance; or, irregularly, from kram (क्रम), to go, with the particle vi (वि), implying variously, prefixed.[*]

[1] Brahmá and the rest is said to apply to the series of teachers through whom this Puráńa was transmitted from its first reputed author, Brahmá, to its actual narrator, the sage Parásara. See, also, b. VI., c. 8.

[2] The Guru or spiritual preceptor is said to be Kapila or Sáraswata. The latter is included in the series of teachers of the Puráńa. Parásara must be considered also as a disciple of Kapila, as a teacher of the Sánkhya philosophy.

---

[*] There seems to be a misunderstanding, here, on the part of the translator; for, in the passage of the *Mahábhárata* referred to by him,— which can be no other than the *Sánti-parvan, Moksha-dharma*, 13170 and 13171 — Vishńu is taken to be derived, with the affix यु, from विशु, "to shine" and also "to move". That passage is subjoined:

नतिष सर्वभूतानां प्रणतश्चापि भारत ।
आत्मा मे रौद्रवी पार्थ शान्तिश्चाभ्यधिका मम ॥
अभिभूतानि भावेषु तद्दिक्षेप्यापि भारत ।
क्रमभावाच्च पार्थ विष्णुरित्यभिसंज्ञितः ॥

Arjuna Miśra, commenting on these verses, derives the word from विशु in the acceptation of "to go". He seems to admit this verb likewise in the Vaidik sense of "to eat." But the latter view is not borne out by the text. His words are: विष्णुपदङ्क्त्यभिमानात् । नतिरिति । विविशर्थः । तेन विश्वति । वेवेष्टीति विष्णुः । अश्नातीति वा निरुक्तम् ।

In the *Nighańtu*, II., 8, वेवेष्टि occurs as a synonym of गति.

Gangádhara, in his metrical gloss on the thousand names of Vishńu, expresses himself as follows, touching the six hundred and fifty-seventh of them:

वेवेष्टि शान्तिम एवं विश्व रौद्रवी वा ।
विष्णुः स विश्वयति सो ऽय हि दीप्यते यु: ॥
भावे मे रौद्रवी पार्थ शान्तिर्भ्यधिका विना ।
क्रमभावाच्च पार्थ विष्णुरित्यभिसंज्ञितः ॥
एतुते भावार्थे हि विश्व दीप्ती च भातुः ।
वीरादिक्षेदलक्षणम् ॥

Maitreya,[1] having saluted him reverentially, thus addressed Parásara,—the excellent sage, the grandson of Vasishťha,[2]—who was versed in traditional history and the Puráńas; who was acquainted with the Vedas and the branches of science dependent upon them, and skilled in law and philosophy;[†] and who had performed the morning rites of devotion.

Maitreya said: Master! I have been instructed, by you, in the whole of the Vedas, and in the institutes of law and of sacred science. Through your favour, other men, even though they be my foes, cannot accuse me of having been remiss in the acquirement of knowledge. I am now desirous, O thou who art profound in piety, to hear from thee how this world was, and how in future it will be? what is its substance, O Brahman; and whence proceeded animate and inanimate things? into what has it been resolved; and into what will its dissolution again occur? how were the elements manifested? whence proceeded the gods and other beings? what are the situation and extent of the oceans and the mountains, the earth, the sun, and the planets? what are the families of the gods and

---

[1] Maitreya is the disciple of Parásara, who relates the Vishńu Puráńa to him. He is also one of the chief interlocutors in the Bhágavata, and is introduced, in the Mahábhárata (Vana Parvan, s. 10), as a great Rishi or sage, who denounces Duryodhana's death. In the Bhágavata, he is also termed Kauśáravi, or the son of Kuśárava.

[2] Literally, "Vasishťha's son's son". Parásara's father, as the commentator remarks, was Śakti. See my second note in p. 8, infra.

[†] "And philosophy" is the commentator's definition of the original, ádi, "and the rest".

others, the Manus, the periods called Manwantaras, those termed Kalpas, and their subdivisions, and the four ages: the events that happen at the close of a Kalpa, and the terminations of the several ages:[1] the histories, O great Muni, of the gods, the sages, and kings; and how the Vedas were divided into branches (or schools), after they had been arranged by Vyása:[*] the duties of the Brahmans and the other tribes, as well as of those who pass through the different orders of life? All these things I wish to hear from you, grandson of Vasishtha.[†] Incline thy thoughts benevolently towards me, that I may, through thy favour, be informed of all I desire to know.

Parásara replied: Well inquired, pious Maitreya. You recall to my recollection that which was of old narrated by my father's father, Vasishtha. I had heard that my father had been devoured by a Rákshasa employed by Viswámitra. Violent anger seized me; and I commenced a sacrifice for the destruction of the Rákshasas. Hundreds of them were reduced to ashes by the rite; when, as they were about to be entirely extirpated, my grandfather Vasishtha thus spoke to me: Enough, my child; let thy wrath be appeased: the Rákshasas are not culpable: thy father's death was the work of destiny. Anger is the passion of fools; it becometh not a wise man. By whom, it may be asked,

---

[1] One copy reads Yugadharma, the duties peculiar to the four ages, or their characteristic properties, instead of Yugánta.

[*] *Vyása-kartṛika* has, rather, the signification of "composed by Vyása".

[†] To the letter, "son of Vásishtha", whose father was Vasishtha.

is any one killed? Every man reaps the consequences
of his own acts. Anger, my son, is the destruction of
all that man obtains, by arduous exertions, of fame
and of devout austerities, and prevents the attainment
of heaven or of emancipation. The chief sages always
shun wrath: be not thou, my child, subject to its influence. Let no more of these unoffending spirits of
darkness be consumed.* Mercy is the might of the
righteous. [1]

---

[1] Sacrifice of Paráśara. The story of Paráśara's birth is
narrated in detail in the Mahábhárata (Ádi Parvan, s. 176). King
Kalmáshapáda, meeting with Śakti, the son of Vasishṭha, in a
narrow path in a thicket, desired him to stand out of his way.
The sage refused; on which the Rájá beat him with his whip;
and Śakti cursed him to become a Rákshasa, a man-devouring
spirit. The Rájá, in this transformation, killed and ate its
author, or Śakti, together with all the other sons of Vasishṭha.
Śakti left his wife, Adriśyanti, pregnant; and she gave birth to
Paráśara, who was brought up by his grandfather. When he
grew up, and was informed of his father's death, he instituted a
sacrifice for the destruction of all the Rákshasas, but was dis-
suaded from its completion by Vasishṭha and other sages, or
Atri, Pulastya, Pulaha, and Kratu. The Mahábhárata adds, that,
when he desisted from the rite, he scattered the remaining sacrificial fire upon the northern face of the Himálaya mountain,
where it still blazes forth, at the phases of the moon, consuming
Rákshasas, forests, and mountains. The legend alludes, possibly, to some trans-himalayan volcano. The transformation of
Kalmáshapáda is ascribed, in other places, to a different cause;
but he is everywhere regarded as the devourer of Śakti † or
Śaktri, as the name also occurs. The story is told in the Linga

---

* Supply: "Let this thy sacrifice cease": एवं ते विरमस्वेति ।
† This is hardly the name of a male. The right word seems to be
Śaktri.

Being thus admonished by my venerable grandsire, I immediately desisted from the rite, in obedience to his injunctions; and Vasishtha, the most excellent of sages, was content with me. Then arrived Pulastya,

---

Puráńa (Púrvárdha, s. 64) in the same manner, with the addition, conformably to the Śaiva tendency of that work, that Parásara begins his sacrifice by propitiating Mahádeva. Vasishtha's dissuasion and Pulastya's appearance are given in the very words of our text; and the story concludes: 'Thus, through the favour of Pulastya and of the wise Vasishtha, Parásara composed the Vaishńava (Vishńu) Puráńa, containing ten thousand stanzas, and being the third of the Puráńa compilations' (Puráńa-samhitá). [*] The Bhágavata (b. III., s. 8) also alludes, though obscurely, to this legend. In recapitulating the succession of the narrators of part of the Bhágavata, Maitreya states, that this first Puráńa was communicated to him by his Guru, Parásara, as he had been desired by Pulastya:

प्रोवाच मह्यं स दयानुदग्धो मुनि: (पराशर:) पुलस्त्येन पुराणमादयम् ।

i. e., according to the commentator, agreeably to the boon given by Pulastya to Parásara, saying, 'You shall be a narrator of Puráńas'; (पुराणवक्ता † भविष्यसि). The Mahábhárata makes no mention of the communication of this faculty to Parásara by Pulastya; and, as the Bhágavata could not derive this particular

---

[*] यथ मया पुलस्त्यस्य सन्निधौ च श्रीमत: ॥
महादेविकयं यन्मे पुराणं वै पराशर: ।
पद्मकारं समस्तार्थसाधकं ज्ञानसंचयम् ॥
इदमाख्यानमखिलं सर्ववेदार्थसंयुतम् ।
मुनीनां हि पुराणेषु संहितासु सुबोधनम् ॥

The lithographed Bombay edition of the *Linga-puráńa* gives the end of this passage differently, so as to reduce the *Vishńu-puráńa* to six thousand stanzas, and to reckon it as the fourth of the Puráńas:

पद्मकारमिदं सर्व वेदार्थेन च संयुतम् ।
षष्ठं हि पुराणानां संहितासु सुबोधनम् ॥

† An oversight of quotation, for पुराणप्रवक्ता. See Goldstücker's *Pániní, His Place in Sanskrit Literature*, pp. 145 et seq.

the son of Brahmá,[1] who was received, by my grandfather, with the customary marks of respect. The
illustrious brother * of Pulaha said to me: Since, in
the violence of animosity, you have listened to the
words of your progenitor, and have exercised clemency,
therefore you shall become learned in every science.
Since you have forborne, even though incensed, to
destroy my posterity, I will bestow upon you another
boon; and you shall become the author of a summary
of the Puráńas.[2] You shall know the true nature of
the deities, as it really is;† and, whether engaged in

---

from that source, it here, most probably, refers, unavowedly, as
the Linga does avowedly, to the Vishńu Puráńa.

[1] Pulastya, as will be presently seen, is one of the Rishis
who were the mind-born sons of Brahmá. Pulaha, who is here
also named, is another. Pulastya is considered as the ancestor
of the Rákshasas; as he is the father of Visravas, the father of
Rávańa and his brethren. Uttara Rámáyańa. Mahábhárata,
Vana Parvan, s. 272. Padma Pur. Linga Pur., s. 63.

[2] पुराणसंहिताकर्ता भवान्वत्स भविष्यति ।

You shall be a maker‡ of the Saṅhitá or compendium of the
Puráńas, or of the Vishńu Puráńa, considered as a summary or
compendium of Pauráńik traditions. In either sense, it is incompatible with the general attribution of all the Puráńas to Vyása.

---

* Read "elder brother". agraja.

† Rather, agreeably to the commentator: "You shall obtain in a proper
manner the highest object derivable from apprehension of deity". This
is said to be "knowledge conducive to emancipation". In the Sanskrit:
देवभावात्परमार्थं मोक्षोपयोगि ज्ञानम् । अथ यथे विदु लाभे ।
The line under exposition is as follows:
देवतायत्परमार्थं च यथावदीक्षसे भवान् ।

‡ Kartŕi is, however, elucidated, in the commentary, by pravartaka,
"publisher" only.

religious rites, or abstaining from their performance,[1] your understanding, through my favour, shall be perfect, and exempt from doubts. Then my grandsire Vasishtha added: Whatever has been said to thee by Pulastya shall assuredly come to pass.

Now truly all that was told me formerly by Vasishtha, and by the wise Pulastya, has been brought to my recollection by your questions; and I will relate to you the whole, even all you have asked. Listen to the complete compendium of the Puránas, according to its tenor. The world was produced from Vishńu: it exists in him: he is the cause of its continuance and cessation:[2] he is the world.[2]

---

[1] Whether performing the usual ceremonies of the Brahmans, or leading a life of devotion and penance, which supersedes the necessity of rites and sacrifices.

[2] These are, in fact, the brief replies to Maitreya's six questions (p. 6), or: How was the world created? By Vishńu. How will it be? At the periods of dissolution, it will be in Vishńu. Whence proceeded animate and inanimate things? From Vishńu. Of what is the substance of the world? Vishńu. Into what has it been, and will it again be, resolved? Vishńu. He is, therefore, both the instrumental and material cause of the universe. 'The answer to the "whence" replies to the query as to the instrumental cause: "He is the world" replies to the inquiry as to the material cause': सर्गेण चमदीनङ्ख निमित्तमन्तकीनारं चमत्र च एतुपादानमन्तकीनारम् । 'And by this explanation of the agency of the materiality, &c. of Vishńu, as regards the universe, (it follows that) all will be produced from, and all will repose in, him': सर्गेण विष्णो: सर्वमनुपादानमङ्ख्यवर्तुंनाहिद्वयेण विष्णोरेषोद्भविष्यति तदेव चासतीति । [dagger] We have

---

[asterisk] *Sańyama.* See the editor's first note in p. 26, *infra.*

[dagger] These two extracts are from the commentary on the *Vishńu-puráńa.* The first is a little abridged.

here precisely the τὸ πᾶν of the Orphic doctrines; and we might fancy, that Brucker was translating a passage from a Puráṇa, when he describes them in these words: "Continuisse Jovem [lege Vishnum] sive summum deum in se omnia, omnibus ortum ex se dedisse; et ** omnia ex se genuisse, et ex sua produxisse essentia; Spiritum esse universi, qui omnia regit, vivificat, eique ** Ex quibus necessario sequitur omnia in cum reditura." Hist. Philos., I., 388. Jamblichus and Proclus also testify that the Pythagorean doctrines of the origin of the material world from the Deity, and its identity with him, were much the same. Cudworth, Intell. Syst., Vol. I., p. 346.

CHAPTER II.

Paráśara said: Glory to the unchangeable, holy,
eternal, supreme Vishńu, of one universal nature, the
mighty over all: to him who is Hiranyagarbha, Hari,
and Sankara,[1] the creator, the preserver, and destroyer

---

[1] The three hypostases of Vishńu. Hiranyagarbha (हिरण्य-
गर्भ) is a name of Brahmá; he who was born from the golden
egg. Hari (हरि) is Vishńu; and Śankara (शंकर), Śiva. The
Vishńu who is the subject of our text is the supreme being in
all these three divinities or hypostases, in his different characters
of creator, preserver, and destroyer. Thus, in the Márkańdeya:[*]
'Accordingly, as the primal all-pervading spirit is distinguished
by attributes in creation and the rest, so he obtains the denomination of Brahmá, Vishńu, and Śiva. In the capacity of Brahmá,
he creates the worlds; in that of Rudra, he destroys them; in
that of Vishńu, he is quiescent. These are the three Avasthás
(lit., hypostases) of the self-born. Brahmá is the quality of activity; Rudra, that of darkness; Vishńu, the lord of the world,
is goodness. So, therefore, the three gods are the three qualities.

[*] XI.VI, 16 et seq. The edition in the *Bibliotheca Indica* gives several
discrepant readings.

of the world: to Vásudeva, the liberator of his worshippers:* to him whose essence is both single and
manifold; who is both subtile and corporeal, indiscrete
and discrete: to Vishńu, the cause of final emancipation.[1] Glory to the supreme Vishńu, the cause

---

They are ever combined with, and dependent upon, one another;
and they are never for an instant separate; they never quit each
other:"

यथा यान्वायव: येपी धर्मादिषु युद्येयुन: ।
तथा व संज्ञामायाति ब्रह्मविष्णुशिवात्मिकाम् ॥
प्रसूति वृद्धि लौकान्द्गुले संहरत्यपि ।
विष्णुस्ते ऽपि चौदासीनजनितो ऽपक्षा: स्वयंभुव: ॥
रक्षो ब्रह्मा तमो रुद्रो विष्णु: सत्त्व जगत्पति: ।
अत एव स्मयो देवा एत एव स्मयो मुदा: ॥
सर्वोऽनिमित्तुना ह्येते सर्वोऽवाबधिकस्यया ।
सर्व वियोगो न ह्येषां न सर्वाणि परस्परम् ॥

The notion is one common to all antiquity, although less philo-
sophically conceived, or, perhaps, less distinctly expressed, in the
passages which have come down to us. The τρεῖς ἀρχικὰς
ὑποστάσεις of Plato are said, by Cudworth (I., III.), upon the
authority of Plotinos, to be an ancient doctrine, παλαιὰ δόξα.
And he also observes: "For, since Orpheus, Pythagoras, and
Plato, who, all of them, asserted a trinity of divine hypostases,
unquestionably derived much of their doctrine from the Egyptians,
it may be reasonably suspected, that these Egyptians did the like
before them." As, however, the Grecian accounts and those of
the Egyptians are much more perplexed and unsatisfactory than
those of the Hindus, it is most probable that we find amongst
them the doctrine in its most original, as well as most methodical
and significant, form.

[1] This address to Vishńu pursues the notion that he, as the
supreme being, is one, whilst he is all. He is Avikára, not sub-

---

of the creation, existence, and end of this world;
who is the root of the world, and who consists of the
world.[1]

Having glorified him who is the support of all
things; who is the smallest of the small;[2] who is in all
created things; the unchanged,[*] imperishable[3] Puru-

---

ject to change: Sadaikarúpa, one invariable nature: he is the
liberator (Tára), or he who bears mortals across the ocean of
existence: he is both single and manifold (Ekánekarúpa): and
he is the indiscrete (Avyakta) cause of the world, as well as
the discrete (Vyakta) effect; or the invisible cause and visible
creation.

[1] Jaganmaya, made up, or consisting substantially (मय), of
the world. Maya is an affix denoting 'made' or 'consisting of';
as Káshthamaya, 'made of wood'. The world is, therefore, not
regarded, by the Paurániks, as an emanation, or an illusion, but
as consubstantial with its first cause.

[2] Aṇíyámsam aṇíyasám (अणीयांसमणीयसां), 'the most atomic
of the atomic'; alluding to the atomic theory of the Nyáya or
logical school.

[3] Or Achyuta (अच्युत); a common name of Vishńu, from a
privative, and Chyuta, fallen; according to our comment, 'he
who does not perish with created things'. The Mahábhárata
interprets it, in one place, to mean 'he who is not distinct from
final emancipation'; and, in another, to signify 'exempt from
decay' (अच्युति). A commentator on the Káśíkhańda of the
Skanda Puráńa explains it 'he who never declines (or varies)
from his own proper nature:' स्वभावादप्रच्यवने ।†

---

[*] In the original there is no term to which this corresponds.

† स्वभावात् प्रच्यवने । ?

shottama;[1] who is one with true wisdom, as truly
known;[2] eternal and incorrupt;[*] and who is known,
through false appearances, by the nature of visible
objects:[3][†] having bowed to Vishńu, the destroyer,

---

[1] This is another common title of Vishńu, implying supreme,
best (Uttama), spirit (Purusha), or male, or sacrifice, or, according to the Mahábh., Moksha Dharma, whatever sense Purusha may bear:

पुरुषो यज्ञ एतेषं यत्परं परिकीर्तितम् ।
यथाब्दनुपुरुषार्थं कालसर्वं तन्पुरुषोत्तम: ॥ ॥

[2] Paramárthatah (परमार्थत:), 'by or through the real object,
or sense; through actual truth.'

[3] Bhrántidarśanatah (भ्रान्तिदर्शनत:), 'false appearances,' in
opposition to actual truth. 'By the nature of visible objects'
(स्वरूपतस्येव): Artha is explained by Dŕiśya (दृश्य), 'visible';
Swarúpeńa, by 'the nature of'. That is, visible objects are not
what they seem to be, independent existences; they are essentially one with their original source; and knowledge of their
true nature, or relation to Vishńu, is knowledge of Vishńu him-

[*] "Who is, essentially, one with intelligence, transcendent, and without
spot:"

ज्ञानस्वरूपमत्यन्तं निर्मलं परमार्थत: ।

[†] Preferably: "Conceived of, by reason of erroneous apprehension,
as a material form":

तमेयार्थस्वरूपेय भ्रान्तिदर्शनत: स्थितम् ।

The commentary runs: स्वरूपस्येव स्मरूपेय गृहजीवभ्रान्तिज्ञानेन
स्थितं प्रतीतम् । The "erroneous apprehension" spoken of is here explained as arising from the conception of the individual soul.

[‡] In the Harivanśa, 11358, we find:

पुरुषो यज्ञ एतेषं यत्परं परिकीर्तितम् ।
यथाप्यनुपुरुषार्थं तु तत्सर्वं पुरुषोत्तम: ॥

"Purusha, that is to say, sacrifice, or whatever else is meant by purusha,
—all that, known for highest (para), is called Purushottama."

The word is a karmadháraya compound, not a tatpurusha.

and lord of creation and preservation; the ruler of the world; unborn, imperishable, undecaying:[*] I will relate to you that which was originally imparted by the great father of all (Brahmá[†]), in answer to the questions of Daksha and other venerable sages; and repeated by them to Purukutsa, a king who reigned on the banks of the Narmadá. It was next related by him to Sáraswata, and by Sáraswata to me.[1]

Who can describe him who is not to be apprehended by the senses: who is the best of all things; the supreme soul, self-existent: who is devoid of all the distinguishing characteristics of complexion, caste, or the like; and is exempt from birth, vicissitude, death, or decay:[‡] who is always, and alone: who exists everywhere, and in whom all things here exist; and who is, thence, named Vásudeva?[2] He is Brah-

---

self. This is not the doctrine of Máyá, or the influence of illusion, which alone, according to Vedánta idealism, constitutes belief in the existence of matter: a doctrine foreign to most of the Puránas, and first introduced amongst them, apparently, by the Bhágavata.

[1] A different and more detailed account of the transmission of the Vishńu Puráńa is given in the last book, c. 8.

[2] The ordinary derivation of Vásudeva has been noticed above (p. 2). Here it is derived from Vas, 'to dwell,' from Vishńu's abiding in all things, and all in him: सर्वाणि वसत्‍ च वसत्येव । The Mahábhárata explains Vásu in the same manner, and Deva to signify radiant, shining: सर्व वसत्‍रानि वास-

---

[*] Achyuta. Here and elsewhere the commentator gives aparikshína, "immutable", as its synonym.

[†] Expressed by Abjayoni, "Lotus-born".

[‡] Add "increase", riddhi.

18 VISHŃU PURÁŃA.

ma,' supreme, lord, eternal, unborn, imperishable, undecaying; of one essence; ever pure, as free from defects. He, that Brahma, was all things; comprehending in his own nature the indiscrete and discrete. He then existed in the forms of Purusha and of Kála. Purusha (spirit) is the first form of the supreme; next proceeded two other forms, the discrete and indiscrete; and Kála (time) was the last.* These four—Pradhána (primary

---

वसति सर्वभूतेषु वसत्यत्र इति वासुः। सूर्य एव हि विम्बमिति इति देवः तं वासुदे-वेति देवेति वासुदेवः। 'He causes all things to dwell in him; and he abides in all: whence he is named Vásu. Being resplendent as the sun, he is called Deva: and he who is both these is denominated Vásudeva.' See also b. VI., c. 5.

' The commentator argues, that Vásudeva must be the Brahma or supreme being of the Vedas, because the same circumstances

तदेव सर्वमेवैतदव्यक्ताव्यक्तरूपवत् ।
तथा पुरुषरूपेण कालरूपेण च स्थितम् ॥
परस्य ब्रह्मणो रूपं पुरुषः प्रथमं द्विज ।
व्यक्ताव्यक्ते तथैवान्ये रूपे कालस्तथापरम् ॥

"That *Brahma*, in its totality, has, essentially, the aspect of *prakriti*, both evolved and unevolved, and also the aspect of spirit, and the aspect of time. Spirit, O twice-born, is the leading aspect of the supreme Brahma. The next is a twofold aspect, *viz., prakriti*, both evolved and unevolved; and time is the last."

It seems, therefore, not that *prakriti*, spirit, and time originated from Brahma, but that Brahma offers itself under these modes of apprehension. These modes are coessential with Brahma.

The last line of the text cited above admitting of two interpretations, that has been chosen which harmonizes the doctrine of the writer of the Puráńa with the doctrine of his quotation in pp. 23—25, *infra*; for on that his own enunciation here undoubtedly is founded.

Professor Wilson adopted the following reading of the first line of the verses in question:

तद्यत्तत्सर्वमेवैतदव्यक्ताव्यक्तरूपवत् ।

† These words have the appearance of being a glossarial expansion of an etymology given in the *Mahábhárata*, or some similar work. The

or crude matter), Purusha (spirit), Vyakta (visible
substance), and Kála (time)—the wise consider to be
the pure and supreme condition of Vishńu.[*] These
four forms, in their due proportions, are the causes of
the production of the phenomena of creation, preservation, and destruction. Vishńu, being thus discrete
and indiscrete substance, spirit, and time, sports like

---

are predicated of both, as eternity, omnipresence, omnipotence,
&c.; but he does not adduce any scriptural text with the name
Vásudeva.

[*] Time is not usually enumerated, in the Puráńas, as an
element of the first cause; but the Padma P. and the Bhágavata
agree with the Vishńu in including it. It appears to have been
regarded, at an earlier date, as an independent cause. The commentator on the Moksha Dharma cites a passage from the Vedas,
which he understands to allude to the different theories of the
cause of creation:

काल: स्वभावो नियतिर्यदृच्छा भूतानि योनि: पुरुष: ।[*]

Time, Inherent nature, consequence of acts, self-will, elementary
atoms, matter, and spirit, asserted, severally, by the Astrologers,
the Buddhists, the Mímáńsakas, the Jainas, the Logicians, the
Sánkhyas, and the Vedántins. *Kρóνος* was also one of the first
generated agents in creation, according to the Orphic theogony.

---

commentary on the *Vishńu-puráńa* has: सर्वमिति । सर्ववासी वसति
सर्वां वाकिन्वसति । * * तत: स वासुदेव एखुच्यते । सर्वाधिवरत-
वीर्यजिति वायुश्मर्थां: । वासुवासी धौतनादैवरैति कर्मधारय: ।
वसनाद्योतनादेव वासुदेव विदुरिति मोक्षधर्मेषु गिरते: ।

In the *Mahábhárata, Sánti-parvan*, 13169, we read:

वादयानि जनयित्वा भूत्वा सूर्यं सगांशुभि: ।
सर्वभूताधिवासश्च वासुदेवस्ततो स्मृतम् ॥

[*] From the *Swetáswatara Upanishad*. See the *Bibliotheca Indica*,
Vol. VII, p. 276.

a playful boy, as you shall learn by listening to his
frolics.[1]

That chief principle (Pradhána), which is the indiscrete cause, is called, by the sages, also Prakŕiti
(nature): it is subtile, uniform, and comprehends what
is and what is not (or both causes and effects);[2] is
durable, self-sustained, illimitable, undecaying, and
stable; devoid of sound or touch, and possessing
neither colour nor form; endowed with the three qualities (in equilibrium); the mother of the world; without beginning;[*] and that into which all that is produced

---

[1] The creation of the world is very commonly considered to
be the Lílá (लीला), sport or amusement, of the supreme being.

[2] The attributes of Pradhána, the chief (principle or element),
here specified, conform, generally, to those ascribed to it by the
Sánkhya philosophy (Sánkhya Káriká, p. 16, &c.); although some
of them are incompatible with its origin from a first cause.† In
the Sánkhya, this incongruity does not occur; for there Pradhána
is independent, and coordinate with primary spirit. The Puráńas
give rise to the inconsistency, by a lax use of both philosophical
and pantheistical expressions. The most incongruous epithets in
our text are, however, explained away in the comment. Thus,
Nitya (नित्य), 'eternal', is said to mean 'uniform, not liable to
increase or diminution': नित्यं सदैकरूपं युगादिहीनम् । Sada-
sadátmaka (सदसदात्मक), 'comprehending what is and what is
not', means 'having the power of both cause and effect' (कार्य-
कारणशक्तियुक्त), as proceeding from Vishńu, and as giving origin
to material things. Anádi (अनादि), 'without beginning', means

---

[*] The literal translation is this: "That which is the unevolved cause
is emphatically called, by the most eminent sages, *pradhána*, *original
base*, which is subtile *prakŕiti*, *viz.*, that which is eternal, and which at
once is and is not, *or is mere process*."

The Sanskrit is in note 2 of this page. I cannot translate *prakŕiti*.

† ?

is resolved.* By that principle all things were in-

'without birth' (अजन्मा), not being engendered by any created
thing, but proceeding immediately from the first cause. 'The
mother', or, literally, 'the womb, of the world' (जगद्योनि),
means 'the passive agent in creation', operated on, or influenced,
by the active will of the creator.† The first part of the passage
in the text is a favourite one with several of the Puráńas; but
they modify it, and apply it after their own fashion. In the
Vishńu, the original is:

यतो यावत्‌ यत्तदख्यानमनुविशसतौ: ।
प्रोच्यते प्रकृति: सूक्ष्मा नित्यं सदसदात्मकम्‌ ॥

rendered as above. The Váyu, Brahmáńda, and Kúrma Puráńas have:

यतो यावत्‌ यतु नित्यं सदसदात्मकम्‌ ।
प्रधानं प्रकृति चैव यमाहुस्तत्त्वचिन्तका: ॥:

'The Indiscrete cause, which is uniform, and both cause and
effect, and whom those who are acquainted with first principles
call Pradhána and Prakŕiti, is the uncognizable Brahma, who
was before all': यद्विशेषं प्रकृते: समवर्तत ।§ But the application
of two synonyms of Prakŕiti to Brahma seems unnecessary, at
least. The Brahma P. corrects the reading, apparently: the first
line is as before; the second is:

---

* *Prabhavápyaya*, "*the place whence is the origination and into which
is the resolution of all things.*" So says the commentator, and rightly.

Jagad-yoni, a little before, is scarcely so much "the mother of the
world", or "the womb of the world", as "the material cause of the
world." The commentator explains it by *káraňa*, "cause".

† It may be generally remarked, with regard to these explanations of
terms used in the text, and expounded by the Hindu commentator, that,
had Professor Wilson enjoyed the advantages which are now at the
command of the student of Indian philosophy, unquestionably he would
here have expressed himself differently. Thus, the reader will not find
the "incongruity" and "inconsistency" complained of, if he bears in
mind, that the text speaks of Brahma, not as putting forth evolutions,
but as exhibiting different aspects of itself.

‡ This is in the fourth chapter of the *Váyu-puráńa*.

§ Compare the *Márkańdeya-puráńa*, XLV., 32 and 34.

vested in the period subsequent to the last dissolution

अभावय प्रधानो व्याजादिव्यक्तं विश्वमीश्वरम् ।

The passage is placed absolutely: 'There was an indiscrete cause,—eternal, and cause and effect,—which was both matter and spirit (Pradhána and Purusha), from which this world was made.' Instead of इदं, 'such' or 'this', some copies read ईश्वर:, 'from which Íswara or god (the active deity or Brahmá) made the world'. The Hari Vaṁśa has the same reading, except in the last term, which it makes ईश्वरं; that is, according to the commentator, 'the world, which is Íswara, was made.' The same authority explains this indiscrete cause, Avyaktakárana, to denote Brahmá, 'the creator'; स वै निमित्तं मह्यार्थं जगारे सर्वभूतानाम् । an identification very unusual, if not inaccurate, and possibly founded on misapprehension of what is stated by the Bhavishya P.:

यत्तत्कारणमव्यक्तं नित्यं सदसदात्मकम् ।
तद्विमिश्र: स पुरुषो लोके ब्रह्मेति कीर्त्यते ।
एवं स भगवानजश्च इति ।

'That male or spirit which is endowed with that which is the indiscrete cause, &c., is known, in the world, as Brahmá: he, being in the egg', &c. The passage is precisely the same in Manu, I., 11.; except that we have 'Viṡishṭa' instead of 'Vi-ṡishṭha'. The latter is a questionable reading, and is, probably, wrong; the sense of the former is, 'detached': and the whole means, very consistently, 'embodied spirit detached from the indiscrete cause of the world, is known as Brahmá'.* The Padma P. inserts the first line, यत्तत्, &c., but has:

महदादि विशेषान्तं सृजतीति विनिश्चय: ।

---

* Viṡishṭa, the only reading recognized by Kullúka and Medhátithi, commentators on the Mánava-dharma-śástra, means, as explained by them, utpádita, "produced" or "created".

The Mánava-dharma-śástra notably differs from the Sánkhya, in that it does not hold a duality of first principles. And still different are the Puránas, in which the dualistic principles are united in Brahma, and — as previously remarked — are not evolutions therefrom, but so many aspects of some supreme deity. See the Translator's first note in p. 15, supra.

of the universe, and prior to creation.[1] For Brahmans learned in the Vedas, and teaching truly their doctrines, explain such passages as the following as intending the production of the chief principle (Pradhána). "There was neither day nor night, nor sky nor earth, nor darkness nor light, nor any other thing, save only One, unapprehensible by intellect, or That which is Brahma and Puṁs (spirit) and Pradhána

---

[1] 'Which creates, undoubtedly, Mahat and the other qualities':[*] assigning the first epithets, therefore, as the Vishṅu does, to Prakṛiti only. The Linga[†] also refers the expression to Prakṛiti alone, but makes it a secondary cause:

यतो ईश्वरादाद्यप्रभवत्तार्व परम् ।
प्रधानं प्रकृतिश्च यदाहुस्तत्वचिन्तकाः ॥

'An indiscrete cause, which those acquainted with first principles call Pradhána and Prakṛiti, proceeded from that Íśwara (Śiva).' This passage is one of very many instances in which expressions are common to several Puráńas, that seem to be borrowed from one another, or from some common source older than any of them; especially in this instance, as the same text occurs in Manu.[‡]

[1] The expression of the text is rather obscure: 'All was pervaded (or comprehended) by that chief principle before (re-creation), after the (last) destruction':

तेनासौ सर्वमेवासीद्ग्रसां वै भगवारतु ।

The ellipses are filled up by the commentator. This, he adds, is to be regarded as the state of things at a Mahápralaya or total dissolution; leaving, therefore, crude matter, nature, or chaos, as a coexistent element with the Supreme. This, which is conformable to the philosophical doctrine, is not, however, that of the Puráńas in general, nor that of our text, which states

---

[*] Read: "Which creates *all*, from *mahat* to individual existences: such is the conclusion *of the scripture*."

[†] Prior Section, LXX., 2.

[‡] See the editor's note in the preceding page.

(matter).[1]   The two forms which are other than

(b. VI., c. 4), that, at a Prákrita or elementary dissolution, Pradhána itself merges into the deity.[*] Neither is it, apparently,
the doctrine of the Vedas, although their language is somewhat
equivocal.

[1] The metre here is one common to the Vedas, Trishṭubh;
but, in other respects, the language is not characteristic of those
compositions. The purport of the passage is rendered somewhat
doubtful by its close and by the explanation of the commentator. The former is: एकं प्राधानिकं ब्रह्म पुमांस्तदासीत् । 'One
Prádhánika Brahma Spirit: THAT, was.' The commentator
explains Prádhánika, Pradhána eva, the same word as Pradhána;
but it is a derivative word, which may be used attributively,
implying 'having, or conjoined with, Pradhána'. The commentator, however, interprets it as the substantive; for he adds:
'There was Pradhána and Brahma and Spirit; this triad was at
the period of dissolution': प्रधानं ब्रह्म च पुमानिति त्रयमेव तदा
सर्वं आसीत् ।† He evidently, however, understands their con-
joint existence as one only; for he continues: 'So, according to
the Vedas, then there was neither the non-existent cause nor the
existent effect': नभा च सृति: । नासदासीन्नो सदासीत्तदानीम् ।‡

----

[*] The evolutionary doctrine is not the Pauránik; and the commentator—
who, on this occasion, does little more than supply ellipses, and does
not call *prakṛiti*, "at a Mahápralaya", "a coexistent element with the
Supreme" — advances nothing in contradiction to the tenor of the
Puránas. See the editor's second note in p. 21, and note in p. 22, *supra*.

† It is the abridged comment that is here cited. In the copy of it to
which I have access, the passage extracted above begins: प्राधानिकं
प्रधानमेव । प्राधानिकं ब्रह्म च । The fuller comment has: प्राधानिकं
स्वार्थे तद्धित: ।

‡ Thus opens a hymn of the *Rig-veda*; X., 129. See Colebrooke's
Miscellaneous Essays, Vol. I., p. 33; Müller's *History of Ancient Sanskrit
Literature*, pp. 559 et seq.; and Goldstücker's *Pánini, His Place in Sanskrit
Literature*, pp. 144 et seq. The Sanskrit of the hymn, accompanied by a
new translation, will be found in *Original Sanskrit Texts*, Part IV., pp. 3
and 4.

the essence of unmodified Vishńu are Pradhána (matter) and Purusha (spirit); and his other form, by which
those two are connected or separated, is called Kála
(time)."[1*] When discrete substance is aggregated in crude
nature, as in a foregone dissolution, that dissolution is

---

meaning that there was only One Being, in whom matter and
its modifications were all comprehended.

' Or it might be rendered: 'Those two other forms (which
proceed) from his supreme nature': विष्णो: स्वरूपात्परत: । that
is, from the nature of Vishńu when he is Nirupádhi or without
adventitious attributes: निरुपाधिर्विष्णो: स्वरूपात् । 'other' (चन्ये);
the commentator states they are other, or separate from Vishńu,
only through Máyá, 'illusion', but here implying 'false notion':
the elements of creation being, in essence, one with Vishńu,
though, in existence, detached and different.

नासीन्न रात्रिर्न नभो न भूमि-
र्नासीत्तमो ज्योतिरभूत्र न चान्यत् ।
श्रोत्रादिबुद्ध्यानुपलभ्यमेकं
प्राधानिकं ब्रह्म पुमांसदासीत् ॥
विष्णो: स्वरूपात्परतो हि ते द्वे
रूपे प्रधानं पुरुषश्च विप्र ।
तदीव ते द्वे न भृते विभुते
रूपादि यत्सर्गकरं कालसंज्ञम् ॥

"There was neither day nor night, neither heaven nor earth, neither
darkness nor light. And there was not aught else apprehensible by the
senses or by the mental faculties. There was then, *however*, one Brahma,
essentially *prakṛiti* and spirit. For the two aspects of Vishńu which are
other than his supreme essential aspect are *prakṛiti* and spirit, O Brahman. *When those two other aspects* of his no longer subsist, *but are
dissolved, then that aspect* whence form and the rest, *i. e.*, *creation*, proceed *anew* is denominated time, O twice-born."

See the editor's first note in p. 18, *supra*.

I have carried forward the inverted commas by which Professor Wilson
indicated the end of the quotation. There can be no question that it
embraces two stanzas. They are in the *trishṭubh* metre, and are preceded
and followed by verses in the *anushṭubh.*

termed elemental (Prákríta). The deity as Time is without beginning, and his end is not known; and from him the revolutions of creation, continuance, and dissolution unintermittingly succeed:[*] for, when, in the latter season, the equilibrium of the qualities (Pradhána) exists, and spirit (Puṁs) is detached from matter, then the form of Vishńu which is Time abides.[1] Then

---

[1] Pradhána, when unmodified, is, according to the Sánkhyas and Pauráńiks, nothing more than the three qualities[†] in equilibrio; or goodness, foulness, and darkness neutralizing each other; (Sánkhya Káriká, p. 52). So in the Matsya P.:

वर्णं रजसमत्वीयं गुणपबमुदाहृतम् ।
साम्यावस्थितिरेषा प्रकृति: परिकीर्तिता ॥

This state is synonymous with the non-evolution of material products, or with dissolution; implying, however, separate existence, and detached from spirit. This being the case, it is asked, What should sustain matter and spirit whilst separate, or renew their combination so as to renovate creation? It is answered, Time, which is when everything else is not, and which, at the end of a certain interval, unites Matter (Pradhána) and Purusha, and

यद्युक्तिमात्मनस्येते धर्मिणस्तत्त्वसंख्या: ।

We here have a reference, apparently, to four—not simply to three—conditions of things, the last of which, saṁyama, "dellitescence", denotes the state that prevails during the nights of Brahmá, when all concrete forms are resolved into their original elements. The word has occurred before: see p. 11, supra. Also see the Márkańdeya-puráńa, XLVI., 7.

The commentator, at first, takes saṁyama—i. e., he says, saṁhára—for the third condition, qualified by anta=ante, "at last". Alternatively, he makes anta the third of the conditions, and governs the names of all three by saṁyamát, in the sense of niyamát. For niyama, in place of saṁyama, in a classification similar to that of the text, see Śankara Áchárya's Commentary on the Śwetáśwatara Upanishad: Bibliotheca Indica, Vol. VII., pp. 275 and 276.

† On rendering the Sánkhya or Pauráńik guńa, as here meant, by "quality", see my translation of Pandit Nehemiah Nílakańṭha Śástrin's Rational Refutation of the Hindu Philosophical Systems, pp. 43 and 44, foot-note, and pp. 219 et seq., foot-note.

the supreme Brahma, the supreme soul, the substance
of the world,[*] the lord of all creatures, the universal
soul, the supreme ruler, Hari, of his own will having
entered into matter and spirit, agitated the mutable
and immutable principles, the season of creation being
arrived. In the same manner as fragrance affects the
mind from its proximity merely, and not from any
immediate operation upon mind itself, so the Supreme
influenced the elements of creation.[1] Purushottama

---

produces creation. Conceptions of this kind are evidently comprised in the Orphic triad, or the ancient notion of the cooperation of three such principles, in creation, as Phanes or Eros,
which is the Hindu spirit or Purusha; Chaos, matter or Pradhána; and Chronos, or Kála, time.

[1] Pradhána is styled Vyaya (व्यय), 'that which may be ex-
pended';[†] or Parinámin (परिणामिन्), 'which may be modified':
and Purusha is called Avyaya (अव्यय), 'inconsumable', or
aparinámin (अपरिणामिन्), 'immutable'. The expressions
प्रविश, 'having entered into', and क्षोभयमास, 'agitated', recall
the mode in which divine intelligence, mens, ροῦς, was conceived, by the ancients, to operate upon matter:

> Φρὴν ... φροντίσι κόσμον ἅπαντα,
> . . . . κατατάσσουσα θνήσιν;

or as in a more familiar passage:

> Spiritus intus alit, totamque infusa per artus,

> Mens agitat molem, et magno se corpore miscet:

or, perhaps, it more closely approximates to the Phœnician cosmogony, in which a spirit, mixing with its own principles, gives
rise to creation. Brucker, I., 240. As presently explained, the
mixture is not mechanical; it is an influence or effect exerted
upon intermediate agents which produce effects; as perfumes do
not delight the mind by actual contact, but by the impression

---

[*] Supply "all-pervading" सर्वगा.
[†] "Passing away", or "perishable", is more literal.

is both the agitator and the thing to be agitated; being
present in the essence of matter, both when it is con-

---

they make upon the sense of smelling, which communicates it to
the mind. The entrance of the supreme Vishńu into spirit, as
well as matter, is less intelligible than the view elsewhere taken
of it, as the infusion of spirit, identified with the Supreme, into
Prakŕiti or matter alone. Thus, in the Padma Puráńa:[*]

मो ऽखो मकाला: पुरुष: मोक्षते च रूराच्युत: ।
स एष भगवान्विष्णु: मक्कालाभिवेश्म ह ॥

'He who is called the male (spirit) of Prakŕiti is here named
Achyuta; and that same divine Vishńu entered into Prakŕiti.'
So the Bŕihan Náradíya:

मक्कती शोभमापद्ये पुरुषाख्ये जगत्पुरी ।

'The lord of the world, who is called Purusha, producing agitation in Prakŕiti.' From the notion of influence or agitation
produced on matter through or with spirit, the abuse of personification led to actual or vicarious admixture. Thus, the Bhágavata, identifying Máyá with Prakŕiti, has:

कालपुरुषा तु मायायां पुरुषमख्यात्मपौरुष: ।
पुरुषेणात्मभूतेन वीर्यमाधत्त वीर्यवान् ॥

'Through the operation of time, the Mighty One, who is present
to the pure, implanted a seed in Máyá endowed with qualities,
as Purusha, which is one with himself.'[†] B. III., s. 5. And the
Bhavishya: 'Some learned men say, that the supreme being,
desirous to create beings, creates, in the commencement of the
Kalpa, a body of soul (or an incorporeal substance); which soul,
created by him, enters into Prakŕiti; and Prakŕiti, being thereby
agitated, creates many material elements':

सर्वे वेदं मनायामो भगवान्ति मखीषिण: ।
यो ऽसावात्मा परमात्मख्यादी सृजति तनुम् ॥

---

* *Uttara-kańda*, XXXIV.

† Burnouf—Vol. I., p. 176—bas: "Lorsque l'action du temps eut déve-
loppé au sein de Máyá les qualités, Adhókrhaja, doué de vigueur, se
manifestant sous la forme de Purucha, déposa en elle sa semence."

For Adhokrhaja, see Goldstücker's *Sanskrit Dictionary*, *sub roce*: also
Original Sanskrit Texts, Part IV., pp. 152 and 153.

tracted and expanded.' Vishṇu, supreme over the
supreme, is of the nature of discrete forms in the
atomic productions, Brahmá and the rest (gods,
men, &c.).

Then from that equilibrium of the qualities (Pradhána), presided over by soul,[2] proceeds the unequal
development of those qualities (constituting the principle Mahat or Intellect) at the time of creation.[3] The

---

पुत्तलश्च महावाहो सिसुर्मूर्विविधा: प्रजा: ।
तेन सृष्ट: पुत्तलग्रं प्रधानं विष्टते नृप ॥
प्रधानं वोभितं तेन सृजते विकारास्यहम् ।

But these may be regarded as notions of a later date. In the
Mahábhárata, the first cause is declared to be 'Intellectual', who
creates by his mind or will:

मानसी नाम पूर्वो ऽपि विभुतो ये महर्षिभि: ।
जनादिनिधनो देवस्तमभेषी ऽयरामर: ॥

'The first (being) is called Mánasa (intellectual), and is so
celebrated by great sages: he is god, without beginning or end,
indivisible, immortal, undecaying.' And again:

प्रजाविसर्गं विविधं मानसो मनसो ऽसृजत् ।

'The Intellectual created many kinds of creatures by his mind.'

[1] Contraction, Sankocha (संकोच), is explained by Sámya
(साम्य), sameness or equilibrium of the three qualities, or inert
Pradhána; and Expansion, Vikása (विकास), is the destruction
of this equipoise, by previous agitation and consequent development of material products.

[2] The term here is Kshetrajna, 'embodied spirit', or that
which knows the Kshetra or 'body'; implying the combination
of spirit with form or matter, for the purpose of creating.

[3] The first product of Pradhána, sensible to divine, though
not to mere human, organs, is, both according to the Sánkhya
and Pauránik doctrines, the principle called Mahat, literally, 'the
Great'; explained in other places, as in our text, 'the production
of the manifestation of the qualities': गुणव्यञ्जनसंभूति । or, as
in the Váyu:

Chief principle then invests that Great principle, Intellect; and it becomes threefold, as affected by the
quality of goodness, foulness, or darkness, and invested

गुणभावादनुक्रमाणो महात्मादुर्यंभूप च ।

We have, in the same Puráńa, as well as in the Brahmáńda and
Linga, a number of synonyms for this term, as:

मनो महानतिर्ब्रह्मा पूर्बुधि: ख्यातिरीश्वर: ।
प्रज्ञा चिति: स्मृति: संविदिपुर चोच्यते बुध: ।*

---

* This stanza occurs in the fourth chapter of the *Váyu-puráńa*. Immediately following it are these definitions, which Professor Wilson has
translated:

मनुते सर्वभूतानां यस्मादेष्टार्थं लभेत् ।
सौक्ष्म्येन विपुलानां तेन मन्तन उच्यते ॥
तत्त्वानामव्ययो यस्मादग्राह्य परिलोचत: ।
बीबिभो गुणात्स्वेभ्यो महानिति तत: स्मृत: ॥
विभर्तिभानं मनुते विभार्यं सर्वते ऽपि च ।
पुत्यभोगर्भबन्धासीन धास्वी मति: स्मृत: ॥
गुणात्मादुन्चलाच भावानां साकल्याश्रयात् ।
यस्मादुच्यते भावान्ब्रह्मा तेन निरुच्यते ॥
आपूरयत्यला यस्माच तत्त्वान्देश्यानुबुधि: ।
तत्त्वभावांश नियतासेन पूरिति चोच्यते ॥
बुध्यते पुत्ययान्च सर्वभावानिबृतानिताम् ।
यस्मादुधयते चैव तेन बुद्धिर्निरुच्यते ॥
ख्याति: प्रत्युपभोगंच यकात्तदवतंते मत: ।
भोगंच ज्ञानिच्छात्तेन ख्यातिरिति स्मृत: ॥
ख्यायते तदुधीर्वापि नामादिभिरनेकय: ।
तस्माच महत: संज्ञा ख्यातिरिखबिधीयते ॥
भावात्सर्वं विजानानि महात्मा तेन चेश्वर: ।
यस्माद्भातगुप्त चैव प्रज्ञा तेन स उच्यते ॥
ज्ञानादीनि च एतानि कनुधर्मफलानि च ।
विजोति यस्माद्वार्यं तेनासौ चितिरुच्यते ॥
वर्तमानाकतीतानि तथा भावानतान्यपि ।
स्मरते सर्वकार्याणि तेनासौ स्मृतिरुच्यते ॥
ज्ञानं च चिन्दुते यस्माद्यस्मानज्ञानत्समनुतम् ।
तस्मादिन्दोर्विदंचैव संविदिखबिधीयते ॥

by the Chief principle (matter), as seed is by its skin.

They are also explained, though not very distinctly, to the
following purport: "Manas is that which considers the conse-

विचते च च धर्षजिग्तर्षं तखिंच चिचते ।
तखात्संविदिति मोक्षो महान्ये मुद्धिमचरैः ॥
ज्ञानेतीजमिखाच भवचाच्ञानचंचिधिः ।
हन्धानां विमुक्तीभावं चिमुरं मोक्षते मुधैः ॥
वर्षेषत्साच चोकाचानबचं च तचेचर: ।
मुत्लाच खुतो ब्रह्म भूतचान्ब्राच उच्चते ॥
चेचपेरचिजानादिचलाच चन: खुत: ।
चखात्पुर्षमुधेते च तचातुच्च उच्चते ॥
चोचादितलात्पुर्षचात्खर्षभूरिति मोच्चते ।
पर्याघवाचैः द्वचैचचमाचमनुत्तमम् ॥

According to Vijnana Bhikshu, at least the first half of the stanza of
synonyms, quoted by Professor Wilson, is in the *Matsya-purana* as well
as in the *Vayu*. See my edition of the *Sankhya-pravachana-bhashya* —
published in the *Bibliotheca Indica* —, p. 117.

The *Linga-purana*, Prior Section, LXX., 12 et seq., differs from the *Vayu*
in having *brahma* and *chit-para* or *chischela* instead of *brahma* and *vipura*.
Its explanations of the terms also present several deviations. For हन्धानां
&c., in definition of *vipura*, it gives:

हन्धानां चित्परीभावाचिल्यरं मोच्चते मुधैः ।

or, agreeably to another reading:

वन्धनादिचपरीभावादीचर: मोच्चते मुधैः ।

With nothing correspondent to the next two stanzas and a half of the
Vayu, it then passes at once to the line beginning with पर्याघवाचैः:.
In the same Purana, Prior Section, VIII., 67—74, we read:

विखरच्च महान्मचा मनो ब्रह्म चिचि: खृति: ।
ख्याति: संविचत: पचारीचरो मतिरेच च ॥
मुच्चेता: चिव्या: चंज्ञा मचत: परिकीर्तिता: ।
वज्ञा मुधैः प्रसादच्च मावाचासेन चिह्यति ॥
विखरो विखरीभावाच्युच्चाना मुनिखत्तमा: ।
चचच: वर्षतत्वाना महाच्च: परिचमत: ॥
चल्ममावाचुता मचा मनच्च मनुते चत: ।
मुचचलात्तुच्चाच मच्च महचिद्वां चर: ॥
सर्वज्ञमारि चौमार्ष पचिचमीति चिचि: खुता ।
चरते चन्चुति: ख़र्ष वांचिद्धि चिच्चते चत: ॥

From the great principle (Mahat) Intellect, threefold

quences of acts to all creatures, and provides for their happiness.
Mahat, the Great principle, is so termed from being the first of
the created principles, and from its extension being greater than
that of the rest. Mati is that which discriminates and distinguishes
objects preparatory to their fruition by Soul. Brahmá implies
that which effects the development and augmentation of created
things. Pur is that by which the concurrence of nature occupies
and fills all bodies. Buddhi is that which communicates to soul
the knowledge of good and evil. Khyáti is the means of individual fruition, or the faculty of discriminating objects by appropriate designations and the like. Íswara is that which knows
all things as if they were present. Prajná is that by which the
properties of things are known. Chiti is that by which the consequences of acts and species of knowledge are selected for the
use of soul. Smṛiti is the faculty of recognizing all things, past,
present, or to come. Samvid is that in which all things are
found or known, and which is found or known in all things: and
Vipura is that which is free from the effects of contrarieties, as
of knowledge and ignorance, and the like. Mahat is also called
Íswara, from its exercising supremacy over all things; Bháva,
from its elementary existence; Eka, or 'the one', from its single-
ness; Purusha, from its abiding within the body; and, from its
being ungenerated, it is called Swayambhu."*   Now, in this

ज्ञायते लिति वऱ्खानिर्गोणादिभिरजेबऱ: ।
र्वंतत्त्वाधिष रऺं विजानाति यदीश्वर: ॥
अनुते मन्वते यऽआऽतिर्मंतिमतां वरऺ: ।
वमबोधयते यत मुऱते मुविऱऱते ॥
यऱा मुते: प्रसादऱु प्रायायामेव विऱाति ।
दोषान्विनिर्दैत्सर्वोऱ्राबायामादृशी यमी ॥

The terms thus enumerated and elucidated — *íswara*, *mahat*, *prajná*,
manas, *brahma*, *chiti*, *smṛiti*, *khyáti*, *samvid*, *íswara*, and *mati* — belong,
as they here stand, to the Yoga philosophy.

  * The reader will be able to verify this translation by the original
given at the beginning of the last note. *Brahma*—which comes between
íswara and *bhára*—was overlooked. Further, for "Eka" read *saka*, meaning
the same thing, "one."

Egotism, (Ahamkára),[1] denominated Vaikárika, 'pure';
Taijasa, 'passionate'; and Bhútádi, 'rudimental',[*] is pro-

---

nomenclature we have chiefly two sets of words; one, as Manas,
Buddhi, Mati, signifying mind, intelligence, knowledge, wisdom,
design; and the other, as Brahmá, Íswara, &c., denoting an
active creator and ruler of the universe: as the Váyu adds,

महात्मूर्तिं विकुरुते बोधमान: विसृचया ।

'Mahat, impelled by the desire to create, causes various creation':
and the Mahábhárata has: महात्सर्वोपकारम् । 'Mahat created
Ahankára.' The Puráńas generally employ the same expression,
attributing to Mahat or Intelligence the act of creating.   Mahat
is, therefore, the divine mind in creative operation, the νοῦς ὁ
διακόσμων τε καὶ πάντων αἴτιος of Anaxagoras; 'an ordering
and disposing mind, which was the cause of all things.'   The
word itself suggests some relationship to the Phœnician Mot,
which, like Mahat, was the first product of the mixture of spirit
and matter, and the first rudiment of creation: "Ex connexione
autem ejus spiritus prodiit Mot … Hinc * * seminium omnis crea-
turæ et omnium rerum creatio."   Brucker, I., 240.   Mot, it is
true, appears to be a purely material substance; whilst Mahat is
an incorporeal[†] substance: but they agree in their place in the
cosmogony, and are something alike in name.   How far, also,
the Phœnician system has been accurately described, is matter
of uncertainty.   See Sánkhya Kárikrá, p. 83.

[1] The sense of Ahankára cannot be very well rendered by any
European term.   It means the principle of individual existence,
that which appropriates perceptions, and on which depend the
notions, I think, I feel, I am.; It might be expressed by the pro-
position of Descartes reversed; "Sum, ergo cogito, sentio", &c.

[*] In strict literality, "origin of the elements." See my edition of the
Sánkhya-sára — In the Bibliotheca Indica —, Preface, p. 31, foot-note.

[†] See, however, the Sánkhya-pravachana, I., 61; and the Sánkhya-
káriká, XXII.

[‡] But see the discussion of the distinction between ahankára and
abhimána in Goldstücker's Sanskrit Dictionary, p. 257.

duced; the origin of the (subtile) elements, and of the organs of sense; invested, in consequence of its three qualities, by Intellect, as Intellect is by the Chief principle.⁴ Elementary Egotism, then becoming productive, as the rudiment of sound, produced from it Ether,⁎ of which sound is the characteristic, investing it with its rudiment of sound.† Ether, becoming productive, en-

---

The equivalent employed by Mr. Colebrooke, egotism, has the advantage of an analogous etymology; Ahankára being derived from Aham (अहं), 'I'; as in the Hari Vanśa:

अहं विमि च होवाच प्रजाः स्रजानि भारत ।

'He (Brahmá), O Bhárata, said, *I* will create creatures.' See also S. Káriká, p. 91.

⁴ These three varieties of Ahankára are also described in the Sánkhya Káriká, p. 92. Vaikárika, that which is productive, or susceptible of production, is the same as the Sáttwika, or that which is combined with the property of goodness. Taijasa Ahankára is that which is endowed with Tejas, 'heat' or 'energy', in consequence of its having the property of Rajas, 'passion' or 'activity'; and the third kind, Bhútádi, or 'elementary', is the Támasa, or has the property of darkness. From the first kind proceed the senses; from the last, the rudimental unconscious elements; both kinds, which are equally of themselves inert, being

⁎ "A characterization of ákáśa will serve to show how inadequately it is represented by 'ether'. In dimension, it is, as has been said, infinite; it is not made up of parts; and colour, taste, smell, and tangibility do not appertain to it. So far forth it corresponds exactly to time, space, Íśwara, and soul. Its speciality, as compared therewith, consists in its being the material cause of sound. Except for its being so, we might take it to be one with vacuity." *Rational Refutation*, &c., p. 120.

"In Hindu opinion, the 'ether' is always essentially colourless and pure, and only from error is supposed to possess hue.⁎⁎ The ignorant, it is said, think the blueness of the sky to be the befoulment of 'ether'." *Ibid.*, p. 272.

† On the translation of this and subsequent passages, see the *Sánkhya-sára*, Preface, p. 33, foot-note.

gendered the rudiment of touch; whence originated
strong wind, the property of which is touch; and Ether,
with the rudiment of sound, enveloped the rudiment
of touch. Then wind, becoming productive, produced
the rudiment of form (colour); whence light (or fire)
proceeded, of which, form (colour) is the attribute;
and the rudiment of touch enveloped the wind with
the rudiment of colour. Light, becoming productive,
produced the rudiment of taste; whence proceed all
juices in which flavour resides; and the rudiment of
colour invested the juices with the rudiment of taste.
The waters, becoming productive, engendered the rudiment of smell; whence an aggregate (earth) originates,
of which smell is the property.[1] In each several ele-

---

rendered productive by the cooperation of the second, the energetic
or active modification of Ahamkára, which is, therefore, said to
be the origin of both the senses and the elements. [*]

[1] The successive series of rudiments and elements, and their
respectively engendering the rudiments and elements next in order,
occur in most of the Puránas, in nearly the same words. The
Bŕihan Náradíya P. observes:

यथामन् भारकसानेकैककोपयान्ति ॥ ।

'They (the elements) in successive order acquire the property of
causality one to the other.' The order is also the same; or,

---

[*] Ahamkára, "the conception of I.", has a preponderance either of
sattwa, "pure quietude", or of rajas, "activity", or of tamas, "sluggancy".
The first species, as likewise the third, becomes productive, when assisted
by the second. Such is the genuine Sánkhya doctrine. In the Puránas,
the second, besides serving as an auxiliary to production, of itself produces; since therefrom arise five "intellectual organs" and five "organs
of action." These organs, with manas, "the organ of imagination", are
derived, in the unmodified Sánkhya, from the first species of ahamkára.
See, for additional details, the Sánkhya-sára, Preface, pp. 30 et seq.,
foot-note.

8*

36   VISHŃU PURÁŃA.

ment resides its peculiar rudiment; thence the property

---

ether (Ákáśa), wind or air (Váyu), fire or light (Tejas), water and
earth; except in one passage of the Mahábhárata (Moksha Dharma,
c. 9), where it is ether, water, fire, air, earth.[*] The order of
Empedocles was: ether, fire, earth, water, air. Cudworth, I., 97.
The investment (Ávarańa) of each element by its own rudiment,
and of each rudiment by its preceding gross and rudimental elements, is also met with in most of the chief Puráńas, as the Váyu,
Padma, Linga, and Bhágavata; and traces of it are found amongst
the ancient cosmogonists; for Anaximander supposed that, 'when
the world was made, a certain sphere or flame of fire, separated
from matter (the Infinite), encompassed the air, which invested
the earth as the bark does a tree': Κατὰ τὴν γένεσιν τοῦδε
τοῦ κόσμου ἀποκριθῆναι, καί τινα ἐκ τούτου φλογὸς σφαῖ-
ραν περιφυῆναι τῷ περὶ τὴν γῆν ἀέρι, ὡς τῷ δένδρῳ φλοιόν.
Euseb., Pr., I., 15. Some of the Puráńas, as the Matsya, Váyu,
Linga, Bhágavata, and Márkańdeya, add a description of a
participation of properties amongst the elements, which is rather
Vedánta than Sánkhya. According to this notion, the elements
add to their characteristic properties those of the elements which
precede them. Ákáśa has the single property of sound: air has
those of touch and sound: fire has colour, touch, and sound:
water has taste, colour, touch, and sound: and earth has smell
and the rest, thus having five properties: or, as the Linga P.[†]
describes the series:

आकाशं शब्दमात्रं तु यतस्तस्मात्समाविशत् ।
विशुद्धं ततो वायुः शब्दस्पर्शात्मकोऽभवत् ॥
रूपं तदविशत्तां शब्दस्पर्शगुणावुभौ ।
विशुद्धं ततस्तदपि च शब्दस्पर्शरूपवान् ॥
शब्दस्पर्शरूपमात्रं रसमात्रं समाविशत् ।
तस्माच्चतुर्गुणा ह्यापो विशेषात्तु रसादिका: ॥

---

* For a related comment, see Goldstücker's *Sanskrit Dictionary*,
pp. 155 and 156, *sub voce* शब्द.
† Prior Section, LXX., 43—47.

of tanmátratá[1] (type or rudiment) is ascribed to these
elements. Rudimental elements are not endowed with
qualities: and therefore they are neither soothing, nor
terrific, nor stupefying."" This is the elemental creation,
proceeding from the principle of egotism affected by

शब्दस्पर्शे च रूपे च रसे गन्धमाविशत् ।
सनुता गन्धमावेव चाविश्वनो महीमिमाम् ॥
तस्मात्पञ्चगुणा भूमिः स्थूलभूतेषु वर्त्तते ।
शान्ता घोराश्च मूढाश्च विशेषाखेन ते गुणाः ॥

[1] Tanmátra, 'rudiment' or 'type', from Tad (तद्), 'that', for
Tasmin (तस्मिन्), 'in that' gross element, and mátri (मात्रा),
'subtile or rudimental form' (मात्रा सूक्ष्म रूपम्).† The rudiments
are also the characteristic properties of the elements: as the
Bhágavata:

तस्य मात्रा गुणः शब्दो लिङ्गं यदूद्रष्टृदृश्ययोः ।

'The rudiment of it (ether) is also its quality, sound;‡ as a common designation may denote both a person who sees an object,
and the object which is to be seen': that is, according to the
commentator, suppose a person behind a wall called aloud, "An
elephant! an elephant!" the term would equally indicate that an
elephant was visible, and that somebody saw it. Bhág., II., 5, 25.

[2] The properties here alluded to are not those of goodness,
&c., but other properties§ assigned to perceptible objects by the
Sánkhya doctrines; or Sánti (शान्ति), 'placidity', Ghoratá (घोरता),
'terror', and Moha (मोह), 'dulness' or 'stupefaction'. S. Káriká,
v. 38, p. 119.

---

* Sánta, ghora, múdha; "placid, commoved, torpid." Probably ghora
is connected with ghúrn, "to whirl."

† With greater likelihood, tan-mátra, "merely transcendental", is
from tanu and mátra, the latter considered as an affix: the u of tanu
being elided, as it is, for instance, in tanmaú for tanumaú, and in similar
conjugational forms of the fifth and eighth classes.

‡ Rather: "Sound is its rudiment and also its quality."

§ "Goodness, &c." are causes; the "other properties", effects.

" And see the Sánkhya-pravachana, III., 1.

the property of darkness. The organs of sense are
said to be the passionate products of the same principle, affected by foulness; and the ten divinities[1] proceed from egotism affected by the principle of goodness; as does Mind, which is the eleventh. The organs
of sense are ten: of the ten, five are the skin, eye, nose,
tongue, and ear; the object of which, combined with
Intellect, is the apprehension of sound and the rest:
the organs of excretion and procreation, the hands,
the feet, and the voice, form the other five; of which
excretion, generation, manipulation, motion, and
speaking are the several acts.

Then, ether, air, light, water, and earth, severally
united with the properties of sound and the rest, existed
as distinguishable according to their qualities, as
soothing, terrific, or stupefying; but, possessing various
energies and being unconnected, they could not, without
combination, create living beings, not having blended
with each other. Having combined, therefore, with
one another, they assumed, through their mutual asso-
ciation, the character of one mass of entire unity; and,
from the direction of spirit, with the acquiescence of
the indiscrete Principle,[2] Intellect and the rest, to the

---

[1] The Bhágavata, which gives a similar statement of the
origin of the elements, senses, and divinities, specifies the last to
be Diś (space), air, the sun, Prachetas, the Aświns, fire, Indra,
Upendra, Mitra, and Ka or Prajápati, presiding over the senses,
according to the comment, or, severally, over the ear, skin, eye,
tongue, nose, speech, hands, feet, and excretory and generative
organs. Bhág., II., 5, 31.

[2] Avyaktánugraheńa (व्यक्तानुग्रहेण). The expression is something equivocal; as Avyakta may here apply either to the First

gross elements inclusive, formed an egg,[1] which gradually expanded like a bubble of water. This vast egg, O sage, compounded of the elements, and resting on the waters, was the excellent natural abode of Vishńu in the form of Brahmá; and there Vishńu, the lord of the universe, whose essence is inscrutable, assumed a perceptible form: and even he himself abided in it, in

---

Cause or to matter. In either case, the notion is the same; and the aggregation of the elements is the effect of the presidence of spirit, without any active interference of the indiscrete principle. The Avyakta is passive, in the evolution and combination of Mahat and the rest. Pradhána is, no doubt, intended; but its identification with the Supreme is also implied. The term Anugraha may also refer to a classification of the order of creation, which will be again adverted to.

[1] It is impossible not to refer this notion to the same origin as the widely diffused opinion of antiquity, of the first manifestation of the world in the form of an egg. "It seems to have been a favourite symbol, and very ancient; and we find it adopted among many nations". Bryant, III., 165. Traces of it occur amongst the Syrians, Persians, and Egyptians; and, besides the Orphic egg amongst the Greeks, and that described by Aristophanes, *Τίκτει πρώτιστον ὑπηνέμιον τί᾽ξ ἡ μελανόπτερος ᾠόν*, part of the ceremony in the Dionysiaca and other mysteries consisted of the consecration of an egg; by which, according to Porphyry, was signified the world: *Ερμηνείει δὲ τὸ ᾠὸν τὸν κόσμον*. Whether this egg typified the ark, as Bryant and Faber suppose, is not material to the proof of the antiquity and wide diffusion of the belief, that the world, in the beginning, existed in such a figure. A similar account of the first aggregation of the elements in the form of an egg is given in all the Puráńas, with the usual epithet Haima or Hiranya, 'golden', as it occurs in Manu., I, 9.

the character of Brahmá.[1]   Its womb, vast as the
mountain Meru, was composed of the mountains;[*] and
the mighty oceans were the waters that filled its cavity.
In that egg, O Brahman, were the continents and seas
and mountains, the planets and divisions of the universe, the gods, the demons, and mankind.   And this
egg was externally invested by seven natural enve-
lopes; or by water, air, fire, ether, and Ahaṃkára,[†] the
origin of the elements, each tenfold the extent of that
which it invested; next came the principle of Intelligence; and, finally, the whole was surrounded by the
indiscrete Principle: resembling, thus, the cocoa-nut,
filled interiorly with pulp, and exteriorly covered by
husk and rind.[‡]

---

[1] Here is another analogy to the doctrines of antiquity relating to the mundane egg: and, as the first visible male being,[*]
who, as we shall hereafter see, united in himself the nature of
either sex, abode in the egg, and issued from it; so "this first-
born of the world, whom they represented under two shapes and
characters, and who sprang from the mundane egg, was the
person from whom the mortals and immortals were derived. He
was the same as Dionysus, whom they styled, πρωτόγονον
διφυῆ, τρίγονον Βακχεῖον Ἄνακτα Ἄγριον ἄρρητον κρύφιον
δικέρωτα δίμορφον:" or, with the omission of one epithet,
δικέρως:

---

[*] The reading of many MSS. and of the commentator, and that which
seems to claim the preference, is:

मेरुरुल्वमभूत्तस्य जरायुश्च महीधराः ।

"Meru was its amnion, and the *other* mountains were its chorion."
† The word *ahaṃkára* is supplied to the original by the translator.
The commentary is silent.
‡ A new translation of this entire paragraph and of the first sentence
of the next will be seen in *Original Sanskrit Texts*, Part IV., pp. 34
and 35.

Affecting then the quality of activity, Hari, the lord of all, himself becoming Brahmá, engaged in the creation of the universe. Vishńu, with the quality of goodness, and of immeasurable power, preserves created things through successive ages, until the close of the period termed a Kalpa; when the same mighty deity, Janárdana,[1] invested with the quality of darkness, assumes the awful form of Rudra, and swallows up the universe. Having thus devoured all things, and converted the world into one vast ocean, the Supreme reposes upon his mighty serpent-couch amidst the deep: he awakes after a season, and, again, as Brahmá, becomes the author of creation.[*]

Thus the one only god, Janárdana, takes the designation of Brahmá, Vishńu, and Śiva, accordingly as he creates, preserves, or destroys.[2] Vishńu, as creator,

---

पूर्वमर्धमनारीयं विष्णुं च प्रजापतिम् ।
ऋषायं कुञ्जनबां ब्रह्माणं च त्रिमूर्निकम् ॥

[1] Janárdana is derived from Jana (जन), 'men', and Ardana (अर्दन),[†] 'worship'; 'the object of adoration to mankind'.

[2] This is the invariable doctrine of the Puráńas, diversified only according to the individual divinity to whom they ascribe identity with Paramátman or Parameśwara. In our text, this is

---

[*] Almost the whole of this chapter and of the next occurs, often nearly word for word, in the *Márkańdeya-puráńa*, XLV. *et seq.*

[†] अर्दन signifies "solicitation". But there are preferable derivations of Janárdana. For instance, Śankara Áchárya, in his gloss on the thousand names of Vishńu enumerated in the *Anuśásana-parvan* of the *Mahábhárata*, takes its constituent *jana*, "people", to stand for "the wicked", and interprets *ardana* by "chastiser or extirpator". His words, in part, are : अनार्युर्जनानर्दयति हिनस्ति । According to the *Mahábhárata* itself, in another place, Vásudeva is called Janárdana because of his striking terror into the Dasyus. *See Original Sanskrit Texts*, Part IV., pp. 182 and 183.

creates himself; as preserver, preserves himself; as
destroyer, destroys himself at the end of all things.
This world of earth, air, fire, water, ether, the senses,
and the mind; all that is termed spirit:[1]—that also is the
lord of all elements, the universal form,[2] and imperishable. Hence he is the cause of creation, preservation,
and destruction; and the subject of the vicissitudes
inherent in elementary nature. He is the object and

Vishńu; in the Śaiva Puráńas, as in the Linga, it is Śiva; in
the Brahma Vaivarta, it is Kŕishńa. The identification of one
of the hypostases with the common source of the triad was an
incongruity not unknown to other theogonies: for Cneph, amongst
the Egyptians, appears, on the one hand, to have been identified
with the supreme being, the indivisible unity; whilst, on the
other, he is confounded with both Emeph and Ptha, the second
and third persons of the triad of hypostases. Cudworth, I., 4. 18.

[1] 'The world that is termed spirit';[*] पुमांसं हि प्रचक्षते ।
explained, by the commentator, पुमर्बुधैः । 'which, indeed,
bears the appellation spirit'; conformably to the text of the
Vedas, पुमान् एवेदं सर्वम् । 'this universe is, indeed, spirit'.[†] This
is rather Vedánta than Sánkhya, and appears to deny the existence
of matter. And so it does, as an independent existence; for the
origin and end of infinite substance is the deity or universal
spirit: but it does not therefore imply the non-existence of the
world as real substance.

[2] Vishńu is both Bhúteśa (भूतेश:), 'lord of the elements',
or of created things, and Viswarúpa (विश्वरूप:), 'universal
substance'.[‡] He is, therefore, as one with sensible things, subject to his own control.

---

[*] Rather: "That which is termed spirit is the world."
[†] See Colebrooke's *Miscellaneous Essays*, Vol. I., p. 47.
[‡] The commentary has: स एव सर्वभूतानामीश: प्रवर्तयिता । वि-
श्वरूप । ततो भूतेषु पितृपुत्रादिषु चितम् । *Viswarúpaḥ*, an adjective
in the masculine, means "omniform".

author of creation: he preserves, destroys, and is preserved. He, Vishńu, as Brahmá, and as all other beings, is infinite form. He is the Supreme, the giver of all good, the fountain of all happiness.[1]

---

[1] Vareńya (वरेण्य:), 'most excellent'; being the same, according to the commentator,[2] with supreme felicity: परमानन्दरूपत्वात् ।

---

[2] He writes: वरेण्यो वरणीयरूप: परमानन्दरूपत्वात् । "Vareńya, i. e., 'of a form to be elected', on account of his being, essentially, supreme felicity."

CHAPTER III.

MAITREYA.—How can creative agency be attributed to that Brahma who is without qualities, illimitable, pure, and free from imperfection?

PARÁŚARA.—The essential properties of existent things are objects of observation, of which no foreknowledge is attainable: and creation and hundreds of properties belong to Brahma,* as inseparable parts of his essence; as heat, O chief of sages, is inherent in fire.[1]

---

[1] Agency depends upon the Rajo-guńa, the quality of foulness or passion, which is an imperfection. Perfect being is void of all qualities, and is, therefore, inert:

> Omnia enim per se divom natura necesse est
> Immortali ævo summa cum pace fruatur.

But, if inert for ever, creation could not occur. The objection is rather evaded than answered. The ascribing to Brahma of innumerable and unappreciable properties is supported, by the com-

श्रमयः सर्वभावानामचिन्त्यज्ञानगोचराः ।
यतो ऽतो ब्रह्मणस्तानु सर्गादा भावशक्तयः ॥
अवस्ति तपतां श्रेष्ठ पावकस्य यथोष्णता ।

"Seeing that the potencies of all existences are understood only through the knowledge of that — i. e., Brahma — which is beyond reasoning, creation and the like, such potencies of existences, are referrible to Brahma", &c.

Professor Wilson preferred ूतास्वो to यतो ऽतो ।

Hear, then, how the deity Náráyańa, in the person of
Brahmá, the great parent of the world, created all
existent things.

---

mentator, with vague and scarcely applicable texts of the Vedas.
'In him there is neither instrument nor effect: his like, his superior, is nowhere seen:'

न तस्य कार्यं करणं च विद्यते।
न तत्समश्चाभ्यधिकश्च दृश्यते॥

'That supreme soul is the subjugator of all, the ruler of all, the
sovereign of all': स वशवर्ती। सर्वस्य वशी सर्वस्येशानः सर्व-
स्याधिपतिः।[*] In various places of the Vedas, also, it is said that
his power is supreme, and that wisdom, power, and action are
his essential properties:

परास्य शक्तिर्विविधैव श्रूयते।
स्वाभाविकी ज्ञानबलक्रिया च॥[†]

The origin of creation is also imputed, in the Vedas, to the rise
of will or desire in the Supreme: सो ऽकामयत बहु स्यां प्रजायेय।:
'He wished, I may become manifold, I may create creatures.'
The Bhágavata expresses the same doctrine: 'The supreme being
was before all things alone, the soul and lord of spiritual substance. In consequence of his own will, he is secondarily defined,
as if of various minds':

भगवानेक आसेदमग्र आत्मात्मनां विभुः।
आत्मेच्छानुगतावात्मा नानामत्यनुपश्यतः॥[§]

---

[*] *Śatapatha-bráhmańa*, XIV., 7, 2, 24. Compare the *Bŕihad-árańyaka
Upanishad*, IV., 4, 22.

[†] These verses are continuous with those above, beginning with न तस्य.
They are from the *Śwetáśwatara Upanishad*, VI., 8.

[‡] See the *Śatapatha-bráhmańa*, XI., 5, 8, 1. The *Chhándogya Upanishad*, p. 398, has: तदैक्षत बहु स्यां प्रजायेय।
The quotations thus far in Professor Wilson's note are taken from the
commentary, which gives no precise clue to their derivation.

[§] *Bhágavata-puráńa*, III., 5, 23. The second line may mean: "Soul—
i. e., *Bhágavat*, *Brahma, or the Absolute*—, when it follows its own desire,
implies a variety of conceptions."

Brahmá is said to be born: a familiar phrase, to signify his manifestation; and, as the peculiar measure
of his presence, a hundred of his years is said to constitute his life. That period is also called Para, and the

---

This will, however, in the mysticism of the Bhágavata, is personified as Máyá:

सा वा एतस्य संद्रष्टुः शक्तिः सदसदात्मिका ।
माया नाम महाभाग ययेदं निर्ममे विभुः ॥ [*]

'She (that desire) was the energy of the Supreme, who was
contemplating (the uncreated world); and, by her, whose name is
Máyá, the lord made the universe.' This, which was, at first, a
mere poetical personification of the divine will, came, in such
works as the Bhágavata, to denote a female divinity, coequal
and coeternal with the First Cause. It may be doubted if the
Vedas authorize such a mystification; and no very decided vestige
of it occurs in the Vishnu Puráńa.

Burnouf translates the stanza in these words: "Au commencement cet
univers était Bhagavat, l'âme et le souverain maître de toutes les âmes;
Bhagavat existait seul sans qu'aucun attribut le manifestât, parce que
tout désir était éteint en son cœur."

The commentator on the Bhágavata, Śrídhara Swámin, explains the latter
part of the stanza in three ways: अथ बुद्धिबीजां वर्षयितुं ततः पूर्व-
पक्षार्थाद् । एदं चित्रकमर्थे बुद्धेः पूर्वं परमात्मा अनपायेव एवास्
आसीत् । आत्मना जीवानामात्मा सदृशं विभुः स्वामी च । नाना-
भूताकारं विचिदसीत् । आत्ममानावस्थे ऽपि पृथक्मतीनाना-
दिलात् । चनानामनुपपन्नः । नानाभूतादि मतिभिनौपनं
इति । तथा यथा । च आत्मैव विधिनायतनं: । यः बुद्धौ नानामति-
भिरुपलक्षते च तदैक एवासीदिति जुभः । सातेच्छा माया । तथा
चनुमती अथे अति । यथा । आत्मन एवाचिकिलिनावना नैजावानुु-
भूतावानिलार्थ: ।

[*] Bhágavata-puráńa, III, 5, 25. Burnouf's translation is as follows:
"Or l'énergie de cet être doué de vue, énergie qui est à la fois ce qui
existe et ce qui n'existe pas [pour nos organes], c'est là ce qui se
nomme Máyá, et c'est par elle, illustre guerrier, que l'Être qui pénètre
toutes choses créa cet univers."

half of it, Parárdha.[1]   I have already declared to you,
O sinless Brahman, that Time is a form of Vishńu.
Hear, now, how it is applied to measure the duration
of Brahmá and of all other sentient beings, as well as
of those which are unconscious; as* the mountains,
oceans, and the like.

O best of sages, fifteen twinklings of the eye make
a Káshťhá: thirty Káshťhás, one Kalá; and thirty Kalás,
one Muhúrta.[2]   Thirty Muhúrtas constitute a day and

---

[1] This term is also applied to a different and still more protracted period. See b. VI., c. 3.

[2] The last proportion is rather obscurely expressed: तासु
त्रिंशद्वियोगेन विधिः। 'Thirty of them (Kalás) are the rule
for the Muhúrta'.   The commentator says it means that thirty
Kalás make a Ghaťiká (or Ghari); and two Ghaťikás, a Muhúrta:
but his explanation is gratuitous, and is at variance with more
explicit passages elsewhere; as in the Matsya: त्रिंशत्कलो मुहूर्तः
अवेणुहर्तः। 'A Muhúrta is thirty Kalás. In these divisions
of the twenty-four hours, the Kúrma, Márkańdeya, Matsya, Váyu,
and Linga Puráńas exactly agree with our authority. In Manu,
I., 64, we have the same computation, with a difference in the
first article, eighteen Nimeshas being one Kásbihá. The Bhavishya P. follows Manu, in that respect, and agrees, in the rest,
with the Padma, which has:

15 Nimeshas = 1 Káshťhá.
30 Káshťhás = 1 Kalá.
30 Kalás   = 1 Kshańa.
12 Kshańas = 1 Muhúrta.
30 Muhúrtas = 1 day and night.

In the Mahábhárata, Moksha Dharma, it is said that thirty Kalás
and one-tenth, or, according to the commentator, thirty Kalás
and three Káshťhás, make a Muhúrta.   A still greater variety,

---

* Supply "the earth", óðd.

night of mortals: thirty such days make a month, divided into two half-months: six months form an Ayana

however, occurs in the Bhágavata* and in the Brahma Vaivarta P. These have:

2 Paramáńus	= 1 Ańu.
3 Ańus	= 1 Trasareńu.
3 Trasareńus	= 1 Truṭi.
100 Truṭis	= 1 Vedha.
3 Vedhas	= 1 Lava.
3 Lavas	= 1 Nimesha.
3 Nimeshas	= 1 Kshańa.
5 Kshańas	= 1 Káshṭhá.
15 Káshṭhás	= 1 Laghu.
15 Laghus	= 1 Nádiká.
2 Nádikás	= 1 Muhúrta.
6 or 7 Nádikás	= 1 Yama† or watch of the day or night.

Allusions to this, or either of the preceding computations, or to any other, have not been found in either of the other Puráńas. Yet the work of Gopála Bhaṭṭa, from which Mr. Colebrooke states he derived his information on the subject of Indian weights and measures (A. R., Vol. V., 105), the Saṅkhyá Parimáńa, cites the Varáha P. for a peculiar computation, and quotes another from the Bhavishya, different from that which occurs in the first chapter of that work, to which we have referred. The principle of the calculation adopted by the astronomical works is different. It is: 6 respirations (Práńa) = 1 Vikalá; 60 Vikalás = 1 Dańda; 60 Dańdas = 1 sidereal day. The Nimesha, which is the base of one of the Pauráńik modes, is a twinkle of the eye of a man at rest; whilst the Paramáńu, which is the origin of the other, and, apparently, more modern, system considering the works in which it occurs, is the time taken by a Paramáńu, or mote in the sunbeam, to pass through a crevice in a shutter. Some indications of this calculation being in common currency occur in the Hindóstání

* III., 11, 5 et seq.

† The *Bhágavata-purána* has *prahara*, a synonym of *yama*.

(the period of the sun's progress north or south of
the ecliptic): and two Ayanas compose a year. The
southern Ayana is a night, and the northern, a day, of
the gods. Twelve thousand divine years, each composed of (three hundred and sixty) such days,* constitute the period of the four Yugas or ages. They
are thus distributed: the Kṛita age has four thousand
divine years; the Tretá, three thousand; the Dwápara,
two thousand; and the Kali age, one thousand: so those
acquainted with antiquity have declared. The period
that precedes a Yuga is called a Sandhyá: and it is of
as many hundred years as there are thousands in the
Yuga: and the period that follows a Yuga, termed the
Sandhyáṃśa, is of similar duration. The interval between the Sandhyá and the Sandhyáṃśa is the Yuga,
denominated Kṛita, Tretá, &c. The Kṛita, Tretá,
Dwápara, and Kali constitute a great age, or aggregate
of four ages: a thousand such aggregates are a day of
Brahmá; and fourteen Manus reign within that term.
Hear the division of time which they measure.[1]

terms Renu (Trasareṇu) and Lamba † (Laghu) in Indian horo-
metry (A. R., Vol. V., 81); whilst the more ordinary system seems
derived from the astronomical works; being 60 Tilas = 1 Vipala;
60 Vipalas = 1 Pala; 60 Palas = 1 Daṇḍa or Ghari. *Ibid.*

[1] These calculations of time are found in most of the Purāṇas,
with some additions, occasionally, of no importance; as that of
the year of the seven Ṛishis, 3030 mortal years, and the year of
Dhruva, 9090 such years, in the Linga P. In all essential points,
the computations accord; and the scheme, extravagant as it may

* There is nothing, in the original, answering to "each .... days".
† This word, لغو, being Arabic, can scarcely have any connexion
with the Sanskrit *laghu.*

I.   4

Seven Ŕishis, certain (secondary) divinities, Indra,[*] Manu, and the kings his sons, are created and perish

---

appear, seems to admit of easy explanation. We have, in the first place, a computation of the years of the gods in the four ages, or:

                Ŕíta Yuga 4000
                        Sandhyá 400
                        Sandhyáṅśa 400

                                            4800
                Tretá Yuga 3000
                        Sandhyá 300
                        Sandhyáṅśa 300

                                            3600
                Dwápara Yuga 2000
                        Sandhyá 200
                        Sandhyáṅśa 200

                                            2400
                Kali Yuga 1000
                        Sandhyá 100
                        Sandhyáṅśa 100

                                            1200

                                            12000

If these divine years are converted into years of mortals, by multiplying them by 360 (a year of men being a day of the gods), we obtain the years of which the Yugas of mortals are respectively said to consist:

$$4800 \times 360 = 1.728.000$$
$$3600 \times 360 = 1.296.000$$
$$2400 \times 360 = 864.000$$
$$1200 \times 360 = 432.000$$
$$4.320.000, \text{ a Maháyuga.}$$

So that these periods resolve themselves into very simple elements: the notion of four ages in a deteriorating series expressed by

---

at one period;[1] and the interval, called a Manwantara,
is equal to seventy-one times the number of years contained in the four Yugas, with some additional years:[2]

---

descending arithmetical progression, as 4, 3, 2, 1; the conversion
of units into thousands; and the mythological fiction, that these
were divine years, each composed of 360 years of men. It does
not seem necessary to refer the invention to any astronomical
computations, or to any attempt to represent actual chronology.

[1] The details of these, as occurring in each Manwantara, are
given in the third book, c. 1 and 2.

[2] चतुर्युगानां सप्ततानां सापिका देवकसप्ततिः ।

'One and seventy enumerations of the four ages, with a surplus.'
A similar reading occurs in several other Puránas; but none of
them state of what the surplus or addition consists. But it is, in
fact, the number of years required to reconcile two computations
of the Kalpa. The most simple, and, probably, the original, calculation of a Kalpa is its being 1000 great ages, or ages of the gods:

सहस्रयुगपर्यन्तं देवानां युगमुच्यते ।
देविकानां युगानां तु सहस्रं परिसंख्यया ॥
ब्राह्मीकल्पमिदं तायती राविरुच्यते ।

Bhavishya P.   Then 4.320.000 years, or a divine age, × 1000 =
4.320.000.000 years, or a day or night of Brahmá. But a day of
Brahmá is also seventy-one times a great age multiplied by fourteen: 4.320.000 × 71 × 14 = 4.294.080.000, or less than the preceding
by 25.920.000; and it is to make up for this deficiency, that a
certain number of years must be added to the computation by
Manwantaras. According to the Súrya Siddhánta, as cited by
Mr. Davis (A. R., Vol. II., 231), this addition consists of a Sandhi to
each Manwantara, equal to the Satya age, or 1.728.000 years; and
one similar Sandhi at the commencement of the Kalpa:[*] thus,
4.320.000 × 71 = 306.720.000 + 1.728.000 = 308.448.000 × 14 = 4.318.272.000
+ 1.728.000 = 4.320.000.000. The Paurániks, however, omit the

---

[*] *Súrya-siddhánta*, I., 13; p. 17 of my edition in the *Bibliotheca
Indica*; p. 10 of the American translation, and p. 4 of Pandit Bápu
Deva Sástrin's translation.

4*

this is the duration of the Manu, the (attendant) divinities, and the rest, which is equal to 852.000 divine years, or to 306.720.000 years of mortals, independent of the additional period. Fourteen times this period constitutes a Bráhma day, that is, a day of Brahmá; the term (Bráhma) being the derivative form. At the end of this day, a dissolution of the universe occurs,[*] when all the three worlds, earth, and the regions of space are consumed with fire. The dwellers of Mahar-loka (the region inhabited by the saints who survive the world), distressed by the heat, repair then to Jana-loka (the region of holy men after their decease). When the three worlds are but one mighty ocean, Brahmá, who is one with Náráyaña, satiate with the demolition of the universe, sleeps upon his serpent-bed—contemplated, the lotos-born, by the ascetic inhabitants of

Sandhi of the Kalpa, and add the whole compensation to the Manwantaras. The amount of this, in whole numbers, is 1.851.428 in each Manwantara, or $4.320.000 \times 71 = 306.720.000 + 1.851.428 = 308.571.428 \times 14 = 4.319.999.992$; leaving a very small inferiority to the result of the calculation of a Kalpa by a thousand great ages. To provide for this deficiency, indeed, very minute subdivisions are admitted into the calculation; and the commentator on our text says that the additional years, if of gods, are 5142 years, 10 months, 8 days, 4 watches, 2 Mahúrtas, 8 Kalás, 17 Káshthás, 2 Nimeshas, and ¼th; if of mortals, 1.851.428 years, 6 months, 24 days, 12 Nádis, 12 Kalás, 25 Káshthás, and 10 Nimeshas. It will be observed that, in the Kalpa, we have the regular descending series 4, 3, 2, with ciphers multiplied ad libitum.

[*] For "the term", &c., read: "At the end of this *day* occurs a recoalescence *of the universe, called Brahmá's contingent recoalescence:*"

ब्राह्मो नैमित्तिको नाम तदाख्यो प्रतिसंचर: ।

Vide infra, VI., 3, *ad init.*: also see the *Márkańdeya-puráńa*, XLVI., 38.

the Janaloka—for a night of equal duration with his
day; at the close of which he creates anew. Of such
days and nights is a year of Brahmá composed; and
a hundred such years constitute his whole life.[1] One
Parárdha,[2] or half his existence, has expired, terminating with the Mahá Kalpa[3] called Pádma. The Kalpa

---

[1] The Brahma Vaivarta says 108 years; but this is unusual.
Brahmá's life is but a Nimesha of Kríshńa, according to that
work; a Nimesha of Śiva, according to the Śaiva Puráńa.

[2] In the last book, the Parárdha occurs as a very different
measure of time; but it is employed here in its ordinary acceptation.*

[3] In theory, the Kalpas are Infinite; as the Bhavishya:

कोटिकोटिसहस्राणि कल्पानां मुनिसत्तमा: ।
यतानि नायधेयानि ॥

'Excellent sages, thousands of millions of Kalpas have passed;
and as many are to come.' In the Linga Puráńa, and others of
the Śaiva division, above thirty Kalpas are named, and some
account given of several; but they are, evidently, sectarial
embellishments. The only Kalpas usually specified are those
which follow in the text: the one which was the last, or
the Pádma, and the present or Váráha. The first is also
commonly called the Bráhma; but the Bhágavata distinguishes
the Bráhma, considering it to be the first of Brahmá's life,
whilst the Pádma was the last of the first Parárdha. The
term Mahá, or great, Kalpa, applied to the Pádma, is attached
to it only in a general sense; or, according to the commentator,
because it comprises, as a minor Kalpa, that in which Brahmá
was born from a lotos. Properly, a great Kalpa is not a day,
but a life, of Brahmá; as in the Brahma Vaivarta:

ब्रह्मणायुषा कल्प: कालविभिर्विंकल्पित: ।
युगकल्पा वसुतराशि संवर्तौदय: स्मृता: ॥

'Chronologers compute a Kalpa by the life of Brahmá. Minor
Kalpas, as Samvarta and the rest, are numerous.' Minor Kalpas

---

* See Goldstücker's *Sanskrit Dictionary*, sub voce वयुन.

(or day of Brahmá) termed Váráha is the first of the
second period of Brahmá's existence.

---

here denote every period of destruction, or those in which the
Samvarta wind, or other destructive agents, operate. Several
other computations of time are found in different Puráńas; but it
will be sufficient to notice one which occurs in the Hari Vaṁśa;[*]
as it is peculiar, and because it is not quite correctly given in
M. Langlois's translation. It is the calculation of the Mánava
time, or time of a Manu:

   10 divine years = a day and night of a Manu.
   10 Mánava days = his fortnight.
   10 Mánava fortnights = his month.
   12 Mánava months = his season.
    6 Mánava seasons = his year.

Accordingly, the commentator says 72000 divine years make up
his year. The French translation has: "Dix années des dieux
font un jour de Manou; dix jours des dieux font un Pakcha de
Manou", &c. The error lies in the expression "jours *des dieux*",
and is evidently a mere inadvertence; for, if ten *years* make a
day, ten *days* can scarcely make a *fortnight*.

* French translation of the *Harivaṁśa*, Vol. I., pp. 43 *et seq.*

CHAPTER IV.

MAITREYA.—Tell me, mighty sage, how, in the commencement of the (present) Kalpa, Náráyańa, who is named Brahmá,* created all existent things.[1]

PARÁŚARA.—In what manner the divine Brahmá, who is one with Náráyańa, created progeny, and is thence named the lord of progeny (Prajápati), the lord god, you shall hear.†

At the close of the past (or Pádma) Kalpa, the divine Brahmá, endowed with the quality of goodness, awoke from his night of sleep, and beheld the universe void. He, the supreme Náráyańa, the incomprehensible, the sovereign of all creatures, invested with the form of

---

[1] This creation is of the secondary order, or Pratisarga (प्रतिसर्ग); water, and even the earth, being in existence, and, consequently, having been preceded by the creation of Mahat and the elements. It is also a different Pratisarga from that described by Manu, in which Swayaṁbhu first creates the waters, then the egg: one of the simplest forms, and, perhaps, therefore, one of the earliest, in which the tradition occurs.

---

* Read "that Brahmá, who is named Náráyańa": ब्रह्मा नारायणा॰ ख्यो हरिः ।

† Read, on the faith of my MSS.: "Hear from me in what manner the divine Brahmá, one with Náráyańa, and the god who is lord of the Progenitors — *prajápati-pati* —, created progeny":

Brahmá, the god without beginning, the creator of
all things; of whom, with respect to his name Náráyańa,
the god who has the form of Brahmá, the imperishable
origin* of the world, this verse is repeated: "The
waters are called Nárá, because they were the offspring
of Nara (the supreme spirit); and, as, in them, his first
(Ayana) progress (in the character of Brahmá) took
place, he is thence named Náráyańa (he whose place
of moving was the waters)."[1]   He, the lord,† conclu-

---

[1] This is the well-known verse of Manu, I., 10,: rendered,
by Sir Wm. Jones: "The waters are called *nárá*, because they
were the production of Nara, *or the spirit of* god; and, since
they were his first *ayana*, *or place of motion*, he thence is named
Náráyańa, *or moving on the waters*." Now, although there can
be little doubt that this tradition is, in substance, the same as
that of Genesis, the language of the translation is, perhaps, more
scriptural than is quite warranted. The waters, it is said in the
text of Manu, were the progeny of Nara, which Kullúka Bhaṭṭa
explains Paramátman, 'the supreme soul'; that is, they were the
first productions of god in creation. Ayana, instead of 'place

प्रजा: सखर्व भगवान्मह्रा नारायणात्मक: ।
प्रजापतिपतिर्देवो यथा तथे निबोधमय ॥

But compare the *Márkańḍeya-puráńa*, XLVII., 1.

* *Prabhavápyaya*. See the editor's first note in p. 21, *supra*.

† Supply "when the world had become one ocean": यदभीकार्वे ।

: आपो नारा इति प्रोक्ता आपो वै नरसूनव: ।
ता यदस्याश्वनं पूर्वं तेन नारायण: स्मृत: ॥

In the *Vishńu-puráńa*, the last line begins: यदयं तस्य ना: ।

The *Harivanśa*—I., 36—takes the stanza from the *Mánava-dharma-
śástra*, without alteration. Compare the *Mahábhárata*, *Vana-parvan*,
12952 and 15819; and the *Śánti-parvan*, 13168. Also see Goldstücker's
Sanskrit Dictionary, *sub voce* यदयम्.

It is beyond doubt that the verses quoted above palter with the
etymology of the word नारायण. On the *taddhita* affix यायन, which
cannot mean "son", see the *gańa* on Páńini, IV, 1, 99.

ding that within the waters lay the earth, and being
desirous to raise it up, created another form for that

---

of motion', is explained by Áśraya, 'place of abiding.' Náráyańa
means, therefore, he whose place of abiding was the deep. The
verse occurs in several of the Puráńas, in general in nearly the
same words, and almost always as a quotation, as in our text:
एवं वा चोदाहरन्ति श्लोकम् । The Linga, Váyu, and Márkańdeya
Puráńas, citing the same, have a somewhat different reading, or:

आपो नारा वै तनव एतेषां नाम शुश्रुम ।
अप्सु शेते यतस्तस्मान्नारायणः स्मृतः ॥ [*]

'Ápah (is the same as) Náráh, or bodies (Tanavah); such, we have
heard (from the Vedas), is the meaning of Ápah. He who sleeps
in them is, thence, called Náráyańa.'[†] The ordinary sense of
Tanu is either 'minute' or 'body'; nor does it occur amongst

---

[*] The *Linga-puráńa*—Prior Section, LXX, 119 and 120—has:

आपो नारा सूनव एतेषां नाम शुश्रुम ।
आपूर्य नाभिरिच्छन्नं जगतामात्मनो यतः ॥
अप्सु शेते जगत्साक्षी वै नारायणः स्मृतः ।

The *Márkańdeya-puráńa*—XLVII., 5—has, in one MS. that has been
consulted:

आपो नारा इति प्रोक्ता आपो वै नरसूनवः ।
तासु शेते स यत्तस्मान्नारायणः स्मृतः ॥

A second MS. has the first line the same, but, for the second:

चधर्म तथा ना: मोक्षार्थं नारायणः स्मृतः ।

And a third MS., while agreeing as to the second line, begins:

आपो नारा वै तनव एतेषां नाम शुश्रुम ।

Three MSS. of the *Váyu-puráńa* have the first verse like this last, and,
as the second:

अप्सु शेते च यत्तस्मान्नारायणः स्मृतः ।

In another place the *Váyu* has, according to all my MSS.:

आपो नराजाः... एतेषां नाम शुश्रुम ।
आपूर्य नाभिरिच्छन्नं वै नारायणः स्मृतः ॥

[†] "Water is the body of Nara: thus we have heard the name of water
explained. Since *Brahmá* rests on the water, therefore he is termed
Náráyańa."

Here, and so in the *Váyu-puráńa*,—see the last note—जगतामात्मन, if
not a copyist's mistake, denotes cause in two kinds, i. e., "hence" in
an absolute sense.

purpose; and, as, in preceding Kalpas, he had assumed
the shape of a fish or a tortoise, so, in this, he took

---

the synonyms of water in the Nirukta of the Vedas. It may,
perhaps, be intended to say, that Náráh or Ápah has the meaning
of 'bodily forms', in which spirit is enshrined, and of which the
waters, with Vishńu resting upon them, are a type; for there is
much mysticism in the Puráńas in which the passage thus occurs.
Even in them, however, it is introduced in the usual manner, by
describing the world as water alone, and Vishńu reposing upon
the deep:

एतावेव तदा सलिलसे सावरवर्जमे ।
तदा व भवति ब्रह्मा बहुखाय: बहुखपात् ॥
बहुखसीर्षा पुरुषो एकमवर्षौ धरनीमित्रुव: ।
ब्रह्मा मारायणाख्य: स सुखाय खलिले तदा ॥

Váyu P.[*] The Bhágavata[†] has, evidently, attempted to explain
the ancient text:

पुरुषो ६ खं विनिर्भिय बहाट्टो व विनिर्गत: ।
खावनो ६ धनमविचछमणो ६ खाचीकुरुष: पुरी: ॥
नालबाल्सीत्सलुहाबु बहुखपरिबसरान् ।
तेन मारायणो नाम पदाय: पुरुषोऽनवा ॥

'When the embodied god, in the beginning, divided the mundane
egg, and issued forth, then, requiring an abiding-place, he created
the waters: the pure created the pure. In them, his own created,
he abode for a thousand years, and thence received the name of
Náráyańa: the waters being the product of the embodied deity:'[‡]
i. e., they were the product of Nara or Vishńu, as the first male

* The same passage occurs in the *Linga-puráńa*, Prior Section, LXX.,
110 and 117. And compare the *Mahábhárata, Vana-parvan,* 15813—15.
  These verses, in an almost identical shape, are found in the *Váyu-
puráńa.* See, further, the *Linga-puráńa,* Prior Section, IV., 59.

† II., 10, 10 and 11.

‡ Burnouf translates: "Purucha, ayant divisé en deux parties l'œuf
[de Brahmá], lorsqu'il en sortit au commencement, réfléchit à se faire un
lieu où il pût se mouvoir; et par, il créa les eaux pures. Il habita sur
ces eaux créées par lui, pendant mille années; de là vient qu'il reçoit le
nom de Náráyańa, parce que les eaux qui sont nées de Purucha [sont
appelées Nárá]."

the figure of a boar. Having adopted a form composed
of the sacrifices of the Vedas,[1] for the preservation of
the whole earth, the eternal,[*] supreme, and universal
soul, the great progenitor of created beings, eulogized
by Sanaka and the other saints who dwell in the sphere
of holy men (Janaloka); he, the supporter of spiritual
and material being, plunged into the ocean. The goddess Earth, beholding him thus descending to the subterrene regions, bowed in devout adoration, and thus
glorified the god:—

Prithivi (Earth).—Hail to thee, who art all creatures;
to thee, the holder of the mace and shell: elevate me
now from this place, as thou hast upraised me in days
of old. From thee have I proceeded; of thee do I
consist; as do the skies and all other existing things.
Hail to thee, spirit of the supreme spirit; to thee, soul

---

or Viráj, and were, therefore, termed Nára: and, from their being
his Ayana or Sthána, his 'abiding-place', comes his epithet of
Náráyaña.

[1] The Varáha form was chosen, says the Váyu P., because it
is an animal delighting to sport in water.[†] But it is described, in
many Puráñas, as it is in the Vishñu, as a type of the ritual of
the Vedas; as we shall have further occasion to remark. The
elevation of the earth from beneath the ocean, in this form, was,
therefore, probably at first an allegorical representation of the
extrication of the world from a deluge of iniquity, by the rites
of religion. Geologists may, perhaps, suspect, in the original and
unmystified tradition, an allusion to a geological fact, or the
existence of lacustrine mammalia in the early periods of the
earth.

[*] *Sthirátman.*

[†] जलक्रीडारुचिरं वाराहं वपुराश्रितम् ।

of soul; to thee, who art discrete and indiscrete matter; who art one with the elements and with time. Thou art the creator of all things, their preserver, and their destroyer, in the forms, O lord, of Brahmá, Vishńu, and Rudra, at the seasons of creation, duration, and dissolution. When thou hast devoured all things, thou reposest on the ocean that sweeps over the world,* meditated upon, O Govinda, by the wise. No one knoweth thy true nature; and the gods adore thee only in the forms it hath pleased thee to assume. They who are desirous of final liberation worship thee as the supreme Brahma;† and who that adores not Vásudeva shall obtain emancipation? Whatever may be apprehended by the mind, whatever may be perceived by the senses, whatever may be discerned by the intellect, all is but a form of thee. I am of thee, upheld by thee; thou art my creator, and to thee I fly for refuge: hence, in this universe, Mádhaví (the bride of Mádhava or Vishńu) is my designation. Triumph to the essence of all wisdom, to the unchangeable,‡ the imperishable: triumph to the eternal; to the indiscrete, to the essence of discrete things: to him who is both cause and effect; who is the universe; the sinless lord of sacrifice;[1] triumph. Thou art sacrifice; thou art the oblation;§ thou art the

---

[1] Yajnapati (यज्ञपति), 'the bestower of the beneficial results of sacrifices.'

* Literally, in place of "thou reposest", &c., "the world having been converted into one ocean, thou reposest": जगत्येकार्णवीभूते भूमि शयन ।
† Read: "Worshipping thee, the supreme Brahma, they who were desirous of final liberation have compassed it":

स्थावरान्त परं ब्रह्म याता मुक्तिं मुमुक्षवः ।

‡ Sthúlamaya, "the gross", "the concrete."
§ Rather, "the formula va-shat", vashatkára,

mystic Oṁkára; thou art the sacrificial fires; thou art the Vedas, and their dependent sciences; thou art, Hari, the object of all worship.[1] The sun, the stars, the planets, the whole world; all that is formless, or that has form; all that is visible, or invisible; all, Purushottama, that I have said, or left unsaid; all this, Supreme, thou art. Hail to thee, again and again! hail! all hail!

PARÁSARA.—The auspicious supporter of the world, being thus hymned by the earth, emitted a low murmuring sound, like the chanting of the Sáma Veda; and the mighty boar, whose eyes were like the* lotos, and whose body, vast as the Níla mountain, was of the dark colour of the lotos-leaves,[2] uplifted upon his ample tusks the earth from the lowest regions. As he reared up his head, the waters shed from his brow purified the great† sages, Sanandana and others, residing in the sphere of the saints. Through the indentations made by his hoofs, the waters rushed into the

---

[1] Yajnapurusha (यज्ञपुरुष), 'the male or soul of sacrifice'; explained by Yajnamúrti (यज्ञमूर्ति), 'the form or personification of sacrifice'; or Yajnárádhya (यज्ञाराध्य), 'he who is to be propitiated by it.'

[2] Varáha Avatára. The description of the figure of the boar is much more particularly detailed in other Puráńas. As in the Váyu: "The boar was ten Yojanas in breadth, a thousand Yojanas high; of the colour of a dark cloud; and his roar was like thunder; his bulk was vast as a mountain; his tusks were white, sharp, and fearful; fire flashed from his eyes like lightning, and he was radiant as the sun; his shoulders were round, fat, and large; he strode along like a powerful lion; his haunches were fat, his loins

* Supply "full-blown", sphuṭa.
† Supply "stoless", apakalmasha.

lower worlds with a thundering noise. Before his
breath the pious denizens of Janaloka were scattered;

---

were slender, and his body was smooth and beautiful." *   The
Matsya P. describes the Varáha in the same words, with one or
two unimportant varieties.   The Bhágavata † indulges in that
amplification which marks its more recent composition, and
describes the Varáha as issuing from the nostrils of Brahmá, at
first of the size of the thumb, or an inch long, and presently
increasing to the stature of an elephant.   That work also sub-
joins a legend of the death of the demon Hirańyáksha,‡ who, in
a preceding existence, was one of Vishńu's doorkeepers, at his
palace in Vaikuńtha.   Having refused admission to a party of
Munis, they cursed him; and he was, in consequence, born as
one of the sons of Diti.   When the earth, oppressed by the weight
of the mountains, sank down into the waters, Vishńu was beheld
in the subterrene regions, or Rasátala, by Hirańyáksha, in the
act of carrying it off.   The demon claimed the earth, and defied
Vishńu to combat; and a conflict took place, in which Hirańyáksha
was slain.   This legend has not been met with in any other
Puráńa, and certainly does not occur in the chief of them, any
more than in our text.   In the Moksha Dharma of the Mahábhárata, c. 35, Vishńu destroys the demons, in the form of the Varáha;
but no particular individual is specified; nor does the elevation
of the earth depend upon their discomfiture.   The Kálika Upapuráńa has an absurd legend of a conflict between Śiva as a

*   सुरयोजनविस्तीर्णं शतयोजनमुच्छ्रितम् ।
नीलमेघप्रतीकाशं मेघस्तनितनिस्वनम् ॥
महापर्वतवर्ष्माणं दीप्तं सीक्ष्णोपदंष्ट्रिणम् ।
विद्युदग्निप्रभाकारमादित्यसमतेजसम् ॥
पीनवृत्तायतस्कन्धं शिग्रविक्रान्तगामिनम् ।
पीनोन्नतकटीदेशं शुभ्रत्वं शुभलक्षणम् ॥
रूपमास्थाय विपुलं वाराहमभितो हरिः ।
भुविभुजरसातलगतां मविवेश रसातलम् ॥

† III., 13, 18 et seq.
‡ III., 18 and 19.

and the Munis sought for shelter amongst the bristles
upon the scriptural body of the boar, trembling as he
rose up, supporting the earth, and dripping with
moisture. Then the great sages, Sanandana and the
rest, residing continually in the sphere of saints, were
inspired with delight; and, bowing lowly, they praised
the stern-eyed upholder of the earth.*

· *The Yogins.*—Triumph, lord of lords supreme; Kesava,
sovereign of the earth, the wielder of the mace, the
shell, the discus, and the sword: cause of production,
destruction, and existence. THOU ART, O god: there is
no other supreme condition but thou. Thou, lord, art
the person of sacrifice: for thy feet are the Vedas; thy
tusks are the stake to which the victim is bound; in
thy teeth are the offerings; thy mouth is the altar; thy
tongue is the fire; and the hairs of thy body are the
sacrificial grass. Thine eyes, O omnipotent, are day
and night; thy head is the seat of all, the place of
Brahma; thy mane is all the hymns of the Vedas; thy
nostrils are all oblations: O thou, whose snout is the
ladle of oblation; whose deep voice is the chanting of
the Sáma Veda; whose body is the hall of sacrifice;
whose joints are the different ceremonies; and whose
ears have the properties of both voluntary and obliga-
tory rites:[1] do thou, who art eternal, who art in size a

Sarabha, a fabulous animal, and Vishńu as the Varáha, in which
the latter suffers himself and his offspring begotten upon earth to
be slain.

[1] This, which is nothing more than the development of the
notion that the Varáha incarnation typifies the ritual of the Vedas,

* Hereabouts the translation is not very literal.

mountain,* be propitious. We acknowledge thee, who hast traversed the world, O universal form, to be the beginning, the continuance, and the destruction of all things: thou art the supreme god. Have pity on us, O lord of conscious and unconscious beings. The orb of the earth is seen seated on the tip of thy tusks, as if thou hadst been sporting amidst a lake where the lotos floats, and hadst borne away the leaves covered with soil. The space between heaven and earth is occupied by thy body, O thou of unequalled glory, resplendent with the power of pervading the universe, O lord, for the benefit of all. Thou art the aim of all: there is none other than thee, sovereign of the world: this is thy might, by which all things, fixed or movable, are pervaded. This form, which is now beheld, is thy form, as one essentially with wisdom. Those who have not practised devotion conceive erroneously of the nature of the world. The ignorant, who do not perceive that this universe is of the nature of wisdom, and judge of it as an object of perception only, are lost in the ocean of spiritual ignorance. But they who know true wisdom, and whose minds are pure, behold this whole world as one with divine knowledge, as one with thee, O god. Be favourable, O universal spirit: raise up this earth, for the habitation of created beings. Inscrutable deity, whose eyes are like lotoses, give us felicity. O lord, thou art endowed with the quality of goodness:

is repeated in most of the Purāṇas, in the same or nearly the same words.

* The MSS. within my reach omit the words answering to "who art in size a mountain".

raise up, Govinda, this earth, for the general good. Grant us happiness, O lotos-eyed. May this, thy activity in creation, be beneficial to the earth. Salutation to thee. Grant us happiness, O lotos-eyed.

PARÁSARA.—The supreme being thus eulogized, upholding the earth, raised it quickly, and placed it on the summit of the ocean, where it floats like a mighty vessel, and, from its expansive surface, does not sink beneath the waters.* Then, having levelled the earth, the great eternal deity divided it into portions, by mountains. He who never wills in vain created, by his irresistible power, those mountains again upon the earth, which had been consumed at the destruction of the world. Having then divided the earth into seven great portions or continents, as it was before, he constructed, in like manner, the four (lower) spheres, earth, sky, heaven, and the sphere of the sages (Maharloka). Thus Hari, the four-faced god, invested with the quality of activity, and taking the form of Brahmá, accomplished the creation. But he (Brahmá) is only the instrumental cause of things to be created; the things that are capable of being created arise from nature as a common material cause. With exception of one instrumental cause alone, there is no need of any other cause; for (imperceptible) substance becomes perceptible substance according to the powers with which it is originally imbued.[1]†

---

[1] This seems equivalent to the ancient notion of a plastic

* A large portion of the present chapter, down to this point, has been translated anew in *Original Sanskrit Texts*, Part IV., pp. 32 and 33.

† निमित्तमात्रमेवासौ सृज्यानां सर्गकर्मणि ।
प्रधानकारणीभूता यतो वै सृज्यशक्तयः ॥

nature; "all parts of matter being supposed able to form themselves artificially and methodically *** to the greatest advantage of their present respective capabilities." This, which Cudworth (c. III.) calls hylozoism, is not incompatible with an active
creator: "not ** that he should αὐτουργεῖν ἅπαντα, set his
own hand ** to every work," which, as Aristotle says, would
be, ἀπρεπές ** τῷ Θεῷ, unbecoming God; but, as in the
case of Brahmá and other subordinate agents, that they should
occasion the various developments of crude nature to take
place, by supplying that will, of which nature itself is incapable.
Action being once instituted by an instrumental medium, or by
the will of an intellectual agent, it is continued by powers, or a
vitality inherent in nature or the matter of creation itself. The
efficiency of such subordinate causes was advocated by Plato,
Aristotle, and others; and the opinion of Zeno, as stated by
Laërtius, might be taken for a translation of some such passage
as that in our text: "Ἔστι δὲ φύσις ἕξις ἐξ αὑτῆς κινουμένη
κατὰ σπερματικοὺς λόγους, ἀποτελοῦσά τε καὶ συνέχουσα
τὰ ἐξ αὑτῆς ἐν ὡρισμένοις χρόνοις, καὶ τοιαῦτα δρῶσα ἀφ'
οἵων ἀπεκρίθη. Nature is a habit moved from itself, according
to ** seminal principles; perfecting and containing those several
things which in determinate times are produced from it, and acting
agreeably to that from which it was secreted." Intell. System,
I., 328. So the commentator illustrates our text, by observing
that the cause of the budding of rice is in its own seed, and its
development is from itself, though its growth takes place only

---

> जिजनिखभार्य जुकिथं जाच्यतिंभिचिहृयेकते ।
> नीयते नयना देउ सष्ठखया बसु नबुनाम् ॥

These rather obscure verses lend themselves, without violence, to some
such interpretation as the following: "He is only the ideal cause of
the potencies to be created in the work of creation; and from him
proceed the potencies to be created, after they have become the real
cause. Save *that* one ideal cause, there is no other to which *the
world* can be referred. Worthiest of ascetics, through its potency—*i. e.,
through the potency of that cause—every created* thing comes by its proper
nature."

In the Vedánta and Nyáya, *nimitta* is the efficient cause, as contrasted
with *upádána*, the material cause. In the Sánkhya, *pradhána* implies

at a determinate season, in consequence of the instrumental
agency of the rain.

---

the functions of both. The author, it appears, means to express, in the
passage before us, that Brahmá is a cause superior to *pradhána*. This
cause he calls *nimitta*. It was necessary, therefore, in the translation,
to choose terms neither Vedánta nor Sánkhya. "Ideal cause" and "real
cause" may, perhaps, answer the purpose.

CHAPTER V.

MAITREYA.—Now unfold to me, Brahman, how this deity created the gods, sages, progenitors, demons, men, animals, trees, and the rest, that abide on earth, in heaven, or in the waters; how Brahmá, at creation, made the world, with the qualities, the characteristics, and the forms of things.[1]

PARÁŚARA.—I will explain to you, Maitreya: listen attentively, how this deity, the lord of all, created the gods and other beings.

---

[1] The terms here employed are for qualities, Guńas; which, as we have already noticed, are those of goodness, foulness, and darkness.[*] The characteristics or Swabhávas are the inherent properties of the qualities, by which they act, as soothing, terrific, or stupefying; and the forms, Swarúpas, are the distinctions of biped, quadruped, brute, bird, fish, and the like.

[*] See Professor Wilson's note in p. 34, supra, and the appended comment.

Whilst he (Brahmá) formerly, in the beginning of the Kalpas,* was meditating on creation, there appeared a creation beginning with ignorance, and consisting of darkness. From that great being appeared fivefold Ignorance, consisting of obscurity, illusion, extreme illusion, gloom, utter darkness.' The creation of the creator thus plunged in abstraction was the fivefold (immovable) world, without intellect or reflection, void of perception or sensation, incapable of feeling, and

---

' Or Tamas (तमस्), Moha (मोह), Mahámoha (महामोह), Támisra (तामिस्र), Andhatámisra (अन्धतामिस्र); they are the five kinds of obstruction, Viparyaya (विपर्यय), of soul's liberation. According to the Sánkhya, they are explained to be: 1. The belief of material substance being the same with spirit; 2. Notion of property or possession, and consequent attachment to objects, as children and the like, as being one's own; 3. Addiction to the enjoyments of sense; 4. Impatience or wrath; and 5. Fear of privation or death. They are called, in the Pátanjala philosophy, the five afflictions, Kleśa (क्लेश), but are similarly explained by Avidyá (अविद्या), 'ignorance'; Asmitá (अस्मिता), 'selfishness', literally 'I-amness'; Rága (राग), 'love'; Dweśha (द्वेष), 'hatred'; and Abhiniveśa (अभिनिवेश), 'dread of temporal suffering'. Sánkhya Káriká, pp. 148-150. This creation by Brahmá in the Váráha Kalpa begins in the same way, and in the same words, in most of the Puránas. The Bhágavata† reverses the order of these five products, and gives them, Andhatámisra, Támisra, Mahámoha, Moha, and Tamas; a variation obviously more immethodical than the usual reading of the text, and adopted, no doubt,‡ merely for the sake of giving the passage an air of originality.

---

* Compare *Original Sanskrit Text*, Part I., p. 20.

† III., 12, 2. In the same Purána, III., 20, 18, we have *támisra andhatámisra, tamas, moha,* and *mahátamas.*

‡ ?

destitute of motion.[1] Since immovable things were
first created, this is called the first creation.[†] Brahmá,

---

[1] This is not to be confounded with elementary creation, although the description would very well apply to that of crude
nature or Pradhána; but, as will be seen presently, we have here
to do with final productions, or the forms in which the previously
created elements and faculties are more or less perfectly aggregated. The first class of these forms is here said to be immovable
things; that is, the mineral and vegetable kingdoms: for the solid
earth, with its mountains, and rivers, and seas, was already prepared for their reception. The 'fivefold' immovable creation is,
indeed, according to the comment, restricted to vegetables, five
orders of which are enumerated, or: 1. trees; 2. shrubs; 3. climb-
ing plants; 4. creepers; and 5. grasses.[‡]

पञ्चभावर्जितः सर्वो धातवो ऽप्रतिबोधवान् ।
बहिरन्तो ऽप्रकाशश्च संवृतात्मा नगादयः ॥

"Of *him* meditating *was* a fivefold creation — *viz.*, *of things* — without
reflection, devoid of clearness in *all matters* external and internal, dull
of nature, essentially immovable."

Another reading of the second line gives बहिरन्तःप्रकाशश्च । अप्र-
तिबोधवान् being taken in connexion with बहिर्, the meaning is,
then: "devoid of reflection on external *objects*, endowed with inward manifestations." This is according to the commentary, which interprets the
"inward manifestations" as being cognitions chiefly of a sensual kind.

The word धातवो, as used in the stanza quoted, is very unusual.

[†] मुख्या जज्ञे यदस्तोषा मुख्यसर्गस्तदुच्यते ।
"Inasmuch as *things* immovable are designated as primary, this is *distinguished as* the primary creation."

The commentator refers to a sacred text for the explanation that immovable things are technically styled "primary", *mukhya*. on the ground
that they were produced at the beginning of the creation of the gods
and others: मुख्ये देवादिवर्गादौ आतस्तायुक्ताः मुख्या निर्मिमीति
देव: ।

See the editor's first note in p. 75, *infra*.

[‡] In the words of the commentary: मुख्यमुख्यसनाथीकृतवनस्पत्यु-
द्भवाय इति । But the grammar here looks very doubtful.

beholding that it was defective,* designed another; and,
whilst he thus meditated, the animal creation was manifested, to the products of which the term Tiryaksrotas
is applied, from their nutriment following a winding
course.[1]† These were called beasts, &c.: and their
characteristic was the quality of darkness; they being
destitute of knowledge, uncontrolled in their conduct,:
and mistaking error for wisdom; being formed of egotism and self-esteem,§ labouring under the twenty-eight kinds of imperfection,[2] manifesting inward sen-

---

[1] Tiryak (तिर्यक्), 'crooked', and Srotas (श्रोतस्), 'a canal'.

[2] Twenty-eight kinds of Badhas (बाध), which, in the Sánkhya
system, mean disabilities, as defects of the senses, blindness, deafness, &c.; and defects of intellect, discontent, ignorance, and the
like. S. Káriká, pp. 148, 151. In place of Badha, however, the
more usual reading, as in the Bhágavata, Váráha, and Márkańdeya Puráńas, is Vidha (विध), 'kind', 'sort',‖ as वडाविधानि-
भावनाः ¶ implying twenty-eight sorts of animals. These are
thus specified in the Bhágavata, III., 10, 20-22: Six kinds have
single hoofs: nine have double, or cloven, hoofs; and thirteen
have five claws, or nails, instead of hoofs. The first are the

* Because, according to the commentator, the universe "did not as
yet possess that which is the purpose of man", namely, sacrificial acts
and the knowledge of Brahmá. The purport is, that human beings were
not yet created: for only they can comply with the ceremonial requirements of the Mimáṉsá, and pursue the study of the Vedánta. The words
of the commentator are: न मुख्यसर्गमवाप्य पुरुषार्थोचितं सुखा ।
See, further, my third note in p. 73, infra.

† "Since the channel for their food is in a horizontal position", agreeably to the commentator, who refers to authority for this explanation.

: "Taking the wrong way", utpathagráhin.

§ वडाभा वडभाना: । Compare the remarks under अभिमान in
Goldstücker's Sanskrit Dictionary.

¶ But see Páńini, IV., 2, 54.

¶ Márkańdeya-puráńa, XLVII., 20.

sations, and associating with each other (according to their kinds). *

Beholding this creation also imperfect, Brahmá again meditated; and a third creation appeared, abounding with the quality of goodness, termed Úrdhwasrotas.[1] The beings thus produced in the Úrdhwasrotas creation were endowed with pleasure and enjoyment, unencumbered internally or externally, and luminous within and without. † This, termed the creation of immortals,‡

---

horse, the mule, the ass, the yak, the Śarabha, and the Gaura or white deer. The second are the cow, the goat, the buffalo, the hog, the gayal, the black deer, the antelope, the camel, and the sheep. The last are the dog, jackal, wolf, tiger, cat, hare, porcupine, lion, monkey, elephant, tortoise, lizard, and alligator.§

[1] Úrdhwa (ऊर्ध्व), 'above', and Srotas, as before; their nourishment being derived from the exterior, not from the interior, of the body; according to the commentator: ऊर्ध्वमुपरि देहादूर्ध्व ऊर्ध्व चाद्यारूपार्थं एव च: । as a text of the Vedas has it: 'Through satiety derived from even beholding ambrosia'; अमृत- दर्शनादेव तृप्ति: ।[1]

* जनाःप्रकाशाश्च सर्वे चाविृताश्च परस्परम् ।
"Endowed with inward manifestations, and mutually in ignorance about *their kind and nature.*"

† ये सुखप्रीतिबहुला बहिरन्तश्च नावृता: ।
प्रकाशा बहिरन्तश्च ऊर्ध्वस्रोतो भवा: स्मृता: ।
"Those beings in which was a preponderance of happy and pleasurable feelings, and that were undull externally and internally, and possessed outward and inward manifestations, were called Úrdhwasrotas."

‡ *Deva-sarga.*

§ "Black deer" is *krishńa;* "antelope", *ruru;* "lizard", *godhá;* and "alligator", *makara.*

‖ The gods are called *úrdhwasrotas,* because they obtain their food extraneously to the body. That is to say, the bare sight of aliment stands, to them, in place of eating it: "for there is satisfaction from the mere beholding of ambrosia". So says—not a Vaidik text, but—the

was the third performance of Brahmá, who, although
well pleased with it, still found it incompetent to fulfil
his end. * Continuing, therefore, his meditations, there
sprang, in consequence of his infallible purpose, † the
creation termed Arváksrotas, from indiscrete nature.
The products of this are termed Arvúksrotas,[1] from
the downward current (of their nutriment). They
abound with the light of knowledge; but the qualities
of darkness and of foulness predominate. Hence they
are afflicted by evil, and are repeatedly impelled to
action. They have knowledge both externally and internally, and are the instruments (of accomplishing the
object of creation, the liberation of soul).‡ These creatures were mankind.§

I have thus explained to you, excellent Muni, six[2]

---

[1] Arvák (अर्वाक्), 'downwards', and Srotas (स्रोतस्), 'canal'. ‖

[2] This reckoning is not very easily reconciled with the crea-

commentator. The quotation from the Veda, which he adds, in support
of his view, is: न ह वै देवा अश्रन्ति नापि पिबन्ति । एतदेवामृतं
रूपं दृष्ट्वा तृप्यन्ति । "The gods do not, indeed, either eat or drink. Having
looked upon this ambrosia, they are satisfied."

* The translation is here somewhat compressed.

† *Satyábhidháyin*,—here an epithet of Brahmá,—"true to his will".
The commentator explains it by *satya-sankalpa*.

‡ The words in brackets are supplied by the translator. The commentator says: व्याख्या: धर्मज्ञानाधिकारित्वात् । Allusion is made,
in the original text, to man's exclusive prerogative to engage in sacrifice
and to explore the nature of spirit. See the editor's first note in p. 71,
supra.

§ For another rendering, see *Original Sanskrit Texts*, Part I., pp. 30
and 31.

‖ Men are called *arváksrotas*, because they are developed by means
of their food going downwards. So says the commentator: यस्मादर्वाग्
गच्छत्यविच्छिन्नाहारादिव अवयते अश्नाति स्राध्यवर्गो जाता: । Possibly
the right word is *aváksrotas*.

creations. The first creation was that of Mahat or Intellect, which is also called the creation of Brahmá.[1]
The second was that of the rudimental principles (Tan-
mátras), thence termed the elemental creation (Bhúta-
sarga). The third was the modified form of egotism,*
termed the organic creation, or creation of the senses
(Aindriyaka). These three were the Prákrita creations,
the developments of indiscrete nature, preceded by the
indiscrete principle.[2] The fourth or fundamental crea-

---

tions described; for, as presently enumerated, the stages of creation
are seven. The commentator, however, considers the Úrdhwasrotas creation, or that of the superhuman beings, to be the same
with that of the Indriyas or senses, over which they preside; by
which the number is reduced to six.†

[1] This creation being the work of the supreme spirit, ब्रह्म
परमात्मा सकर्तृकः सर्गो विशेष एवर्ष: । according to the commentator: or it might have been understood to mean, that Brahmá
was then created, being, as we have seen, identified with Mahat,
'active intelligence', or the operating will of the Supreme. See
note in p. 83, supra.

[2] The text is: सर्गः संभूतो बुद्धिपूर्वक: । which is, as rendered
in the text, 'creation preceded by, or beginning with, Buddhi, in-

----

* "Modified form of egotism" here translates vaikárika; and this is
synonymous with sáttwika, the adjective of sattwa. See Professor Wilson's
note in p. 34, and the editor's comment in p. 35, supra.

† Mention has been made, in the second chapter, of three creations,
denominated mahattattwa, bhúta, and indriya; and we have just read of
four, the mukhya, tiryaksrotas, úrdhwasrotas, and arváksrotas. The indriya comprehends the úrdhwasrotas, according to the commentator. He
speaks of a reading "seven", instead of "six"; when, he says, the úrdhwasrotas is not comprised in the indriya; and the order of the creations is as follows: mahattattwa, bhúta, indriya, mukhya, tiryaksrotas,
úrdhwasrotas, and arváksrotas.

‡ Most of my copies of the commentary have: यदा मद्दा परमात्मा
सकर्तृकः सर्गो एवर्ष: ।

tion (of perceptible things) was that of inanimate
bodies.* The fifth, the Tairyagyonya creation, was
that of animals. The sixth was the Úrdhwasrotas creation, or that of the divinities. The creation of the
Arváksrotas beings was the seventh, and was that of
man. There is an eighth creation, termed Anugraha,
which possesses both the qualities of goodness and

telligence.' The rules of euphony would, however, admit of a
mute negative being inserted, or संभूतो (बुद्धिपूर्वक: । 'preceded
by Ignorance'; that is, by the chief principle, crude nature or
Pradhána, which is one with ignorance: but this seems to depend
on notions of a later date and more partial adoption than those
generally prevailing in our authority; and the first reading, therefore, has been preferred. It is also to be observed, that the first
unintellectual creation was that of immovable objects (as in p. 69,
supra), the original of which is

बुद्धिपूर्वक: सर्व: प्रादुर्भूतसमीभवः ।

and all ambiguity of construction is avoided. The reading is also
established by the text of the Linga Puráńa, which enumerates
the different series of creation in the words of the Vishńu, except
in this passage, which is there transposed, with a slight variation
of the reading. Instead of

प्रथमो महत: सर्वो विशेषो महत्तत्त्व च: । †

it is

प्रथमो महत: सर्व: संभूती बुद्धिपूर्वक: ।

'The first creation was that of Mahat; Intellect being the first in
manifestation.' The reading of the Váyu P. is still more tautological, but confirms that here preferred:

प्रथमो महत: सर्वो विशेषो महत्तत्त्व च: ।

See also note 2 in the next page.

* मूलसर्गश्चतुर्थेषु मुक्ता वै भावरा: भूता: ।
"And the fourth creation is *here* the primary; *for things immovable*
are emphatically known as primary."
See the editor's second note in p. 70, *supra.*
† *Linga-puráńa*, Prior Section, LXX, 162.

darkness.[1] Of these creations five are secondary and
three are primary.[2] But there is a ninth, the Kaumára

---

[1] The Anugraha creation, of which no notice has been found
in the Mahábhárata, seems to have been borrowed from the Sánkhya philosophy. It is more particularly described in the Padma,
Márkańdeya,[*] Linga,[†] and Matsya Puráńas; as:

पञ्चमोऽनुग्रहः सर्गः स चतुर्धा व्यवस्थितः ।
विपर्ययेणाशक्त्या च सिद्ध्या मुख्या तथैव च ॥

'The fifth is the Anugraha creation, which is subdivided into four
kinds; by obstruction, disability, perfectness, and acquiescence.'
This is the Pratyayasarga or intellectual creation of the Sánkhyas
(S. Káriká, v. 46, p. 146); the creation of which we have a notion,
or to which we give assent (Anugraha), in contradistinction to
organic creation, or that existence of which we have sensible perception. In its specific subdivisions, it is the notion of certain
inseparable properties in the four different orders of beings: obstruction or stolidity in inanimate things; inability or imperfection
in animals; perfectibility in man; and acquiescence or tranquil
enjoyment in gods. So also the Váyu P.:

तामसे विपर्ययाख्येन वैकृतोऽनुग्रहः स्मृता ।
सिद्ध्यात्मानो मनुष्याश्च तुष्टिर्देवेषु जायते ॥

[2] Or Vaikŕita, derived mediately from the first principle, through
its Vikŕitis, 'productions' or 'developments'; and Prákŕita, derived
more immediately from the chief principle itself. Mahat and the
two forms of Ahaṁkára, or the rudimental elements and the
senses, constitute the latter class; inanimate beings, &c. compose
the former: or the latter are considered as the work of Brahmá,
whilst the three first are evolved from Pradhána. So the Váyu:

---

[*] XLVII., 28; where, however, the second half of the stanza is read:

विपर्ययेण सिद्धा च शक्त्या मुख्या तथैव च ।

[†] Prior Section, LXX., 157.

[‡] The Váyu-puráńa, to the same effect—only that it substitutes "eighth"
for "fifth"—as the verses given above, is cited by the commentator.
Then follows the stanza with which the note concludes.

creation, which is both primary and secondary.' These
are the nine creations of the great progenitor of all,

ब्राह्मास्तु पयः सर्गाः प्रकृतो तुविपूर्वकाः ।
तुविपूर्वं प्रवर्तंते वह्नर्गा प्रह्मवतु ते ॥

'The three creations beginning with Intelligence are elemental;
but the six creations which proceed from the series of which Intellect is the first are the work of Brahmá.'

' We must have recourse, here also, to other Puráńas, for the
elucidation of this term. The Kaumára creation is the creation
of Rudra or Nílalohita, a form of Śiva, by Brahmá, which is subsequently described in our text, and of certain other mind-born
sons of Brahmá, of whose birth the Vishńu P. gives no further
account. They are elsewhere termed Sanatkumára, Sananda, Sanaka, and Sanátana, with sometimes a fifth, Ribhu, added. These,
declining to create progeny, remained, as the name of the first
implies, ever boys, Kumáras; that is, ever pure and innocent;
whence their creation is called the Kaumára. Thus the Váyu:

चतो एवर्ज ये ब्रह्मा मानसानाबन: समान् ।
समबुन सखनव्धं धिद्वांशं व सनातनम् ॥
समक्लुमारमिव व म ते लोके तु सर्वले ।
निरपेषा: सनातना: * * * ॥

And the Linga has:

यवीत्यब: सद्दा एव कुमार: स एोच्यते ।
तस्मात्सनुक्लुमारेति नामासीत प्रकीर्तित: ॥*

'Being ever as he was born, he is here called a youth; and hence
his name is well known as Sanatkumára.' This authority makes
Sanatkumára and Ribhu the two first born of all:

चमु: समक्लुमारएव द्वाविमावूर्धरितबी ।
पूर्वोत्यक्षी पुरा मेध: संवेषामपि पूर्वजी ॥†

whilst the text of the Hari Vamśa limits the primogeniture to
Sanatkumára:

समक्लुमारे व विभुं पूर्वेषामपि पूर्वजम् ।

In another place, however, it enumerates, apparently, six, or the

* Prior Section, LXX., 174.
† Prior Section, LXX., 170 and 171.

and, both as primary and secondary, are the radical
causes of the world, proceeding from the sovereign
creator. What else dost thou desire to hear?

above four, with Sana, and either Ŕibhu or another Sanátana:
for the passage is corrupt. The French translation* ascribes a
share in creation to Sanatkumára: 'Les sept Pradjápatis, Roudra,
Scanda (son fils), et Sanatcoumára se mirent à produire les êtres,
répandant partout l'inépuisable énergie du Dieu.' The original is:

बहिति जनयन्ति च प्रजा रुद्र आरन ।
सनत्कुमारश्च नैव: संयम्य तिष्ठत: ॥†

Sankshipya is not 'répandant', but 'restraining'; and Tishťhatah,
being in the dual number, relates, of course, to only two of the
series. The correct rendering is: 'Those seven (Prajápatis) created
progeny; and so did Rudra: but Skanda and Sanatkumára, restraining their power, abstained (from creation).' So the commentator: बुद्धिबालमयें संयम्य निगृह्य बुद्धिमनुपूर्वत्वादेव तिष्ठत: ।
These sages, however, live as long as Brahmá; and they are only
created by him in the first Kalpa, although their generation is
very commonly, but inconsistently, introduced in the Váráha or
Pádma Kalpa. This creation, says the text, is both primary
(Prákrita) and secondary (Vaikrita). It is the latter, according
to the commentator, as regards the origin of these saints from
Brahmá: it is the former, as affects Rudra, who, though proceeding from Brahmá, in a certain form was in essence equally an
immediate production of the first principle. These notions, the
birth of Rudra and the saints, seem to have been borrowed from
the Śaivas, and to have been awkwardly engrafted upon the Vaishńava system. Sanatkumára and his brethren‡ are always described, in the Śaiva Puráńas, as Yogins: as the Kúrma, after
enumerating them, adds:

पञ्चैते योगिनो विप्रा: परे वैराग्यमाश्रिता: ।

* Vol. I., p. 6.
† Stanza 44.
‡ On the subject of these personages, see *Original Sanskrit Texts*,
passim, and the *Sánkhya-sára*, Preface, pp. 13 *et seq.*, foot-note.

MAITREYA.—Thou hast briefly related to me, Muni, the creation of the gods and other beings. I am desirous, chief of sages, to hear from thee a more ample account of their creation.

PARÁSARA.—Created beings, although they are destroyed (in their individual forms) at the periods of dissolution, yet, being affected by the good or evil acts of former existence, they are never exempted from their consequences; and, when Brahmá creates the world anew, they are the progeny of his will, in the fourfold condition of gods, men, animals, or inanimate things. Brahmá then, being desirous of creating the four orders of beings, termed gods, demons, progeni-

---

'These five, O Brahmans, were Yogins, who acquired entire exemption from passion:' and the Ilari Vaṁśa, although rather Vaishṇava than Śaiva, observes, that the Yogins celebrate these six, along with Kapila, in Yoga works:

सनत्कुमारो वामन एव वेदोक्तानुभवयोगिनः ।
ततो योगमयेषु वाम्युवति द्विजातयः ॥ *

The idea seems to have been amplified also in the Śaiva works; for the Linga P. describes the repeated birth of Śiva, or Váma-deva, as a Kumára, or boy, from Brahmá, in each Kalpa, who again becomes four. Thus, in the twenty-ninth Kalpa, Sweta-lohita is the Kumára; and he becomes Sananda, Nandana, Viswa-nanda, Upanandana; all of a white complexion: in the thirtieth, the Kumára becomes Virajas, Vivahu, Viśoka, Viśwabhávana; all of a red colour: in the thirty-first, he becomes four youths of a yellow colour; and, in the thirty-second, the four Kumáras were black. All these are, no doubt, comparatively recent additions to the original notion of the birth of Rudra and the Kumáras; itself obviously a sectarial innovation upon the primitive doctrine of the birth of the Prajápatis or will-born sons of Brahmá.

---

* Stanza 12439.

tors, and men, collected his mind into itself.[1] Whilst
thus concentrated, the quality of darkness pervaded
his body; and thence the demons (the Asuras) were
first born, issuing from his thigh. Brahmá then abandoned that form which was composed of the rudiment
of darkness, and which, being deserted by him, became
night. Continuing to create, but assuming a different
shape, he experienced pleasure; and thence from his
mouth proceeded the gods, endowed with the quality
of goodness. The form abandoned by him became day,
in which the good quality predominates; and hence by
day the gods are most powerful, and by night the demons. He next adopted another person, in which the
rudiment of goodness also prevailed; and, thinking of
himself as the father of the world, the progenitors (the

---

[1] These reiterated, and not always very congruous, accounts
of the creation are explained, by the Puráṇas, as referring to different Kalpas or renovations of the world, and therefore involving
no incompatibility. A better reason for their appearance is, the
probability that they have been borrowed from different original
authorities. The account that follows is evidently modified by
the Yogi Śaivas, by its general mysticism, and by the expressions
with which it begins:

मनो देवासुरपितृमानुषांश्च चतुष्टयम् ।
सिसृक्षुरम्भांस्येतानि समाराममयुयुजत् ॥

'Collecting his mind into itself', मनो समाधत्ते । according to the
comment, is the performance of the Yoga (Yúyuje). The term
Ambhánsi, lit., 'waters', for the four orders of beings, gods, demons, men, and Pitṛis, is, also, a peculiar, and, probably, mystic,
term. The commentator says it occurs in the Vedas, as a synonym
of gods, &c.: एतानि वस्तार्घ्यानि । देवा मनुजा: पितरो ऽसुरा
इति बुधै:. The Váyu Puráṇa derives it from भा 'to shine'; because the different orders of beings shine, or flourish, severally,
by moonlight, night, day, and twilight: भाति वक्रारभतोऽर्धानि। &c.

Pitris) were born from his side.* The body, when he
abandoned it, became the Sandhyá (or evening twilight), the interval between day and night. Brahmá
then assumed another person, pervaded by the quality
of foulness; and from this, men, in whom foulness (or
passion) predominates, were produced. Quickly aban-
doning that body, it became morning twilight, or the
dawn. At the appearance of this light of day, men
feel most vigour; while the progenitors are most powerful in the evening season. In this manner, Maitreya,
Jyotsná (dawn), Rátri (night), Ahan (day), and Sandhyá
(evening), are the four bodies of Brahmá invested by
the three qualities.[1]

---

[1] This account is given in several other Puráńas: in the Kúrma,
with more simplicity; in the Padma, Linga, and Váyu, with more
detail. The Bhágavata, as usual, amplifies still more copiously,
and mixes up much absurdity with the account. Thus, the person
of Sandhyá, 'evening twilight', is thus described: "She appeared
with eyes rolling with passion, whilst her lotos-like feet sounded
with tinkling ornaments; a muslin vest depended from her waist,
secured by a golden zone: her breasts were protuberant and close
together; her nose was elegant; her teeth, beautiful; her face
was bright with smiles, and she modestly concealed it with the
skirts of her robe; whilst the dark curls clustered round her
brow."† The Asuras address her, and win her to become their

---

* "Of the world" and "from his side" are adopted from the commentary.

† *Bhágavata-puráńa*, III., 20, 29-31:

सा ज्ष्वरलोचोनां मदविह्वलवोषनाम् ।
जाघीक्वमार्यिनमदुकुमाक्षम रोधमम् ।
ववोयावेचलोगुर्निरमर्पवोधराम् ।
कुमानां सुद्विषां स्निग्धशासलीजावलोकनाम् ॥
गृह्णती मीत्पावाज्ञान नीजावलदवर्छविणीम ।

Next, from Brahmá, in a form composed of the quality of foulness, was produced hunger, of whom anger
was born: and the god put forth, in darkness, beings
emaciate with hunger, of hideous aspects, and with
long beards. Those beings hastened to the deity. Such
of them as exclaimed Oh preserve us! were, thence,
called Rákshasas:[1*] others, who cried out Let us eat,

---

bride. To the four forms of our text the same work adds:
Tandri, 'sloth'; Jrimbhaña, 'yawning'; Nidrá, 'sleep'; Unmáda,
'insanity'; Antardhána, 'disappearance'; Pratibimba,† 'reflexion';
which become the property of Pisáchas, Kimnaras, Bhútas, Gandharvas, Vidyádharas, Sádhyas, Pitris, and Manus. The notions
of night, day, twilight, and moonlight being derived from Brahmá
seem to have originated with the Vedas. Thus, the commentator
on the Bhágavata observes: यास्य तनुरासीत्तामपाहत सा नासि-
कामभवदिति श्रुति: । 'That which was his body, and was left, was
darkness: this is the Sruti.' All the authorities place night before
day, and the Asuras or Titans, before the gods, in the order of
appearance; as did Hesiod and other ancient theogonists.

[1] From Raksh (रक्ष्), 'to preserve.'

---

* मैत्रो भो रक्षतामेष पैदर्भ राक्षास्तु ये ।
"Those among them that called out 'Not so: ah! let him be saved!'
were named Rákshasas."

It is related, in the Bhágavata-purána, III., 20, 19-21, that Brahmá
transformed himself into night, invested with a body. This the Yakshas
and Rákshasas seized upon, exclaiming "Do not spare it; devour it."
Brahmá cried out "Don't devour me; spare me."

The original of Brahmá's petition is: मा मां जहत रक्षत ।

For yaksha, as implied in jakshata, see the editor's fourth note in
the next page.

† The Bhágavata-purána has the strange term pratyátmya. Pratibimba
occurs in Srídhara Swámin's elucidation of it.

Jrimbhaña, just above, has been substituted for Professor Wilson's
jrimbhiká.

were denominated, from that expression, Yakshas.[1] Beholding them so disgusting, the hairs of Brahmá* were shrivelled up, and, first falling from his head, were again renewed upon it. From their falling, they became serpents, called Sarpa, from their creeping, and Ahi, because they had deserted the head.[2] The creator of the world, being incensed, then created fierce beings, who were denominated goblins, Bhútas (malignant fiends), and eaters of flesh.† The Gandharvas were next born, imbibing melody. Drinking of the goddess of speech, they were born, and thence their appellation.[3]

The divine Brahmá, influenced by their material energies, having created these beings, made others of his own will. Birds he formed from his vital vigour; sheep, from his breast; goats, from his mouth; kine, from his belly and sides; and horses, elephants, Śarabhas, Gayals, deer, camels, mules, antelopes,‡ and other

---

[1] From Yaksh (यक्ष),§ 'to eat.'

[2] From Sŕip (सृप्), serpu, 'to creep', and from Há (हा), 'to abandon.'

[3] Gám dhayantak (गां धयन्तः), 'drinking speech.'

* Vedhas, in the Sanskrit.

† These creatures were "fiends, frightful from being monkey-coloured, and carnivorous:"

वर्णेन कपिपिङ्गेनाथा भूताश्च पिशिताशिनः ।

‡ *Nyanku.*

§ Professor Wilson's "from that expression", in the text, answers to *jakshadrit.* According to the commentator, this word means "from eating"; for he takes *jaksh,* its base, to be a substitute for *yaksh.* The sense of *yaksh,* in classical Sanskrit, is "to venerate".

For the derivation of the words *rákshasa* and *yaksha,* see the *Linga-puráńa,* Prior Section, LXX., 227 and 228.

animals, from his feet; whilst from the hairs of his body sprang herbs, roots, and fruits.

Brahmá, having created, in the commencement of the Kalpa, various* plants, employed them in sacrifices, in the beginning of the Tretá age. Animals were distinguished into two classes, domestic (village) and wild (forest). The first class contained the cow, the goat, the hog,† the sheep, the horse, the ass, the mule; the latter, all beasts of prey,‡ and many animals with cloven hoofs, the elephant, and the monkey. The fifth order were the birds; the sixth, aquatic animals; and the seventh, reptiles and insects. [1]§

From his eastern mouth Brahmá then created the Gáyatrá metre, the Ŕig-veda, the collection of hymns termed Trivŕit, the Rathantara portion of the Sáma-veda, and the Agnishtoma sacrifice: from his southern mouth he created the Yajur-veda, the Traishťubha metre, the collection of hymns called Panchadasa, the Bŕihat Sáman, and the portion of the Sáma-veda termed Ukthya: from his western mouth he created

---

[1] This and the preceding enumeration of the origin of vegetables and animals occurs in several Puráńas, precisely in the same words. The Linga adds a specification of the Árańya or wild animals, which are said to be the buffalo, gayal, bear, monkey, Sarabha, wolf, and lion.

---

* Insert "sacrificial animals", pasú.

† The MSS. consulted by me have "man" purusha. The commentator observes, that, in the nara-medha, or human sacrifice, man is accounted a sacrificial animal. His words are: पुरुषो मनुष्य: । नरमेधे तख पशु-त्वकल्पनात् ।

‡ Swápada.

§ "Reptiles and Insects", sarishipa.

the Sáma-veda, the Jagatí metre, the collection of
hymns termed Saptadaśa, the portion of the Sáman
called Vairúpa, and the Atirátra sacrifice: and from his
northern mouth he created the Ekaviṅśa collection of
hymns, the Atharva-veda, the Áptoryáman rite, the
Anushṭubh metre, and the Vairája portion of the Sáma-
veda.[1][*]

---

[1] This specification of the parts of the Vedas that proceed
from Brahmá occurs, in the same words, in the Váyu, Linga,
Kúrma, Padma, and Márkańdeya Puráńas. The Bhágavata offers
some important varieties: "From his eastern and other mouths
he created the Ṛich, Yajus, Sáman, and Atharva Vedas; the
Sastra (शस्त्र) or 'the unuttered incantation'; Ijyá (इज्या), 'oblation'; Stuti (स्तुति) and Stoma (स्तोम), 'prayers' and 'hymns';
and Práyaśchitta (प्रायश्चित्त), 'explation', or 'sacred philosophy'
(Bráhma): also the Vedas of medicine, arms, music, and mechanics; and the Itihásas and Puráńas, which are a fifth Veda:
also the portions of the Vedas called Shodaśín, Ukthya, Purīshin,
Agnishṭut, Áptoryáman, Atirátra, Vájapeya, Gosava;[†] the four

---

[*] It is on the authority of the commentator, as supplementing the
text, that Gáyatra and Anushṭubh are here said to be metres; that
Agnishṭoma, Atirátra, and Áptoryáman are taken to denote parts of a
sacrifice, viz., of the Jyotishṭoma; and that Vairúpa and Vairája denominate sundry verses of the Sáma-veda. But the commentator also says
that Ukthya is, here, a stage of a sacrifice: सोमसंस्थाविशेष. He means
the Jyotishṭoma.

As to Áptoryáman, both in the *Vishńu-puráńa* and in the *Bhágavata*,
it is to be regarded as a Pauráńik alteration of the Vaidik Áptoryáma.

For Vairúpa and Vairája, see Benfey's Index to the Sáma-veda: *Indische
Studien*, Vol. III., p. 238.

Professor Wilson's "Gáyatrí", "Trishṭubh", and "Ukths" have been
corrected to Gáyatra, Traishṭubha, and Ukthya.

See, regarding the passage thus annotated, *Original Sanskrit Texts*,
Part III., pp. 6 and 7.

[†] These are not characterized, in the original, as "portions of the
Vedas". They are sacrificial proceedings.

In this manner, all creatures, great or small, proceeded from his limbs. The great progenitor of the

---

parts of virtue, purity, liberality, piety, and truth; the orders of life, and their institutes and different religious rites and professions; and the sciences of logic, ethics, and polity. The mystic words and monosyllable proceeded from his heart; the metre Ushńih, from the hairs of his body; Gáyatrí, from his skin; Trishťubh, from his flesh; Anushťubh, from his tendons; Jagatí, from his bones; Pankti, from his marrow; Brihatí, from his breath. The consonants were his life; the vowels, his body; the sibilants, his senses; the semi-vowels, his vigour."* This mysticism, although, perhaps, expanded and amplified by the Pauráńiks, appears to originate with the Vedas; as in the text यजुष्टमस्यायुषात्। 'The metre was of the tendons.' The different portions of the Vedas specified in the text are yet, for the most part, uninvestigated.

---

* *Bhágavata-puráńa*, III., 12, 37–41 and 44·47:

मैत्रेय उवाच।
ऋग्यजुःसामाथर्वाख्यान्वेदान्पूर्वादिभिर्मुखैः।
शास्त्रमिज्यां स्तुतिस्तोमं प्रायश्चित्तं व्यधात्क्रमात्॥
आयुर्वेदं धनुर्वेदं गान्धर्वं वेदमात्मनः।
स्थापत्यं चासृजद्वेदं क्रमात्पूर्वादिभिर्मुखैः॥
इतिहासपुराणानि पञ्चमं वेदमीश्वरः।
सर्वेभ्य एव वक्त्रेभ्यः ससृजे सर्वदर्शनः॥
षोडश्युक्थौ पूर्ववक्त्रात्पुरीष्याग्निष्टुतावथ।
आप्तोर्यामातिरात्रौ च वाजपेयं सगोसवम्॥
विद्या दानं तपः सत्यं धर्मस्येति पदानि च।
आश्रमांश्च यथासंख्यमसृजत्सह वृत्तिभिः॥
* * * * * * * *
सांवित्रिकी विद्या वार्ता दण्डनीतिस्तथैव च।
एवं व्याहृतयश्चासन्प्रणवो ह्यस्य दह्रतः॥
तस्योष्णिगासील्लोमभ्यो गायत्री च त्वचो विभोः।
त्रिष्टुम्मांसात्स्नुतोऽनुष्टुब्जगत्यस्थ्नः प्रजापतेः॥
मज्जायाः पङ्क्तिरुत्पन्ना बृहती प्राणतोऽभवत्।
स्पर्शस्तस्याभवज्जीवः स्वरो देह उदाहृतः॥
ऊष्माणमिन्द्रियाण्याहुरन्तःस्था बलमात्मनः।

world, having formed the gods, demons, and Pitṛís,* created, in the commencement of the Kalpa, the Yakshas, Piśáchas (goblins), Gandharvas, and the troops of Apsarasas, the nymphs of heaven, Naras (centaurs, or beings with the limbs of horses and human bodies), and Kiṃnaras (beings† with the heads of horses), Rákshasas, birds, beasts, deer, serpents, and all things permanent or transitory, movable or immovable. This did the divine Brahmá, the first creator and lord of all. And these things, being created, discharged the same functions as they had fulfilled in a previous creation,‡ whether malignant or benign, gentle or cruel, good or evil, true or false; and, accordingly as they are actuated by such propensities, will be their conduct.

And the creator§ displayed infinite variety in the objects of sense, in the properties of living things, and in the forms of bodies. He determined, in the beginning, by the authority of the Vedas, the names and forms and functions of all creatures, and of the gods; and the names and appropriate offices of the Rishis, as they also are read in the Vedas.‖

In like manner as the products of the seasons designate, in periodical revolution, the return of the same season, so do the same circumstances indicate the recurrence of the same Yuga or age; and thus, in the beginning of each Kalpa, does Brahmá repeatedly create the world, possessing the power that is derived

---

* Add "men", *manushyn.*

† Literally, "men", *manushya.*

‡ See *Original Sanskrit Texts*, Part I., p. 21.

§ Supply Dhátṛí, a name of Brahmá.

‖ See *Original Sanskrit Texts*, Part III., p. 4, second foot-note.

from the will to create, and assisted by the natural and essential faculty of the object to be created.*

* यथर्तावृतुलिङ्गानि नानारूपाणि पर्य्यये ।
दृश्यन्ते तानि तान्येव तथा भावा युगादिषु ॥
करोतेर्वंविधां सृष्टिं कल्पादौ च पुन: पुन: ।
सिसृक्षाशक्तियुक्तोऽसौ सृज्यशक्तिप्रचोदित: ॥

"As, in every season, multifarious tokens are, in turn, beheld thereof, so, at the beginnings of the Yugas, it is with their products. Possessed of the desire and of the power to create, and impelled by the potencies of what is to be created, again and again does he, at the onset of a Kalpa, put forth a similar creation."

The writer may have had in mind a stanza of the *Mánava-dharma-śástra*: I., 30.

CHAPTER VI.

MAITREYA.—Thou hast briefly noticed, illustrious sage, the creation termed Arváksrotas, or that of mankind. Now explain to me more fully how Brahmá accomplished it; how he created the four different castes;* what duties he assigned to the Brahmans and the rest.[1]

PARÁSARA.—Formerly, O best of Brahmans, when the truth-meditating† Brahmá was desirous of creating the world, there sprang, from his mouth, beings especially endowed with the quality of goodness; others, from his breast, pervaded by the quality of foulness; others, from his thighs, in whom foulness and darkness prevailed; and others, from his feet, in whom the quality of darkness predominated. These were, in succession, beings of the several castes,—Brahmans, Kshatriyas, Vaisyas, and Súdras; produced from the mouth,

---

[1] The creation of mankind here described is rather out of its place, as it precedes the birth of the Prajápatis, or their progenitors. But this want of method is common to the Puráńas, and is evidence of their being compilations from various sources.

* Add "and with what qualities": गुणांश्च ।

† *Satyábhidháyin,* "true to his will." The commentator here, for the second time, explains it by *satya-sankalpa.* See my second note in p. 73, *supra.*

the breast, the thighs, and the feet, of Brahmá.[1] These
he created for the performance of sacrifices; the four
castes being the fit instruments of their celebration.[*]
By sacrifices, O thou who knowest the truth, the gods
are nourished; and, by the rain which they bestow,
mankind are supported:[2] and thus sacrifices, the source
of happiness, are performed by pious men, attached to
their duties, attentive to prescribed obligations, and
walking in the paths of virtue. Men acquire (by them)
heavenly fruition, or final felicity: they go, after death,
to whatever sphere they aspire to, as the consequence
of their human nature. The beings who were created
by Brahmá, of these four castes, were, at first, endowed
with righteousness and perfect faith; they abode wherever they pleased, unchecked by any impediment; their
hearts were free from guile; they were pure, made free
from soil, by observance of sacred institutes. In their
sanctified minds Hari dwelt; and they were filled with
perfect wisdom, by which they contemplated the glory

---

[1] This original of the four castes is given in Manu,† and in
most of the Puráṇas. We shall see, however, that the distinctions
are subsequently ascribed to voluntary election, to accident, or
to positive institutions.

[2] According to Manu, oblations ascend to and nourish the
sun; whence the rain falls upon earth, and causes the growth of
corn.‡ Burnt-offerings are, therefore, the final causes of the support
of mankind.

---

[*] See *Original Sanskrit Texts*, Part I., pp. 21 and 22.
† In the *Mánava-dharma-śástra*, I., 31, the Kshatriya is said to have
proceeded from the arms of Brahmá. And so state the *Purusha-súkta*
of the *Rig-veda*, &c.
‡ *Mánava-dharma-śástra*, III., 76.

of Vishńu.[1] After a while, (after the Tretá age had
continued for some period), that portion of Hari which
has been described as one with Kála (time) infused into
created beings sin, as yet feeble, though formidable,
or passion and the like—the impediment of soul's liberation, the seed of iniquity, sprung from darkness and
desire. The innate perfectness of human nature was
then no more evolved: the eight kinds of perfection,
Rasollásá and the rest, were impaired;[2] and, these

---

[1] This description of a pure race of beings is not of general
occurrence in the Puráńas. It seems here to be abridged from a
much more detailed account in the Brahmáńda, Váyu, and Márkańdeya Puráńas. In those works, Brahmá is said to create, in
the beginning of the Kalpa, a thousand pairs of each of the four
classes of mankind, who enjoy perfect happiness during the Kríta
age, and only gradually become subject to infirmities, as the
Tretá or second age advances.

[2] These eight perfections or Siddhis are not the supernatural
faculties obtained by the performance of the Yoga. They are
described, the commentator says, in the Skanda and other works;
and from them he extracts their description: 1. Rasollásá, the
spontaneous or prompt evolution of the juices of the body, inde-
pendently of nutriment from without: 2. Trípti, mental satisfaction, or freedom from sensual desire: 3. Sámya, sameness of
degree: 4. Tulyatá, similarity of life, form, and feature: 5. Visoká,
exemption alike from infirmity or grief: 6. Consummation of
pannnce and meditation, by attainment of true knowledge: 7. The
power of going everywhere at will: 8. The faculty of reposing
at any time or in any place.[*] These attributes are alluded to,

---

[*] I add the text from MSS, at my disposal. To judge from Professor
Wilson's translation, his text must have been rather different.

एष सत एवाम्रद्राष: श्रान्त्यो युमे ।
एषोत्रात्रात्रा श्रा त्रिव्रिक्तया त्रृति युष्र नर: ॥

being enfeebled, and sin gaining strength, mortals were
afflicted with pain, arising from susceptibility to con-
trasts, (as heat and cold, and the like)." They therefore
constructed places of refuge, protected by trees, by
mountains, or by water; surrounded them by a ditch
or a wall, and formed villages and cities: and in them
erected appropriate dwellings, as defences against the
sun and the cold.' Having thus provided security

though obscurely, in the Váyu, and are partly specified in the
Márkańdeya Puráńa. †

' In the other three Puráńas, in which this legend has been
found, the different kinds of inhabited places are specified and
introduced by a series of land measures. Thus, the Márkańdeya;
states that 10 Paramáńus = 1 Parasúkshma; 10 Parasúkshmas =
1 Trasareńu; 10 Trasareńus = 1 particle of dust or Mahírajas;

स्थ्यादिभिरपेषेव सदा मृत्राः प्रजास्तदा ।
द्वितीया सिद्धिरहिता वा भूमिर्मुनिसत्तमैः ॥
यधमौक्तमलं नास्त्वार्धा वा तृतीयाभिधीयते ।
चतुर्थी तुक्ला नाधामायुः शुभरूपधीः ॥
रैवाम्यवक्वाकृर्च विशोका नाम पञ्चमी ।
परमार्थपरस्त्रेन तपोध्यानादिनिछना ॥
यथी निकामचारित्वं सप्तमी विविच्यते ।
यद्धमी च तथा मोक्षा यथक्रवन याथिता ॥

* See Original Sanskrit Texts, Part I., pp. 22 and 23.
† XLIX., 18, et seq.   : XLIX., 36-40.

मानार्थानि प्रमाथानि साधु पूर्वं प्रचक्षिरे ॥
परमाणुः परं सूक्ष्मं त्रसरेणुर्महीरजः ।
बालाग्रं चैव लिक्षा च यूका याव यवोदरम् ॥
क्रमादष्टगुणाम्बाह्यर्धयान्यष्टो ततो ४ ङुलम् ।
बहुगुलं पदं तच्च वितस्तिर्विर्गुणं स्मृतम् ॥
द्वे वितस्ती तथा हस्तो ब्रह्मनीर्घार्दिर्घाहत: ।
चतुर्हस्तं धनुर्दण्डो नालिका युगमेव च ॥
क्रोशो धनुःसहस्रे द्वे गव्यूतिश्च चतुर्गुलम् ।
मौलं च योजनं प्राहुः संख्यानार्थमिदं परम् ॥

against the weather, men next began to employ themselves in manual labour, as a means of livelihood, (and

---

10 Mahírajasas = 1 Bálágra, 'hair's point'; 10 Bálágras = 1 Likhyá; 10 Likhyás = 1 Yúká; 10 Yúkás = 1 heart of barley (Yavodara); 10 Yavodaras = 1 grain of barley of middle size; 10 barley-grains = 1 finger, or inch; 6 fingers = a Pada or foot (the breadth of it); 2 Padas = 1 Vitasti or span; 2 spans = 1 Hasta or cubit; 4 Hastas = a Dhanus, a Daúda or staff, or 2 Nádikás; 2000 Dhanusas = a Gavyúti; 4 Gavyútis = a Yojana. The measurement of the Brahmáńda is less detailed. A span from the thumb to the first finger is a Pradeśa; to the middle finger, a Tála;* to the third finger, a Gokarńa; and, to the little finger, a Vitasti, which is equal to twelve Angulas or fingers; understanding, thereby, according to the Váyu, a joint of the finger (अङ्गुलपर्वाणि). According to other authorities, it is the breadth of the thumb at the tip.

For this passage, I have used manuscripts, in preference to the Calcutta edition of the *Márkańdeya-puráńa*. According to my text, the measures noted are as follows:

A *paramáńu* is a *para súkshma*, ultimate minimum; or the sense may be

8 *paramáńu*	= 1 *para súkshma*.
8 *para súkshma*	= 1 *trasareńu*.
8 *trasareńu*	= 1 *mahírajas*.
8 *mahírajas*	= 1 *bálágra*.
8 *bálágra*	= 1 *likhá*.
8 *likhá*	= 1 *yúká*.
8 *yúká*	= 1 *gavodara*.
8 *gavodara*	= 1 *angula*.
8 *angula*	= 1 *pada*.
2 *pada*	= 1 *vitasti*.
2 *vitasti*	= 1 *hasta*, long cubit.
4 *hasta*	= 1 *dhanurdańda*, bow-staff.
2 *dhanurdańda*	= 1 *náliká*.
2000 *dhanus*	= 1 *krośa*.
2 *krośa*	= 1 *gavyúti*.
4 *gavyúti*	= 1 *yojana*.

Compare Colebrooke, *Asiatic Researches*, Vol. V., pp. 103 and 104.
* Corrected from Professor Wilson's "Nala".

cultivated) the seventeen kinds of useful grain—rice,
barley, wheat, millet, sesamum, panic,* and various

(A. R., Vol. V., 104.) The Váyu, giving similar measurements,† upon
the authority of Manu: (मनोर्वाणि प्रमाणानि), although such a
statement does not occur in the Manu Sanhitá, adds, that 21
fingers = 1 Ratni; 24 fingers = 1 Hasta or cubit; 2 Ratnis = 1 Kishku;
1 Hastas = 1 Dhanus; 2000 Dhanusas = 1 Gavyúti; and 8000 Dhanusas = 1 Yojana. Durgas or stronghold are of four kinds; three
of which are natural, from their situation in mountains, amidst
water, or in other inaccessible spots. The fourth is the artificial
defences of a village (Gráma), a hamlet (Khetaka), or a city
(Pura or Nagara), which are, severally, half the size of the next
in the series. The best kind of city is one which is about a mile
long by half a mile broad, built in the form of a parallelogram,
facing the north-east, and surrounded by a high wall and ditch.
A hamlet should be a Yojana distant from a city; a village, half
a Yojana from a hamlet. The roads leading to the cardinal points
from a city should be twenty Dhanusas (above 100 feet) broad:

---

* "Millet" and "panic", *aṇu* and *priyangu*.

† अष्टाभ्यदैर्गाव्वा बालः प्रादेय उच्यते ।
ताल: कृतो मध्यमया गौवर्षिशाखानामया ॥
कानिष्ठया वितस्तिस्तु प्रादेशस्तु उच्यते ।
रत्निर्भुजपर्वाणि संख्यया त्रिविंशतिः ॥
चतुर्विंशतिभिश्च एता: खादहुनानि (-नां ?) तु ।
किष्कु: कृतो द्वारत्निस्तु द्विपलार्घादहुस्तम् ॥
चतुर्दशं धनुर्दण्डो नालिका पुगमेव च ।
धनु:सहस्रे द्वे तन गव्युतिर्विभाव्यते ॥
षष्टौ धनु:सहस्राणि योजनं निर्दिश्यते ।

‡ In one of the four MSS. of the *Váyu-puráṇa* that I have consulted,
the verses quoted in the last note are introduced by a stanza and a half,
at the beginning of which are the words मनोर्वाणि प्रमाणानि । But
these words mean nothing; and there is no reference to Manu. We here
simply have a clerical error. In place of the opening words of the passage
cited, in p. 92, from the *Márkaṇḍeya-puráṇa*. The forementioned MS. of
the *Váyu-puráṇa* must have been transcribed from a somewhat ancient
copy, or from one in the Bengali character.

sorts of lentils, beans, and pease.[1] These are the kinds
cultivated for domestic use. But there are fourteen
kinds* which may be offered in sacrifice. They are: rice,
barley, Másha, wheat, millet, and sesamum; Priyangu
is the seventh, and Kulatthaka, pulse, the eighth. The
others are: Syámáka, a sort of panic; Nívára, unculti-
vated rice; Jartila, wild sesamum; Gavedhuká (coix
barbata); Markaťaka, wild panic; and (a plant called)
the seed or barley of the Bambu (Veńnyava).† These,

a village road should be the same: a boundary road, ten Dhanusas: a royal or principal road or street should be ten Dhanusas
(above fifty feet) broad: a cross or branch road should be four
Dhanusas. Lanes and paths amongst the houses are two Dhanusas
in breadth; footpaths, four cubits; the entrance of a house, three
cubits; the private entrances and paths about the mansion, of still
narrower dimensions.‡ Such were the measurements adopted by
the first builders of cities, according to the Puránas specified.

[1] These are enumerated in the text, as well as in the Váyu
and Márkańdeya Puránas, and are: Udára, a sort of grain with
long stalks (perhaps a holcus); Koradúsha (Paspalum kora);
Chínaka, a sort of panic (Paspalum miliaceum); Másha, kidney
bean (Phaseolus radiatus); Mudga (Phaseolus mungo); Masúra,
lentil (Ervum hirsutum); Nishpáva, a sort of pulse; Kulatthaka
(Dolichos biflorus); Ádhakí (Cytisus cajanus); Chańaka, chick
pea (Cicer arietinum); and Sańa (Crotolaria).

* Supply "cultivated and wild", घान्यारएशाच ।

† The *Márkańdeya-purána*, XLIX., 70, *et seq.*, omits *udaka*, but, by
compensation, inserts *kurubinda* between *gavedhuká* and *markaťaka*. The
MSS. I have seen of that Puráńa afford no warrant for such readings of
the edition in the *Bibliotheca Indica* as *yartila* for *jartila*, *velugradha*
for *veńvyava*, and, in the preceding list, *gaúa* for *úúúa*.

The *Váyu-puráńa*, though professing to name only fourteen vegetable
productions that may be used in sacrifice, names all that are mentioned
in the *Vishńu-puráńa*, and one more. The fifteenth is *kurubinda*.

‡ *Márkańdeya-puráńa*, XLIX., 41, *et seq.*

cultivated or wild, are the fourteen grains that were produced for purposes of offering in sacrifice; and sacrifice (the cause of ruin) is their origin also. They, again, with sacrifice, are the great cause of the perpetuation of the human race; as those understand who can discriminate cause and effect. Thence sacrifices were offered daily; the performance of which, O best of Munis, is of essential service to mankind, and expiates the offences of those by whom they are observed. Those, however, in whose hearts the drop of sin derived from Time (Kála) was still more developed, assented not to sacrifices, but reviled both them and all that resulted from them, the gods, and the followers of the Vedas. Those abusers of the Vedas, of evil disposition and conduct, and seceders from the path of enjoined duties, were plunged in wickedness.[1]*

The means of subsistence having been provided for the beings he had created, Brahmá prescribed laws suited to their station and faculties, the duties of the several castes and orders,[2] and the regions of those of

---

[1] This allusion to the sects hostile to the Vedas—Buddhists or Jainas—does not occur in the parallel passages of the Váyu and Márkańdeya Puráńas.

[2] The Váyu goes further than this, and states that the castes were now first divided according to their occupations; having, indeed, previously stated that there was no such distinction in the Krita age:

वर्णाश्रमव्यवस्थां च तदासीच्च शंकर: ।

Brahmá now appointed those who were robust and violent to be Kshatriyas, to protect the rest; those who were pure and pious he made Brahmans; those who were of less power, but industrious,

* See *Original Sanskrit Texts*, Part I., p. 23.

the different castes who were observant of their duties.[*]
The heaven of the Pitris is the region of devout Brahmans; the sphere of Indra, of Kshatriyas who fly not
from the field. The region of the winds is assigned to
the Vaisyas who are diligent in their occupations; and
submissive Súdras are elevated to the sphere of the
Gandharvas. Those Brahmans who lead religious lives
go to the world of the eighty-eight thousand saints;
and that of the seven Rishis is the seat of pious anchorets and hermits. The world of ancestors is that
of respectable householders; and the region of Brahmá

---

and addicted to cultivate the ground, he made Vaisyas; whilst
the feeble and poor of spirit were constituted Súdras. And he
assigned them their several occupations, to prevent that interference with one another which had occurred as long as they recognized no duties peculiar to castes.†

[*] See *Original Sanskrit Texts*, Part I., p. 23. The original has Praja
pati in place of "Brahmá". "Orders" renders *ásrama*.

† [illegible Sanskrit verses]

For another translation of this passage, and several various readings,
see *Original Sanskrit Texts*, Part I., pp. 30 and 31.

is the asylum of religious mendicants.'* The imperishable region of the Yogins is the highest seat of Vishńu, where they perpetually meditate upon the supreme being,† with minds intent on him alone. The sphere where they reside the gods themselves cannot behold.‡ The sun, the moon, the planets,§ shall repeatedly be and cease to be; but those who internally repeat the mystic adoration of the divinity shall never know decay.

---

¹ These worlds, some of which will be more particularly described in a different section, are the seven Lokas or spheres above the earth: 1. Prájápatya or Pitri-loka: 2. Indra-loka or Swarga: 3. Marut-loka or Diva-loka, heaven: 4. Gandharva-loka, the region of celestial spirits; also called Mahar-loka: 5. Jana-loka or the sphere of saints. Some copies read eighteen thousand; others, as in the text, which is also the reading of the Padma Puráńa: 6. Tapo-loka, the world of the seven sages: and 7. Brahma-loka or Satya-loka, the world of infinite wisdom and truth. The eighth, or high world of Vishńu, विष्णो: परमं पदम् । is a sectarial addition, which, in the Bhágavata, is called Vaikuńṭha, and, in the Brahma Vaivarta, Go-loka; both, apparently, and, most certainly, the last, modern inventions.

---

* "Heaven of the Pitṛis" and "world of ancestors": in the original, Prájápatya. "Region of the winds" and "sphere of the Gandharvas", Márnta and Gándharva. "Brahmans who lead religious lives", gururdsin; which the commentator explains as meaning conventuals abiding for life with a spiritual guide, and devoted to theology. They are said to inherit the region of the Válikhilyas and other high saints. "Pious anchorets and hermits", vanaukas; the same as vánaprastha. "Religious mendicants", mydsin; one with sannyásin. The original leaves "householders" unqualified.

† Brahma, in the Sanskrit.

‡ Such MSS. as I have consulted exhibit the reading:

तेषां मध्यरतं ज्ञानं वयु पश्यन्ति सूरय: ।

§ "The sun, the moon, and other planets." The original is in the note following.

For those who neglect their duties, who revile the
Vedas, and obstruct religious rites, the places assigned,
after death, are the terrific regions of darkness, of deep
gloom, of fear, and of great terror, the fearful hell of
sharp swords, the hell of scourges and of a waveless
sea.[1][2]

---

[1] The divisions of Naraka or hell, here named, are again more
particularly enumerated, b. II., c. 6.

---

[2] यस्मा यस्मा विषयांके चक्षुसूर्यादयो यथा: ।
 यदापि न विषयांके द्वादशाक्षरीयकमका: ॥
 नामिखन्यतामिषं महारौरवरौरवौ ।
 यक्षियकयं चौरं आज्ञकूषमयीचिमत् ॥
 विमिबृकानां वेदेख यज्ञव्याघातकारिणाम् ।
 ग्राम्मैतत्समाख्यातं खधर्मत्यागिनश्च ॥

The द्वादशाक्षर, or "*spell of twelve syllables*",—Professor Wilson's
"mystic adoration of the divinity",—consists of the words ॐ नमो
भगवते वासुदेवाय । Also see the Professor's *Sanskrit Dictionary*, sub
voce द्वादशाक्षरमन्त्र.

CHAPTER VII.

PARÁŚARA.—From Brahmá, continuing to meditate,
were born mind-engendered progeny, with forms and
faculties derived from his corporeal nature; embodied
spirits, produced from the person* of that all-wise† deity.
All these beings, from the gods to inanimate things, appeared as I have related to you;[1] being the abode of the
three qualities. But, as they did not multiply themselves,
Brahmá created other mind-born sons, like himself;
namely: Bhrígu, Pulastya, Pulaha, Kratu, Angiras,
Maríchi, Daksha, Atri, and Vasishtha. These are the
nine Brahmás (or Brahmarshis) celebrated in the Puránas.[2]‡ Sanandana and the other sons of Brahmá§

---

[1] It is not clear which of the previous narratives is here referred to; but it seems most probable that the account in pp. 70-72
is intended.

[2] Considerable variety prevails in this list of Prajápatis, Brah-
maputras, Brahmás, or Brahmarshis; but the variations are of

---

* Literally, "limbs", *gátra*.
† *Dhímat.*
‡ See *Original Sanskrit Texts*, Part I., pp. 24, 25, and 30.
§ Vedhas, in the Sanskrit.

were previously created by him. But they were without
desire or passion, inspired with holy wisdom, estranged

---

the nature of additions made to an apparently original enumera-
tion of but seven, whose names generally recur. Thus, in the
Mahábhárata, Moksha Dharma, we have, in one place, Marichi,
Atri, Angiras, Pulastya, Pulaha, Kratu, and Vasishtha:

मरीचि: सप्त वै पुत्रा महात्मान: स्वयम्भुव: ।[*]

'the seven high-minded sons of the self-born Brahmá.' In another
place of the same, however, we have Daksha substituted for
Vasishtha:

मनसैवसृजे पुत्रान् मानसान् स्वेन तेजसा ।
मरीचिमत्र्यंगिरसौ पुलस्त्यं पुलहं क्रतुम् ॥[†]

'Brahmá then created mind-begotten sons, of whom Daksha was
the seventh, with Marichi', &c. These seven sons of Brahmá are
also identified with the seven Rishis; as in the Váyu:

भृगु: समर्यङस्तीव अत्यश्वा: समानबा: ।
पुलहे वसिष्ठश्चैव सर्वमेव स्वयम्भुव: ॥

although, with palpable inconsistency, eight are immediately
enumerated; or: Bhrigu, Marichi, Atri, Angiras, Pulastya, Pulaha,
Kratu, and Vasishtha. The Uttara Kháńda of the Padma Puráńa
substitutes Kardama for Vasishtha. The Bhágavata includes
Daksha, enumerating nine.[‡] The Matsya agrees with Manu, in
adding Nárada to the list of our text. The Kúrma Puráńa adds
Dharma and Sankalpa. The Linga, Brahmáńda, and Váyu Puráńas also add them, and extend the list to Adharma and Ruchi.
The Hari Vamśa, in one place, inserts Gautama, and, in another,
Manu. Altogether, therefore, we have seventeen, instead of seven.
But the accounts given of the origin of several of these show
that they were not, originally, included amongst the Mánasaputras
or sons of Brahmá's mind; for even Daksha, who finds a place
in all the lists except one of those given in the Mahábhárata, is

---

[*] Śánti-parvan, 7569, 7570; and see 13075.

[†] Ibid., 7534.

[‡] The Bhágavata-puráńa, III., 12, 22, includes Daksha and Nárada;
thus enumerating ten.

from the universe, and undesirous of progeny. This
when Brahmá perceived, he was filled with wrath

---

uniformly said to have sprung from Brahmá's thumb: and the
same patriarch, as well as Dharma, is included, in some accounts,
as in the Bhágavata and Matsya Puráńas, amongst a different
series of Brahmá's progeny, or virtues and vices; or: Daksha
(dexterity), Dharma (virtue), Káma (desire), Krodha (passion),
Lobha (covetousness), Moha (infatuation), Mada (insanity), Pra-
moda (pleasure), Mrityu (death), and Angaja (lust). These are
severally derived from different parts of Brahmá's body; and the
Bhágavata, adding Kardama (soil, or sin) to this enumeration,
makes him spring from Brahmá's shadow. The simple statement
that the first Prajápatis sprang from the mind, or will, of Brahmá,
has not contented the depraved taste of the mystics; and, in some
of the Puráńas, as the Bhágavata, Linga, and Váyu, they also
are derived from the body of their progenitor; or: Bhrigu, from
his skin; Marichi, from his mind; Atri, from his eyes; Angiras,
from his mouth; Pulastya, from his ear; Pulaha, from his navel;
Kratu, from his hand; Vasishťha, from his breath; Daksha, from
his thumb; and Nárada, from his hip. They do not exactly agree,
however, in the places whence these beings proceed; as, for instance, according to the Linga, Marichi springs from Brahmá's
eyes, not Atri, who, there, proceeds, instead of Pulastya, from
his ears. The Váyu has, also, another account of their origin,
and states them to have sprung from the fires of a sacrifice offered
by Brahmá; an allegorical mode of expressing their probable
original,—considering them to be, in some degree, real persons,—
from the Brahmanical ritual, of which they were the first institu-
tors and observers. The Váyu Puráńa also states, that, besides
the seven primitive Rishis, the Prajápatis are numerous, and
specifies Kardama, Kaśyapa, Sesha, Vikránta, Suśravas, Bahu-
putra, Kumára, Viraswat, Suchiśravas, Prácheta (Daksha),
Arishťanemi, Bahula. These and many others were Prajápatis:

रुद्रवमाद्योऽङैऽपि बहुषु प्रवित्रता: ।

In the beginning of the Mahábhárata (Ádi Parvan), we have, again,
a different origin; and, first, Daksha, the son of the Prachetasas, is

capable of consuming the three worlds, the flame of which invested, like a garland, heaven, earth, and hell. Then from his forehead, darkened with angry frowns, sprang Rudra,[1] radiant as the noon-tide sun, fierce,

---

is said, had seven sons, after whom the twenty-one Prajápatis were born, or appeared. According to the commentator, the seven sons of Daksha were the allegorical persons Krodha, Tamas, Dama, Vikrita, Angiras, Kardama, and Aśwa; and the twenty-one Prajápatis, the seven usually specified,—Maríchi and the rest,—and the fourteen Manus. This looks like a blending of the earlier and later notions.

[1] Besides this general notice of the origin of Rudra and his separate forms, we have, in the next chapter, an entirely different set of beings so denominated; and the eleven alluded to in the text are also more particularly enumerated in a subsequent chapter. The origin of Rudra, as one of the agents in creation, is described in most of the Puránas. The Mahábhárata, indeed, refers his origin to Vishńu; representing him as the personification of his anger, whilst Brahmá is that of his kindness:

तमः: सर्वे अनाटाव तुतो देवज यै तथा ।
कोपाविाद्य सर्वे रुद्र: संहारकारक: ।
एतौ हौ विशुभमेषी प्रसादक्रोधजावुभी ।
तदादितिनयमायौ सृष्टिसंहारकारकौ ।[a]

The Kúrma Puráńa makes him proceed from Brahmá's mouth, whilst engaged in meditating on creation. The Varáha Puráńa makes this appearance of Rudra the consequence of a promise made by Śiva to Brahmá, that he would become his son. In the parallel passages in other Puránas, the progeny of the Rudra created by Brahmá is not confined to the eleven, but comprehends infinite numbers of beings, in person and equipments like their parent; until Brahmá, alarmed at their fierceness, numbers, and immortality, desires his son Rudra, or, as the Matsya calls him, Vámadeva, to form creatures of a different and mortal nature. Rudra refusing to do this, desists; whence his name Sthánu, from Sthá, 'to stay'. Linga, Váyu Puráńas, &c.

[a] *Mahábhárata, Sánti-parvan,* 13146-7.

and of vast bulk, and of a figure which was half male,
half female. Separate yourself, Brahmá said to him,
and, having so spoken, disappeared; obedient to which
command, Rudra became twofold, disjoining his male
and female natures. His male being he again divided
into eleven persons, of whom some were agreeable,
some hideous; some fierce, some mild.* And he multiplied his female nature manifold, of complexions black
or white.'†

Then Brahmá' created, himself, the Manu Swáyam-

---

¹ According to the Váyu, the female became, first, twofold,
or one half white, and the other, black; and each of these, again,
becomes manifold, being the various energies or Śaktis of Mahádeva, as stated by the Kúrma, after the words एतस्यैतर्जिनी: चिते: ।
which are those of our text:

ता वै विभूतयो विश्रा विभुताः: प्रभवो भुवि ।

The Linga and Váyu specify many of their names. Those of
the white complexion, or mild nature, include Lakshmi, Saraswati,
Gaurí, Umá, &c.; those of the dark hue, and fierce disposition,
Durgá, Káli, Chańdi, Maháráiri, and others.

* Brahmá, after detaching from himself the property of anger,
in the form of Rudra, converted himself into two persons, the
first male, or the Manu Swáyańbhuva, and the first woman, or
Śatarúpá. So, in the Vedas: सवात्मा वै पुत्रो नामासीत् ।: 'So
himself was indeed (his) son.' The commencement of production
through sexual agency is here described with sufficient distinctness; but the subject has been rendered obscure by a more com-

---

* According to the commentator, "fierce" and "mild" are exepegetical
of "agreeable" and "hideous".

† See *Original Sanskrit Texts*, Part IV., p. 331.

: This quotation requires to be slightly altered. The commentator,
after citing चात्रात्मनेव from the *Vishńu-purána*, proceeds: चात्रा वै
पुत्रनामावीति श्रुति: । These words, ending with पुत्रनामावि, are
from the *Śatapatha-bráhmańa*, XIV., 9, 4, 26.

bhuva, born of, and identical with, his original self,
for the protection of created beings: and the female

---

plicated succession of agents, and, especially, by the introduction
of a person of a mythic or mystical character, Viráj. The notion
is thus expressed in Manu: "Having divided his own substance,
the mighty power Brahmá became half male and half female;
and from that female he produced Viráj. Know me to be that
person whom the male Viráj produced by himself." I. 32, 33. [*]
We have, therefore, a series of Brahmá, Viráj, and Manu, instead
of Brahmá and Manu only; also the generation of progeny by
Brahmá, begotten on Śatarúpá, instead of her being, as in our
text, the wife of Manu. The idea seems to have originated with
the Vedas, as Kullúka Bhaṭṭa quotes a text: ततो विराडजायत ।
'Then (or thence) Viráj was born'. The procreation of progeny
by Brahmá, however, is at variance with the whole system,
which, almost invariably, refers his creation to the operation of
his will: and the expression, in Manu, तस्यां स विराजमसृजत् ।
'he created Viráj in her', does not necessarily imply sexual intercourse. Viráj also creates, not begets, Manu. And in neither
instance does the name of Śatarúpá occur. The commentator on
Manu, however, understands the expression Asŕijat to imply the
procreation of Viráj: मैथुनेन धर्मेण । and the same interpretation
is given by the Matsya Puráṇa, in which the incestuous passion
of Brahmá for Śatarúpá,—his daughter, in one sense, his sister,
in another,—is described; and by her he begets Viráj, who there
is called, not the progenitor of Manu, but Manu himself:

ततः कायेन मनुना तस्याः पुत्रोऽसमभवत् ।
स्वायंभुव इति ख्यातः स विराडिति यः सुतम् ॥ [†]

This, therefore, agrees with our text, as far as it makes Manu
the son of Brahmá, though not as to the nature of the connexion.

---

[*] द्विधा कृत्वात्मनो देहमर्धेन पुरुषोऽभवत् ।
अर्धेन नारी तस्यां स विराजमसृजत्प्रभुः ॥
तपस्तप्त्वासृजद्यं तु स स्वयं पुरुषो विराट् ।
तं मां वित्तास्य सर्वस्य स्रष्टारं द्विजसत्तमाः ॥

[†] *Matsya-puráṇa*, III., 49, 50.

portion of himself he constituted Śatarúpá, whom
austerity purified from the sin (of forbidden nuptials),

The reading of the Agni and Padma Puráńas is that of the
Vishńu: and the Bhágavata agrees with it, in one place; stating,
distinctly, that the male half of Brahmá was Manu, the other
half, Śatarúpá:

यस्य नप पुमास्तोऽभूयत्: स्त्वर्धभुव: सरात् ।
स्त्री यासीकुसद्रुपाज्ञा महिबज महाक्रम: ॥

Bhágavata, III., 12, 53, 54: and, although the production of Viráj
is elsewhere described, it is neither as the son of Brahmá nor
the father of Manu. The original and simple idea, therefore,
appears to be, the identity of Manu with the male half of Brahmá,
and his being, thence, regarded as his son. The Kúrma Puráńa
gives the same account as Manu, and in the same words. The
Linga Puráńa and Váyu Puráńa describe the origin of Viráj and
Śatarúpá from Brahmá; and they intimate the union of Śatarúpá
with Purusha or Viráj, the male portion of Brahmá, in the first
instance, and, in the second, with Manu, who is termed Vairája,
or the son of Viráj: वैराजस्य मनुः सुतः । The Brahma Puráńa,
the words of which are repeated in the Hari Vaṃśa, introduces
a new element of perplexity, in a new name, that of Ápava.
According to the commentator, this is a name of the Prajápati
Vaśishťha: वायवर्यविविशापदनात: प्रजापति: । As, however, he
performs the office of Brahmá, he should be regarded as that
divinity. But this is not exactly the case, although it has been
so rendered by the French translator. Ápava becomes twofold,
and, in the capacity of his male half, begets offspring by the female. Again, it is said Vishńu created Viráj, and Viráj created
the male, which is Vairája or Manu; who was, thus, the second
interval (Antara) or stage in creation. That is, according to the
commentator, the first stage was the creation of Ápava, or Vaśishťha, or Viráj, by Vishńu, through the agency of Hiraṇyagarbha
or Brahmá; and the next was that of the creation of Manu by
Viráj. Śatarúpá appears as, first, the bride of Ápava, and then
as the wife of Manu. This account, therefore, although obscurely
expressed, appears to be essentially the same with that of Manu;

and whom the divine Manu Swáyambhuva took to wife.
From these two were born two sons, Priyavrata and

---

and we have Brahmá, Viráj, Manu, instead of Brahmá and Manu.
It seems probable that this difference, and the part assigned to
Viráj, has originated, in some measure, from confounding Brahmá
with the male half of his individuality, and considering as two
beings that which was but one. If the Purusha or Viráj be distinct from Brahmá, what becomes of Brahmá? The entire whole
and its two halves cannot coexist; although some of the Paurániks and the author of Manu seem to have imagined its possibility, by making Viráj the son of Brahmá. The perplexity,
however, is still more ascribable to the personification of that
which was only an allegory. The division of Brahmá into two
halves designates, as is very evident from the passage in the
Vedas given by Mr. Colebrooke, (As. R., VIII., 425,*) the distinction of corporeal substance into two sexes; Viráj being all
male animals, Śatarúpá, all female animals. So the commentator
on the Hari Vanśa explains the former to denote the horse, the
bull, &c., and the latter, the mare, the cow, and the like. In the
Bhágavata, the term Viráj implies Body collectively, as the commentator observes: यथा हि पुरुषो रविः स्वशरीरं प्रकाशयति वहिः
प्रकाशयत्येव विराजं मूर्तेर्वापयत्यन्तर्बहिः पुमान् । 'As the sun
illuminates his own inner sphere, as well as the exterior regions,
so soul, shining in body (Virája), irradiates all without and within.'
विराजो प्रकाशयन्नन्तराख्यं प्रकाशयति । All, therefore, that
the birth of Viráj was intended to express, was, the creation of
living body, of creatures of both sexes; and, as, in consequence,
man was produced, he might be said to be the son of Viráj, or
bodily existence. Again, Śatarúpá, the bride of Brahmá, or of
Viráj, or of Manu, is nothing more than beings of varied or
manifold forms, from Śata, 'a hundred', and रूप 'form'; explained,
by the annotator on the Hari Vanśa, by Anantarúpá (अनन्तरूपा),
'of infinite', and Viridharúpá (विविधरूपा), 'of diversified shape';
being, as he states, the same as Máyá, 'illusion', or the power

---

* *Miscellaneous Essays*, Vol. I., p. 64.

Uttánapáda,[1] and two daughters, named Prasúti and
Ákúti, graced with loveliness and exalted merit.[2] Prasúti he gave to Daksha, after giving Ákúti to the patriarch Ruchi,[3] who espoused her.* Ákúti bore to
Ruchi twins, Yajna and Dakshiná,[4] who afterwards

---

of multiform metamorphosis: वनेबहुपधारलसामर्घ । The Matsya
Puráńa has a little allegory of its own, on the subject of Brahmá's
intercourse with Satarúpá; for it explains the former to mean the
Vedas, and the latter, the Sáritri or holy prayer, which is their
chief text; and in their cohabitation there is, therefore, no evil:

वेदराशि: सुतो ब्रह्मा सावित्री तदुपस्थिता ।
मखाख परिद्दोव: आत्मसाविदीयबलं विभो: ॥†

[1] The Brahma Puráńa has a different order, and makes Vira
the son of the first pair, who has Uttánapáda, &c. by Kámyá.
The commentator on the Hari Vaṁśa quotes the Váyu for a
confirmation of this account. But the passage there is:

वेराजात्सुदपधारीरो ब्रह्मरूपा बयायात ।
मियवलीतागपादो पुत्री पुवदता वरी ॥

'Satarúpá bore to the male Vairája (Manu) two Viras', i. e.,
heroes, or heroic sons, Uttánapáda and Priyavrata. It looks as if
the compiler of the Brahma Puráńa had made some very un-
accountable blunder, and invented, upon it, a new couple, Vira
and Kámyá. No such person as the former occurs in any other
Puráńa; nor does Kámyá, as his wife.

[2] The Bhágavata adds a third daughter, Devahúti; for the
purpose, apparently, of introducing a long legend of the Rishi
Kardama, to whom she is married, and of their son Kapila: a
legend not met with anywhere else.

[3] Ruchi is reckoned amongst the Prajápatis, by the Linga
and Váyu Puráńas.

[4] These descendants of Swáyambhuva are, all, evidently, allegorical. Thus, Yajna (यत्न) is 'sacrifice', and Dakshiná (दक्षिणा),
'donation' to Brahmans.

---

* See *Original Sanskrit Texts*, Part I., p. 25.

† *Matsya-puráńa*, IV., 10, 11.

became husband and wife, and had twelve sons, the deities called Yámas,[1] in the Manwantara of Swáyambhuva.

The patriarch Daksha had, by Prasúti, twenty-four daughters.[2] Hear from me their names: Śraddhá (faith), Lakshmí (prosperity), Dhŕiti (steadiness), Tushťi (resignation), Pushťi (thriving), Medhá (intelligence), Kriyá (action, devotion), Buddhi (intellect), Lajjá (modesty), Vapus (body), Śánti (expiation), Siddhi (perfection), Kírtti (fame). These thirteen daughters of Daksha, Dharma (righteousness) took to wife. The other eleven bright-eyed and younger daughters of the patriarch were: Khyáti (celebrity), Satí (truth), Sambhúti (fitness), Smŕiti (memory), Príti (affection), Kshamá (patience), Saňnati (humility), Anasúyá (charity), Úrjá (energy), with Swáhá (offering), and Swadhá (oblation). These maidens were respectively wedded to the Munis Bhŕigu, Bhava, Maríchi, Angiras, Pulastya, Pulaha, Kratu, Atri, and Vasishťha, to Fire (Vahni),[4] and to the Pitris (progenitors).[3]†

---

[1] The Bhágavata (b. IV. c. 1) says the Tushitas: but they are the divinities of the second, not of the first, Manwantara; as appears also in another part of the same, where the Yámas are likewise referred to the Swáyambhava Manwantara.

[2] These twenty-four daughters are of much less universal occurrence in the Puráńas than the more extensive series of fifty or sixty, which is subsequently described, and which appears to be the more ancient legend.

[3] The twenty-four daughters of Daksha are similarly named

---

[4] For Vahni's wife, Swáhá, and for other allegorical females here mentioned, as originating from particles of *prakŕiti*, see the *Brahmavaivartapuráńa*, in Prof. Aufrecht's *Catalog. Cod. Manuscript.*, &c., p. 23.

† See *Original Sanskrit Texts*, Part IV., p. 324.

The progeny of Dharma, by the daughters of Daksha, were as follows: by Śraddhá, he had Káma (desire); by Lakshmí,* Darpa (pride); by Dhṛiti, Niyama (precept); by Tushṭi, Santosha (content); by Pushṭi, Lobha (cupidity); by Medhá, Śruta (sacred tradition); by Kriyá, Danda, Naya, and Vinaya (correction, polity, and prudence); by Buddhi, Bodha (understanding); by Lajjá, Vinaya (good behaviour); by Vapus, Vyavasáya (perseverance). Śánti gave birth to Kshema (prosperity); Siddhi, to Sukha (enjoyment); and Kírtti, to

and disposed of in most of the Puráṇas which notice them. The Bhágavata, having introduced a third daughter of Swáyambhuva, has a rather different enumeration, in order to assign some of them, the wives of the Prajápatis, to Kardama and Devahúti. Daksha had, therefore, it is there said (b. IV. c. 1), sixteen daughters, thirteen of whom were married to Dharma, named Śraddhá, Maitrí (friendship), Dayá (clemency), Śánti, Tushṭi, Pushṭi, Kriyá, Unnati (elevation), Buddhi, Medhá, Titikshá (patience), Hrí (modesty), Múrti (form); and three, Satí, Swáhá, and Swadhá, married, as in our text. Some of the daughters of Devahúti repeat these appellations; but that is of slight consideration. They are: Kalá (a moment), married to Marichi; Anasúyá, to Atri; Śraddhá, to Angiras; Havirbhú (oblation-born), to Pulastya; Gati (movement), to Pulaha; Kriyá, to Kratu; Khyáti, to Bhṛigu; Arundhatí, to Vasishṭha; and Śánti, to Atharvan.† In all these instances, the persons are, manifestly, allegorical, being personifications of intelligences and virtues and religious rites, and being, therefore, appropriately wedded to the probable authors of the Hindu code of religion and morals, or to the equally allegorical representation of that code, Dharma, moral and religious duty.

* In the original, Chalá.

† The *Bhágavata-puráṇa*, in the texts that I have examined, pairs Urjá with Vasishṭha, and Chitti with Atharvan.

Yaśas (reputation).[1] These were the sons of Dharma; one of whom, Káma, had Harsha (joy) by his wife Nandí (delight).

The wife of Adharma[2] (vice) was Himsá (violence), on whom he begot a son, Anrita (falsehood), and a daughter, Nikríti (immorality). They intermarried, and had two sons, Bhaya (fear) and Naraka (hell); and

---

[1] The same remark applies here. The Puránas that give these details generally concur with our text. But the Bhágavata specifies the progeny of Dharma in a somewhat different manner; or, following the order observed in the list of Dhárma's wives, their children are: Ríta* (truth), Prasáda (favour), Abhaya (fearlessness), Sukha, Muda (pleasure), Smaya (wonder), Yoga (devotion), Darpa, Artha (meaning†), Smriti (memory), Kshema, Prasraya (affection), and the two saints Nara and Náráyana, the sons of Dharma by Múrti. We have occasional varieties of nomenclature in other authorities; as, instead of Sruta, Sama; Kúrma Puráńa: instead of Dańdanaya, Samaya; and, instead of Budha, Apramáda; Linga Puráńa: and Siddha, in place of Sukha: Kúrma Puráńa.

[2] The text rather abruptly introduces Adharma and his family. He is said, by the commentator, to be the son of·Brahmá; and the Linga Puráńa enumerates him amongst the Prajápatis, as well as Dharma. According to the Bhágavata, he is the husband of Mrishá (falsehood), and the father of Dambha (hypocrisy) and Máyá (deceit), who were adopted by Nirriti. The series of their descendants is, also, somewhat varied from our text; being, in each descent, however, twins, which intermarry, or: Lobha (covetousness) and Nikríti, who produce Krodha (wrath) and Himsá: their children are Kali (wickedness) and Durukti (evil speech): their progeny are Mrityu and Bhí (fear); whose offspring are Niraya (hell) and Yátaná (torment).

---

* The MSS. which I have inspected give Subha, "felicity".

† ?

twins to them, two daughters, Máyá (deceit) and Ve-
danú (torture), who became their wives. The son of
Bhaya and Máyá was the destroyer of living creatures,
or Mrityu (death); and Duḥkha (pain) was the offspring
of Naraka* and Vedaná. The children of Mrityu were:
Vyádhi (disease), Jará (decay), Śoka (sorrow), Tŕishńá
(greediness), and Krodha (wrath). These are all called
the inflictors of misery, and are characterized as the
progeny of Vice† (Adharma).‡ They are all without
wives, without posterity, without the faculty to pro-
create. They are the terrific forms of Vishńu, and
perpetually operate as causes of the destruction of this
world. On the contrary, Daksha and the other Ŕishis,§
the elders of mankind, tend perpetually to influence
its renovation; whilst the Manus and their sons,‖ the
heroes endowed with mighty power, and treading in
the path of truth, as constantly contribute to its preservation.

Maitreya.—Tell me, Brahman, what is the essential
nature of these revolutions, perpetual preservation,
perpetual creation, and perpetual destruction.

Parásara.—Madhusúdana, whose essence is incomprehensible, in the forms of these (patriarchs and
Manus), is the author of the uninterrupted vicissitudes
of creation, preservation, and destruction. The dissolu-

---

* Raurava, in the original.

† अधर्मवत्सला:, "essentially vicious". The commentator says:
पापरूपा: । यद्वा प्राचीनाधर्मवत्सला: । तत्फलत्वात् ।

‡ For some additions, including Nirriti and Alakshmí, see the *Márkańḍeya-puráńa*, L., 33, *et seq.*

§ Four are named in the Sanskrit: Daksha, Marichi, Atri, and Bhŕigu.

‖ An epithet is here omitted: *bhúpa*, "kings".

tion of all things is of four kinds: Naimittika,[*] 'occasional'; Prákṛitika, 'elemental'; Átyantika, 'absolute';
Nitya, 'perpetual'.[1] The first, also termed the Bráhma

---

[1] The three first of these are more particularly described in
the last book. The last, the Nitya or constant, is differently
described by Colonel Vans Kennedy (Researches Into the Nature
and Affinity of Ancient and Hindu Mythology, p. 224, note). "In
the seventh chapter, however", he observes, "of the first part of
the Vishṇu Puráṇa, it is said that the *naimittika, prákṛitika, átyantika,* and *nitya* are the four kinds of *pralaya* to which created
things are subject. The *naimittika* takes place when Brahmá
slumbers; the *prákṛitika,* when this universe returns to its original
nature; *átyantika* proceeds from divine knowledge, and consequent
identification with the supreme spirit; and *nitya* is the extinction
of life, like the extinction of a lamp, in sleep at night." For this
last characteristic, however, our text furnishes no warrant. Nor
can it be explained to signify, that the Nitya Pralaya means no
more than "a man's falling into sound sleep at night". All the
copies consulted on the present occasion concur in reading:

नित्य: सदैव जातानां यो विनाशो दिवानिशम् ।

as rendered above. The commentator supplies the illustration,
दीपज्वालावत् । 'like the flame of a lamp'; but he also writes:
जातानां दिवानिशं यो विनाश: स नित्य: । 'That which is the
destruction of all that are born, night and day, is the Nitya or
constant.' Again, in a verse presently following, we have the
Nitya Sarga, 'constant or perpetual creation', as opposed to cou-
stant dissolution:

भूतान्वनुदिनं यच जायन्ते मुनिसत्तमा: ।
नित्य: सर्ग: स तु प्रोक्त: पुराणार्थविचक्षणै: ॥

'That in which, O excellent sages, beings are daily born, is termed
constant creation, by those learned in the Puráṇas.' The commentator explains this: यदहरादिवृद्धिमवाप्तौ नित्यसर्ग एवं: ।
'The constant flow or succession of the creation of ourselves and
other creatures is the Nitya or constant creation. This is the

---

[*] See the editor's note in p. 52, *supra.*

I.   8

dissolution, occurs when the sovereign of the world reclines in sleep. In the second, the mundane egg resolves into the primary element, from whence it was derived. Absolute non-existence of the world is the absorption of the sage,* through knowledge, into supreme spirit. Perpetual destruction is the constant disappearance, day and night, of all that are born. The productions of Prakriti form the creation that is termed the elemental (Prákrita). That which ensues after a minor dissolution is called ephemeral creation; and the daily generation of living things is termed, by those who are versed in the Puránas, constant creation. In this manner, the mighty Vishnu, whose essence is the elements, abides in all bodies, and brings about production, existence, and dissolution.† The faculties of Vishnu, to create, to preserve, and to destroy, operate successively, Maitreya, in all corporeal beings, and at all seasons; and he who frees himself from the influence of these three faculties, which are essentially composed of the three qualities (goodness, foulness, and darkness), goes to the supreme sphere, from whence he never again returns.

----

meaning of the text.' It is obvious, therefore, that the alternation intended is that of life and death, not of waking and sleep.

----

* *Yogin.*
† *Sankyana.*

CHAPTER VIII.

PARÁSARA.—I have described to you, O great Muni,
the creation of Brahmá in which the quality of darkness prevailed. I will now explain to you the creation
of Rudra.[1]

In the beginning of the Kalpa, as Brahmá purposed
to create a son, who should be like himself, a youth
of a purple complexion[2] appeared; crying with a low
cry, and running about.[3] Brahmá, when he beheld him
thus afflicted, said to him: "Why dost thou weep?"
"Give me a name", replied the boy. "Rudra be thy
name", rejoined the great father of all creatures: "be
composed; desist from tears." But, thus addressed,

---

[1] The creation of Rudra has been already adverted to; and
that seems to be the primitive form of the legend. We have,
here, another account, grounded, apparently, upon Śaiva or Yoga
mysticism.

[2] The appearance of Rudra as a Kumára, 'a boy', is described,
as of repeated occurrence, in the Linga and Váyu Puráńas, as
already noticed (pp. 76, *et seq.*); and these Kumáras are of different
complexions in different Kalpas. In the Vaishńava Puráńas,
however, we have only one original form, to which the name of
Nilalohita, 'the blue and red or purple complexioned', is assigned.
In the Kúrma, this youth comes from Brahmá's mouth; in the
Váyu, from his forehead.

[3] This is the Paurániḳ etymology: रोदनाद्रवणाच्च रुद्रः ।
or Rud, 'to weep', and Dru, 'to run'. The grammarians derive
the name from Rud, 'to weep', with Rak affix.

8*

the boy still wept seven times; and Brahmá therefore
gave to him seven other denominations: and to these
eight persons regions and wives and posterity belong.
The eight manifestations, then, are named Rudra,
Bhava, Śarva, Íśána, Paśupati, Bhíma, Ugra, and Mahádeva, which were given to them by their great progenitor.* He also assigned to them their respective
stations, the sun, water, earth, air, fire,† ether, the
ministrant Brahman, and the moon; for these are their
several forms.[1] The wives of the sun and the other

---

[1] The Váyu details the application of each name severally.
These eight Rudras are, therefore, but one, under as many appellations, and in as many types. The Padma, Márkańdeya,
Kúrma, Linga, and Váyu agree with our text in the nomenclature
of the Rudras, and their types, their wives, and progeny. The
types are those which are enumerated in the Nándi or opening
benedictory verse of Śakuntalá; and the passage of the Vishńu
Puráńa was found, by M. Chezy, on the envelope of his copy.
He has justly corrected Sir William Jones's version of the term
धीरजी, 'the sacrifice is performed with solemnity'; as the word
means, 'Brahmane officiant', दीरिजमी आहूयः। 'the Brahman
who is qualified, by initiation (Díkshá), to conduct the rite.' These
are considered as the bodies, or visible forms, of those modifications of Rudra which are variously named, and which, being
praised in them, severally abstain from harming them: तेषु
पूजयत वस्यः। आसु। एरूजास तिष्ठति थे। Váyu Puráńa.
The Bhágavata, III., 12, 11-13, has a different scheme, as
usual; but it confounds the notion of the eleven Rudras, to
whom the text subsequently adverts, with that of the eight

---

* See an almost identical passage, from the *Márkańdeya-puráńa*, LII., 2,
et seq., translated in *Original Sanskrit Texts*, Part IV., p. 286.

† In most MSS. seen by me the order is "fire, air"; and so in other
Puráńas than the Vishńu.

manifestations, termed Rudra and the rest, were, respectively: Suvarchalá, Ushá,[*] Vikeśí, Sivá, Swáhá, Disás, Díkshá, and Rohiní. Now hear an account of their progeny, by whose successive generations this world has been peopled. Their sons, then, were, severally: Sanaischara (Saturn), Śukra (Venus), the fiery-bodied [†] (Mars), Manojava (Hanumat:[‡]), Skanda, Swarga,[§] Santána, and Budha (Mercury).

It was the Rudra of this description that married Satí, who abandoned her corporeal existence in consequence of the displeasure of Daksha.[1] She after-

---

here specified. These eleven It terms Manyu, Manu, Mahínasa, Mahat, Siva, Ritadhwaja,[‖] Ugraretas, Bhava, Kála, Vámadeva, and Dhṛitavrata; their wives are Dhí, Dhṛiti, Rasalomá, Niyut, Sarpi,[¶] Ilá, Ambiká, Irávatí, Swadhá, Dikshá, Rudráni; and their places are the heart, senses, breath, ether, air, fire, water, earth, sun, moon, and tapas or ascetic devotion. The same allegory or mystification characterizes both accounts.

[1] See the story of Daksha's sacrifice at the end of the chapter.

[*] Several of the MSS. inspected by me have Swavarchalá and Umá. The *Márkańdeya-puráńa*, LII., 9, has Umá.

[†] *Lohitánga.*

[‡] The commentator says that Manojava is "a certain wind". Hanumat is called, however, Anilátmaja, Pavanatanaya, Váyuputra, &c., "Son of the Wind"; and Marutwat.

[§] Some MSS. have Sarga; and so has the *Márkańdeya-puráńa*, LII., 11.

[‖] The Bombay editions of the *Bhágavata-puráńa* have Kratudhwaja.

ऋ श्रीधृतिरुषणोमा च नियुत्सर्पिरिलाम्बिका ।
एरावती सुधा दीक्षा रुद्राण्यो रुद्र ते स्त्रियः ॥

"Dhí, Dhṛiti, Úsaná, Umá, Niyut, Sarpi, Ilá, Ambiká, Irávati, Sudhá, and Diksha, the Rudráńís, are thy wives, Rudra."

Vritti is a variant, of common occurrence, for Dhṛiti. "Rasalomá" and "Swadha" are not found in any MS. that I have seen. Sarpi must be feminine. Sarpis would be neuter.

wards was the daughter of Himavat (the snowy mountains) by Mená; and, in that character, as the only Umá, the mighty Bhava again married her[1]." The divinities Dhátṛi and Vidhátṛi were born to Bhṛigu by Khyáti; as was a daughter, Srí, the wife of Náráyaṇa, the god of gods.[2]

MAITREYA.—It it commonly said that the goddess Srí was born from the sea of milk, when it was churned for ambrosia. How, then, can you say that she was the daughter of Bhṛigu by Khyáti?

PARÁSARA.—Srí, the bride of Vishṇu, the mother of the world, is eternal, imperishable. In like manner as he is all-pervading, so also is she, O best of Brahmans, omnipresent. Vishṇu is meaning; she is speech. Hari is polity (Naya); she is prudence (Níti). Vishṇu is understanding; she is intellect. He is righteousness; she is devotion. He is the creator; she is creation. Srí is the earth; Hari, the support of it. The deity is content; the eternal Lakshmí is resignation. He is desire; Srí is wish. He is sacrifice; she is sacrificial donation (Dakshiṇá). The goddess is the invocation which attends the oblation;† Janárdana is the obla-

---

[1] The story of Umá's birth and marriage occurs in the Siva Puráṇa, and in the Kási Khaṇḍa of the Skanda Puráṇa: it is noticed briefly, and with some variation from the Puráṇas, in the Rámáyaṇa, first book: it is also given, in detail, in the Kumára Sambhava of Kálidása.

[2] The family of Bhṛigu is more particularly described in the tenth chapter. It is here mentioned merely to introduce the story of the birth of the goddess of prosperity, Srí.

---

* See *Original Sanskrit Texts*, Part IV., p. 324.

† For "the invocation which attends the oblation", read "the oblation of clarified butter", *ájyáhuti*, not *ájyáhṛti*.

tion.* Lakshmí is the chamber where the females are
present (at a religious ceremony); Madhusúdana, the
apartment of the males of the family. Lakshmí is the
altar; Hari, the stake (to which the victim is bound).
Srí is the fuel; Hari, the holy grass (Kuśa). He is the
personified Sáma-veda; the goddess, lotos-throned, is
the tone of its chanting.† Lakshmí is the prayer of
oblation (Swáhá); Vásudeva, the lord of the world, is
the sacrificial fire. Sauri (Vishńu) is Sankara (Siva);
and Srí: is the bride of Siva (Gaurí). Keśava, O Maitreya, is the sun; and his radiance is the lotos-seated
goddess. Vishńu is the tribe of progenitors (Pitríguńa);
Padmá is their bride (Swadhá), the eternal bestower
of nutriment.§ Srí is the heavens; Vishńu, who is one
with all things, is wide-extended space. The lord of
Srí is the moon; she is his unfading light. She is called
the moving principle of the world; he, the wind which
bloweth everywhere. Govinda is the ocean; Lakshmí,
its shore. Lakshmí is the consort of Indra (Indráńí);
Madhusúdana is Devendra. The holder of the discus
(Vishńu) is Yama (the regent of Tartarus); the lotos-
throned goddess is his dusky spouse (Dhúmorńá). Srí
is wealth; Srídhara (Vishńu) is, himself, the god of
riches (Kubera). Lakshmí, illustrious Brahman, is
Gaurí; and Keśava is the deity of ocean (Varuńa). Srí

---

* To render *purodáśa*, "a sacrificial cake of ground rice". See Colebrooke's *Two Treatises on the Hindu Law of Inheritance*, p. 234, first
annotation, and p. 337, second annotation.

† "The tone of its chanting", *udgíti*.

: Here called Bháíl, in several of the MSS. I have examined.

§ Most of the MSS. consulted by me have, not सततान्नपूर्णदा, "the
eternal bestower of nutriment", but सततान्नपूर्णदा, "the perpetual bestower of contentment".

is the host of heaven (Devasená); the deity of war, her
lord, is Hari. The wielder of the mace is resistance;
the power to oppose is Śrí. Lakshmí is the Kásht́há
and the Kalá; Hari, the Nimesha and the Muhúrta.
Lakshmí is the light; and Hari, who is all, and lord of
all, the lamp. She, the mother of the world, is the
creeping vine; and Vishńu, the tree round which she
clings. She is the night; the god who is armed with
the mace and discus is the day. He, the bestower of
blessings, is the bridegroom; the lotos-throned goddess
is the bride. The god is one with all male, the goddess
one with all female, rivers. The lotos-eyed deity is the
standard; the goddess seated on a lotos, the banner.
Lakshmí is cupidity; Náráyańa, the master of the world,
is covetousness. O thou who knowest what righteousness is, Govinda is love; and Lakshmí, his gentle
spouse,* is pleasure.† But why thus diffusely enume-
rate their presence? It is enough to say, in a word,
that, of gods, animals, and men, Hari is all that is called
male; Lakshmí is all that is termed female. There is
nothing else than they.

SACRIFICE OF DAKSHA.[1]
(From the Váyu Puráńa.)

"There was formerly a peak of Meru, named Sávitra,
abounding with gems, radiant as the sun, and celebrated

---

[1] The sacrifice of Daksha is a legend of some interest, from
its historical and archæological relations. It is, obviously, intended

---

* There is nothing, in the MSS. I have seen, answering to "his gentle
spouse".   † *Rága*, "love"; *rati*, "pleasure".

throughout the three worlds; of immense extent, and
difficult of access, and an object of universal veneration.
Upon that glorious eminence, rich with mineral treasures, as upon a splendid couch, the deity Śiva reclined,
accompanied by the daughter of the sovereign of
mountains, and attended by the mighty Ádityas, the
powerful Vasus, and by the heavenly physicians, the

---

to intimate a struggle between the worshippers of Śiva and of
Vishńu, in which, at first, the latter, but, finally, the former,
acquired the ascendancy. It is, also, a favourite subject of Hindu
sculpture, at least with the Hindus of the Śaiva division, and
makes a conspicuous figure both at Elephanta and Ellora. A representation of the dispersion and mutilation of the gods and
sages by Virabhadra, at the former, is published in the Archæo-
logia, Vol. VII., 326, where it is described as the Judgment of
Solomon! A figure of Virabhadra is given by Niebuhr, Vol. II.,
tab. 10; and the entire group, in the Bombay Transactions, Vol. I.,
p. 220. It is described, p. 229: but Mr. Erskine has not verified
the subject, although it cannot admit of doubt. The group described, p. 224, probably represents the introductory details given
in our text. Of the Ellora sculptures, a striking one occurs in
what Sir C. Malet calls the Doomar Leyna cave, where is "Veer
Budder, with eight hands. In one is suspended the slain Rajah
Dutz." A. R. Vol. VI., 396. And there is also a representation
of 'Ehr Badr' in one of the colonnades of Kailas; being, in fact,
the same figure as that at Elephanta. Bombay Tr., Vol. III., 287.
The legend of Daksha, therefore, was popular when those cavern
temples were excavated. The story is told in much more detail
in several other Puráńas, and with some variations, which will
be noticed: but the above has been selected as a specimen of the
style of the Váyu Puráńa, and as being a narration which, from
its inartificial, obscure, tautological, and uncircumstantial construction, is, probably, of an ancient date. The same legend, in
the same words, is given in the Brahma Puráńa.

sons of Aświní; by Kubera,* surrounded by his train of Guhyakas, the lord of the Yakshas, who dwells on Kailása. There also was the great Muni Uśanas: there were Rishis of the first order, with Sanatkumára at their head; divine Rishis, preceded by Angiras; Viśwávasu, with his bands of heavenly choristers; the sages Nárada and Parvata; and innumerable troops of celestial nymphs. The breeze blew upon the mountain, bland, pure, and fragrant; and the trees were decorated with flowers that blossomed in every season. The Vidyádharas and Siddhas, affluent in devotion, waited upon Mahádeva, the lord of living creatures;† and many other beings, of various forms, did him homage. Rákshasas of terrific semblance, and Piśáchas of great strength, of different shapes and features, armed with various weapons, and blazing like fire, were delighted to be present, as the followers of the god. There stood the royal Nandin,‡ high in the favour of his lord, armed with a fiery trident,§ shining with inherent lustre; and there the best of rivers, Gangá, the assemblage of all holy waters,‖ stood adoring the mighty deity. Thus worshipped by all the most excellent of sages and of gods, abode the omnipotent and all-glorious¶ Mahádeva.

"In former times Daksha commenced a holy sacrifice on the side of Himavat, at the sacred spot Gangá-

---

* In the original, Vaiśravaṇa.

† *Paśupati*; rather, "lord of sacrificial animals"; and so in p. 125, l. 3.

‡ In the Sanskrit, Nandíśwara.

§ *Śúla*, "a pike"; and so wherever "trident" occurs in the present extract from the *Váyu-purána*.

‖ The more literal rendering would be: "rising from the water of all holy places situate on streams": सर्वतीर्थजलोद्गता ।

¶ Instead of "omnipotent and all-glorious", read "divine", *bhagavat*.

dwára, frequented by the Ŕishis. The gods, desirous
of assisting at this solemn rite, came, with Indra* at
their head, to Mahádeva, and intimated their purpose,
and, having received his permission, departed, in their
splendid chariots, to Gangádwára, as tradition reports.[1]
They found Daksha, the best of the devout, surrounded
by the singers and nymphs of heaven, and by numerous
sages, beneath the shade of clustering trees and climb-
ing plants; and all of them, whether dwellers on earth,
in air, or in the regions above the skies, approached
the patriarch with outward gestures of respect. The
Ádityas, Vasus, Rudras,† Maruts, all entitled to partake
of the oblations, together with Jishńu, were present.
The (four classes of Pitŕis) Úshmapas, Somapas, Ájyu-
pas, and Dhúmapas, (or those who feed upon the flame,
the acid juice, the butter, or the smoke of offerings),
the Aświns, and the progenitors, came along with
Brahmá. Creatures of every class, born from the womb,
the egg, from vapour, or vegetation, came upon their
invocation; as did all the gods, with their brides, who,
in their resplendent vehicles, blazed like so many fires.

---

[1] Or this may be understood to imply, that the original story
is in the Vedas; the term being, as usual in such a reference,
इति श्रुति: । Gangádwára, the place where the Ganges descends
to the plains — or Haridwár, as it is more usually termed — is
usually specified as the scene of action. The Linga is more
precise, calling it Kanakhala, which is the village still called
Kankhal, near Haridwár (Megha Dúta, p. 59). It rather inaccu-
rately, however, describes this as upon Hamsa peak, a point of
the Himálaya: हंसे हिमवच्छिखरे ।

---

* The Sanskrit has Kratu.
† Add Sádhyas.

Beholding them thus assembled, the sage Dadhícha was filled with indignation, and observed: 'The man who worships what ought not to be worshipped, or pays not reverence where veneration is due, is guilty, most assuredly, of heinous sin.' Then, addressing Daksha, he said to him: 'Why do you not offer homage to the god who is the lord of life* (Paśubhartri̇)?' Daksha spake: 'I have already many Rudras present, armed with tridents, wearing braided hair, and existing in eleven forms. I recognize no other Mahádeva.' Dadhícha spake: 'The invocation that is not addressed to Íśa is, for all, but a solitary (and imperfect) summons. Inasmuch as I behold no other divinity who is superior to Śankara, this sacrifice of Daksha will not be completed.'† Daksha spake: 'I offer, in a golden cup, this entire oblation, which has been consecrated by many prayers, as an offering ever due to the unequalled Vishńu,‡ the sovereign lord of all.'[1]

---

[1] The Kúrma Puráńa gives also this discussion between Dadhícha and Daksha; and their dialogue contains some curious matter. Daksha, for instance, states that no portion of a sacrifice is ever allotted to Śiva, and no prayers are directed to be addressed to him, or to his bride:

* Rather, "the guardian of animals fit for sacrifice".

† सर्वेषामेव यज्ञानां देवेशो न निर्मितः ।
यथायं शंकरादूर्ध्वं भागं पश्यामि दैवतम् ॥
तथा रुद्रस्य विमुखो यज्ञोऽयं न अभिचाति ।

For the text, from the *Mahábhárata*, of a passage nearly identical with that in which these verses occur, accompanied by a very different rendering from that given above, see *Original Sanskrit Texts*, Part IV., pp. 314, *et seq.*

‡ The epithet *makhela*, "lord of sacrifice", is here omitted.

"In the meanwhile the virtuous daughter of the mountain king, observing the departure of the divinities, addressed her lord, the god of living beings, and said — Umá spake — 'Whither, O lord, have the gods, preceded by Indra,[*] this day departed? Tell me truly,

---

वर्वेषिष हि यज्ञेषु न भाग: परिकल्पित: ।
न मह्या भार्यया सार्धं शंकरेति निगद्यते ॥

Dadhícha apparently evades the objection, and claims a share for Rudra, consisting of the triad of gods, as one with the sun, who is, undoubtedly, bymned by the several ministering priests of the Vedas:

स पूज्यो यज्ञाद्यु: सामवाभ्यर्घोऽनुगि: ।
यज्ञे विज्ञधर्मार्थं एष मूर्तिचतीचयम् ॥

Daksha replies that the twelve Ádityas receive special oblations; that they are all the sons; and that he knows of no other. The Munis, who overbear the dispute, concur in his sentiments:

य एते द्वादशादित्या आदित्यजयश्रभाविन: ।
तेषां सूर्या एति देवा न अन्यो विद्यते रवि: ॥
एवमुक्ते तु मुनय: समायाता द्विजवर: ।
पादमिजयुरूप्यं तथा साद्यकबारिष: ॥

These notions seem to have been exchanged for others, in the days of the Padma Puráńa and Bhágavata; as they place Daksha's neglect of Śiva to the latter's filthy practices, — his going naked, smearing himself with ashes, carrying a skull, and behaving as if he were drunk or crazed; alluding, no doubt, to the practices of Śaiva mendicants, who seem to have abounded in the days of Sankara Áchárya, and since. There is no discussion in the Bhágavata; but Rudra is described as present at a former assembly, when his father-in-law censured him before the guests, and, in consequence, he departed in a rage. His follower Nandin[†] curses the company; and Bhríga retorts in language descriptive of the Vámácharins or left hand worshippers of Śiva. "May all those",

---

O thou who knowest all truth; for a great doubt perplexes me.' Maheśwara spake: 'Illustrious goddess,
the excellent patriarch Daksha celebrates the sacrifice
of a horse; and thither the gods repair.' Deví spake:
'Why, then, most mighty god, dost thou also not proceed to this solemnity? By what hinderance is thy
progress thither impeded?' Maheśwara spake: 'This
is the contrivance, mighty queen, of all the gods, that,
in all sacrifices, no portion should be assigned to me.
In consequence of an arrangement formerly devised,
the gods allow me, of right, no participation of sacrificial
offerings.' Deví spake: 'The lord god lives in all bodily
forms;[*] and his might is eminent through his superior
faculties. He is unsurpassable, he is unapproachable, in
splendour and glory and power. That such as he should
be excluded from his share of oblations fills me with
deep sorrow; and a trembling, O sinless, seizes upon

he says,[†] "who adopt the worship of Bhava (Śiva), all those
who follow the practices of his worshippers, become heretics, and
oppugners of holy doctrines. May they neglect the observances
of purification; may they be of infirm intellects, wearing clotted
hair, and ornamenting themselves with ashes and bones; and may
they enter the Śaiva initiation, in which spirituous liquor is the
libation."

[*] Professor Wilson doubtless read सर्वदेषु ; but the MSS. which I
have consulted give सर्वदेवेषु, "in all the gods".

[†] *Bhágavata-puráṇa*, IV., 2, 28—29:

भवव्रतधरा ये च ये च तान्समनुव्रताः।
पाषण्डिनो भवन्तु स्मशास्त्रपरिपन्थिनः॥
जटाधरा भस्मधरा बटाभस्मास्थिधारिणः।
विशन्तु शिवदीक्षायां यत्र दैवं सुरासवम्॥

This passage will be found translated in *Original Sanskrit Texts*,
Part IV., p. 321.

my frame. Shall I now practise bounty, restraint, or
penance, so that my lord, who is inconceivable, may
obtain a share,—a half, or a third portion,—of the
sacrifice?"[1]

"Then the mighty and incomprehensible deity, being
pleased, said to his bride, thus agitated and speaking:
'Slender-waisted queen of the gods, thou knowest not
the purport of what thou sayest. But I know it, O thou
with large eyes; for the holy declare all things by meditation. By thy perplexity this day are all the gods,

---

[1] This simple account of Sati's share in the transaction is
considerably modified in other accounts. In the Kúrma, the
quarrel begins with Daksha the patriarch's being, as he thinks,
treated, by his son-in-law, with less respect than is his due. Upon
his daughter Sati's subsequently visiting him, he abuses her husband, and turns her out of his house. She, in spite, destroys
herself: हृदामात्मनमाक्षण । Śiva, hearing of this, comes to
Daksha, and curses him to be born as a Kshatriya, the son of
the Prachetasas, and to beget a son on his own daughter:

सर्वा कुलाया भूतास्यनुषद्सुखादविवसि ।

It is in this subsequent birth that the sacrifice occurs. The Linga
and Matsya allude to the dispute between Daksha and Sati, and
to the latter's putting an end to herself by Yoga:

भक्षीकमालमनी देहं योनमानेव वा पुन: ।

The Padma, Bhágavata, and Skanda,—in the Káśi Khaṅda,—
relate the dispute between father and daughter in a like manner,
and in more detail. The first refers the death of Sati, however,
to a prior period; and that and the Bhágavata both ascribe it to
Yoga:

एवं देवी वावस्वान: सती
वव: प्रभजाव समाधिवातिमा ।[a]

The Káśi Khaṅda, with an improvement indicative of a later age,
makes Sati throw herself into the fire prepared for the solemnity.

---

[a] *Bhágavata-puráṇa*, IV., 4, 27.

with Mahendra and all the three worlds, utterly confounded. In my sacrifice, those who worship me repeat my praises, and chant the Rathantara song of the Sámaveda. My priests worship me in the sacrifice of true wisdom, where no officiating Brahman is needed; and, in this, they offer me my portion.'* Deví spake: 'The lord is the root of all,† and, assuredly, in every assemblage of the female world, praises or hides himself at will.' Mahádeva spake: 'Queen of the gods, I praise not myself. Approach, and behold whom I shall create for the purpose of claiming my share of the rite.'

"Having thus spoken to his beloved spouse, the mighty Maheśwara created, from his mouth, a being like the fire of fate;‡ a divine being, with a thousand heads, a thousand eyes, a thousand feet; wielding a thousand clubs, a thousand shafts; holding the shell, the discus, the mace, and bearing a blazing bow and battle-axe;§ fierce and terrific, shining with dreadful splendour, and decorated with the crescent moon; clothed in a tiger's skin dripping with blood, having a capacious stomach, and a vast mouth armed with formidable tusks. His ears were erect; his lips were pendulous; his tongue was lightning; his hand brandished the thunder bolt; flames streamed from his hair; a necklace of pearls wound round his neck; a garland of flame descended on his breast. Radiant with lustre, he looked like the final fire that consumes the world. Four tremendous tusks projected from a mouth which

* See *Original Sanskrit Texts*, Part IV., p. 316, note 281.
† *Suprakhita.*
‡ *Kálágni.* Some MSS. have *krodhágni*, "the fire of wrath".
§ Add "sword", *asi.*

extended from ear to ear. He was of vast bulk, vast
strength, a mighty male and lord, the destroyer of the
universe, and like a large fig-tree in circumference;
shining like a hundred moons at once; fierce as the
fire of love; having four heads, sharp white teeth, and
of mighty fierceness, vigour, activity, and courage;
glowing with the blaze of a thousand fiery suns at the
end of the world; like a thousand undimmed moons;
in bulk, like Himádri, Kailása, or Sumeru, or Mandara,
with all its gleaming herbs; bright as the sun of destruction at the end of ages; of irresistible prowess
and beautiful aspect; irascible, with lowering eyes, and
a countenance burning like fire; clothed in the hide of
the elephant and lion,* and girt round with snakes;
wearing a turban on his head, a moon on his brow;
sometimes savage, sometimes mild; having a chaplet
of many flowers on his head, anointed with various
unguents, adorned with different ornaments and many
sorts of jewels, wearing a garland of heavenly Karṇi-
kára flowers, and rolling his eyes with rage. Sometimes
he danced; sometimes he laughed aloud; sometimes
he stood wrapt in meditation; sometimes he trampled
upon the earth; sometimes he sang; sometimes he
wept repeatedly. And he was endowed with the faculties of wisdom, dispassion, power, penance, truth, en-
durance, fortitude, dominion, and self-knowledge.

"This being then knelt down upon the ground, and,
raising his hands respectfully to his head, said to
Mahádeva: 'Sovereign of the gods, command what it

---

* The original, in the MSS. known to me, is मृगेन्द्रचर्म्मवसनं, in
the accusative. That is to say, there is no mention of "the elephant".

is that I must do for thee'; to which Maheśwara replied: 'Spoil the sacrifice of Daksha.' Then the mighty Vírabhadra, having heard the pleasure of his lord, bowed down his head to the feet of Prajápati,* and, starting like a lion loosed from bonds, despoiled the sacrifice of Daksha; knowing that he had been created by the displeasure of Deví. She, too, in her wrath, as the fearful goddess Rudrakálí, accompanied him, with all her train, to witness his deeds. Vírabhadra, the fierce, abiding in the region of ghosts, is the minister of the anger of Deví. And he then created, from the pores of his skin, powerful demigods,† the mighty attendants upon Rudra, of equal valour and strength, who started, by hundreds and thousands, into existence. Then a loud and confused clamour filled all the expanse of ether, and inspired the denizens of heaven with dread. The mountains tottered, and earth shook; the winds roared, and the depths of the sea were disturbed; the fires lost their radiance, and the sun grew pale; the planets of the firmament shone not, neither did the stars give light; the Rishis censed their hymns, and gods and demons were mute; and thick darkness eclipsed the chariots of the skies.[1]:

-'Then from the gloom emerged fearful and numerous forms, shouting the cry of battle; who instantly

---

[1] The description of Vírabhadra and his followers is given in other Puráńas, in the same strain, but with less detail.

* In the original, Umápati.

† The original calls them Raumás.

सोऽबुबहूरोमकूपेभ्यो रोमाजान्‌ बभेदराम् ।

: Hereabouts the translation is somewhat free.

broke or overturned the sacrificial columns, trampled
upon the altars, and danced amidst the oblations.
Running wildly hither and thither, with the speed of
wind, they tossed about the implements and vessels
of sacrifice, which looked like stars precipitated from
the heavens. The piles of food and beverage for the
gods, which had been heaped up like mountains; the
rivers of milk; the banks of curds and butter; the sands
of honey, and butter-milk, and sugar; the mounds of
condiments and spices of every flavour; the undulating
knolls of flesh and other viands; the celestial liquors,
pastes, and confections, which had been prepared; these
the spirits of wrath devoured, or defiled, or scattered
abroad. Then, falling upon the host of the gods, these
vast and resistless Rudras beat or terrified them, mocked
and insulted the nymphs and goddesses, and quickly
put an end to the rite, although defended by all the
gods; being the ministers of Rudra's wrath, and similar
to himself.[1] Some then made a hideous clamour, whilst
others fearfully shouted, when Yajna was decapitated.
For the divine Yajna, the lord of sacrifice, then began
to fly up to heaven, in the shape of a deer; and Virabhadra, of immeasurable spirit, apprehending his power,

---

[1] Their exploits, and those of Virabhadra, are more particularly specified elsewhere, especially in the Linga, Kúrma, and
Bhágavata Puráńas. Indra is knocked down and trampled on;
Yama has his staff broken; Saraswatí and the Mátris have their
noses cut off; Mitra or Bhaga has his eyes pulled out; Púshan
has his teeth knocked down his throat; Chandra is pummelled;
Vahni's hands are cut off; Bhrigu loses his beard; the Brahmans
are pelted with stones; the Prajápatis are beaten; and the gods
and demigods are run through with swords, or stuck with arrows.

cut off his vast head, after he had mounted into the
sky.[1] Daksha, the patriarch, his sacrifice being destroyed, overcome with terror, and utterly broken in
spirit, fell, then, upon the ground, where his head was
spurned by the feet of the cruel Vírabhadra.[2] The
thirty scores[a] of sacred divinities were all presently

[1] This is also mentioned in the Linga and in the Hari Vaṃśa:
and the latter thus accounts for the origin of the constellation
Mṛigaśiras; Yajna, with the head of a deer, being elevated to the
planetary region, by Brahmá.

[2] As he prays to Śiva presently, it could not well be meant,
here, that Daksha was decapitated, although that is the story in
other places. The Linga[1] and Bhágavata both state that Virabhadra cut off Daksha's head, and threw it into the fire. After
the fray, therefore, when Śiva restored the dead to life, and the
mutilated to their limbs, Daksha's head was not forthcoming. It
was, therefore, replaced by the head of a goat, or, according to
the Káśi Khaṇḍa, that of a ram. No notice is taken, in our
text, of the conflict elsewhere described between Vírabhadra and
Vishṇu. In the Linga, the latter is beheaded; and his head is
blown, by the wind, into the fire. The Kúrma, though a Śaiva
Puráṇa, is less irreverent towards Vishṇu, and, after describing
a contest in which both parties occasionally prevail, makes
Brahmá interpose, and separate the combatants. The Káśi
Khaṇḍa of the Skanda Puráṇa describes Vishṇu as defeated, and
at the mercy of Vírabhadra, who is prohibited, by a voice from
heaven, from destroying his antagonist; whilst, in the Hari Vaṃśa,
Vishṇu compels Śiva to fly, after taking him by the throat and
nearly strangling him. The blackness of Śiva's neck arose from
this throttling, and not, as elsewhere described, from his drinking
the poison produced at the churning of the ocean.

[a] "Three hundred and thirty millions". The original is:

यथाखिलहरिवलानां शा: कोट्यो त्रिनवात्रया: ।
वाद्येनाचिवकेनानु यदा: त्रिंशवीन च ॥

bound, with a band of fire, by their lion-like foe; and they all then addressed him, crying: 'O Rudra, have mercy upon thy servants! O lord, dismiss thine anger!' Thus spake Brahmá, and the other gods, and the patriarch Daksha; and, raising their hands, they said: 'Declare, mighty being, who thou art.' Vírabhadra said: 'I am not a god, nor an Áditya; nor am I come hither for enjoyment, nor curious to behold the chiefs of the divinities. Know that I am come to destroy the sacrifice of Daksha, and that I am called Vírabhadra, the issue of the wrath of Rudra. Bhadrakálí, also, who has sprung from the anger of Devi, is sent here, by the god of gods, to destroy this rite. Take refuge, king of kings, with him who is the lord of Umá. For better is the anger of Rudra than the blessings of other gods.'

"Having heard the words of Vírabhadra, the righteous Daksha propitiated the mighty god, the holder of the trident, Maheswara. The hearth of sacrifice, deserted by the Brahmans, had been consumed; Yajna had been metamorphosed to an antelope; the fires of Rudra's wrath had been kindled; the attendants, wounded by the tridents of the servants of the god, were groaning with pain; the pieces of the uprooted sacrificial posts were scattered here and there; and the fragments of the meat-offerings were carried off by flights of hungry vultures and herds of howling jackals. Suppressing his vital airs, and taking up a posture of meditation, the many-sighted victor of his foes, Daksha, fixed his eyes everywhere upon his thoughts. Then the god of gods appeared from the altar, resplendent as a thousand suns, and smiled upon him, and said: 'Daksha, thy sacrifice has been destroyed

134

through sacred knowledge. I am well pleased with
thee.' And then he smiled again, and said: 'What shall
I do for thee? Declare, together with the preceptor
of the gods.'

"Then Daksha, frightened, alarmed, and agitated,
his eyes suffused with tears, raised his hands reverentially to his brow, and said: 'If, lord, thou art pleased;
if I have found favour in thy sight; if I am to be the
object of thy benevolence; if thou wilt confer upon
me a boon, this is the blessing I solicit, that all these
provisions for the solemn sacrifice, which have been
collected with much trouble, and during a long time,
and which have now been eaten, drunk, devoured,
burnt, broken, scattered abroad, may not have been
prepared in vain.' 'So let it be', replied Hara, the sub-
duer of Indra.* And thereupon Daksha knelt down
upon the earth, and praised, gratefully, the author of
righteousness, the three-eyed god Mahádeva, repeating
the eight thousand names of the deity whose emblem
is a bull."

---

* Bhaganetra is here used, in the Sanskrit, for "Indra". See the
article बहुवाच in Professor Wilson's *Sanskrit Dictionary*.

CHAPTER IX.

Parásara.—But, with respect to the question thou hast asked me, Maitreya, relating to the history of Śrí, hear from me the tale, as it was told to me by Maríchi.

Durvásas, a portion of Śankara (Śiva),[1] was wandering over the earth; when he beheld, in the hands of a nymph of air,[2] a garland of flowers culled from the trees of heaven, the fragrant odour of which spread throughout the forest, and enraptured all who dwelt beneath its shade. The sage, who was then possessed by religious phrensy,[3] when he beheld that garland, demanded it of the graceful and full-eyed nymph, who,

---

[1] Durvásas was the son of Atri by Anasúyá, and was an incarnation of a portion of Śiva.

[2] A Vidyádharí. These beings, male and female, are spirits of an inferior order, tenanting the middle regions of the atmosphere. According to the Váyu, the garland was given to the nymph by Deví.

[3] He observed the Vrata, or vow of insanity, उन्मत्तव्रतम् । equivalent to the ecstasies of some religious fanatics. 'In this state', says the commentator, 'even saints are devils': योगिनो हि मनोन्मना: पिशाचा एव वर्तन्ते ।[*]

---

[*] The MSS. of the commentary which I have had access to read: योगिनो हि अतीव मनःपिशाचा एव वर्तन्ते ।

bowing to him reverentially, immediately presented
it to him. He, as one frantic, placed the chaplet upon
his brow, and, thus decorated, resumed his path: when
he beheld (Indra) the husband of Sachi, the ruler of
the three worlds, approach, seated on his infuriated
elephant, Airávata, and attended by the gods. The
phrensied sage, taking from his head the garland of
flowers, amidst which the bees collected ambrosia,
threw it to the king of the gods, who caught it, and
suspended it on the brow of Airávata, where it shone
like the river Jáhnaví, glittering on the dark summit
of the mountain Kailása.* The elephant, whose eyes
were dim with inebriety, and attracted by the smell,
took hold of the garland with his trunk, and cast it on
the earth. That chief of sages, Durvásas, was highly
incensed at this disrespectful treatment of his gift, and
thus angrily addressed the sovereign of the immortals:
"Inflated with the intoxication of power, Vásava,
vile of spirit, thou art an idiot not to respect the garland I presented to thee, which was the dwelling of
Fortune (Srí). Thou hast not acknowledged it as a
largess; thou hast not bowed thyself before me; thou
hast not placed the wreath upon thy head, with thy
countenance expanding with delight. Now, fool, for
that thou hast not infinitely prized the garland that I
gave thee, thy sovereignity over the three worlds shall
be subverted. Thou confoundest me, Sakra, with other
Brahmans; and hence I have suffered disrespect from

----

* The original is simply:

गृहीत्वामरराजेन जैरावतमधूर्धनि ।
यथा रराज कैलासशिखरे जाह्नवी यथा ॥

thy arrogance. But, in like manner as thou hast cast the garland I gave thee down on the ground, so shall thy dominion over the universe be whelmed in ruin. Thou hast offended one whose wrath is dreaded by all created things, king of the gods, even me, by thine excessive pride."

Descending hastily from his elephant, Mahendra endeavoured to appease the sinless Durvásas. But, to the excuses and prostrations of the thousand-eyed, the Muni answered: "I am not of a compassionate heart, nor is forgiveness congenial to my nature. Other Munis may relent; but know me, Śakra, to be Durvásas. Thou hast in vain been rendered insolent by Gautama and others; for know me, Indra, to be Durvásas, whose nature is a stranger to remorse. Thou hast been flattered by Vasishtha and other tender-hearted saints, whose loud praises have made thee so arrogant that thou hast insulted me.* But who is there in the universe that can behold my countenance, dark with frowns, and surrounded by my blazing hair, and not tremble? What need of words? I will not forgive, whatever semblance of humility thou mayest assume."

Having thus spoken, the Brahman went his way; and the king of the gods, remounting his elephant, returned to his capital, Amarávatí. Thenceforward, Maitreya, the three worlds and Śakra lost their vigour; and all vegetable products, plants, and herbs were withered and died; sacrifices were no longer offered; devout exercises no longer practised; men were no more addicted to charity, or any moral or religious

* See *Original Sanskrit Texts*, Part I., p. 95, note.

obligation; all beings became devoid of steadiness;[1] all the faculties of sense were obstructed by cupidity; and men's desires were excited by frivolous objects. Where there is energy[*] there is prosperity; and upon prosperity energy depends. How can those abandoned by prosperity be possessed of energy? And without energy where is excellence? Without excellence there can be no vigour or heroism amongst men. He who has neither courage nor strength will be spurned by all; and he who is universally treated with disgrace must suffer abasement of his intellectual faculties.

The three regions being thus wholly divested of prosperity, and deprived of energy, the Dánavas and sons of Diti, the enemies of the gods, who were incapable of steadiness, and agitated by ambition, put forth their strength against the gods. They engaged in war with the feeble and unfortunate divinities; and Indra and the rest, being overcome in fight, fled, for refuge, to Brahmá, preceded by the god of flame (Hutáśana). When the great father of the universe had heard all that had come to pass, he said to the deities: "Repair, for protection, to the god of high and low; the tamer of the demons; the causeless cause of creation, preservation, and destruction; the progenitor of the progenitors; the immortal, unconquerable Vishńu; the cause of matter and spirit, of his unengendered products; the remover of the grief of all who humble themselves before him. He will give you aid." Having

---

[1] They became (निःसत्त्व), Niḥsattwa; and Sattwa is explained, throughout, by Dhairya (धैर्य), 'steadiness', 'fortitude'.

---

[*] Here and below, this represents sattwa.

thus spoken to the deities, Brahmá proceeded, along with them, to the northern shore of the sea of milk, and, with reverential words, thus prayed to the supreme Hari:—

"We glorify him who is all things; the lord supreme over all; unborn, imperishable; the protector of the mighty ones of creation; the unperceived,* indivisible Náráyańa; the smallest of the smallest, the largest of the largest, of the elements; in whom are all things; from whom are all things; who was before existence; the god who is all beings; who is the end of ultimate objects; who is beyond final spirit, and is one with supreme soul; who is contemplated, as the cause of final liberation, by sages anxious to be free; in whom are not the qualities of goodness, foulness, or darkness, that belong to undeveloped nature. May that purest of all pure spirits this day be propitious to us. May that Hari be propitious to us, whose inherent might is not an object of the progressive chain of moments, or of days, that make up time. May he who is called the supreme god, who is not in need of assistance, Hari, the soul of all embodied substance, be favourable unto us. May that Hari, who is both cause and effect; who is the cause of cause, the effect of effect; he who is the effect of successive effect; who is the effect of the effect of the effect, himself; the product of the effect of the effect of the effect, (or elemental substance).[1] To him I bow. The cause of the cause; the cause of the cause

---

[1] The first effect of primary cause is nature, or Prakŕiti; the effect of the effect, or of Prakŕiti, is Mahat; effect in the third

---

* *Aprakáśa*; explained, by the commentator, to mean "self-illuminated".

of the cause: the cause of them all: to him I bow. To
him who is the enjoyer and thing to be enjoyed; the
creator and thing to be created; who is the agent and
the effect: to that supreme being I bow. The infinite
nature of Vishñu is pure, intelligent, perpetual, unborn,
undecayable, inexhaustible, inscrutable, immutable; it
is neither gross nor subtile, nor capable of being defined: to that ever holy nature of Vishñu I bow. To
him whose faculty to create the universe abides in but
a part of but the ten-millionth part of him; to him who
is one with the inexhaustible supreme spirit, I bow:
and to the glorious nature of the supreme Vishñu,
which nor gods, nor sages, nor I, nor Śankara appre-
hend; that nature which the Yogins, after incessant
effort, effacing both moral merit and demerit, behold
to be contemplated in the mystical monosyllable Om:
the supreme glory of Vishñu, who is the first of all;
of whom, one only god, the triple energy is the same
with Brahmá, Vishñu, and Śiva: O lord of all, great
soul of all, asylum of all, undecayable, have pity upon
thy servants! O Vishñu, be manifest unto us."

Parásara continued.—The gods, having heard this
prayer uttered by Brahmá, bowed down, and cried:
"Be favourable to us! Be present to our sight. We

---

degree is Ahaṁkára; in the fourth, or the effect of the effect
(Ahaṁkára) of the effect (Mahat) of the effect (Prakṛiti), is elementary substance, or Bhúta. Vishñu is each and all. So, in
the succeeding ascending scale, Brahmá is the cause of mortal
life; the cause of Brahmá is the egg, or aggregate elementary
matter; its cause is, therefore, elementary matter; the cause of
which is subtile or rudimental matter, which originates from
Ahaṁkára; and so on. Vishñu is, also, each and all of these.

bow down to that glorious nature which the mighty
Brahmá does not know; that which is thy nature, O
imperishable, in whom the universe abides." Then,
the gods having ended, Brihaspati and the divine
Rishis thus prayed: "We bow down to the being entitled to adoration; who is the first object of sacrifice;
who was before the first of things; the creator of the
creator of the world; the undefinable. O lord of all
that has been or is to be; imperishable type of sacrifice;
have pity upon thy worshippers! Appear to them prostrate before thee. Here is Brahmá; here is Trilochana
(the three-eyed Śiva), with the Rudras; Púshan (the
sun), with the Ádityas; and Fire, with all the mighty
luminaries.* Here are the sons of Aświní (the two
Aświní Kumáras), the Vasus and all the winds, the
Sádhyas, the Viśwadevas, and Indra, the king of the
gods; all of whom bow lowly before thee. All the
tribes of the immortals, vanquished by the demon host,
have fled to thee for succour.".

Thus prayed to, the supreme deity, the mighty
holder of the conch and discus, showed himself to them;
and, beholding the lord of gods, bearing a shell, a discus, and a mace, the assemblage of primeval form, and
radiant with embodied light, Pitámaha and the other
deities, their eyes moistened with rapture, first paid
him homage, and then thus addressed him: "Repeated
salutation to thee, who art indefinable! Thou art Brahmá; thou art the wielder of the Pináka bow (Śiva);
thou art Indra; thou art fire, air, the god of waters,†

____

* "Fire, with all its forms": वायवो ऽर्त्र सहार्चिषि: ।

† Varuńa, in the original.

the sun,[*] the king of death (Yama), the Vasus, the
Máruts (the winds), the Sádhyas, and Viśwadevas.
This assembly of divinities, that now has come before
thee, thou art; for, the creator of the world, thou art
everywhere. Thou art the sacrifice, the prayer of oblation,[†] the mystic syllable Om, the sovereign of all
creatures. Thou art all that is to be known, or to be
unknown. O universal soul, the whole world consists
of thee. We, discomfited by the Daityas, have fled to
thee, O Vishńu, for refuge. Spirit of all,[‡] have compassion upon us! Defend us with thy mighty power.
There will be affliction, desire, trouble, and grief, until
thy protection is obtained: but thou art the remover
of all sins. Do thou, then, O pure of spirit, show favour
unto us, who have fled to thee! O lord of all, protect
us with thy great power, in union with the goddess
who is thy strength."[§] Hari, the creator of the universe, being thus prayed to by the prostrate divinities,
smiled, and thus spake: "With renovated energy, O
gods, I will restore your strength. Do you act as I
enjoin. Let all the gods, associated with the Asuras,
cast all sorts of medicinal herbs into the sea of milk;
and then, taking the mountain Mandara for the churn-
ing-stick, the serpent Vásuki for the rope, churn the

---

[1] With thy Śakti, or the goddess Śri or Lakshmí.

---

[*] In the Sanskrit, Savitri.
[†] *Vashatkára*, "the exclamation at a sacrifice".
[‡] These words, and "universal soul", just above, are to render sar-
vátman.
[§] "Lord of all energies, make us, by thy power, to prosper":
सर्व्वां नाथ सर्व्वेषां लक्ष्म्यालिगिनं कुरु ।

ocean together for ambrosia; depending upon my aid. To secure the assistance of the Daityas, you must be at peace with them, and engage to give them an equal portion of the fruit of your associated toil; promising them, that, by drinking the Amrita that shall be produced from the agitated ocean, they shall become mighty and immortal. I will take care that the enemies of the gods shall not partake of the precious draught; that they shall share in the labour alone."

Being thus instructed by the god of gods, the divinities entered into alliance with the demons: and they jointly undertook the acquirement of the beverage of immortality. They collected various kinds of medicinal herbs, and cast them into the sea of milk, the waters of which were radiant as the thin and shining clouds of autumn. They then took the mountain Mandara for the staff, the serpent Vásuki for the cord, and commenced to churn the ocean for the Amrita. The assembled gods were stationed, by Krishna, at the tail of the serpent; the Daityas and Dúnavas, at its head and neck. Scorched by the flames emitted from his inflated hood, the demons were shorn of their glory; whilst the clouds, driven towards his tail by the breath of his mouth, refreshed the gods with revivifying showers. In the midst of the milky sea, Hari himself, in the form of a tortoise, served as a pivot for the mountain, as it was whirled around. The holder of the mace and discus was present, in other forms, amongst the gods and demons, and assisted to drag the monarch of the serpent race; and, in another vast body, he sat upon the summit of the mountain. With one portion of his energy, unseen by gods or demons,

he sustained the serpent-king, and, with another, infused vigour into the gods.

From the ocean, thus churned by the gods and
Dánavas, first uprose the cow Surabhi, the fountain
of milk and curds, worshipped by the divinities, and
beheld by them and their associates with minds disturbed and eyes glistening with delight. Then, as the
holy Siddhas in the sky wondered what this could be,
appeared the goddess Váruńí (the deity of wine), her
eyes rolling with intoxication. Next, from the whirl-
pool of the deep, sprang the celestial Párijáta tree, the
delight of the nymphs of heaven; perfuming the world
with its blossoms. The troop of Apsarasas (the nymphs
of heaven), were then produced, of surprising loveliness,
endowed with beauty and with taste. The cool-rayed
moon next rose, and was seized by Mahádeva; and
then poison was engendered from the sea, of which
the snake-gods (Nágas) took possession. Dhanwantari, robed in white, and bearing in his hand the cup
of Amṛita, next came forth; beholding which, the sons
of Diti and of Danu, as well as the Munis, were filled
with satisfaction and delight. Then, seated on a full-
blown lotos, and holding a water-lily in her hand, the
goddess Śrí, radiant with beauty, rose from the waves.
The great sages, enraptured, hymned her with the
song dedicated to her praise.[1][2] Viśwávasu and other

---

[1] Or with the Súkta, or hymn of the Vedas, commencing,
"Hirańyavarńám", &c.

[2] "The song dedicated to her praise" translates *Śrí-súkta*. For the
hymn so called, with its commentary, edited by me, see Müller's *Ṛig-veda*,
Vol. IV., Varietas Lectionis, pp. 5, *et seq.*

heavenly quiristers sang, and Ghṛitáchí and other celestial nymphs danced before her. Gangá and other holy streams attended for her ablutions; and the elephants of the skies, taking up their pure waters in vases of gold, poured them over the goddess, the queen of the universal world. The sea of milk, in person, presented her with a wreath of never-fading flowers; and the artist of the gods (Viśwakarmma) decorated her person with heavenly ornaments. Thus bathed, attired, and adorned, the goddess, in the view of the celestials, cast herself upon the breast of Hari, and, there reclining, turned her eyes upon the deities, who were inspired with rapture by her gaze. Not so the Daityas, who, with Viprachitti at their head, were filled with indignation, as Vishńu turned away from them: and they were abandoned by the goddess of prosperity (Lakshmí).

The powerful and indignant Daityas then forcibly seized the Amṛita-cup, that was in the hand of Dhanwantari. But Vishńu, assuming a female form, fascinated and deluded them, and, recovering the Amṛita from them, delivered it to the gods. Śakra and the other deities quaffed the ambrosia. The incensed demons, grasping their weapons, fell upon them. But the gods, into whom the ambrosial draught had infused new vigour, defeated and put their host to flight; and they fled through the regions of space, and plunged into the subterraneous realms of Pátála. The gods thereat greatly rejoiced, did homage to the holder of the discus and mace, and resumed their reign in heaven. The sun shone with renovated splendour, and again discharged his appointed task; and the celestial luminaries again circled, O best of Munis, in their respective orbits. Fire once more blazed aloft, beautiful in splendour; and the minds of all beings were animated by devotion. The three worlds again were rendered happy by prosperity; and Indra, the chief of the gods, was restored to power.[1] Seated upon his throne, and once more in

---

[1] The churning of the ocean does not occur in several of the Puráńas, and is but cursorily alluded to in the Śiva, Linga, and Kúrma Puráńas. The Váyu and Padma have much the same narrative as that of our text; and so have the Agni and Bhágavata, except that they refer only briefly to the anger of Durvásas, without narrating the circumstances; indicating their being posterior, therefore, to the original tale. The part, however, assigned to Durvásas appears to be an embellishment added to the original; for no mention of him occurs in the Matsya Puráńa or even in the Hari Vaṁśa. Neither does it occur in what may be considered the oldest extant versions of the story, those of the Rámáyańa and Mahábhárata. Both these ascribe the occurrence to the desire of the gods and Daityas to become immortal. The Matsya assigns a similar motive to the gods, instigated by observing that the Daityas slain by them in battle were restored to life, by Śukra, with the Sanjíviní or herb of immortality, which he had discovered. The account in the Hari Vaṁśa is brief and obscure, and is explained, by the commentator, as an allegory, in which the churning of the ocean typifies ascetic penance, and the ambrosia is final liberation. But this is mere mystification. The legend of the Rámáyańa is translated, Vol. I., p. 410, of the Serampore edition, and that of the Mahábhárata, by Sir C. Wilkins, in the notes to his translation of the Bhagavad Gítá. See, also, the original text, Calcutta edition, p. 40. It has been presented to general readers, in a more attractive form, by my friend, H. M. Parker, in his Draught of Immortality, printed, with other poems, London, 1827. The Matsya Puráńa has many of the stanzas of the Mahábhárata interspersed with others. There is some variety in the order and number of articles produced from

heaven, exercising sovereignty over the gods, Śakra thus eulogized the goddess who bears a lotos in her hand:

---

the ocean. As I have observed elsewhere (Hindu Theatre, Vol. I., p. 59, London edition), the popular enumeration is fourteen. But the Rámáyaña specifies but nine; the Mahábhárata, nine; the Bhágavata, ten; the Padma, nine; the Váyu, twelve: the Matsya, perhaps, gives the whole number. Those in which most agree are: 1. the Hálahála or Kálakúta poison, swallowed by Śiva; 2. Váruńí or Surá, the goddess of wine, who being taken by the gods, and rejected by the Daityas, the former were termed Suras, and the latter, Asuras; 3. the horse Uchchaihśravas, taken by Indra; 4. Kaustubha, the jewel worn by Vishńu; 5. the moon; 6. Dhanwantari, with the Amŕita in his Kamańdalu or vase; and these two articles are, in the Váyu, considered as distinct products; 7. the goddess Padmá or Śrí; 8. the Apsarasas or nymphs of heaven; 9. Surabhi or the cow of plenty; 10. the Párijáta tree or tree of heaven; 11. Airávata, the elephant taken by Indra. The Matsya adds: 12. the umbrella taken by Varuńa; 13. the ear-rings taken by Indra, and given to Aditi; and, apparently, another horse, the white horse of the sun. Or the number may be completed by counting the Amŕita separately from Dhanwantari. The number is made up, in the popular lists, by adding the bow and the conch of Vishńu. But there does not seem to be any good authority for this; and the addition is a sectarial one. So is that of the Tulasí tree, a plant sacred to Kŕishńa, which is one of the twelve specified by the Váyu Puráńa. The Uttara Khańda of the Padma Puráńa has a peculiar enumeration, or: Poison; Jyeshthá or Alakshmí, the goddess of misfortune, the elder born to fortune; the goddess of wine; Nidrá or sloth; the Apsarasas; the elephant of Indra; Lakshmí; the moon; and the Tulasí plant. The reference to Mohiní, the female form assumed by Vishńu, is very brief in our text; and no notice is taken of the story told in the Mahábhárata and some of the Puráńas, of the Daitya Ráhu's insinuating himself amongst

" I bow down to Śrí, the mother of all beings, seated
on her lotos-throne, with eyes like full-blown lotoses,
reclining on the breast of Vishńu. Thou art Siddhi
(superhuman power); thou art Swadhá and Swáhá;
thou art ambrosia (Sudhá), the purifier of the universe;
thou art evening, night, and dawn; thou art power,
intellect, faith;* thou art the goddess of letters (Saraswatí). Thou, beautiful goddess, art knowledge of devotion, great knowledge, mystic knowledge, and spiritual knowledge,¹ which confers eternal liberation.
Thou art the science of reasoning,† the three Vedas,
the arts and sciences;² thou art moral and political

---

the gods, and obtaining a portion of the Amŕíta. Being beheaded,
for this, by Vishńu, the head became Immortal, in consequence
of the Amŕíta having reached the throat, and was transferred, as
a constellation, to the skies: and, as the sun and moon detected
his presence amongst the gods, Ráhu pursues them, with impla-
cable hatred, and his efforts to seize them are the causes of
eclipses; Ráhu typifying the ascending and descending nodes.
This seems to be the simplest and oldest form of the legend.
The equal immortality of the body, under the name Ketu, and
his being the cause of meteorical phenomena, seems to have been
an afterthought. In the Padma and Bhágavata, Ráhu and Ketu
are the sons of Siṁhiká, the wife of the Dánava Viprachiti.

¹ The four Vidyás or branches of knowledge are said to be:
Yajna-vidyá, knowledge or performance of religious rites; Mahá-
vidyá, great knowledge, the worship of the female principle, or Tántrika worship; Guhya-vidyá, knowledge of mantras, mystical prayers,
and incantations; and Átma-vidyá, knowledge of soul, true wisdom.

² Or Várttá, explained to mean the Śilpa-śástra, mechanics,
sculpture, and architecture; Áyur-veda, medicine; &c.

* Bhúti, medhá, and śraddhá.
† Ánvíkshikí.

science.† The world is peopled, by thee, with pleasing or displeasing forms. Who else than thou, O goddess, is seated on that person of the god of gods, the wielder of the mace, which is made up of sacrifice, and contemplated by holy ascetics? Abandoned by thee, the three worlds were on the brink of ruin: but they have been reanimated by thee. From thy propitious gaze, O mighty goddess, men obtain wives, children, dwellings, friends, harvests, wealth. Health and strength, power, victory, happiness are easy of attainment to those upon whom thou smilest. Thou art the mother of all beings; as the god of gods, Hari, is their father: and this world, whether animate or inanimate, is pervaded by thee and Vishńu. O thou who purifiest all things, forsake not our treasures, our granaries, our dwellings, our dependants, our persons, our wives. Abandon not our children, our friends, our lineage, our jewels, O thou who abidest on the bosom of the god of gods. They whom thou desertest are forsaken by truth, by purity, and goodness, by every amiable and excellent quality; whilst the base and worthless upon whom thou lookest favourably become immediately endowed with all excellent qualifications, with families, and with power. He on whom thy countenance is turned is honourable, amiable, prosperous, wise, and of exalted birth, a hero of irresistible prowess. But all his merits and his advantages are converted into worthlessness, from whom, beloved of Vishńu, mother of the world, thou avertest thy face. The tongues of Brahmá are unequal to celebrate thy excellence. Be

---

† *Dakshańi.*

propitious to me, O goddess, lotos-eyed; and never forsake me more."

Being thus praised, the gratified Śrí, abiding in all creatures, and heard by all beings, replied to the god of a hundred rites (Śatakratu): "I am pleased, monarch of the gods, by thine adoration. Demand from me what thou desirest. I have come to fulfil thy wishes." "If, goddess", replied Indra, "thou wilt grant my prayers; if I am worthy of thy bounty; be this my first request,—that the three worlds may never again be deprived of thy presence. My second supplication, daughter of Ocean, is, that thou wilt not forsake him who shall celebrate thy praises in the words I have addressed to thee." "I will not abandon", the goddess answered, "the three worlds again. This thy first boon is granted: for I am gratified by thy praises. And, further, I will never turn my face away from that mortal who, morning and evening, shall repeat the hymn with which thou hast addressed me."

Parásara proceeded.—Thus, Maitreya, in former times the goddess Śrí conferred these boons upon the king of the gods, being pleased by his adorations. But her first birth was the daughter of Bhrigu by Khyáti. It was at a subsequent period that she was produced from the sea, at the churning of the ocean, by the demons and the gods, to obtain ambrosia.[1] For, in

---

[1] The cause of this, however, is left unexplained. The Padma Puráńa inserts a legend to account for the temporary separation of Lakshmí from Vishńu, which appears to be peculiar to that work. Bhrigu was lord of Lakshmípura, a city on the Narmadá, given him by Brahmá. His daughter Lakshmí instigated her husband to request its being conceded to her, which offending

like manner as the lord of the world, the god of gods, Janárdana, descends amongst mankind (in various shapes), so does his coadjutrix Śrí. Thus, when Hari was born as a dwarf, the son of Aditi, Lakshmí appeared from a lotos (as Padmá or Kamalá). When he was born as Ráma, of the race of Bhrigu (or Paraśuráma), she was Dharańí. When he was Rághava (Rámachandra), she was Sítá. And, when he was Krishńa, she became Rukminí. In the other descents of Vishńu, she is his associate. If he takes a celestial form, she appears as divine: if a mortal, she becomes a mortal, too; transforming her own person agreeably to whatever character it pleases Vishńu to put on. Whosoever hears this account of the birth of Lakshmí, whosoever reads it, shall never lose the goddess Fortune from his dwelling, for three generations; and misfortune, the fountain of strife, shall never enter into those houses in which the hymns to Śrí are repeated.

Thus, Brahman, have I narrated to thee, in answer to thy question, how Lakshmí, formerly the daughter of Bhrigu, sprang from the sea of milk. And misfortune shall never visit those amongst mankind who daily recite the praises of Lakshmí, uttered by Indra, which are the origin and cause of all prosperity.

Bhrigu, he cursed Vishńu to be born upon earth ten times, to be separated from his wife, and to have no children. The legend is an insipid modern embellishment.

CHAPTER X.

MAITREYA.—Thou hast narrated to me, great Muni, all that I asked of thee. Now resume the account of the creation subsequently to Bhrigu.

PARÁSARA.—Lakshmí, the bride of Vishńu, was the daughter of Bhrigu by Khyáti. They had also two sons, Dhátri and Vidhátri, who married the two daughters of the illustrious Meru, Áyati and Niyati, and had, by them, each, a son, named Práńu and Mrikańda.* The son of the latter was Márkańdeya, from whom Veda-siras was born.[1] The son of Práńa was named Dyuti-

---

[1] The commentator interprets the text तनो वेदशिरा अभू to refer to Práńa: प्राणाब वेदशिरा अभू । 'Vedasiras was born the son of Práńa.' So the Bhágavata † has:

मार्कण्डेयो मृकण्डस्य प्राणाद्वेदशिरा मुनि; ।

The Linga, the Váyu, and Márkańdeya, however, confirm our reading of the text; making Vedasiras the son of Márkańdeya. Práńa, or, as read in the two former, Páńdu, was married to Puńdarika. and had, by her, Dyutimat, whose sons were Srija-vána and Asruta or Asrutavrana. Mrikańda (also read Mrikańdu) married Manaswiní, and had Márkańdeya, whose son, by Múr-dhanyá, was Vedasiras. He married Pivari, and had many children, who constituted the family or Brahmanical tribe of the Bhárgavas, sons of Bhrigu. The most celebrated of these was Usanas. the preceptor of the Daityas, who, according to the Bhá-gavata, was the son of Vedasiras. But the Váyu makes him the son of Bhrigu by Paulomi, and born at a different period.

---

* All the MSS. seen by me have Mrikańdu.
† IV, 1, 45.

mat; and his son was Rájavat; after whom the race of Bhrigu became infinitely multiplied.

Sambhúti, the wife of Maríchi, gave birth to Paurnamása, whose sons were Virajas and Sarvaga. I shall hereafter notice his other descendants, when I give a more particular account of the race of Maríchi.[1]

The wife of Angiras, Smriti, bore daughters named Siníválí, Kuhú, Ráká, and Anumati (phases of the moon).[2] Anasúyá, the wife of Atri, was the mother

---

[1] Alluding especially to Kaśyapa, the son of Marichi, of whose posterity a full detail is subsequently given. The Bhágavata adds a daughter, Devakulyá; and the Váyu and Linga, four daughters, Tushti, Pushti, Twishá, and Apachiti. The latter inserts the grandsons of Paurnamása. Virajas, married to Gauri, has Sudháman, a Lokapála, or ruler of the east quarter; and Parvasa (quasi Sarvaga) has, by Parvasá, Yajuvama and Kaśyata,[*] who were, both, founders of Gotras or families.[†] The names of all these occur in different forms[‡] in different MSS.

[2] The Bhágavata adds, that, in the Swárochisha Manwantara,

---

[*] Professor Wilson had "Parvasi". Instead of his "Kaśyata", I find, in MSS., Kaśyapa: and there is a *gotra* named after the latter. And see my next note.

[†] The words of the *Váyu-puráńa*, in the MSS. within my reach, are:

पर्वस: सर्वबधानां प्रविष: स महायया: ।
पर्वस: पर्वसाला तु बमयामास वै श्रुती ॥
यह्वानां च श्रीमन्तं सुतं काश्यपमेव च ।
तयोर्नीचघरी पुत्री तौ आनी धर्मोजिचिती ॥

The first line of this quotation is, in some MSS. that I have seen, पर्वस: सर्वबधानामविष: &c.; and one MS. has, instead of प्रविष:, प्रविष:. All those MSS. have स महायया:, or स महायच:. But, without conjectural mending, the line in question yields no sense. Professor Wilson's "quasi Sarvaga" seems to imply that the MS., or MSS., which he followed had some such lection as सर्वग एव.

[‡] These names and forms of names—and so throughout the notes to this work—are very numerous; and a fully satisfactory account of them, in the absence of critical editions of the Puráńas, is impracticable.

of three sinless sons: Soma (the moon), Durvásas, and
the ascetic* Dattátreya.[1] Pulastya had, by Príti, a
son, called, in a former birth, or in the Swáyambhuva
Manwantara, Dattoli,† who is now known as the sage
Agastya.[2] Kshamá, the wife of the patriarch Pulaha,
was the mother of three sons: Karmaśa,‡ Arvarivat,§

the sages Utathya and Brihaspati were also sons of Angiras;
and the Váyu, &c. specify Agni and Kirttimat as the sons of the
patriarch, in the first Manwantara. Agni, married to Sadwati,
has Parjanya, married to Márichi; and their son is Hiranyaroman,
a Lokapála. Kirttimat has, by Dhenuká, two sons, Charishńu
and Dhritimat.

[1] The Bhágavata gives an account of Atri's penance, by which
the three gods, Brahmá, Vishńu, and Śiva, were propitiated, and
became, in portions of themselves, severally his sons, Soma,
Datta, and Durvásas. The Váyu has a totally different series,
or five sons: Satyanetra, Havya, Ápomúrti, Śani, and Soma;
and one daughter, Śruti, who became the wife of Kardama.

[2] The text would seem to imply that he was called Agastya
in a former Manwantara: but the commentator explains it as
above. The Bhágavata calls the wife of Pulastya, Havirbhú,
whose sons were the Muni Agastya, called, in a former birth,
Dahrágni (or Jatharágni) and Viśravas. The latter had, by
Idavidá, the deity of wealth, Kuvera, and, by Keśini, the Rákshasas Rávańa, Kumbhakarńa, and Vibhishańa. The Váyu

* Yogin.
† Variants of this name are Dattáli, Dattotli, Dattotri, Dattobhri,
Dambhobhi, and Dambholi
‡ Kardama seems to be a more common reading than "Karmaśa".
§ Also written Avarivat, and Arvaríyat.
, The text is as follows;

प्रीत्या पुलस्त्यभार्य्यायां दत्तोलिर्यस्तनूजोऽभवत् ।
पूर्व्वजन्मनि सोऽगस्त्यः पुनः स्वायंभुवेऽत्ररे ॥

And the commentator observes: तस्तूनः पुलस्त्यपुत्रः पूर्व्वजन्मनि स्वा-
यंभुवमन्वन्तरे दत्तोलिः स दत्तोलिर्मुनस्तुः पुनः एतस्यः ।

and Sahishńu.[1] The wife of Kratu, Samnati, brought forth the sixty thousand Válikhilyas, pigmy sages,[*] no bigger than a joint of the thumb, chaste, pious, resplendent as the rays of the sun.[2] Vasishtha had seven sons, by his wife Urjá: Rajas, Gátra, Urdhwabáhu, Savana,[†] Anagha, Sutapas, and Śukra, the seven pure sages.[3] The Agni named Abhimánin, who is the eldest

---

specifies three sons of Pulastya,—Dattoli, Vedabáhu,[‡] and Vinita, and one daughter, Sadwati, married (see p. 153, note 2) to Agni.

[1] The Bhágavata reads Karmaśreshtha, Variyas, and Sahishńu. The Váyu and Linga have Kardama and Ambarisha, in place of the two first, and add Vanakapivat and a daughter, Pivarí, married to Vedaśiras (see p. 152, note). Kardama married Śruti (p. 154, note 2), and had, by her, Sankhapáda, one of the Lokapálas, and a daughter, Kámyá, married to Priyavrata (p. 108, note 1). Vanakapivat (also read Dhanakapivat and Ghanakapivat) had a son, Sahishńu, married to Yaśodhará; and they were the parents of Kámadeva.

[2] The different authorities agree in this place. The Váyu adds two daughters, Punyá and Sumati, married to Yajnaváma (see p. 153, note 1).

[3] The Bhágavata has an entirely different set of names, or: Chitraketu, Surochis, Virajas, Mitra, Ulbańa, Vasubhridyána, and Dyumal. It also specifies Śaktri and others, as the issue of a different marriage. The Váyu and Linga have the same sons as in our text; reading Putra and Hasta, in place of Gátra. They add a daughter, Puńdariká, married to Páńda (see p. 152, note). The eldest son, according to the Váyu, espoused a daughter of Márkańdeya, and had, by her, the Lokapála of the west, Ketumat. The seven sons of Vasishtha are termed, in the text, the seven Rishis; appearing, in that character, in the third Manwantara.

* Yati.
† Vasana is another reading.
‡ I find Devabáhu in one MS. of the Váyu-puráńa.

born of Brahmá, had, by Swáhá, three sons of surpass-
ing brilliancy: Pávaka, Pavamána, and Śuchi, who
drinks up water. They had forty-five sons, who, with
the original son of Brahmá, and his three descendants,
constitute the forty-nine fires.[1] The progenitors (Pitŕis),
who, as I have mentioned, were created by Brahmá,
were the Agnishwáttas and Barhishads; the former
being devoid of, and the latter possessed of, fires.[2] By

---

[1] The eldest son of Brahmá, according to the commentator,
upon the authority of the Vedas: ब्रह्मणो ज्येष्ठोऽपत्यो मुसादृपित्रा-
पतेति श्रुते; । The Váyu Puráńa enters into a very long detail
of the names and places of the whole forty-nine fires. According
to that, also, Pávaka is electric or Vaidyuta fire; Pavamána is
that produced by friction, or Nirmathya; and Śuchi is solar
(Saura) fire. Pavamána was the parent of Kavyaváhana, the fire
of the Pitŕis; Śuchi, of Havyaváhana, the fire of the gods; and
Pavamána, of Saharaksha, the fire of the Asuras. The Bhágavata explains these different fires to be so many appellations of
fire employed in the invocations with which different oblations
to fire are offered in the ritual of the Vedas:

एतानि कर्माणि यज्ञामभिर्ब्रह्मवादिभिः ।
यायेब हेतयो यज्ञे निरूप्यन्तेऽपयचु ते ॥

explained, by the commentator; वेदिते कर्माणि यज्ञे येषां नामभि-
रविदेवताका हेतयो निरूप्यन्ते कियन्तो न एते ऽपयो न लौकिका: ।

[2] According to the commentator, this distinction is derived
from the Vedas. The first class, or Agnishwáttas, consists of
those householders who, when alive, did not maintain their domestic fires, nor offer burnt-sacrifices; the second, of those who
kept up the household flame, and presented oblations with fire.
Manu† calls these Agnidagdhas and the reverse, which Sir William
Jones renders 'consumable by fire', &c. Kullúka Bhaṭṭa gives
no explanation of them. The Bhágavata adds other classes of

---

* *Bhágavata-puráńa*, IV., 1, 61.   † III., 198.

them Swadhá had two daughters, Mená and Dháriní,
who were, both, acquainted with theological truth, and
both addicted to religious meditation, both accomplished in perfect wisdom, and adorned with all esti-
mable qualities.[1] Thus has been explained the progeny
of the daughters of Daksha.[2] He who, with faith, recapitulates the account shall never want offspring.

Pitrís; or, the Ájyapas, 'drinkers of ghee', and Somapas, 'drinkers
of the acid juice.' The commentator, explaining the meaning of
the terms Ságni and Anagni, has: येषामग्नी सरसमग्नि ते
सायव:। बहुविनास्तरनयव:। which might be understood to signify
that the Pitrís who are 'without fire' are those to whom oblations
are not offered, and those 'with fire' are they to whom oblations
are presented.

[1] The Váyu carries this genealogy forward. Dháriní was
married to Meru, and had, by him, Mandara and three daughters,
Niyati, Áyati, and Velá. The two first were married to Dhátri
and Vidhátri (p. 152). Velá was the wife of Samudra, by whom
she had Sámudri, married to Práchínabarhis, and the mother of
the ten Prachetasas, the fathers of Daksha, as subsequently narrated. Mená was married to Himavat, and was the mother of
Maináka, and of Gangá, and of Párvati or Umá.

[2] No notice is here taken of Satí, married to Bhava, as is
intimated in c. 8 (pp. 117, 118), when describing the Rudras. Of
these genealogies the fullest and, apparently, the oldest account
is given in the Váyu Purána. As far as that of our text extends,
the two nearly agree; allowing for differences of appellation,
originating in inaccurate transcription; the names frequently varying
in different copies of the same work, leaving it doubtful which
reading should be preferred. The Bhágavata, as observed above
(p. 109 note 3), has created some further perplexity by substitu-
ting, as the wives of the patriarchs, the daughters of Kardama,
for those of Daksha. Of the general statement it may be observed,
that, although, in some respects, allegorical, as in the names of
the wives of the Rishis (p. 109), and, in others, astronomical, as

In the denominations of the daughters of Angiras (p. 153), yet it seems probable that it is not altogether fabulous, but that the persons, in some instances, had a real existence; the genealogies originating in imperfectly preserved traditions of the families of the first teachers of the Hindu religion, and of the descent of individuals who took an active share in its propagation.

CHAPTER XI.

PARÁSARA continued.—I mentioned to you that the
Manu Swáyambhuva had two heroic and pious sons,
Priyavrata and Uttánapáda. Of these two the latter
had a son, whom he dearly loved, Uttama, by his
favourite wife, Suruchi. By his queen, named Suniti,
to whom he was less attached, he also had a son, called
Dhruva.[1] Observing his brother Uttama on the lap of
his father, as he was seated upon his throne, Dhruva
was desirous of ascending to the same place; but, as
Suruchi was present, the Raja did not gratify the desire
of his son, respectfully wishing to be taken on his
father's knee. Beholding the child of her rival thus
anxious to be placed on his father's lap, and her own
son already seated there, Suruchi thus addressed the
boy: "Why, child, do you vainly indulge in such presumptuous hopes? You are born from a different
mother, and are no son of mine, that you should aspire
inconsiderately to a station fit for the excellent Uttama
alone. It is true you are the son of the Raja: but I

---

[1] The Matsya, Brahma, and Váyu Puráńas speak of but one
wife of Uttánapáda, and call her Súníti. They say, also, that she
had four sons: Apaspati (or Vasu), Áyushmat, Kírttimat, and
Dhruva. The Bhágavata, Padma, and Náradíya have the same
account as that of the text.

have not given you birth. This regal throne, the seat of the king of kings, is suited to my son only. Why should you aspire to its occupation? Why idly cherish such lofty ambition, as if you were my son? Do you forget that you are but the offspring of Suníti?"

The boy, having heard the speech of his step-mother, quitted his father, and repaired, in a passion, to the apartment of his own mother; who, beholding him vexed, took him upon her lap, and, gently smiling, asked him what was the cause of his anger, who had displeased him, and if any one, forgetting the respect due to his father, had behaved ill to him. Dhruva, in reply, repeated to her all that the arrogant Suruchi had said to him, in the presence of the king. Deeply distressed by the narrative of the boy, the humble Suníti, her eyes dimmed with tears, sighed, and said: "Suruchi has rightly spoken. Thine, child, is an unhappy fate. Those who are born to fortune are not liable to the insults of their rivals. Yet be not afflicted, my child. For who shall efface what thou hast formerly done, or shall assign to thee what thou hast left undone? The regal throne, the umbrella of royalty, horses, and elephants are his whose virtues have deserved them. Remember this, my son, and be consoled. That the king favours Suruchi is the reward of her merits in a former existence. The name of wife alone belongs to such as I, who have not equal merit. Her son is the progeny of accumulated piety, and is born as Uttama. Mine has been born as Dhruva, of inferior moral worth. Therefore, my son, it is not proper for you to grieve. A wise man will be contented with that degree which appertains to him. But, if you continue to feel hurt at the words of Suruchi, endeavour to augment that religious merit which bestows all good. Be amiable; be pious; be friendly; be assiduous in benevolence to all living creatures. For prosperity descends upon modest worth, as water flows towards low ground."

Dhruva answered: "Mother, the words that you have addressed to me, for my consolation, find no place in a heart that contumely has broken. I will exert myself to obtain such elevated rank, that it shall be revered by the whole world. Though I be not born of Suruchi, the beloved of the king, you shall behold my glory, who am your son. Let Uttama, my brother, her child, possess the throne given to him by my father. I wish for no other honours than such as my own actions shall acquire, such as even my father has not enjoyed."

Having thus spoken, Dhruva went forth from his mother's dwelling. He quitted the city, and entered an adjoining thicket, where he beheld seven Munis, sitting upon hides of the black antelope, which they had taken from off their persons, and spread over the holy Kuśa grass. Saluting them reverentially, and bowing humbly before them, the prince said: "Behold, in me, venerable men, the son of Uttánapáda, born of Suníti. Dissatisfied with the world, I appear before you." The Ŕishis replied: "The son of a king, and but four or five years of age, there can be no reason, child, why you should be dissatisfied with life. You cannot be in want of anything, whilst the king, your father, reigns. We cannot imagine that you suffer the pain of separation from the object of your affections;

L   11

nor do we observe, in your person, any sign of disease. What is the cause of your discontent? Tell us, if it is known to yourself."

Dhruva then repeated to the Rishis what Suruchi had spoken to him; and, when they had heard his story, they said to one another: "How surprising is the vehemence of the Kshatriya nature, that resentment is cherished even by a child, and he cannot efface from his mind the harsh speeches of a step-mother! Son of a Kshatriya, tell us, if it be agreeable to thee, what thou hast proposed, through dissatisfaction with the world, to accomplish. If thou wishest our aid in what thou hast to do, declare it freely: for we perceive that thou art desirous to speak."

Dhruva said: "Excellent sages, I wish not for riches; neither do I want dominion. I aspire to such a station as no one before me has attained. Tell me what I must do, to effect this object; how I may reach an elevation superior to all other dignities." (The Rishis severally thus replied.) Maríchi said: "The best of stations is not within the reach of men who fail to propitiate Govinda. Do thou, prince, worship the undecaying (Achyuta)." Atri said: "He with whom the first of spirits, Janárdana, is pleased, obtains imperishable dignity. I declare unto you the truth." Angiras said: "If you desire an exalted station, worship that Govinda in whom, immutable and undecaying, all that is exists." Pulastya said: "He who adores the divine Hari, the supreme soul, supreme glory, who is the supreme Brahma, obtains what is difficult of attainment, eternal liberation." "When that Janárdana", observed Kratu, "who, in sacrifices, is the soul of sacrifice, and who, in

abstract contemplation, is supreme spirit,* is pleased,
there is nothing man may not acquire." Pulaha said:
"Indra, having worshipped the lord of the world, obtained the dignity of king of the celestials. Do thou
adore, pious youth, that Vishńu, the lord of sacrifice."
"Anything, child, that the mind covets", exclaimed
Vasishťha, "may be obtained by propitiating Vishńu,—
even though it be the station that is the most excellent in the three worlds."

Dhruva replied to them: "You have told me, humbly
bending before you, what deity is to be propitiated.
Now inform me what prayer is to be meditated by me,
that will offer him gratification. May the great Rishis,
looking upon me with favour, instruct me how I am
to propitiate the god." The Rishis answered: "Prince,
thou deservest to hear how the adoration of Vishńu
has been performed by those who have been devoted
to his service. The mind must first be made to forsake
all external impressions; and a man must then fix it
steadily on that being in whom the world is. By him
whose thoughts are thus concentrated on one only
object, and wholly filled by it; whose spirit is firmly
under control; the prayer that we shall repeat to thee
is to be inaudibly recited: 'Om! Glory to Vásudeva,
whose essence is divine wisdom; whose form is in-

* यज्ञस्याप ।
यो यज्ञपुरुषो यज्ञे योनि य: परम: पुमान् ।
तमिंसुरे तु नाम्ना यं किंचिदर्शि अनार्हमे ॥
The commentator says: यज्ञे यज्ञप्रतिपादके शास्त्रे । योनि योनयास्त्रे ।
यदा । येनो य: मीयत एवेत्यर्थ: ।
The meaning is, then: "who, in *the śástra of* sacrifice, *is called* the
soul of the sacrifice, and, in the Yoga *śástra*, the supreme spirit."

scrutable, or is manifest as Brahmá, Vishńu, and Śiva!"
This prayer, which was formerly uttered by your
grandsire, the Manu Swáyambhuva, and propitiated by
which, Vishńu conferred upon him the prosperity he
desired, and which was unequalled in the three worlds,
is to be recited by thee. Do thou constantly repeat
this prayer, for the gratification of Govinda."[*]

---

[*] The instructions of the Ŕishis amount to the performance
of the Yoga. External impressions are, first, to be obviated by
particular positions, modes of breathing, &c. The mind must
then be fixed on the object of meditation: this is Dhárańá. Next
comes the meditation or Dhyána; and then the Japa or inaudible
repetition of a Mantra or short prayer: as in the text. The subject of the Yoga is more fully detailed in a subsequent book.

हिरण्यगर्भपुरुषप्रधानाव्यक्तरूपिणे ।
ॐ नमो वासुदेवाय शुद्धज्ञानस्वरूपिणे ॥
एतज्जाप भगवाञ्जग्य सायंभुवो मनुः ।
पितामहस्त्व पुरा तस्य तुष्टो जनार्दनः ॥
इदो यत्राभिलषितामूर्तिं त्रैलोक्यदुर्लभाम् ।
तथा त्वमपि गोविन्दं तोषयैतत्तदा जपन् ॥

"'Om! Glory to Vásudeva, who has the form of Hirańyagarbha, and
of soul, and of *pradhána* when not yet evolved, and who possesses the
nature of pure intelligence!' Mann, the holy son of the Self-existent
Brahmá, muttered this prayer. Janárdana, thy grandsire, of yore, propitiated, bestowed on him wealth to his wish, such as is hard to be
acquired in the three worlds. Therefore, daily muttering this *prayer*,
do thou, too, propitiate Govinda."

For Hirańyagarbha and *pradhána*, see pp. 13, 20, 39, and 40, *supra.*

CHAPTER XII.

THE prince, having received these instructions, respectfully saluted the sages, and departed from the forest, fully confiding in the accomplishment of his purposes. He repaired to the holy place, on the banks of the Yamuná, called Madhu or Madhuvana, (the grove of Madhu), after the demon of that name, who formerly abided there. Śatrughna (the younger brother of Ráma) having slain the Rákshasa Lavańa, the son of Madhu, founded a city on the spot, which was named Mathurá. At this holy shrine—the purifier from all sin, which enjoyed the presence of the sanctifying god of gods—Dhruva performed penance, as enjoined by Maríchi and the sages. He contemplated Vishńu, the sovereign of all the gods, seated in himself. Whilst his mind was wholly absorbed in meditation, the mighty Hari, identical with all beings and with all natures, (took possession of his heart). Vishńu being thus present in his mind, the earth, the supporter of elemental life, could not sustain the weight of the ascetic. As he stood upon his left foot, one hemisphere bent beneath him; and, when he stood upon his right, the other half of the earth sank down. When he touched the earth with his toes, it shook, with all its mountains; and the rivers and the seas were troubled: and the gods partook of the universal agitation.

The celestials called Yámas, being excessively alarmed, then took counsel with Indra, how they should interrupt the devout exercises of Dhruva; and the divine beings termed Kushmáńdas. in company with their king. commenced anxious efforts to distract his meditations. One, assuming the semblance of his mother, Suníti, stood weeping before him, and calling in tender accents: "My son, my son, desist from destroying thy strength by this fearful penance. I have gained thee, my son, after much anxious hope. Thou canst not have the cruelty to quit me, helpless, alone, and unprotected, on account of the unkindness of my rival. Thou art my only refuge. I have no hope but thou. What hast thou, a child but five years old, to do with rigorous penance? Desist from such fearful practices, that yield no beneficial fruit. First comes the season of youthful pastime; and, when that is over, it is the time for study. Then succeeds the period of worldly enjoyment; and, lastly, that of austere devotion. This is thy season of pastime, my child. Hast thou engaged in these practices to put an end to thine existence? Thy chief duty is love for me. Duties are according to time of life. Lose not thyself in bewildering error. Desist from such unrighteous actions. If not, if thou wilt not desist from these austerities, I will terminate my life before thee."

But Dhruva, being wholly intent on seeing Vishńu, beheld not his mother weeping in his presence, and calling upon him; and the illusion, crying out, "Fly, fly, my child: the hideous spirits of ill are crowding

into this dreadful forest, with uplifted weapons", quickly
disappeared. Then advanced frightful Rákshasas, wielding terrible arms, and with countenances emitting fiery
flame; and nocturnal fiends thronged around the prince,
uttering fearful noises, and whirling and tossing their
threatening weapons. Hundreds of jackals, from
whose mouths gushed flame,' as they devoured their
prey, were howling aloud, to appal the boy, wholly
engrossed by meditation. The goblins called out: "Kill
him, kill him: cut him to pieces; eat him, eat him."
And monsters, with the faces of lions and camels and
crocodiles. roared and yelled, with horrible cries, to
terrify the prince. But all these uncouth spectres, ap-
palling cries, and threatening weapons made no impression upon his senses, whose mind was completely
intent on Govinda. The son of the monarch of the
earth, engrossed by one only idea, beheld, uninter-
ruptedly. Vishńu seated in his soul. and saw no other
object.

All their delusive stratagems being thus foiled, the
gods were more perplexed than ever. Alarmed at
their discomfiture. and afflicted by the devotions of
the boy, they assembled, and repaired, for succour, to
Hari, the origin of the world, who is without beginning
or end, and thus addressed him: "God of gods, sovereign of the world, god supreme, and infinite spirit,'

' A marginal note, by a Bengali Pandit, asserts it to be a
fact. that, when a jackal carries a piece of meat in his mouth,
it shows. in the dark, as if it was on fire.

' *Purushottama*, in the original. See my third note in p. 16, *supra*.

distressed by the austerities of Dhruva, we have come
to thee for protection. As the moon increases in his
orb day by day, so this youth advances incessantly
towards superhuman power, by his devotions. Terrified
by the ascetic practices of the son of Uttánapáda, we
have come to thee for succour. Do thou allay the
fervour of his meditations. We know not to what
station he aspires—to the throne of Indra, the regency
of the solar or lunar sphere, or to the sovereignty of
riches or of the deep. Have compassion on us, lord:
remove this affliction from our breasts. Divert the
son of Uttánapáda from persevering in his penance."
Vishṅu replied to the gods: "The lad desireth neither
the rank of Indra, nor the solar orb, nor the sovereignty of wealth or of the ocean. All that he solicits
I will grant. Return, therefore, deities, to your man-
sions, as ye list; and, be no more alarmed. I will put
an end to the penance of the boy, whose mind is immersed in deep contemplation."

The gods, being thus pacified by the supreme, saluted
him respectfully, and retired, and, preceded by Indra,
returned to their habitations. But Hari, who is all
things, assuming a shape with four arms, proceeded
to Dhruva, being pleased with his identity of nature,
and thus addressed him: "Son of Uttánapáda, be prosperous. Contented with thy devotions, I, the giver of
boons, am present. Demand what boon thou desirest.
In that thou hast wholly disregarded external objects,
and fixed thy thoughts on me, I am well pleased with
thee. Ask, therefore, a suitable reward." The boy,
hearing these words of the god of gods, opened his
eyes, and, beholding that Hari, whom he had before

seen in his meditations, actually in his presence, bearing, in his hands, the shell, the discus, the mace, the bow, and scimetar, and crowned with a diadem, he bowed his head down to earth: the hair stood erect on his brow, and his heart was depressed with awe. He reflected how best he should offer thanks to the god of gods, what he could say in his adoration, what words were capable of expressing his praise; and, being overwhelmed with perplexity, he had recourse, for consolation, to the deity. "If", he exclaimed, "the lord is contented with my devotions, let this be my reward,—that I may know how to praise him as I wish. How can I, a child, pronounce his praises, whose abode is unknown to Brahmá and to others learned in the Vedas? My heart is overflowing with devotion to thee. O lord, grant me the faculty worthily to lay mine adorations at thy feet."

Whilst lowly bowing, with his hands uplifted to his forehead, Govinda, the lord of the world, touched the son of Uttánapáda with the tip of his conch-shell. And immediately the royal youth, with a countenance sparkling with delight, praised respectfully the imperishable protector of living beings. "I venerate", exclaimed Dhruva, "him whose forms are earth, water, fire, air, ether, mind, intellect, the first element* (Ahaṅkára), primeval nature, and the pure, subtile, all-pervading soul, that surpasses nature.† Salutation to that spirit that is void of qualities; that is supreme over all the elements and all the objects of sense, over intellect,

---

* *Bhuddhi.* See my first note in p. 33, *supra.*

† Here, and in the next sentence, "nature" is for *pradhána.* See my first note in p. 20, *supra.*

over nature and spirit. I have taken refuge with that
pure form of thine, O supreme, which is one with
Brahma, which is spirit, which transcends all the world.
Salutation to that form which, pervading and supporting all, is designated Brahma, unchangeable, and contemplated by religious sages. Thou art the male with
a thousand heads, a thousand eyes, a thousand feet,
who traversest the universe, and passest ten inches
beyond its contact.[1] Whatever has been, or is to be,
that, Purushottama, thou art. From thee sprang Viráj,
Swaráj, Samráj, and Adhipurusha.[2] The lower, and
upper, and middle parts of the earth are not independent of thee. From thee is all this universe, all
that has been, and that shall be; and all this world is
in thee, assuming this universal form.[3] From thee is

---

[1] The commentator understands this passage to imply merely,
that the supreme pervades both substance and space; being infinitely vast, and without limit. 'Having a thousand heads', &c.
denotes only infinite extension; and the 'ten inches beyond the
contact of the universe' expresses merely non-restriction by its
boundaries. दृष्टान्तमिदमधिकमपरम् । यतोऽयमर्वः । सर्वं
महत्वं सुष्ठभिवाच महत्तित्वाच निरवधिर्मवाच्चित इति ।

[2] Explained, severally, the Brahmáńda or material universe;
Brahmá, the creator; Manu, the ruler of the period; and supreme
or presiding spirit.

[3] So the inscription upon the temple of Sais: Ἐγώ εἰμι πᾶν
τὸ γεγονὸς, καὶ ὄν, καὶ ἐσόμενον. So the Orphic verse, cited
by Eusebius, beginning:
    "Ἐν δὲ δέμας βασιλειον ἐν ᾧ τάδε πάντα κυκλεῖται, κ. τ. λ.
'One regal body in which all things are comprehended (viz.,
Viráj), fire, and water, and earth, and air, and night, and day,
and Intelligence (viz., Mahat), the first generator, and divine love:
for all these does Jupiter include in his expansive form.' It proceeds, also, precisely in the Pauráńik strain, to describe the mem-

sacrifice derived, and all oblations, and curds, and ghee, and animals of either class (domestic or wild). From thee the Rig-veda, the Sáman, the metres (of the Vedas), and the Yajur-veda are born. Horses, and cows having teeth in one jaw only,[1] proceed from thee; and from thee come goats, sheep, deer. Brahmans sprang from thy mouth; warriors, from thy arms; Vaiśyas, from thy thighs; and Śúdras, from thy feet. From thine eyes come the sun: from thine ears, the wind; and, from thy mind, the moon; the vital airs. from thy central vein; and fire, from thy mouth; the sky. from thy navel; and heaven, from thy head; the regions. from thine ears; the earth. from thy feet. All this world was derived from thee. As the wide-spreading Nyagrodha (Indian fig) tree is compressed in a small seed,[2] so, at the time of dissolution,* the whole universe is comprehended in thee. as its germ. As the Nyagrodha germinates from the seed, and becomes. first, a shoot. and then rises into loftiness, so the created world proceeds from thee, and expands into magnitude. As the bark and leaves of the plantain—tree are to be seen in its stem. so thou art the stem of the universe: and all things are visible in thee. The faculties of the intellect, that are the cause of pleasure and of pain, abide in

hers of this universal form. The heaven is his head; the stars, his hair; the sun and moon, his eyes, &c.

[1] A piece of natural history quite correct, as applied to the front teeth, which, in the genus ox, occur in the lower jaw only.

[2] This is. also, conformable to the doctrine, that the rudiments of plants exist in their cotyledons.

* Sáyana.

thee, as one with all existence. But the sources of
pleasure and of pain, singly, or blended, do not exist
in thee, who art exempt from all qualities.[1] Salutation
to thee, the subtile rudiment, which, being single, becomes manifold. Salutation to thee, soul of existent
things, identical with the great elements. Thou, imperishable, art beheld, in spiritual knowledge, as perceptible objects, as nature, as spirit, as the world, as
Brahmá, as Manu, by internal contemplation.[2] But
thou art in all, the element of all: thou art all, assuming
every form: all is from thee: and thou art from thyself.
I salute thee, universal soul. Glory be to thee! Thou
art one with all things, O lord of all, thou art present

---

[1] In life, or living beings, perception depends not, according
to Hindu metaphysics, upon the external senses; but the impressions made upon them are communicated to the mental organ
or sense, and by the mind to the understanding—Saṁvid (संविद्)
in the text—by which they are distinguished as pleasurable, pain-
ful, or mixed. But pleasure depends upon the quality of goodness; pain, on that of darkness; and their mixture, on that of
foulness, inherent in the understanding: properties belonging to
Jíveśwara, or god as one with life, or to embodied spirit, but not
as Parameśwara or supreme spirit.

[2] चराचरभूतात्मविराडहङ्काराद्यना ।
विभाव्यतेऽक्षरे सर्वे पुरुषेष्वव्ययो भवान् ॥

"Thou art regarded, in mental action, as the evolved, as *pradhána*,
as spirit; as *viráj*, *samráj*, and *swaráj*; as, among souls, the imperishable
soul."

For *pradhána*, the same as *prakṛiti*, see my first note in p. 15, and
the first in p. 20, *supra*. It is *ahankára*, &c. that is meant by "the
evolved", *viz.*, *pradhána*. *Pradhána*, unqualified, is here to be taken as
unevolved. *Viráj*, *samráj*, and *swaráj* are well-known technicalities of
the Vedánta philosophy.

The Supreme, under various aspects, is described in this couplet.

in all things. What can I say unto thee? Thou knowest
all that is in the heart, O soul of all, sovereign lord of
all creatures, origin of all things. Thou, who art all
beings, knowest the desires of all creatures. The desire
that I cherished has been gratified, lord, by thee. My
devotions have been crowned with success, in that I
have seen thee."

Vishṅu said to Dhruva: "The object of thy devotions
has, in truth, been attained, in that thou hast seen me:
for the sight of me, young prince, is never unproductive.
Ask, therefore, of me what boon thou desirest: for
men in whose sight I appear obtain all their wishes."
To this, Dhruva answered: "Lord god of all creatures,
who abidest in the hearts of all, how should the
wish that I cherish be unknown to thee? I will confess
unto thee the hope that my presumptuous heart has
entertained; a hope that it would be difficult to gratify,
but that nothing is difficult, when thou, creator of the
world, art pleased. Through thy favour, Indra* reigns
over the three worlds. The sister-queen of my mother
has said to me, loudly and arrogantly: 'The royal
throne is not for one who is not born of me': and I
now solicit of the support of the universe an exalted
station, superior to all others, and one that shall endure
for ever." Vishṅu said to him: "The station that thou
askest thou shalt obtain: for I was satisfied with thee,
of old, in a prior existence. Thou wast, formerly, a
Brahman, whose thoughts were ever devoted to me,
ever dutiful to thy parents, and observant of thy duties.
In course of time, a prince became thy friend, who was

---

* Maghavat, in the original.

in the period of youth, indulged in all sensual pleasures, and was of handsome appearance and elegant form. Beholding, in consequence of associating with him, his affluence, you formed the desire that you might be subsequently born as the son of a king; and, according to your wish, you obtained a princely birth, in the illustrious mansion of Uttánapáda. But that which would have been thought a great boon by others, birth in the race of Swáyambhuva, you have not so considered, and, therefore, have propitiated me. The man who worships me obtains speedy liberation from life. What is heaven to one whose mind is fixed on me? A station shall be assigned to thee, Dhruva, above the three worlds;[1] one in which thou shalt sustain the stars and the planets; a station above those of the sun, the moon, Mars, the son of Soma (Mercury), Venus, the son of Súrya (Saturn), and all the other constellations; above the regions of the seven Rishis and the divinities

---

[1] The station or sphere is that of the north pole, or of the polar star. In the former case, the star is considered to be Suniti, the mother of Dhruva. The legend, although, as it is related in our text, it differs, in its circumstances, from the story told, by Ovid, of Callisto and her son Arcas, whom Jove

Imposuit cælo vicinaque sidera fecit,

suggests some suspicion of an original identity. In neither of the authorities have we, perhaps, the primitive fable. It is evident, from the quotation, that presently follows in the text, of a stanza by Usanas, that the Puráná has not the oldest version of the legend; and Ovid's representation of it is after a fashion of his own. All that has been retained of the original is the conformity of the characters and of the main incident, the translation of a mother and her son to the heavens, as constellations, in which the pole-star is the most conspicuous luminary.

who traverse the atmosphere.[1] Some celestial beings endure for four ages; some, for the reign of a Manu. To thee shall be granted the duration of a Kalpa. Thy mother, Suníti, in the orb of a bright star, shall abide near thee for a similar term; and all those who, with minds attentive, shall glorify thee at dawn, or at eventide, shall acquire exceeding religious merit.

Thus, the sage Dhruva, having received a boon from Janárdana, the god of gods, and lord of the world, resides in an exalted station. Beholding his glory, Usanas, the preceptor of the gods and demons, repeated these verses: "Wonderful is the efficacy of this penance, marvellous is its reward, that the seven Rishis should be preceded by Dhruva. This, too, is the pious Suníti, his parent, who is called Súnritá."[2] Who can celebrate her greatness, who, having given birth to Dhruva, has become the asylum of the three worlds, enjoying, to all future time, an elevated station, a station eminent above all? He who shall worthily describe the ascent into the sky of Dhruva, for ever shall be freed from all sin, and enjoy the heaven of Indra. Whatever be his dignity, whether upon earth, or in heaven, he shall never fall from it, but shall long enjoy life, possessed of every blessing.[3]

---

[1] The Vaimánika devas, the delties who travel in Vimánas, 'heavenly ears', or, rather, 'moving spheres.'

[2] The text says merely: सुनीतिनीतम सुनृता । The commentator says: 'Perhaps* formerly so called'; पुर्वनाम वा । We have already remarked, that some Puránas so denominate her.

[3] The legend of Dhruva is narrated in the Bhágavata, Padma

---

* The वा, here rendered "perhaps", connects two interpretations, and means "or else".

(Swarga Khańda), Agni, and Náradíya, much to the same purport, and partly in the same words, as our text. The Brahma, and its double, the Hari Vaṃśa, the Matsya, and Váyu, merely allude to Dhruva's having been transferred, by Brahmá, to the skies, in reward of his austerities. The story of his religious penance and adoration of Vishńu seems to be an embellishment interpolated by the Vaishńava Puráńas; Dhruva being adopted, as a saint, by their sect. The allusion to Súnítá, in our text, concurs with the form of the story as it appears elsewhere, to indicate the priority of the more simple legend.

CHAPTER XIII.

PARÁSARA.—The sons of Dhruva, by his wife Sam-
bhu, were Bhavya and Slishti. Suchchháyá, the wife
of the latter, was the mother of five virtuous sons;
Ripu, Ripunjaya, Vipra, Vrikala, and Vrikatejas. The
son of Ripu, by Brihatí, was the illustrious Chakshusha,
who begot the Manu Chákshusha on Pushkariní, of the
family of Varuna, the daughter of the venerable patriarch Anaranya. The Manu had, by his wife Nadvalá,[*]
the daughter of the patriarch Vairája, ten noble sons:
Úru, Puru,[†] Satadyumna, Tapaswin, Satyavách, Kavi,
Agnishtoma, Atirátra, Sudyumna, and Abhimanyu.
The wife of Úru, Ágneyí, bore six excellent sons:
Anga, Sumanas, Swáti, Kratu, Angiras, and Siva. Anga
had, by his wife Sunithá, only one son, named Vena,
whose right arm was rubbed, by the Rishis, for the
purpose of producing from it progeny. From the arm
of Vena, thus rubbed, sprang a celebrated monarch,

---

* Professor Wilson inadvertently put "Navalá".

† Púru is the older form of this word, as, for instance, in the *Rig-
veda*, *Sákuntala*, &c.

named Pṛithu, by whom, in olden time, the earth was
milked for the advantage of mankind.[1]

---

[1] The descent of Pṛithu from Dhruva is similarly traced in
the Matsya Puráńa, but with some variety of nomenclature. Thus,
the wife of Dhruva is named Dhanyá, and the eldest son of the
Manu, Taru. The Váyu introduces another generation; making
the eldest son of Slishṭi,—or, as there termed, Pushṭi,—father of
Udáradhí, and the latter, the father of Ripu, the father of Chakshusha, the father of the Manu. The Bhágavata [*] has an almost
entirely different set of names, having converted the family of
Dhruva into personifications of divisions of time and of day and
night. The account there given is: Dhruva had, by his wife
Bhrami (revolving), the daughter of Sisumára (the sphere), Kalpa
and Vatsara. The latter married Swarvíthi, and had six sons:
Pushpárńa, Tigmaketu, Isha, Úrja, Vasu, Jaya. The first married
Prabhá and Doshá, and had, by the former, Prátas (dawn),
Madhyandina (noon), and Sáya (evening), and, by the latter,
Pradosha, Nisitha, and Vyushta, or the beginning, middle, and
end, of night. The last has, by Pushkariní, Chakshus, married
to Ákúti, and the father of Chákshusha Manu. He has twelve sons:
Puru, Kutsa, Trita, Dyumna, Satyavat, Ṛita,[†] Vrata, Agnishṭoma,
Atirátra, Pradyumna, Sibi, and Ulmuka. The last is the father
of six sons, named as in our text, except the last, who is called
Gaya.[‡] The eldest, Anga, is the father of Vena, the father of
Pṛithu. These additions are, evidently, the creatures of the author's
imagination. The Brahma Puráńa and Hari Vaṃśa have the
same genealogy as the Vishńu; reading, as do the Matsya and
Váyu, Pushkariní or Viraní, the daughter of Virańa, instead of
Varuńa. They, as well as copies of the text, present several

---

[*] IV., 10 and 13.

[†] Professor Wilson had "Kṛituna", "Ṛita", and "Dhṛita", instead of
Kutsa, Trita, and Ṛita.

[‡] The *Bhágavata-puráńa* also has Khyáti, instead of Swáti. And see
my second note in the next page.

MAITREYA.—Best of Munis, tell me why was the right hand of Vena rubbed by the holy sages, in consequence of which the heroic Prithu was produced.

PARÁSARA.—Suníthá was, originally,* the daughter of Mŕityu, by whom she was given to Anga to wife. She bore him Vena, who inherited the evil propensities of his maternal grandfather. When he was inaugurated, by the Rishis, monarch of the earth, he caused it to be everywhere proclaimed, that no worship should be performed, no oblations offered, no gifts bestowed upon the Brahmans. "I, the king", said he, "am the lord of sacrifice. For who but I am entitled to the oblations?" The Rishis, respectfully approaching the sovereign, addressed him in melodious accents, and said: "Gracious prince, we salute you. Hear what we have to represent. For the preservation of your kingdom and your life, and for the benefit of all your subjects, permit us to worship Hari, the lord of all sacrifice, the god of gods, with solemn and protracted rites,[1]—a por-

---

other varieties of nomenclature. † The Padma Puráńa (Bhúmi Khańḍa) says Anga was of the family of Atri; in allusion, perhaps, to the circumstance, mentioned in the Brahma Puráńa, of Uttánapáda's adoption by that Rishi.

[1] With the Dirghasatra, 'long sacrifice'; a ceremony lasting a thousand years.

---

* Some MSS. have, instead of मृत्योः प्रथमतोऽभवत्, मृत्योः प्रथमजाभवत् । It seems, therefore, better to substitute: "Suníthá was Mŕityu's eldest daughter."

† The principal variants of the Vishṇu-puráṇa are as follows: for "Slishṭi", Sishṭi; for "Varuńa", Viriṇa; for "Anaraṇya", Araṇya; for "Kavi", Suchi; for "Agnishṭoma", Agnishṭat; for "Kudyumna", Pradyumna; for "Swáti", Khyáti; for "Siva", Ushij.

tion of the fruit of which will revert to you.[1] Vishṇu,
the god of oblations,[*] being propitiated with sacrifice
by us, will grant you, O king, all your desires. Those
princes have all their wishes gratified, in whose realms
Hari, the lord of sacrifice, is adored with sacrificial
rites." "Who", exclaimed Vena, "is superior to me?
Who besides me is entitled to worship? Who is this
Hari, whom you style the lord of sacrifice? Brahmá,
Janárdana, Saṃbhu, Indra, Váyu, Yama, Ravi (the
sun), Hutabhuj (fire), Varuṇa, Dhátṛi, Púshan (the
sun), Bhúmi (earth), the lord of night (the moon),—
all these, and whatever other gods there be who listen
to our vows,—all these are present in the person of a
king. The essence of a sovereign is all that is divine.[†]
Conscious of this, I have issued my commands: and
look that you obey them. You are not to sacrifice, not
to offer oblations, not to give alms. As the first duty
of women is obedience to their lords, so observance
of my orders is incumbent, holy men, on you." "Give
command, great king", replied the Rishis, "that piety
may suffer no decrease. All this world is but a trans-

---

[1] That is, the land will be fertile in proportion as the gods
are propitiated; and the king will benefit accordingly, as a sixth
part of the merit and of the produce will be his. So the commentator explains the word 'portion': वंश: वशो भाग: ।

[*] Yajnapurusha. See my note in p. 163, supra.

[†] एते चान्ये च ये देवा: शापानुग्रहकारिण: ।
नृपशरीरस्था: सर्वदेवमयो नृप: ॥
In place of "whatever other gods there be who listen to our vows",
read "whatever other gods bestow curses or blessings."

The end of the stanza signifies, literally: "A king is made up of all
that is divine."

mutation of oblations; and, if devotion be suppressed, the world is at an end." But Vena was entreated in vain: and, although this request was repeated by the sages, he refused to give the order they suggested. Then those pious Munis were filled with wrath, and cried out to each other: "Let this wicked wretch be slain. The impious man who has reviled the god of sacrifice,* who is without beginning or end, is not fit to reign over the earth." And they fell upon the king, and beat him with blades of holy grass, consecrated by prayer, and slew him, who had first been destroyed by his impiety towards god.

Afterwards the Munis beheld a great dust arise; and they said to the people who were nigh: "What is this?" And the people answered and said: "Now that the kingdom is without a king, the dishonest men have begun to seize the property of their neighbours. The great dust that you behold, excellent Munis, is raised by troops of clustering robbers, hastening to fall upon their prey."† The sages, hearing this, consulted, and together rubbed the thigh of the king, who had left no offspring, to produce a son. From the thigh, thus rubbed, came forth a being of the complexion of a charred stake, with flattened features (like a negro), and of dwarfish stature. "What am I to do?" cried he eagerly to the Munis. "Sit down" (nishída), said they: and thence his name was Nisháda. His descendants, the inhabitants of the Vindhya mountain, great Muni, are still called Nishádas, and are characterized by

* Yajnapurusha.
† There is here considerable compression in the translation.

the exterior tokens of depravity.[1] By this means the wickedness of Vena was expelled; those Nishádas being

[1] The Matsya says there were born outcast or barbarous races, Mlechchhas (म्लेच्छजातयः), as black as collyrium. The Bhágavata describes an individual of dwarfish stature, with short arms and legs, of a complexion as black as a crow, with projecting chin, broad flat nose, red eyes, and tawny hair; whose descendants were mountaineers and foresters.* The Padma (Bhúmi Khańda) has a similar description; adding to the dwarfish stature and black complexion, a wide mouth, large ears, and a protuberant belly. It also particularizes his posterity as Nishádas, Kirátas, Bhillas, Bahanakas, Bhrahmaras, Pulindas, and other barbarians or Mlechchhas, living in woods and on mountains. These passages intend, and do not much exaggerate, the uncouth appearance of the Gonds, Koles, Bhils, and other uncivilized tribes, scattered along the forests and mountains of central India, from Behar to

* *Bhágavata-puráńa*, IV., 14, 43-46:

विनिश्चित्यैवमृषयो विपन्नस्य महीपतेः ।
ममन्थुरूरुं तरसा तत्रासीद्बाहुको नरः ॥
काककृष्णोऽतिह्रस्वाङ्गो ह्रस्वबाहुर्महाहनुः ।
ह्रस्वपान्निम्ननासाग्रो रक्ताक्षस्ताम्रमूर्धजः ॥
तं तु तेऽवनतं दीनं किं करोमीति वादिनम् ।
निषीदेत्यब्रुवंस्तात स निषादस्ततोऽभवत् ॥
तस्य वंश्यास्तु नैषादा गिरिकाननगोचराः ।
येनाहरज्जायमानो वेनकल्मषमुल्बणम् ॥

Burnouf's translation is in these words:

"Ayant pris cette résolution, les Ŕichis secouèrent rapidement la cuisse du roi qu'ils avaient tué, et il en sortit un nain

"Noir comme un corbeau, ayant le corps d'une extrême petitesse, les bras courts, les mâchoires grandes, les pieds petits, le nez enfoncé, les yeux rouges et les cheveux cuivrés.

"Prosterné devant eux, le pauvre nain s'écria: Que faut-il que je fasse? Et les Bráhmanes lui répondirent: Assieds-toi, ami. De là lui vint le nom de Nichâda.

"C'est de sa race que sont sortis les Nâichâdas qui habitent les cavernes et les montagnes; car c'est lui dont la naissance effaça la faute terrible de Véna."

born of his sins, and carrying them away. The Brahmans then proceeded to rub the right arm of the king,
from which friction was engendered the illustrious son
of Vena, named Prithu, resplendent in person, as if the
blazing deity of Fire had been manifested.

There then fell from the sky the primitive bow (of
Mahádeva) named Ájagava, and celestial arrows, and
panoply from heaven. At the birth of Prithu, all living
creatures rejoiced; and Vena, delivered, by his being
born, from the hell named Put, ascended to the realms
above.* The seas and rivers, bringing jewels (from
their depths), and water to perform the ablutions of
his installation, appeared. The great parent of all,
Brahmá, with the gods and the descendants of Angiras
(the fires), and with all things animate or inanimate,
assembled, and performed the ceremony of consecrating
the son of Vena. Beholding in his right hand the
(mark of the) discus of Vishńu, Brahmá recognized
a portion of that divinity in Prithu, and was much
pleased. For the mark of Vishńu's discus is visible in
the hand of one who is born to be a universal emperor,[1]
one whose power is invincible even by the gods.

Khandesh, and who are, not improbably, the predecessors of the
present occupants of the cultivated portions of the country. They
are always very black, ill-shapen, and dwarfish, and have countenances of a very African character.

[1] A Chakravartin, or, according to the text, one in whom the
Chakra (the discus of Vishńu) abides (vartate); such a figure being
delineated by the lines of the hand. The grammatical etymology
is: 'He who abides in, or rules over, an extensive territory called
a Chakra.'

---

* See *Original Sanskrit Texts*, Part I., pp. 60-63.

The mighty Pṛithu, the son of Vena, being thus invested with universal dominion by those who were skilled in the rite, soon removed the grievances of the people whom his father had oppressed; and, from winning their affections, he derived the title of Rájá or king.[1] The waters became solid, when he traversed the ocean: the mountains opened him a path: his banner passed unbroken (through the forests): the earth needed not cultivation; and, at a thought, food was prepared: all kine were like the cow of plenty: honey was stored in every flower. At the sacrifice of the birth of Pṛithu, which was performed by Brahmá, the intelligent Súta (herald or bard) was produced, in the juice of the moon-plant, on the very birth-day.[2] At that great sacrifice also was produced the accomplished Mágadha. And the holy sages said to these two persons: "Praise ye the king Pṛithu, the illustrious son of Vena. For this is your especial function, and here is a fit subject for your praise." But they respectfully replied to the Brahmans: "We know not the acts of the new-born king of the earth. His merits are not understood by us: his fame is not spread abroad. Inform us upon what subject we may dilate in his praise." "Praise the king", said the Rishis, "for the acts this

---

[1] From Rága (राग), 'passion' or 'affection.' But the more obvious etymology is Ráj (राज्), 'to shine' or 'be splendid.'

[2] The birth of Pṛithu is to be considered as the sacrifice, of which Brahmá, the creator, was the performer. But, in other places, as in the Padma, it is considered that an actual sacrificial rite was celebrated, at which the first encomiasts were produced. The Bhágavata does not account for their appearance.

heroic monarch will perform: praise him for the virtues he will display."

The king, hearing these words, was much pleased, and reflected, that persons acquire commendation by virtuous actions, and that, consequently, his virtuous conduct would be the theme of the eulogium which the bards were about to pronounce. Whatever merits, then, they should panegyrize, in their encomium, he determined that he would endeavour to acquire; and, if they should point out what faults ought to be avoided, he would try to shun them. He, therefore, listened attentively, as the sweet-voiced encomiasts celebrated the future virtues of Pṛithu, the enlightened son of Vena.

"The king is a speaker of truth, bounteous, an observer of his promises. He is wise, benevolent, patient, valiant, and a terror to the wicked. He knows his duties; he acknowledges services; he is compassionate and kind-spoken. He respects the venerable; he performs sacrifices; he reverences the Brahmans. He cherishes the good, and, in administering justice, is indifferent to friend or foe."

The virtues thus celebrated by the Súta and the Mágadha were cherished in the remembrance of the Raja, and practised, by him, when occasion arose. Protecting this earth, the monarch performed many great sacrificial ceremonies, accompanied by liberal donations. His subjects soon approached him, suffering from the famine by which they were afflicted; as all the edible plants had perished during the season of anarchy. In reply to his question of the cause of their coming, they told him that, in the interval in which the earth was without a king, all vegetable products had been withheld, and that, consequently, the people had perished. "Thou", said they, "art the bestower of subsistence to us: thou art appointed, by the creator, the protector of the people. Grant us vegetables, the support of the lives of thy subjects, who are perishing with hunger."

On hearing this, Príthu took up his divine bow Ájagava, and his celestial arrows, and, in great wrath, marched forth to assail the Earth. Earth, assuming the figure of a cow, fled hastily from him, and traversed, through fear of the king, the regions of Brahmá and the heavenly spheres. But, wherever went the supporter of living things, there she beheld Vainya with uplifted weapons. At last, trembling (with terror), and anxious to escape his arrows, the Earth addressed Príthu, the hero of resistless prowess. "Know you not, king of men", said the Earth, "the sin of killing a female, that you thus perseveringly seek to slay me?" The prince replied: "When the happiness of many is secured by the destruction of one malignant being, the death of that being is an act of virtue." "But", said the Earth, "if, in order to promote the welfare of your subjects, you put an end to me, whence, best of monarchs, will thy people derive their support?" "Disobedient to my rule", rejoined Príthu, "if I destroy thee, I will support my people by the efficacy of my own devotions." Then the Earth, overcome with apprehension, and trembling in every limb, respectfully saluted the king, and thus spoke: "All undertakings are successful, if suitable means of effecting them are employed. I will impart to you means of success, which you can make use of, if you please. All vege

table products are old, and destroyed by me: but, at
your command, I will restore them, as developed from
my milk. Do you, therefore, for the benefit of mankind,
most virtuous of princes, give me that calf by which
I may be able to secrete milk. Make, also, all places
level, so that I may cause my milk, the seed of all
vegetation, to flow everywhere around."

Prithu, accordingly, uprooted the mountains, by
hundreds and thousands, for myriads of leagues; and
they were, thenceforth, piled upon one another. Before
his time there were no defined boundaries of villages
or towns, upon the irregular surface of the earth; there
was no cultivation, no pasture, no agriculture, no high-
way for merchants. All these things (or all civilization)
originated in the reign of Prithu. Where the ground
was made level, the king induced his subjects to take
up their abode. Before his time, also, the fruits and
roots which constituted the food of the people were
procured with great difficulty; all vegetables having
been destroyed: and he, therefore, having made Swáyambhuva Manu the calf,[1] milked the Earth, and re-

---

[1] 'Having willed or determined the Manu Swáyambhava to
be the calf:'

स वत्सयित्वा वत्सं तु मनुं स्वायंभुव प्रभु: ।

So the Padma Puráńa:

* * * * * * * * वत्सं तस्या: मर्विचिनम् ।
मनुं स्वायंभुव पूर्वं परिचिंत्य गुण: गुज: ॥

The Bhágavata[*] has: वत्सं कृत्वा मनुम् । 'Having made the Manu
the calf.' By the 'calf', or Manu in that character, is typified,
the commentator observes, the promoter of the multiplication of
progeny: प्रजाभिवृद्धिप्रवर्तकं ।

---

[*] IV., 18, 19.

ceived the milk into his own hand, for the benefit of
mankind. Thence proceeded all kinds of corn and
vegetables upon which people subsist now and perpetually. By granting life to the Earth, Prithu was
as her father; and she thence derived the patronymic
appellation Prithiví (the daughter of Prithu). Then
the gods, the sages, the demons, the Rákshasas, the
Gandharvas, Yakshas, Pitris, serpents, mountains, and
trees, took a milking vessel suited to their kind, and
milked the earth of appropriate milk. And the milker
and the calf were both peculiar to their own species.[1]

---

[1] The Matsya, Brahma, Bhágavata, and Padma enter into a
greater detail of this milking, specifying, typically, the calf, the
milker, the milk, and the vessel. Thus, according to the Matsya,
the Rishis milked the earth through Brihaspati; their calf was
Soma; the Vedas were the vessel; and the milk was devotion.
When the gods milked the earth, the milker was Mitra (the sun);
Indra was the calf; superhuman power was the produce. The
gods had a gold, the Pitris, a silver, vessel: and, for the latter,
the milker was Antaka (death); Yama was the calf; the milk
was Swadhá or oblation. The Nágas or snake-gods had a gourd
for their pail; their calf was Takshaka; Dhritaráshtra (the serpent)
was their milker; and their milk was poison. For the Asuras,
Máyá was the milk; Virochana, the son of Prahláda, was the
calf; the milker was Dwimúrdhan; and the vessel was of iron.
The Yakshas made Vaisravańa their calf; their vessel was of
unbaked earth: the milk was the power of disappearing. The
Rákshasas and others employed Raupyanábha as the milker;
their calf was Sumálin; and their milk was blood. Chitraratha
was the calf, Vasuruchi, the milker, of the Gandharvas and nymphs,
who milked fragrant odours into a cup of lotos-leaves. On behalf
of the mountains, Meru was the milker; Himavat, the calf; the
pail was of crystal; and the milk was of herbs and gems. The
trees extracted sap in a vessel of the Palása; the Sál being the

This Earth—the mother, the nurse, the receptacle, and nourisher, of all existent things—was produced from

milker, and the Plaksha, the calf. The descriptions that occur in the Bhágavata,* Padma, and Brahma Puráńas are, occasionally, slightly varied; but they are, for the most part, in the same words as that of the Matsya. These mystifications are, all, probably, subsequent modifications of the original simple allegory, which typified the earth as a cow, who yielded to every class of beings the milk they desired, or the object of their wishes.

* The account given in the *Bhágavata-puráńa*—IV., 18, 12-27—is in these words:

इति प्रियं हितं वाक्यं भुव आदाय भूपतिः ।
वत्सं कृत्वा मनुं पाणावदुहत्सकलौषधीः ॥
तथापरे च सर्वत्र सारमाददते बुधाः ।
ततोऽन्ये च यथाकामं दुदुहुः पृथुभाविताम् ॥
ऋषयो दुदुहुर्देवीमिन्द्रियेष्वथ सत्तम ।
वत्सं बृहस्पतिं कृत्वा पयश्छन्दोमयं शुचि ॥
कृत्वा वत्सं सुरगणा इन्द्रं सोममदूदुहन् ।
हिरण्मयेन पात्रेण वीर्यमोजो बलं पयः ॥
दैतेया दानवा वत्सं प्रह्लादमसुरर्षभम् ।
विधायादूदुहन्क्षीरमयःपात्रे सुरासवम् ॥
गन्धर्वाप्सरसोऽधुक्षन्पात्रे पद्ममये पयः ।
वत्सं विश्वावसुं कृत्वा गान्धर्वं मधुसौभगम् ॥
वत्सेन पितरोऽर्यम्णा कव्यं क्षीरमधुक्षत ।
आमपात्रे महाभागाः श्रद्धया श्राद्धदेवताः ॥
प्रकल्प्य वत्सं कपिलं सिद्धाः संकल्पनामयीम् ।
सिद्धिं नभसि विद्यां च ये च विद्याधरादयः ॥
अन्ये च मायिनो मायामन्तर्धानाद्भुतात्मनाम् ।
मयं प्रकल्प्य वत्सं ते दुदुहुर्धारणामयीम् ॥
यक्षरक्षांसि भूतानि पिशाचाः पिशिताशनाः ।
भूतेशवत्सा दुदुहुः कपाले क्षतजासवम् ॥
तथाहयो दन्दशूकाः सर्पा नागाश्च तक्षकम् ।
विधाय वत्सं दुदुहुर्बिलपात्रे विषं पयः ॥
पशवो यवसं क्षीरं वत्सं कृत्वा च गोवृषम् ।
अरण्यपात्रे चाधुक्षन्मृगेन्द्रेण च दंष्ट्रिणः ॥

the sole of the foot of Vishńu. And thus was born the mighty Pŕithu, the heroic son of Vena, who was

कवादाः माविनः कर्व सुरुजः हरकसेवरे ।
सुपर्वबत्सा विश्वभावर वावरमेव च ॥
पढवत्सा पनस्ततयः पुबयस्मयं पयः ।
निर्दुदो द्विजमद्वत्सा नानाधातूस्तथायुग ॥
सर्वे समुज्जबत्सेन ते हि पारे पुबल्पयः ।
सर्वकामदुघा पुथी दुदुजः पुबुभाविताम् ॥
एवं पुबादयः पुबीमद्राहाः सद्याक्षाजन् ।
दौबवत्सादिभेदेन वीरमेद दुह्वह ॥

Burnouf's translation of this passage is as follows:

"Se conformant au conseil amical et utile de la terre, le roi lui donna pour veau le Manu, et se mettant à la traire de sa main, il en tira toutes les plantes annuelles.

"C'est ainsi que d'autres sages ont su, comme ce roi, retirer de toutes choses une substance précieuse; les autres êtres vinrent également traire, selon leurs désirs, la terre soumise par Ṕŕithu.

"Les Ŕichis, ô sage excellent, lui donnant Bŕihaspati pour veau, vinrent aussi traire la vache divine; leurs organes étaient le vase dans lequel ils reçurent le pur lait des chants sacrés.

"Les troupes des Suras, lui amenant Indra comme veau, en tirèrent le Sôma, ce lait qui donne la force, l'énergie, la vigueur, et le reçurent dans un vase d'or.

"Les Dăityas et les Dănavas, prenant comme veau Prahrăda, chef des Asuras, vinrent la traire, et reçurent dans un vase de fer le lait des liqueurs spiritueuses et des sucs fermentés.

"Les Gandharvas et les Apsaras, prenant un lotus pour vase, vinrent aussi traire la vache; Viçvâvasu fut le veau; le lait fut la douceur de la voix et la beauté des Gandharvas.

"Les Pitŕis, dont Aryaman était le veau, eurent pour lait l'offrande qu'on présente aux Mânes; les Divinités des funérailles, ô grand sage, la recueillirent avec foi dans un vase d'argile crue.

"Kapila fut le veau des Siddhas et des Vidyâdharas; le ciel fut le vase dans lequel ils reçurent les charmes et la puissance surnaturelle qui consiste dans l'acte seul de la volonté.

"D'autres Dieux livrés à la magie, prenant Maya pour veau, reçurent la Mâyâ, simple acte de la réflexion, que connaissent les êtres merveilleux qui peuvent disparaître à leur gré.

"Les Yakchas, les Râkchasas, les Bhûtas, les Piçâichas et les Démons qui se nourrissent de chair, prirent pour veau le chef des Bhûtas, et reçurent dans un crâne le sang dont ils s'enivrent.

the lord of the earth, and who, from conciliating the affections of the people, was the first ruler to whom the title of Rájá was ascribed. Whoever shall recite this story of the birth of Prithu, the son of Vena, shall never suffer any retribution for the evil he may have committed. And such is the virtue of the tale of Prithu's birth, that those who hear it repeated shall be relieved from affliction.[1]

---

[1] Another reading is, दुःस्वप्नोपघातं * * * करोति । 'It counteracts evil dreams.' The legend of Prithu is briefly given in the Mahábhárata, Rája Dharma, and occurs in most of the Puráńas, but in greatest detail in our text, in the Bhágavata, and, especially, in the Padma, Bhúmi Khańda, s. 29, 30. All the versions, however, are, essentially, the same.

"Les reptiles, les serpents, les animaux venimeux, les Nágas prirent Takchaka pour veau, et reçurent dans leur bouche le poison qu'ils avaient trait de la vache.

"Prenant pour veau le taureau, et pour vase les forêts, les bestiaux reçurent l'herbe des pâturages. Accompagnées du roi des animaux, les bêtes féroces,

"Qui se nourrissent de chair, prirent la viande chacune dans leur corps; et les volatiles, ayant comme veau Suparńa, eurent pour leur part l'insecte qui se meut et le fruit immobile.

"Les arbres, rois des forêts, prenant le figuier pour veau, recueillirent chacun le lait de leur propre sève; les montagnes, ayant l'Himavat, recueillirent chacune sur leurs sommets les métaux variés.

"Toutes les créatures enfin, prenant comme veau le chef de leur espèce, reçurent chacune dans leur vase le lait qu'elles étaient venues traire de la vache, mère féconde de tous biens, qu'avait domptée Prithu.

"C'est ainsi, ô descendant de Kuru, que Prithu et les autres êtres, avides de nourriture, trouvèrent tous d'excellents aliments dans les diverses espèces de lait qu'ils reçurent, en présentant chacun à la terre son veau et son vase."

CHAPTER XIV.

Prithu had two valiant sons, Antardhi and Pálin.[1]
The son of Antardhána, by his wife Sikhańdiní, was
Havirdhána, to whom Dhishańá, a princess of the race
of Agni, bore six sons: Práchínabarhis, Sukra, Gaya,

---

[1] The text of the Váyu and Brahma (or Hari Vaṁśa) read,
like that of the Vishńu:

मुष्टी मुषी मधाधीयीं मधामेकार्षिगातिनी ।

M. Langlois[*] understands the two last words as a compound
epithet: "Et jouirent du pouvoir de se rendre invisibles." The
construction would admit of such a sense:[†] but it seems more
probable that they are intended for names. The lineage of Prithu
is immediately continued through one of them, Antardhána, which
is the same as Antardhi; as the commentator states, with regard
to that appellation: मधार्धिरेवान्तर्धानः । and as the commentator
on the Hari Vaṁśa remarks, of the succeeding name: मधार्धाना-
मधार्धिनंभान् । 'One of the brothers being called Antardhána
or Antardhi' leaves no other sense for Pálin but that of a proper
name. The Bhágavata[‡] gives Prithu five sons: Vijitáśwa, Dhúmra-
keśa, Haryaksha, Draviña, and Vríka; and adds,[§] that the elder
was also named Antardhána, in consequence of having obtained,
from Indra, the power of making himself invisible:

मधार्धानवर्ति मकाहच्युाकार्धानवर्जित: ।

---

* Vol. I., p. 10.
† The alternative sense implies, rather, that they had the disposition
to render themselves invisible.
‡ IV., 22, 54.
§ IV., 24, 3.

Kŕishńa, Vŕaja, and Ajina.[1] The first of these was a
mighty prince and patriarch, by whom mankind was
multiplied after the death of Havirdhána. He was
called Práchínabarhis, from his placing upon the earth
the sacred grass, pointing to the east.[2] At the termina-

[1] The Bhágavata, as usual, modifies this genealogy. Antardhána has, by Śikhańdiní, three sons, who were the three fires,
Pávaka, Pavamána, and Śuchi,* condemned, by a curse of Vasishtha,
to be born again. By another wife, Nabhaswatí, he has Havirdhána, whose sons are the same† as those of the text; only
giving another name, Barhishad, as well as Práchínabarhis, to
the first. According to the Mahábhárata (Moksha Dharma), which
has been followed by the Padma Puráńa, Práchínabarhis was
born in the family of Atri:

अत्रिवंशे समुत्पन्नो ब्रह्मयोनिः सनातनः ।
प्राचीनबर्हिर्भगवान् ॥

[2] The text is,

प्राचीनाग्राः कुशास्तस्य पृथिव्यामभवन्मुने ।

Kuśa or Barhis is, properly, 'sacrificial grass' (Poa); and Práchi-
nágra, literally, 'having its tips towards the east'; the direction
in which it should be placed upon the ground, as a seat for the
gods, on occasion of offerings made to them. The name, therefore, intimates either that the practice originated with him, or,
as the commentator explains it, that he was exceedingly devout,
offering sacrifices, or invoking the gods, everywhere: सर्वत्र ब्रह्म-
कुशानाम् । The Hari Vaṁśa‡ adds a verse to that of our text,
reading:

प्राचीनाग्राः कुशास्तस्य पृथिव्यां समकल्पयत् ।
प्राचीनबर्हिर्भगवानापृथिव्यीतलबर्हिषः ।

* *Bhágavata-puráńa*, IV., 24, 4. At IV., 1, 69, they are spoken of
as sons of Agni by Swáhá. And see pp. 155 and 156, *supra*.

† The *Bhágavata-puráńa*, IV., 24, 8, gives their names as follows:
Barhishad, Gaya, Śukla, Kŕishńa, Satya, and Jitavrata.

‡ Stanza 85.

I. 13

tion of a rigid penance, he married Savarńá, the daughter of the ocean, who had been previously betrothed

---

which M. Langlois[*] has rendered: 'Quand il marchait sur la terre, les pointes de cousa étaient courbées vers l'orient'; which he supposes to mean, 'que ce prince avait tourné ses pensées et porté sa domination vers l'est:" a supposition that might have been obviated by a little further consideration of the verse of Manu[†] to which he refers: "If he have sitten on culms of *kuśa*, with their points toward the east, and be purified by *rubbing* that holy grass on both his hands, and be further prepared by three suppressions of breath, *each equal, in time, to five short vowels*, he then may fitly pronounce om.":[‡] The commentary explains the passage as above, referring पूर्ववीनवारिका: to कुशा:, not to तत्त्वा; as: पूर्विबा तत्त्व प्राचीनाया: कुशा: पूर्ववीनवारिको भुव: सक्षे प्रधरत्न: आत्तवूमखनवापिन आसन् । तत्त: स प्राचीनवर्हि: । 'He was called Práchínabarhis, because his sacred grass, pointing east, was going upon the very earth, or was spread over the whole earth.'§ The text of the Bhágavata also explains clearly what is meant:

यस्येदं देवयजनमनुयर्ष्ठं वितन्वत: ।
प्राचीनाग्रे: कुशैरासीदाच्छन्नं वसुधातलम् ॥

'By whose sacred grass, pointing to the east, as he performed sacrifice after sacrifice, the whole earth, his sacrificial ground, was overspread.'¶

माकुशान्पर्युपासीन: पविषैरैव पावित: ।
प्राणायामैस्त्रिभि: पूतमल ओंकारमर्हति ॥

‡ This rendering, which is that of Sir William Jones, is not altogether in keeping with the commentary of Kullúka Bhaţţa.

§ Rather: "On his land the sacred grass, pointing towards the east, was forthcoming on the face of the earth, as it were, *that is to say*, was filling the entire circuit of the earth. Hence he *was called* Práchínabarhis."

‖ IV., 24, 10.

¶ Burnouf—Vol. II., Preface, p. III., note—renders thus: "C'est lui qui, faisant succéder les sacrifices aux sacrifices, couvrit de tiges de Kaça

to him, and who had, by the king, ten sons, who were all styled Prachetasas, and were skilled in military science. They all observed the same duties, practised religious austerities, and remained immersed in the bed of the sea for ten thousand years.

MAITREYA.—You can inform me, great sage, why the magnanimous Prachetasas engaged in penance in the waters of the sea.

PARÁŚARA.—The sons of Práchínabarhis were, originally, informed, by their father, who had been appointed as a patriarch, and whose mind was intent on multiplying mankind, that he had been respectfully enjoined, by Brahmá, the god of gods, to labour to this end, and that he had promised obedience. "Now, therefore", continued he, "do you, my sons, to oblige me, diligently promote the increase of the people: for the orders of the father of all creatures are entitled to respect." The sons of the king, having heard their father's words, replied: "So be it." But they then inquired of him, as he could best explain it, by what means they might accomplish the augmentation of mankind. He said to them: "Whoever worships Vishńu, the bestower of good, attains, undoubtedly, the object of his desires. There is no other mode. What further can I tell you? Adore, therefore, Govinda, who is Hari, the lord of all beings, in order to effect the increase

<hr>

dont les extrémités regardaient l'orient, la surface de la terre, dont il faisait ainsi un terrain consacré."

Also see the *Bhágavata-puráńa*, IV., 29, 49.

Śrídhara Swámin's comment on IV., 24, 10, is as follows: एवं बहु-भावं देवयजनं यज्ञवाटं वितन्वतो यस्यां यज्ञः जगत्समीप एव यज्ञावारं कुर्वन्तः सतः । अत एव प्राचीनबर्हिरित्युच्यते ।

of the human race, if you wish to succeed. The eternal Purushottama is to be propitiated by him who wishes for virtue, wealth, enjoyment, or liberation. Adore him, the imperishable, by whom, when propitiated, the world was first created; and mankind will assuredly be multiplied."

Thus instructed by their father, the ten Prachetasas plunged into the depths of the ocean, and, with minds wholly devoted to Náráyaṇa, the sovereign of the universe, who is beyond all worlds, were engrossed by religious austerity for ten thousand years. Remaining there, they, with fixed thoughts, praised Hari, who, when propitiated, confers on those who praise him all that they desire.

MAITREYA.—The excellent praises that the Prachetasas addressed to Vishṇu, whilst they stood in the deep, you, O best of Munis, are qualified to repeat to me.

PARÁŚARA.—Hear, Maitreya, the hymn which the Prachetasas, as they stood in the waters of the sea, sang, of old, to Govinda, their nature being identified with him:—

"We bow to him whose glory is the perpetual theme of every speech; him first, him last; the supreme lord of the boundless world; who is primeval light; who is without his like; indivisible and infinite; the origin of all existent things, movable or stationary. To that supreme being who is one with time, whose first forms, though he be without form, are day and evening and night, be adoration! Glory to him, the life of all living things, who is the same with the moon, the receptacle of ambrosia, drunk daily by the gods and progenitors;

to him who is one with the sun, the cause of heat and cold and rain, who dissipates the gloom, and illuminates the sky with his radiance: to him who is one with earth, all-pervading, and the asylum of smell and other objects of sense, supporting the whole world by its solidity! We adore that form of the deity Hari which is water, the womb of the world, the seed of all living beings. Glory to the mouth of the gods, the eater of the Havya; to the eater of the Kavya, the mouth of the progenitors; to Vishńu, who is identical with fire; to him who is one with air, the origin of ether, existing as the five vital airs in the body, causing constant vital action: to him who is identical with the atmosphere, pure, illimitable, shapeless, separating all creatures! Glory to Kŕishńa, who is Brahmá in the form of sensible objects; who is ever the direction of the faculties of sense! We offer salutation to that supreme Hari who is one with the senses, both subtile and substantial, the recipient of all impressions, the root of all knowledge: to the universal soul, who, as internal intellect, delivers the impressions, received by the senses, to soul; to him who has the properties of Prakŕiti; in whom, without end, rest all things: from whom all things proceed; and who is that into which all things resolve. We worship that Purushottoma, the god who is pure spirit, and who, without qualities, is ignorantly considered as endowed with qualities. We adore that supreme Brahma, the ultimate condition of Vishńu, unproductive, unborn, pure, void of qualities, and free from accidents; who is neither high nor low, neither bulky nor minute, has neither shape, nor colour, nor shadow, nor substance, nor affection, nor body; who

is neither ethereal nor susceptible of contact, smell, or
taste; who has neither eyes, nor ears, nor motion, nor
speech, nor breath, nor mind, nor name, nor race, nor
enjoyment, nor splendour; who is without cause, without fear, without error, without fault, undecaying,
immortal, free from passion, without sound, imperceptible, inactive, independent of place or time, detached
from all investing properties; but (illusively) exercising
irresistible might, and identified with all beings, dependent upon none. Glory to that nature of Vishńu,
which tongue cannot tell, nor has eye beheld!"

Thus glorifying Vishńu, and intent in meditation on
him, the Prachetasas passed ten thousand years of
austerity in the vast ocean; on which, Hari, being
pleased with them, appeared to them amidst the waters,
of the complexion of the full-blown lotos-leaf. Beholding him mounted on the king of birds, (Garuda), the
Prachetasas bowed down their heads in devout homage; when Vishńu said to them: "Receive the boon
you have desired; for I, the giver of good, am content
with you, and am present." The Prachetasas replied
to him with reverence, and told him that the cause of
their devotions was the command of their father to
effect the multiplication of mankind. The god, having,
accordingly, granted to them the object of their prayers,
disappeared; and they came up from the water.

CORRIGENDA, &c.

P. VII., notes, l. 4. So runs the stanza in the *Matsya*, *Kúrma*, and other Puránas. The *Márkaṇḍeya-puráṇa*, in its concluding chapter, has the same, with the exception of वंशा: for वंशः. The *Vishṇu-puráṇa*, III., 6, 17, reads:

सर्वेषु प्रतिसर्गेषु वंशो मन्वन्तराणि च ।
सर्वेष्वेतेषु कथ्यन्ते वंशानुचरितं च यत् ॥

For the second line, II gives, at VI., 8, 21:

वंशानुचरितं चैव भवतो वर्णितं मया ।

P. XXX., ll. 6 and 32. *Read* Bhúmi Khaṇḍa.

P. XLII., l. 18, *Read* Vena.

P. XLV., notes, l. 4. *Read* editor's note in p. LV., *infra*.

P. LVII., notes, l. 2. *Read* Venkaṭa.

P. LXIII, l. 11. *Read* Swáyaṃbhó.

P. LXVI., note, l. 2. *For* स भवर्ष (?) *read* सत्त्ववर्ष.

P. LXXXVII., l. 2. "Durvásasa" is the reading of Professor Wilson's MS. But it is ungrammatical.

P. XCV., ll. 15 and 29. *Read* Satarúpá.

P. CII., notes, l. 4. *Read* Christa Sangítá.

P. CXXII., l. 2 *ab infra*. *Read* Maruta.

P. 6. The Translator's note is here misnumbered. And the same is the case at pp. 19 and 34.

P. 22, notes, l. 2 *ab infra*. *For* p. 15 *read* p. 18.

P. 25, notes, l. 13. Professor Wilson must have adopted the following reading, that of a few MSS. which I have seen:

योगादिमुख्यमुपलभ्यमेव ।

Dr. Muir does the same, where he translates the stanza in which this line occurs. See *Original Sanskrit Texts*, Part IV., p. 8, first foot-note.

P. 25, notes, l. 16. *Read* पुरुषं.

P. 31, notes, l. 5. *Read*:

जागतिर्ज्ञानमिताद्या भवन्त्यज्ञानसंनिधि: ।

P. 36, note, l. 9. Cudworth's very words are: "When this world was made, a certain sphere of flame or fire did first arise and encompass the air which surrounds this earth, (as a bark doth a tree)", &c.
But both the Greek and the English are inadequately quoted.

P. 44, Editor's note. I ought to have added, that the commentator's view approaches more nearly that of the translator than my own. His rendering, however, of परिवृढ—which, in the Vedánta, is a stereotype epithet of Brahma—by कुतर्कासहिष्णु makes it doubtful, to my mind, whether his interpretation is preferable to that which I have proposed. The commentary runs as follows: परिवृढति प्रभवति इति सार्थेन । लोके हि सर्वेषां भावानां महिमन्यादीनां वास्तवो ऽपिचित्तज्ञानगोचरा:। परिवृढं कुतर्कासहिष्णु यज्ज्ञानं कार्यांवया-गुपर्यगाद्यद्यर्थं तत्र गोचरा:। वास्तव यत एतमतो ब्रह्मणो ऽपि नाच-

द्विधा: धर्मावा: धर्मादिहेतुभूता: । भावश्रतय: स्वभावसिद्धा:
घातय: सर्व्वेष वर्ज्जेर्द्देषयन्त्रिकत् । अतो मुख्यादिहीनत्वादपि तद्दव:
धर्म्मादिकार्त्तृत्वं वहत्न एति भाव: । तथा च श्रुति: । न तस्य, &c., and
परराज, &c., quoted at p. 45.　माया तु प्रकृतिं विद्याभावयितं तु
महेश्वरिमत्यादि: । अतो मायाख्यप्रकृतिनिष्ठधर्म्महेतुत्वं परमात्मन
उपचर्य्यत एति भाव: । तथा । निर्गुणस्यावश्वधर्म्मित्वद्वष्ट मुजे
ऽपरिक्तिप्तखायाकायादे: शब्दादावघरीरखायाघात्मन: शरीरिमेरघ
रागादिरहितकायकात्माबादिर्म्मोहप्रमघादीं हेतुत्वं यथा तथा
ब्रह्मणोऽपि तादृशाच संसर्व्वादिहेतुत्वं भविष्यतीनि । नघ सर्व्वादि-
हेतुत्वरूपमैश्वर्य्यं ब्रह्ममुखलष्वश्वमत्वादिर्धर्म्म विहत्वत एति निरूह-
मैध । स वा ऽवयमात्मा, &c., quoted at p. 45. तपतां श्चेति शंबोधेन
तप:प्रकृत्या स्वयमेवेदं ज्ञातव्यमिति सूचयति । यत एवमतो ब्रह्मण
एव हेतो: धर्म्मावा भवन्ति नावाजुपपत्तिरित्वर्थ: ।

The passage thus annotated will be found translated in *Original
Sanskrit Texts*, Part IV., p. 31, foot-note.

P. 56, l. 5. *Read* Narāh.

P. 69, notes, l. 12. *Read* Lam-ness.

P. 85, notes, l. 6. Referring to this place, Professor Wilson has written:
"M. Burnouf renders *śastra, les prières (mentales) qui sont comme la
glaive*; and, in a note in the *Vishnu Purána*, I have translated the
same expression of the *Bhágavata*, 'the uttered incantation'. But
it may be doubted if this is quite correct. The difference between
śastra and *stoma* seems to be, that one is recited, whether audibly
or inaudibly; the other, sung." Translation of the *Rig-veda*, Vol. I.,
p. 29, note.

P. 86, notes, l. 16. *Read* ब्रह्मयज्ञः.साम*.　l. 27. *For* वार्ता *read* वार्त्ता.

P. 110, notes, l. 2 *ab infra.* The passage to which I refer is IV., 1, 40
and 42. At III., 21, 23 and 24, as Professor Wilson says, Arundhatí
is married to Vasishtha, and Śánti, to Atharvan.

P. 111, notes, l. 4. *Read* Dharma's.

P. 124, notes, l. 6 *ab infra.* *Read* सूयख.

P. 125, notes, l. 3 *ab infra.* *Read* Vámáchárins.

P. 135, notes, l. 3 *ab infra.* *Read* वर्त्ते.

P. 136, l. 4. *Read* Sachi.

P. 142, l. 2. *Read* Maruts. Notes, l. 6 *ab infra.* *Read* Savitrí.

P. 152, notes, l. 6 *ab infra.* What is really stated is, that Prána had
two sons, Vedaśiras and Kavi; and the latter was father of Uśanas.
See Burnouf's *Bhágavata-purána*, Vol. II., Preface, pp. VI-IX.

P. 156, notes, l. 12. *Read* Puñja.

P. 164, notes, l. 4. *Read* Dhárana.

P. 170, notes, l. 6. *Read* -आयघरम्.

Berlin, printed by Unger brothers, Printers to the King.